Y0-BZJ-254

Praise for *Twenty-Two Ocean View*

The author has written a timely and informative novel. The sweep of developments, the trajectory of moving parts, the arc of time all give it a sense of immediacy—and unsettledness. That the story ended the way it did truly conveys a sense of dire seriousness. No happily-ever-after, tied up with a silk bow. (Bravo for that.) Through the author's story-telling, the reader is forced to acknowledge a changed world, one in which there is no guarantee of safety from harm. (A personal aside, having grown up overseas and evacuated from three countries by the time I was 16, it was especially potent and resonated in more ways than I wish.)

L. Kahn

Twenty-Two Ocean View is a high adventure page turner. I was hooked from the first page until the end. Very much a plot driven book, and a good one, reflecting the author's years of experience and in-depth research on a wide variety of topics concerning the many complex forces affecting our world today.

T. White

A remarkable story that sheds light on the dark spots of our era, and reflects that the author must have had some amazing experiences in the course of his career.

L. Smith

I loved *Twenty-Two Ocean View*, especially since I've been to many of the places mentioned. It is a good story, full of intrigue.

J. Wren

In reading *Twenty-Two Ocean View* I found myself eager to discover what would be happening next. I felt I was involved in history. Kevin was an engaging character, and kept my interest.

S. Wright

Overall I greatly enjoyed reading *Twenty-Two Ocean View*. It captured my attention and I thought the story was compelling, full of details, especially about foreign matters, and also about sailing. The intrigue was compelling.

T. Nielsen

Twenty-Two Ocean View is a good story with twists of plot. It has a nice combination of current history and past history, with nice transitions between settings and dates.

D. Roff

Twenty-Two Ocean View was very interesting and I was intrigued by the mixture of fictional and non-fictional elements. The historical setting was accurate and made what was apparently fiction all the more realistic. I believe that many familiar with the background of the Middle East conflicts will find this book one that is difficult to put down.

P. Mark

Also by Craig B. Smith

Non Fiction

Energy Management Principles

How the Great Pyramid Was Built

Extreme Waves

Lightning: Fire from the Sky

Counting the Days: POWs, Internees, and Stragglers of WWII in the Pacific

In the Wake of Cabrillo

Fiction

House of Miracles

Malaika's Miracle

Iwa Tales: Legends for Our Times

Stirrings: Three Novellas

TWENTY-TWO OCEAN VIEW

VIEW

Terrorists Among Us

A Novel

Craig B. Smith

Dockside Sailing Press

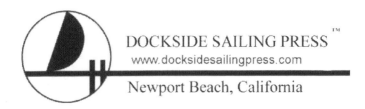

DOCKSIDE SAILING PRESS ™
www.docksidesailingpress.com
Newport Beach, California

1

Copyright 2017 by Craig B. Smith

All rights reserved. No part of this book may be reproduced
in any form without permission in writing from the
publisher, except by a reviewer who wishes to quote brief
passages in connection with the review published in printed
or electronic media.

Printed in the United States of America

DEDICATION

This book is dedicated to innocent victims worldwide who have suffered at the hands of terrorists.

AUTHOR'S INTRODUCTION

As may be apparent to the reader, I have drawn heavily on my professional experiences and global travels to write this novel. I chose to set a fictional story in a historical context to support how I believe the story might have unfolded. Readers will recognize a backdrop of some historical events such as 9/11, the invasion of Kuwait, and the Arab Spring and its aftermath.

However, Kevin, Juliana, Kidd and the other principal characters and what happens to them are all products of my imagination.

Nonetheless, recent events have shown that this story rings true and suggests a frightening future for peace-loving people everywhere.

Craig B. Smith, Balboa 2017

iv

THE RETIREMENT DINNER

The retirement dinner was at Twenty-Two Ocean View, an elegant oceanfront restaurant in Newport Beach. It was a warm, humid evening and the windows were open. There was a heaviness to the air, perhaps an impending thunderstorm. Outside, Kevin could hear the surf crashing on the shore.

There was a toast and Ray was saying, "Now you can spend more time on your boat, sailing to the islands," when the restaurant lights flickered and went out.

No one said anything for a moment. "It must be the Edison Company," Juliana said, "they're putting the power lines underground in this neighborhood."

Sitting in the darkness, Kevin said nothing. He had suppressed that memory for many years. Now, in the darkened room, it suddenly came back. Why the fear? Another time, another place, waking to darkness....

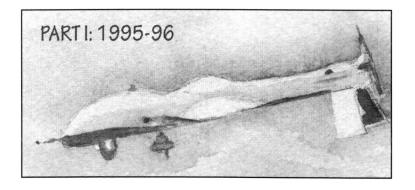

PART I: 1995-96

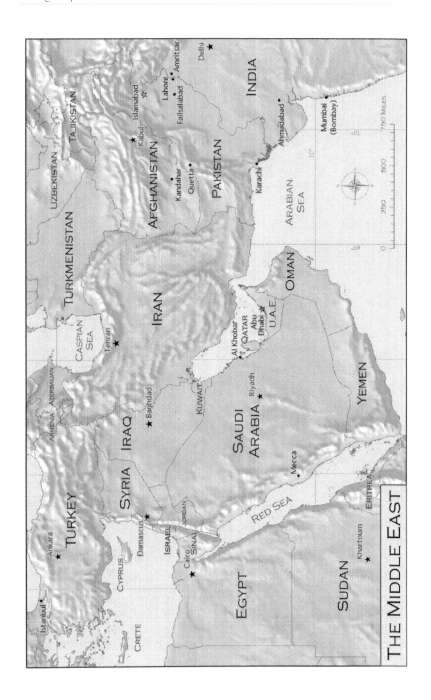

THE MIDDLE EAST

THE CABIN

Kevin was vaguely conscious of the vehicle bouncing over a dirt road. He couldn't see anything. His head hurt with a sharp, pounding pain. As the vehicle negotiated tight turns in the road, he rolled from one side to the other, crashing into the wall. He passed out again.

When he came to, it was dark and quiet. He was lying on a concrete floor. He tried to recall what happened and how he came to be in this strange place. He couldn't concentrate—it was like waking from a bad dream. He felt totally disoriented and terrified.

Fragments of memory came back to him. He'd been attacked, although he couldn't remember where or why or what he had been doing at the time. The thought of danger surged into the forefront of his mind. He had to be careful; he had to escape. At this point, he opened his eyes. It was pitch dark. He couldn't sort out what had happened and where he was, but recognized certain smells. There was the odor of an old wood fire, the smell of ashes, a musty odor, as in an old unoccupied building. Not totally unoccupied, because the odor of food lingered.

He listened but heard no sound. He attempted to move. Quietly, he struggled into a sitting position, but realized that his hands and feet were tied. He managed to turn on his side and draw his knees up into a fetal position. His head pounded and he couldn't see out of one eye. He tried to wipe his forehead with his bound hands and felt something sticky and wet. Blood.

He relaxed for a moment, trying to get his thoughts together, trying to focus. He listened carefully for any noise that would indicate people nearby.

All was quiet. There was a faint murmur of a breeze blowing outside. In the distance he could hear the hooting of an owl. Otherwise there was no sound whatsoever.

He brought his hands up to his mouth and closed his teeth on the knot. He worked on various strands until he felt one loop give. He kept pulling, and at the same time pulled his hands apart. One hand slid free. He removed the cord that bound his hands.

Once again, he lay still and listened, but heard nothing. He turned over on his back and forced himself up into a sitting position. The pain in his head was sharp when he sat up, and he felt a brief moment of nausea. Though it was dark, the room seemed to be whirling. After a moment, the feeling passed and the pain returned to a steady throbbing. He raised his arm to his face and used his sleeve to wipe the blood from his eyes.

His vision became clearer and he tried to identify where he was. It was apparent that he was in some sort of cabin. There was no light except faint moonlight that illuminated gaps in a curtain that covered a window. He could make out the outlines of furniture—a couch, a crude bench, possibly a table. He had been dumped on the floor near the end of the couch.

He pulled his legs up and began working on the

knot that bound his ankles together. When his legs were free, he tried to pull himself up on his feet but the effort exhausted him and left him disoriented. Again, he slumped back down on the floor to rest and try to collect his thoughts.

He felt better lying down. Rather than stand up, he crawled. In the darkness he couldn't see anything, so he dragged himself over toward the faint glimmer of light from the window. He slowly inched his way across the floor to the light, each movement causing a sharp pain in his head. His progress was slow and he stopped several times when he became dizzy.

The next time he reached out his hand to pull himself forward, he felt cloth and someone's leg. He stopped and jerked his hand back, listening. Still no sound.

"Hey," he whispered. "Are you okay?" There was no answer.

He reached out again and pushed on the leg. "Hey you," he said. "We've got to get out of here. Please help me." There was no response.

He crawled closer. It was a man's body. Kevin could feel that he was dressed in a suit. The body was cold and the person very likely dead.

Kevin wondered…what to do now?

Maybe it was adrenaline, or maybe just fear, but his finding the body suddenly galvanized him into action. He staggered to his feet in the darkness, hands out in front like a blind man, groping toward what he thought was the window. He tripped over the corpse and fell forward, crashing into a wall that broke his fall. He stepped over the body and worked his way along the wall to the window.

He pulled one edge of the heavy canvas curtain aside and looked out into the night. He could see a porch, surrounded by a stone wall, a clearing, and trees fading away into total darkness. There was no vehicle, no lights, no sign of any person.

He pulled the curtain aside to let more of the faint

light into the cabin. Now he could see a large fireplace at one end of the room, the couch, a pair of reclining chairs by the fireplace, a table with wooden benches and, at the other end of the room, a wood-burning cook stove and a sink. He made his way to the sink. There was a faucet but when he opened the valve no water came out. There was a large kettle on the stove. He lifted the lid and found it full of water. He opened a cupboard, found a coffee mug, and dipped out water to wash his face. He drank a cup of water.

He again felt tired and nauseated. He staggered to the table, sat on a bench, and put his head down.

When Kevin next awoke, the early light of dawn was filtering into the cabin. His head still hurt, but the throbbing had diminished. He tried to stand and found that his sense of balance was better. He walked to the cabin door, opened it quietly, looked out and listened. He stepped out on the porch. No one was in sight. The cabin was set against a hill. There were oak trees behind it. Not far away a windmill stood silent, a pipe leading from it up to a tank on the hillside. In front of the cabin there were some pine trees and a meadow. A dirt road went from the cabin past the windmill and disappeared down a narrow valley.

Kevin could see tracks in the dirt where a vehicle had come up the road, parked under the pine trees, then backed out, turned around, and returned the way it came.

Who brought us here and then left, he wondered? What did it mean? He presumed they'd be returning and knew he'd better not be there when they come back. He went back into the cabin and looked through cupboards and found a six-inch knife in one of the drawers. He filled an empty plastic bottle with water from the kettle on the stove and grabbed a handful of wooden matches from a box by the fireplace. Then he turned his attention to the man on the floor. He rolled the body over and recognized him as Robert Beske, the CIA agent he'd met the evening before. He'd been shot once in the chest.

Kevin went through Beske's pockets and found a

wallet, which he removed and put in his pocket. His own wallet was gone. He turned the body back over to the position he'd found it, and went to the door, where he paused.

He hated to leave without doing something to safeguard the body. But what could he do? He doubted that he could carry it very far. Even if he removed it from the cabin, all he could do would be to hide it somewhere, and then it could be damaged further by scavengers. The best option was to get out of there, report the murder as quickly as possible, and let the authorities deal with it. He took one last look inside the cabin. He picked up the ropes he'd been tied with, cleaned up the sink, and tried to make it look like he had never been there. If the kidnappers returned, he wanted his disappearance to worry them. He took a rag he found under the sink and wiped the kettle lid, the faucet, the drawer and cupboard handles, and the cabin doorknob. He closed the door and left.

He climbed off the side of the porch, taking care to step on some rocks that formed a border on one side of the cabin. He climbed up the hillside at the back of the cabin, stepping on stones to reach the top. That section of the hillside was a limestone ridge. He followed it, stepping carefully to make sure he left no tracks. After walking for about a mile, he dropped down into the canyon, carefully making his way through thick brush and up another hillside to a ridge that ran in an easterly direction, roughly parallel to the dirt road. He could see the road, a half mile off to his left. Keeping it in sight, he walked as fast as he could in the direction he hoped would lead him out of this place.

Suddenly, he stopped and listened. He thought he'd heard the sound of an approaching car. He crouched down behind a small manzanita bush and watched the road. A black SUV came up the road, trailing a long plume of dust and headed toward the cabin. Once it was out of sight, Kevin took a swallow of water and continued walking rapidly towards the east.

❧

At 7 a.m. the phone rang, waking Juliana.

An unfamiliar voice asked, "Is this Mrs. Hunter?"

She hesitated. "Yes… who's calling?"

"This is Officer Johnson from the Sheriff's department. We have a wallet with an ID for a Kevin Hunter. You know him?"

"Yes. He's my husband. Is he all right?"

"We don't know. That's why we're calling. Is he at home with you?"

"No. He had a dinner meeting last night and was headed directly for the airport. I was surprised he didn't call me from the airport, but I expect him to call this morning."

"We have reason to believe he may be in some kind of trouble. I don't want to worry you unnecessarily, but it would help us if you would identify his wallet."

"Oh my god, you have his wallet? Where is he?"

"We don't know."

"How did you get his wallet?"

"Can we discuss that when we see you?"

"Yes, of course."

"I will send the wallet over with one of our detectives in about fifteen minutes. We'll fill you in with what we know."

"You're worrying me. What could be wrong? Is there anything else that you can tell me?"

"I'm afraid not, ma'am."

Minutes later the bell rang and Juliana answered the door. A heavyset man in a dark suit stood there.

"Mrs. Hunter?"

"Yes."

"I'm Officer Johnson. Could you step out to our vehicle for a moment and tell us if the wallet my partner has belongs to your husband? It will just take a moment and we'll be on our way."

Worried about Kevin, Juliana didn't think to ask for an ID, saying, "of course."

He escorted Juliana out to a dark blue sedan. Johnson opened the rear door and spoke to another man in the rear seat. "Jim, this is Mrs. Hunter, would you show her the wallet?"

Johnson stepped aside so Juliana could look in. Jim held up a wallet in a plastic bag. "That looks like it," she said, "but can you take it out of the bag?"

"Sorry, we haven't checked it for fingerprints. Slide in and you can have a closer look."

Juliana got in the car. Johnson closed the door and quickly walked around to the driver's door.

"What are you doing?" she yelled, as Johnson started the car and pulled away from the curb. Juliana tried to grab for the door handle, but Jim pinned her arms to her side.

"Let me out here," she screamed, knowing something was terribly wrong.

"Calm down lady," Jim said, restraining her. "Just a short ride and a few questions and we'll bring you right back."

Kevin continued along the crest of the hill, following the road. After another mile or so the terrain flattened out, and he descended from the hills down into a large meadow. The road turned left. He continued to follow it, staying off to the right, far enough away that he could drop out of sight if he heard a vehicle coming. Up ahead he saw a clump of cottonwood trees and an old corral.

He approached carefully, but saw there were no structures nearby. The corral had been used as a holding pen for cattle. There was a chute that once had been used to load cattle onto a truck. Part of the fence railing had collapsed, and it was now clear the corral had not been used for years.

Where the road passed by the corral there was a gate. It looked new, made of aluminum bars and fastened with a heavy chain and combination lock. A barbed wire fence on either side of the gate extended off into the distance. Kevin slipped through barbed wire and continued, keeping the road in sight.

In the meadow a covey of quail flew up right in front of him with thundering wings. He was so startled he dropped to the ground and froze. When he realized what it was, he stood and continued.

From the meadow, the road led up into some low hills. They were dotted with manzanita bushes but there were enough open spaces that he could walk easily. The road turned left again and began ascending the hills. With the sun at his back now, Kevin knew he was headed west. At the crest of the hills the road descended into another long valley. He had just started down when he heard a vehicle coming.

He dropped out of sight until it passed. When it had gone by, he looked cautiously through an opening in the brush. It was the black SUV, traveling fast. In the distance he saw the tail lights flash red as it stopped. Someone got out of the passenger side and walked in front of the vehicle. The SUV pulled forward and he saw the brake lights come on again. The passenger got back in and the car accelerated out of sight around a bend in the road.

So there is another gate, Kevin thought. He started walking downhill at a fast pace. He crawled through another fence at the second gate and continued. He came to a cabin set back from the road. An old mobile home was parked next to it. The door was open and the windows were broken. The place looked deserted, so he skirted it and continued on his way. After another fifteen or twenty minutes he came to a paved road. A dilapidated sign pointing to the right said "Cherry Valley." He decided that turning left was more likely to lead to civilization. He got off the road on the right side and followed it south.

He estimated he'd been walking for three hours. Given the ups and downs, he thought he'd come about six miles. He needed to remember the landmarks. He regretted he'd never been close enough to see the license plate on the black SUV.

He came to an intersection. He saw that he was on Oak Glen Road and Orchard Street. As he crossed Orchard Street, an ancient Ford pickup truck approached. He stepped out in Oak Glen Road and held out his thumb. The pickup stopped.

The driver looked out at him. He appeared to be about seventy years old, unshaven, with two or three days of growth on his chin. He had on a Dodgers baseball cap, a blue work shirt, and bib overalls.

"You okay, son?" he asked. "You look kinda beat up. What happened?"

"I'd be grateful for a ride into town," Kevin said. "I had a car problem. Tire blew, ran off the road, hit my head. I need to get somewhere where I can make a call."

"Get in, son. I'm driving down to Beaumont to pick up some feed. Will that do for you?"

"Much appreciated. How far is it?"

"From here, about three or four miles. Won't take long. Where is your car?"

"I'm not exactly sure. I was out looking around. A friend said I might find an old cabin out here I could buy and fix up, you know, a weekend place. He gave me directions, but I think I got on the wrong road or missed a turn off. Back north of here a mile or two, I turned right on the dirt road. Up there I saw what looked like an abandoned shack and an old mobile home."

"Yeah, that's probably Pat Murphy's old place. He was a prospector, or so he said. I heard he did most of his prospecting down in the Beaumont bars. Every now and then I'd see him staggering back up this road to his place.

But he's dead now. Been gone a couple years."

"Anything further up the road? I saw a gate."

"Not much up there. You might've seen old man Westmoreland's place. He ran a few cattle until it got to be too much for him. He had a nice little place there with a spring and a windmill for water. Always had water, even in the dry season. I heard his daughter couldn't wait to sell the place. As soon as he passed on, she sold to some big shot lawyer in L.A. He was going to fix it up, but all he did so far was put a new gate on the road and keep it locked. Most of us up here in these parts are neighborly and trust each other. This guy doesn't seem to be the friendly type. But maybe he wants his privacy.

"By the way, my name's Hank," the driver said, reaching over to shake Kevin's hand. "Kevin," he replied. "I really appreciate the lift." Up ahead, Kevin could see buildings and decided they were nearing the town. "Say Hank, on second thought, is there a police department or sheriff's station in Beaumont? I probably should report the accident."

"Sure. There is the California Highway Patrol over on Highland Springs Road, or the Beaumont Police Department is down ahead of us on Orange Street."

"If it's not out of your way, could you drop me at the police station?"

"Glad to. What are you going to do about your car?"

"I've got Automobile Club," Kevin replied. "I'll get it towed here and fixed up and be on my way."

A few minutes later Hank pulled up in front of the Beaumont police station.

"Well, here you go," Hank said. "Good luck with the car. Have somebody take a look at that noggin of yours. That's a nasty cut, may need some stitches."

Kevin stepped out of the pickup. "Thanks for the ride Hank. I'm feeling better now and I think I'll be okay. I'll take your advice."

When Hank drove away, Kevin looked at the entrance to the Beaumont police station. This will be interesting, he thought.

❦

As the car drove off Juliana fought back her desire to scream again and forced herself to calm down before Jim did serious harm.

"Please let go; you're hurting my arm. I'll do whatever you want. Just tell me where my husband is."

"He's fine," Jim said. "You just take it easy, and we'll take you to him." He stuck the plastic bag with Kevin's wallet into the pocket on the back of the car seat.

The morning traffic was heavy with people going to work. Juliana watched the street signs as Johnson drove, trying to determine where they were headed. She could tell they were moving west toward Santa Monica.

"You work down here somewhere, don't you?" Jim said. "At that think tank where they do all the secret stuff."

"No," she said. "I don't know what you're talking about. You've got me mixed up with someone else."

Yeah, right," he replied, leering at her.

"Let go of my arm, now."

Jim released his grip on her arm and put his arm around her shoulders, his right hand clasping her breast. She recoiled from his touch but said nothing. "That's better," he said. "We'll be there soon."

They turned left and were on Cloverfield Street, approaching the east bound on-ramp for the Santa Monica Freeway. Once on the freeway, Juliana knew she would be in trouble with no possibility of escape.

Johnson stopped the car in a long line of traffic. Jim looked out the left window at the traffic, stopped both ways.

With the traffic at a standstill, Juliana thought that this might be her only chance. She swung her left arm as hard as she could, crashing her elbow into Jim's Adam's apple, at the same time ducking under his arm and jerking the car door open. She grabbed the bag with Kevin's wallet as she dove head first out of the car, got to her feet, ran behind the car, dashed through the stopped cars on the other side of the street, and darted through the driveway of an auto repair shop and into the alley behind.

Inside the car, Jim gasped for breath, with Johnson swearing at him for being stupid. "Get the back door closed, you dumb shit. We've got to get out of here."

In the rearview mirror Johnson could see a woman in the car behind dialing a number on her car phone. The traffic started moving, and he accelerated onto the freeway, the only direction he could go.

Shit, he thought, we lost the girl. That broad behind us was calling someone. He hoped she didn't get their license number. He thought about trying to go back and locate Juliana. It was a mile down the freeway to the first exit where he could backtrack. By then no telling where she would've gone. He decided the best thing was to get the hell out of there and tell Saleh what had happened.

Kevin walked up to the officer at the desk.

"Can I help you?"

"I hope so, Kevin replied. "I'd like to report a kidnapping and murder."

The officer looked up from his desk at Kevin. "You what? I'm sorry, what is your name sir?"

"Kevin Hunter."

"Okay Mr. Hunter, can you wait a minute while I locate the Sergeant?"

"Certainly."

Kevin was ushered into a room where he met Sergeant Rhinefeld. The sergeant asked him to take a seat at a table.

"What's this about a kidnapping and murder? First, who was kidnapped?"

"That would be me," Kevin replied. "But I escaped."

"And who was murdered?"

"This man," Kevin said. He handed over the CIA agent's wallet. "His name is Robert Beske. I didn't know him well. I spoke briefly with him on the phone, and met him once. It was just after our meeting that all this started."

The sergeant looked at the ID in the wallet. "I need to talk to one of our detectives, Mr. Hunter. Will you excuse me for a moment?" He returned a few minutes later, accompanied by another man. "This is Detective Jeff Palk."

Kevin stood, shook hands. "Glad to meet you."

The detective stared at Kevin's head, noted the injury. "Mr. Hunter, would you like some water, maybe some coffee?"

"Coffee would be great." The sergeant left the room, returning shortly with a mug of coffee. "It's not Starbucks, but it's warm."

"Thanks."

"If you don't mind, we'd like to tape record your statement and then we'll get someone to take a look at your head. That's a nasty cut you've got there. To start with, would you state your full name and address for the record?" Kevin gave his name and address. Then Detective Palk gave his name and the date. "Mr. Hunter, you have any ID with you?"

"No. My wallet was stolen, I assume by the kidnappers."

"Okay. Let's start at the beginning. Tell us what you can remember about your meeting with Mr. Beske."

After Kevin finished his statement, Detective Palk said, "So when you left the cabin this morning at dawn, Mr. Beske's body was lying there?"

"Yes. But as I told you, I saw a black SUV go up the road, and a little later come back down. I think you should get someone up there as soon as possible, but I would not be surprised if you find the cabin empty."

"Suppose it is empty. How can we be sure that you were there? I'm not doubting your story; it's just that we need to tie up all the loose ends. You can understand how it might look, since you were the last person to see Mr. Beske alive, you end up with his wallet, and you've obviously been injured—by someone."

Kevin reached in his pocket and pulled out the knife and matches he'd taken from the cabin and the ropes he'd been tied with. He handed them to Detective Palk. "I wasn't sure how long I'd be wandering in the hills, so I took these from the cabin. The matches are from a box by the fireplace. I found the knife in the drawer by the sink. I'm pretty sure that you'll find some more just like it. These are the ropes I was tied up with."

"Mr. Hunter, are you willing to accompany us back up to the cabin?"

"I guess so," Kevin replied, hesitation showing in his voice.

"Okay, I appreciate that. We'll make sure you're safe. I'm going to make some calls because Mr. Beske is a federal officer, and I will need to notify the authorities. Sergeant Rhinefeld will take you to emergency and get someone to look at your head. Let's try to meet back here in an hour. Sarge, you know where the old Westmoreland place is located?"

"Yes, I'm pretty sure I can find it. We probably should bring some bolt cutters for the gate lock."

"Good point. I'll get the crime scene crew organized and find some bolt cutters."

"Anything else we can do for you at the moment, Mr. Hunter?"

"Yes, I'd like to phone my wife. She's got to be worrying."

There was no answer at the house when Kevin called. He left a message, saying that there'd been a problem and he'd missed his flight. He gave a call back number.

The police crew found the cabin without difficulty. As Kevin suspected, Beske's body had been removed. The floor had been cleaned. It was so clean, in fact, it stood out in comparison to the rest of the dusty interior of the cabin. Using a reagent known as luminol, the detectives were able to detect traces of blood where Kevin indicated the body had lain. Also, as Kevin said, the knife matched a set in the cabin. The detectives were able to get a good casting of the SUV tire tracks and also several promising fingerprints.

Juliana made her way through several alleyways until she reached a chain-link fence at the back of a manufacturing plant that made water heaters. It seemed that the kidnappers had not followed her, but she did not want to take any chances. She hurried along the fence until there was a place where she could climb over and enter the plant. She found herself in a storage yard filled with rusty abandoned equipment and shipping containers. She slipped inside one of the containers and sat down to catch her breath.

She was confused, frightened, and sick with worry about Kevin. She forced herself to take deep breaths, to calm down, to push away the panic.

Certainly it would be unwise to go home. The kidnappers might expect that. Would they be bold enough to make a second attempt? And what was the story about Kevin? Clearly they had his wallet, but what did that mean? Had he been robbed, kidnapped, or worse? She didn't want to think about what might have happened to him. Her first priority was to get somewhere safe. She'd left the house in such a hurry that the front door was unlocked with her purse inside, and she had no money, no identification. What would happen if someone found her hiding in the storage area? She didn't like the idea of trying to explain to some plant security guard what she was doing there.

She looked at her watch. It'd been thirty minutes with no sign of the kidnappers. She decided to climb back over the fence, walk up to Olympic Boulevard, and head to Santa Monica where one of her girlfriends lived. From there she would call 911, report the kidnapping, and then have the police drive her home so she could get her purse, lock the house, and get her car. She'd go to a local hotel. She didn't want to stay in the house without Kevin. Also there was the issue of finding out about him. Maybe the police would have some information.

Back at the police station, Kevin told the officers about his contact with Hank.

"He seemed familiar with the various property owners up on that road. He mentioned that the owner of the cabin had recently died and his daughter had sold the place to a Los Angeles attorney. Do you know anything about this lawyer?" he asked.

"We've been working on that while you were gone," replied detective Palk. From what we've been able to find out, he's a Saudi named Saleh, very successful it would appear, as he lives in Beverly Hills. He represents a lot of Middle East companies. He is rumored to have Iranian connections. We're asking Beverly Hills PD to look into that, because we know the Iranians use a lot of middlemen and third-party dummy corporations to try to get around the economic sanctions. When we contacted Beverly Hills, they got interested very quickly. Apparently they have him tagged as 'person of interest.'"

By the time the LAPD officer arrived where Juliana was staying at her girlfriend's house, she had calmed down. The officer introduced himself as detective Roger Mead and asked her to tell him what had happened. When she was done, he had a few questions.

"Have you ever seen these two men before?"

"No."

"You think you'd recognize them if you saw them again?"

"I think so."

"Did they hurt you in any way?"

"No, other than to just shove me into the car and grope me."

"How about the car? Could you describe it?"

"I'm not good on cars. But it was dark blue, a four-door sedan, not real old, but not new. It smelled of cigarettes inside. It was big, so I think it was an American car, maybe a Buick or a Lincoln. Thinking back, I should've realized that it didn't look like a police car."

"Why do you think they wanted you?"

"I can't think of any reason, except that it must've had something to do with my husband, since they had his wallet."

"What does he do?"

"He's an engineer, and works for Consolidated Engineers and Constructors. They do large engineering and construction projects, both in the U.S. and overseas, some government work, some classified projects, but I can't think of any reason why anybody would want to harm him."

"Do you suppose that kidnapping you might've been a way to put pressure on him for some reason?"

"Possibly, but I don't know what he could have that would interest anyone. I'm really worried about him. Can you see if you can find out anything?"

"Certainly. I'll see if there is any information about your husband, but should warn you that it may take a little while. That's enough questions for now, Mrs. Hunter. I'll take you back to your home and let you get your things and lock the house. I suggest you stay with friends for a few days while I see what we can find out. You need to call me right away if you think of anything else or if you hear from your husband." He gave Juliana his card.

Twenty minutes later, Officer Mead parked the police car in front of the house. He asked her to wait in the car while he checked the house.

In a few minutes he returned. "Looks okay. No one was there and it doesn't look like anything's been disturbed."

"Thank you so much for checking," Juliana said. "Please come in for a few minutes while I get some things, and then I'll lock up and you can leave. I really appreciate your help. Sorry to be such a bother."

Juliana went to their bedroom and threw some clothes in a small suitcase. She grabbed her purse. As she started to leave the house, she noticed the message light blinking on the phone.

"Julie, it's me. I'm okay, but there's been a problem and I missed my flight. I'm in the Beaumont Police Department. As soon as you get this message, call this number. I need you to drive out and pick me up. Don't worry, but call as soon as you can. I love you."

In the Beaumont police station, Kevin introduced Juliana to detective Palk. "I think you're going to want to hear what happened to her. It appears that when I disappeared from the cabin, somebody decided to snatch her so they could force me to cooperate."

Juliana repeated the details of the kidnapping and the fact that the kidnappers had Kevin's wallet. "That's why I thought they were really policeman. I still don't know how they got your wallet."

"I knew it was gone," Kevin said, "and I assume they took it from me at the airport. I don't know what happened that night. I had a meeting scheduled with Bob Beske at the L.A. airport and we went to a bar in the terminal to have a drink before I had to board my flight. That's the last thing I remember before waking up in the cabin."

"What time was your flight?"

"It was a redeye back to Washington D.C., so it was 11 p.m. or 12 p.m. I can't remember, but Juliana has a copy of my itinerary at home.

"So that would put you in the bar at around 10 p.m."

"That sounds about right, but I can't remember anything after that."

"So between 10 p.m. and say 12 p.m. you were walked or carried out of the airport, driven out to Beaumont, tossed into the cabin, say between midnight and 2 a.m. You awoke at dawn so you were out for six to eight hours. It sounds like you were drugged. Before leaving us, do you mind giving a urine sample?"

"No, not at all. I'll cooperate in any way to help you find these guys."

"We also need to take care of some administrative matters and get your statement printed so you can sign it, and then you're free to go. I'd also like to get the contact information for the L.A. detective who spoke with Mrs. Hunter. Also, Kevin, please fax me a copy of your itinerary and tell us in what terminal the bar was located. We'll have someone contact them and see if anyone remembers any unusual activity at the time you were there."

On the drive back to Los Angeles, Juliana put her head on Kevin's shoulder and stroked his arm as he drove. "I'm so relieved that you're okay. You can't imagine what was going through my mind. Even though you said you were fine on the phone, you didn't sound right. I worried all the way out here that something was terribly wrong. At the same time, I couldn't stop thinking about those two fake cops. I should have known better. I was stupid to open the door for them without at least asking for some identification." She reached up to touch his head. "What about this? With all the excitement, I didn't ask about that cut."

"Just a small one. The police took me to emergency, and a doctor looked at it and cleaned it up. I'll be fine.

"What a terrifying sequence of events. I can't believe this happened to me and worse, what happened to you—you were so brave. Also, poor Bob Beske, dead, and for what reason?"

"What about your meeting?"

"I don't know, I can't remember anything."

"Do you think he was trying to protect you?

"Maybe."

"It's sad that he got caught up in this," Juliana said.

"Thank God you got my wallet back. I had some cash with me—probably about five hundred bucks for my expenses in Washington. Your buddies obviously removed that. I'm also missing my carry-on bag with my clothes. Nothing really valuable in it, just my suit and some shirts. There was my briefcase too, with some reports, nothing confidential or important, but it's also gone."

"My car! I just realized—it's still in the L.A. airport parking lot, or at least I hope it is. Let's go there when we get back to L.A."

"I'm worried about going home. I think we should check into a hotel for a few days, give the cops a chance to see what they can find out," Juliana said. "I'll call the airport lost and found and see if anyone turned in your briefcase or carry-on bag. Chances are they ended up in a trash can somewhere."

"Good idea. First I'll need to get a few things from the house."

Kevin located his car where he'd left it in parking lot "C" at LAX and followed Juliana home. She was nervous about entering the darkened house, so he went first to check it out while she waited outside, locked in her car with the motor running. When he came to the front door and turned on the porch light, she parked the car and came inside. She gave Kevin a big hug.

"I'm so glad that you're okay, and I don't have to sleep alone. I don't know if I can sleep. When I close my eyes my brain kicks in and I start thinking about those two bastards. I feel stupid that I fell for their line of bullshit."

"It's been a rough time for both of us. Try to put it out of your mind, if you can. Let's get out of here and go to a hotel. In the morning I'll go to the office and call the police and see what they know. I haven't called my boss yet. He must know by now that I never got to Washington."

At his office in L.A. the next morning, Kevin asked for a private meeting with Howard Clark, his boss.

"You're back early. I thought you'd be in Washington a few days longer," Howard said, with a hint of a smile that suggested sarcasm. Howard was an impressive man. Six feet, 2 inches, balding, and at age sixty had a body made hard by years of working construction. People were respective around Howard.

"That's why I wanted to talk to you," Kevin said. "I never went to Washington. As crazy as this sounds, I was kidnapped, taken right out of the airport. The police said that tests showed I'd been drugged. Worse yet, the guy I was meeting with also was kidnapped. He was killed. I managed to get away. I'm lucky to be alive."

"Kevin, that's terrible! But why you?" Howard asked. "What have you been up to?"

"Nothing illegal, if that's what you mean. Because of my meeting at the airport, I think it was related to those drone parts Juliana and I found on Santa Barbara Island. I told you about turning them over to the Coast Guard. Remember?"

"Yes. I assumed that was the end of it."

"So did I. But somebody wanted those parts bad enough to kidnap me in plain sight of dozens of people from the airport, and later, they tried to kidnap Juliana."

"Juliana? Is she okay?"

"Yes, she got away from them when they were stuck in traffic."

"Why her?"

"We don't know. Possibly to put pressure on me. Fortunately, she's shaken up but otherwise fine. I'm sorry about missing Washington. What needs to be done about that?"

"Oh hell, don't worry about that. I think the submittal has been delayed, so it doesn't matter. More important, what about you and Juliana?"

"When you and I are done talking, I'm going to call the cops and see what they know. If they haven't found those guys, I'm going to request that they watch our house. I don't want a repeat of what we've been through. In the meantime, we're staying at the Holiday Inn."

"My God, Kevin, that's a hell of a story. Tell Juliana I'm really relieved that you are both okay. As for you, you need to watch your backside until the cops locate those guys. If you need to take some time off, let me know."

"Thanks. I'll keep you posted."

After meeting with Howard, Kevin went to his own office, where he was greeted by his secretary Holly. She held a manila folder stuffed with papers.

"Everything okay?" she asked. "I heard you missed your flight. Travel called me. I figured something came up, so I didn't mention it to Howard."

"Yes, you could say something came up," he said, filling her in on what had happened.

"My god, Kevin, that's shocking. Both you and Juliana. Who could imagine…."

Thanks for covering for me. Howard's up to speed. It looks like the trip is off for now. Tell travel we want a credit on the plane ticket. If they need a reason, tell them 'family emergency.' Meanwhile, is anything else pressing?"

Holly looked in the folder. "Bill Quade wants you to come out to Cal State Northridge this afternoon on the FEMA project. There are more questions about who pays for what on the damage from the 1994 Northridge earthquake. Bill likes how you are able to explain all that seismic stuff to the FEMA claims guy."

"Okay, I can do that. Right now I need to make some calls, so chase everyone else away, except for Howard, of course."

"You got it." Holly left, closing the door behind her.

Kevin's first call was to the Beaumont Police Department. There had been some new developments. Kevin listened and made a few notes as detective Palk summarized the latest findings.

When he was finished with the police, Kevin called Holly.

"I need some help," he said. "My briefcase and carry-on bag went missing at the airport. It was in the American Airlines terminal at LAX. Julie reported them missing. Please call airport lost and found and see if anything has turned up. See if they check the trash cans; somebody may have just tossed them. They both have nametags and they have my business cards inside. After lunch I'll go see Mr. Quade. Based on past experience, I'll probably be there all afternoon. If you need me for anything important, call Quade's office. My pager is gone, so don't call that number. His office will know where to find me."

Kevin took out the business card he'd removed from Bob Beske's wallet. It was a plain white card with his name, a phone number, and a PO Box address printed on it. That was it—no street address, no company name.

He stared at the card, thinking. He picked up his phone again and dialed the number on the card. The phone rang twice. A voice came on at the other end of the line. The voice repeated the number he'd dialed and asked, "How may I help you?"

I want to speak with Robert Beske."

"Your name?"

"Kevin Hunter."

"One moment."

The line went dead for a few minutes and then another voice came on.

"I'm sorry Mr. Hunter, Mr. Beske is not available at this time. Can I have a number where he can get back to you?"

"You can have my number, but he will not be getting back to me. I was with him when he was killed."

Silence. Then the voice came on again. "Let me have your number and someone will get in touch with you."

Kevin gave his office phone number. It was repeated and then the line went dead. He held the phone, stared at it. What's this, he thought, that's it? No reaction, no "What do you know?" No "Thanks for calling?" He hung the phone up, thinking, *What the hell?*

The next day at work Holly stuck her head into his office. "There is a Robert Beske calling for you. He wouldn't tell me why. He said it was personal."

"Thanks," Kevin said, "put the call through." He picked up the phone when it rang. "Kevin Hunter."

"Mr. Hunter, thank you for taking my call. I'm not Robert Beske, but I thought that if you heard that name you'd be willing to speak with me."

"Who are you?"

"My name is Brown. I'm an associate of Robert's, and I'm trying to gather information about what happened in the airport. It would be helpful if you told us what you can remember about that evening.

"I've already told the police as much as I can recall. I'm not sure I can be of any further assistance."

"We have a copy of your statement to the police. There are a few points we'd like to clarify."

"What are they?"

"I don't think we should discuss this matter over the phone. Could we meet for lunch?"

"Yes, I could do that," Kevin said. "Today?"

"Yes, if possible."

"Fine, where?"

"Could you be at the Pacific Dining Car restaurant at 11:45? You know, the one over on Sixth Street?"

"Yes, that would work."

"Thank you. I'll see you there."

The caller disconnected. Kevin again sat there, staring at the phone, then slowly hung it up. Strange. How was he supposed to find this Mr. Brown? How would Brown find him? He'd play the game and see what happened.

At 11:40 Kevin entered the restaurant. It was known as a meeting place for local politicians and business leaders. About half of the tables were already full.

At the front desk he was greeted by the hostess.

"Good morning. Do you have a reservation?"

"No."

"Your name?"

"Kevin Hunter."

She scanned some lists, and then looked up, smiling. "Right this way, Mr. Hunter," she said, grabbing some menus. She led him to a booth at one end of the car, somewhat isolated from the other tables. "Enjoy your lunch."

Kevin noticed that she placed three menus on the table. The waiter appeared and Kevin ordered iced tea. This will be interesting, he thought. A moment after the waiter left, two men arrived.

"Mr. Hunter?"

Kevin stood to greet them. "Yes. And who are you?"

"My name is Charles Kidd. This is my associate George Taylor. Please be seated. We are very grateful you were willing to talk to us. Before we proceed, you need to see this."

Each man handed Kevin a small leather wallet. Inside was an identification card with a photo and a badge that read Central Intelligence Agency. Kevin glanced at the photo and looked up at each man, then handed the ID back.

"I gather 'Mr. Brown' will not be joining us...."

The faintest trace of a smile passed over Kidd's face.

"We've been assigned to find out what happened to agent Beske. We're in touch with the police in Beaumont and in Los Angeles. It appears that you were the last person to see Beske alive at the airport, before you discovered his body in the cabin. We know that he was meeting with you because of some aircraft parts you found on Santa Barbara Island. Let's order lunch and then we'd like to hear all you can remember about your contacts with Mr. Beske."

The waiter reappeared and took orders. After he left, Kevin said, "Mr. Beske called me to follow up on 'the Coast Guard matter,' as he called it. He said he was with *the CIA. I was very busy getting ready to go to Washington D.C. I told him I didn't have time to meet that day because I was taking a redeye flight east that night, and I had a lot to do. He asked me if we could meet in the airport before my flight. I got the idea he thought it was urgent, so I said yes. We agreed to meet at the American Airlines counter at 9:30 p.m. He said he'd have a small sign with my name."

"So you met as planned?"

"Yes. He got a gate pass that let him in. We agreed to go back in the terminal corridor to a bar there, very near the American gate. From then on my mind is blank, until I woke up the next morning. I keep thinking back, but I can't remember what happened. There have been a few times I've woken up at night with the sensation that I'm falling, in a crowded place, people looking down at me, but then it fades."

"We checked with the bar," Kidd said. "The bartender recalled a customer passing out. The man he was with tried to help him to his feet. Two other men volunteered to help him out of the bar. The three left, supporting the fourth man, who appeared to be drunk. As they left, one man returned, picked up a briefcase and travel bag, and carried them out. That's all the bartender knew."

"Do you know why Beske wanted to meet with me?" Kevin asked.

"The aircraft parts you found—they were stolen from a U.S. Navy laboratory on San Nicolas Island. They were essential parts of the guidance system of a new drone the military is testing. We think the intent was to use the information to develop a way to take control of the drone in flight and redirect it to a different destination."

"But how and why did they get to Santa Barbara Island?"

"We think they were removed from the laboratory by a civilian technician, an electronics engineer, Iranian-born naturalized U.S. citizen. He did not come to work the next morning and was nowhere to be found, although his room and the island were searched. He may have passed the package to some folks in a boat; he may have left with them. No one knows. It's possible that he was killed and dumped in the ocean on the way to Santa Barbara Island. Stashing the package on Santa Barbara Island probably had something to do with money—after payment received, we tell you where the goods are, that kind of thing."

"So Beske was going to meet with me and tell me all this?"

"Not exactly. He was tasked with seeing what else you could remember about the boat, any description of the men, the time they arrived and left, where they seemed to be headed, that kind of information."

"I'd already told the Coast Guard most of that when we got back to the mainland. I went to the station in Marina del Rey and gave them a statement."

"Yes, we knew that. Beske was following up, trying to make sure we had all the facts, seeing if you might have remembered anything else. There was one other thing."

"What was that?"

"He wanted to warn you. It seems that somebody identified your boat. They may have picked up your call sign during the radio chatter. Someone called the Coast Guard and gave your name, wanting to know 'if there was any new information.' Fortunately, the guy that took the call did the easy thing and said he couldn't discuss it, and the caller hung up. The Coasties record these calls and we listened to the recording. It definitely wasn't you. The caller had an accent of some kind. We believe the bad guys may think you kept the package. In any case, they probably wanted to find out what you knew."

"Then why would Beske help them in the bar, knowing all this?"

"We think they came looking for you. They were going to dope you up and haul you out of there. Beske was a surprise, something they hadn't planned on. They no doubt gave him some line of bullshit about helping you. At some point, they probably stuck a gun in his ribs. Once you were all out of the airport, they probably shot him."

"Why leave me at the cabin?"

"They probably overdid the drug dosage. They couldn't get the info they needed from you. Maybe they had to report in? Maybe they went to get someone else to interrogate you? Our guess is that they didn't think you'd be able to get out of there before they returned. When they found you gone, they paid a call on Mrs. Hunter. Fortunately, that plan backfired."

"I don't think I can add anything," Kevin said. "It seems that you already know more than I do."

"We'd like you to contact us immediately if you think of something else," Kidd said "We want you to be careful. As you've seen, these are not nice people."

"Certainly. I'll contact you if I think of anything else. I feel really bad about Beske. I only have the barest recollection of our meeting, but he seemed like a nice guy."

"Mr. Hunter, there's one more thing."

"What?"

"We have a couple of choices. We can go public with the fact that the Coast Guard recovered these materials after an anonymous tip. That would eliminate any pressure on you."

"The other choice?"

"We could continue to keep the recovery quiet. That would mean you are still possibly of interest to the bad guys. It might encourage them to make another effort."

"I'd be bait."

"Yes, in a manner of speaking. We'd keep a close eye on you and Mrs. Hunter, of course, but there would be some risk."

Kevin was silent as he thought about this. He recalled rolling over in the dark cabin and finding Beske's body. He wondered if Beske was married, or had kids. What happened to his body? How terrible to not know, how difficult for the family.

"Are you trying to find Beske's body?" he asked.

"Yes, you can be certain we will do everything possible. We're searching the area around the cabin. The morning your wife was abducted a woman called 911 to report what appeared to be two men assaulting a woman. The victim jumped out of the car and ran. The caller had a partial license number. We're getting a description from her and we expect to locate that vehicle. If we find it, we may be able to locate the black SUV you saw. It may tell us if Beske was transported a second time."

"I'd like to nail these bastards. What do I need to do?"

"The first thing will be to set up some private communication channels. We would like you to spend a day with our trainers. They'll go over communications and some other practical matters, such as how you can tell if you are under surveillance and what to do about it."

"What about Juliana?"

"We'll keep an eye on her. But we think that if there is any attempt, it will be on you. You are the obvious target. Starting today, without being obvious, you need to change your routines. Don't go to the office or leave it at the same time every day. Use different routes. If you go to lunch, stay in public places and don't go alone. That kind of thing, common sense. Be a little unpredictable."

"Okay, I think I understand. By the way, we're staying in a hotel for a few days this week."

"Are you free this Saturday?"

"Yes, we'll be back by then."

"Good. We'll pick you up at 8 a.m. at your house. Wear casual clothes. We'll bring you back by 5 p.m. It's best to just say you have to inspect a job site with a client."

"I understand. Let me give you my address."

"No need to do that," Kidd said. "We need to get going. Don't worry about the check, it's being taken care of. We'd appreciate it if you kept this meeting and our discussions to yourself. Probably better Mrs. Hunter doesn't know. That okay?"

"Yes. I understand. The less she knows, the safer we both are."

"Exactly."

"Meanwhile, think back over your sailing trip to Santa Barbara Island. You may recall something. Anything that you remember about the boat or its occupants would be very helpful to us."

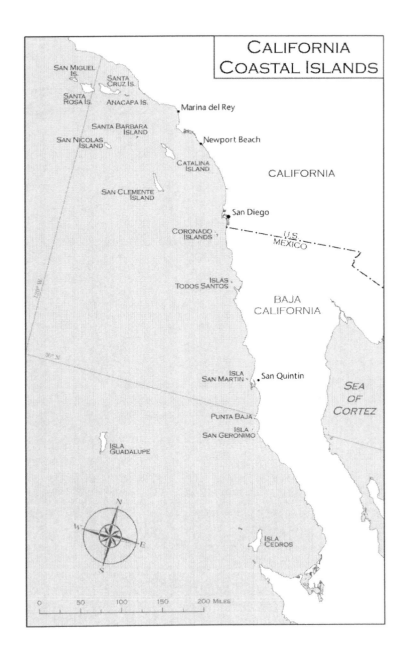

SANTA BARBARA ISLAND

That night Kevin lay awake in bed revisiting every aspect of the trip out to Santa Barbara Island, trying to recollect if there was some trivial detail he might have overlooked, something useful to pass on to Kidd. The trip had been planned for months. Kevin had always wanted to take Juliana there, but for one reason or another—weather, work, or something else—the trip had been postponed. At last, in 1995, the timing worked out and they sailed for the island on a Friday, the week after Easter.

They'd left Marina del Rey early in the morning. It was cloudy and overcast most of the way across to the island. As they got closer, the island rose from the leaden sky, first as a low gray smudge on the horizon, then gradually taking shape as the boat drew closer. Kevin steered to the port side of the island to avoid a shallow where kelp grew. In the distance, beyond Santa Barbara Island, Kevin could barely make out the low silhouette of San Nicolas Island.

He could see the cove on his starboard bow. It was empty—no other boats. "We're here," he shouted below to Juliana. "Come take the wheel."

He turned into the wind and began furling the jib. When Juliana stepped up into the cockpit he went forward and lowered the mainsail. When this was done, he returned to the cockpit and started the engine. The boat moved slowly forward into the cove.

"There," he said, pointing to the right as they entered the cove, "see the arch? We want to be in there, a little to the left of that spot. Watch the depth. We need to be about six or eight fathoms. When we're there, put it in neutral and I'll drop the anchor." He slowed the engine until the boat was barely moving, just enough to respond to the rudder, and went forward.

Standing in the bow, Kevin looked down into the clear water. Below he saw an occasional flash of orange as a garibaldi swam away, disturbed by the passage of the yacht.

Juliana called out "six fathoms" and he released the heavy Delta anchor. When fifty feet of chain had run out he yelled, "Reverse now."

She backed the boat up while he let out another hundred feet of chain. He shouted, "Neutral."

Kevin secured the anchor and returned to the cockpit. He put the engine in reverse and again backed down on the anchor until he felt the chain go taut and the anchor grab the bottom. He shut down the engine.

"We're here," he said. "You can go back to your book. I want to dive and check on the anchor and make sure it set okay. I'll put on the bridle so we won't hear the chain banging in the middle of the night. With that done, we can break out the Champagne."

The next day was a quiet one. Kevin rigged up a fishing pole and caught a four-pound sheepshead. The boat was immediately surrounded by diving and screaming gulls fighting for the scraps as he cleaned the fish. In the midst of all the confusion, a sea lion appeared and grabbed the carcass of the fish before the gulls could squabble over it. He went below and put the fillets in a plastic bag in the refrigerator.

"Dinner is on ice," he said. "I caught it, you cook it. How does that sound?"

"Perfect," Juliana replied.

That evening, while Kevin sat in the boat cockpit enjoying a beer as the sun went down and Juliana fixed dinner in the galley, he saw a strange sight. A low-profile, very fast boat, running without lights, appeared out of the overcast to the west of the island. It slowed down and came to stop near the boat landing on the other side of the cove. Two men launched an inflatable boat and rowed over to the landing ladder. They were dressed in black and in the fading light were difficult to see. They each carried a small backpack.

In a moment, they scrambled up the ladder and disappeared somewhere up on the hillside overlooking the cove. About twenty minutes later they returned. By now it was becoming dark, but Kevin observed that they no longer had the backpacks. They descended quickly, climbed into the inflatable, and rowed quietly back to their boat. Within minutes they had climbed on board, hoisted the inflatable out of the water, and the boat crept quietly out of the cove. Once clear, the engines went to full throttle, and the boat rapidly disappeared into the darkness, again showing no lights.

At that moment Juliana came to the companionway. "Do we have company? I thought I heard a boat."

"They came and left," Kevin replied. "It was weird. Two guys climbed up the ladder with backpacks, came back about twenty minutes later without them, and then took off, headed back towards the mainland. They left traveling fast, with no lights."

"Maybe it was a delivery for the Park Ranger," she said.

"I don't think the Ranger is here this weekend. Maybe they are smuggling drugs."

"Don't worry about it now. Dinner is served, Captain," she said. "That fine sheepshead you caught has been converted to fish tacos. They're going to get cold so you should come and eat now."

Kevin went below. The table was set, a plate of fish tacos was ready, along with a salad. Juliana had candles on the table. She turned off the overhead light.

"Let's save the batteries," she said, "besides, it's more romantic. You want a Mexican beer or Margarita to go with dinner?"

"I like romantic," he said, giving her a hug. "The

tacos look great. I think I'll just have a beer—one of those Carta Blancas."

"What are we doing tomorrow?" she asked.

"We'll sleep in, enjoy the nice calm seas we have for a change. Later, I thought we'd take a hike on the island, if you'd like. Although I like all the Channel Islands, for some reason Santa Barbara Island has always been my favorite."

After dinner, Juliana cleared the table. "I cooked, you clean up."

He laughed. "Fair enough." Kevin dipped a bucket overboard and used salt water to wash the dishes and the pans Juliana had used for dinner. He rinsed them with fresh water, dried them, and put them away.

Through the open hatch the night sky was visible, full of stars. The moon had not risen.

"Are you ready for bed?" she asked, her voice full of promise.

"In a minute. I want to check the anchor and turn on the anchor light, then I'll be there."

Kevin stepped on deck. The cove was quiet, the sea making faint swishing sounds as it crept past the boat and ran up against the rocky shore of the cove. In the distance a sea lion started barking. He stood on deck for a few minutes, taking it all in. There was nothing better than being on a boat at sea, or anchored when the weather was good. The quiet, gentle rocking of the boat, the smell of seaweed and salt air, brought him a sense of peacefulness.

The anchor was fine, their position had not changed in the last twenty-four hours. He stepped below, sliding the hatch cover partially closed. Juliana had left the candle burning on the galley table. She was forward, just emerging from the head after brushing her teeth. She wore a thin nightgown that showed the outline of her breasts and the dark triangle below her navel.

"Hmmm," Kevin said, "don't you look lovely." He stepped up and embraced her. "I love you so much, more than you'll ever know."

She kissed him. "I love you too, so hurry and come to bed."

He continued to hold her. "It's a warm night; I don't think you'll need this nightgown."

"You're probably right," she said, pulling away from him. "So hurry up and get in bed so you can take it off."

Kevin woke with the sun, got up, pulled on some shorts, and went on deck to check their position. Everything was fine. The tide had ebbed, and the boat had swung around to face away from the island, but all was peaceful. They were still alone in the cove. He went below to make coffee.

When the coffee was ready, he poured a cup and went up to sit in the cockpit. Juliana was still sleeping.

Kevin sat in the cockpit drinking his coffee and watching the sea. The sky was grey, slightly overcast except to the east where the sun had turned it pink. A few gulls flew over the cove, looking for an unwary fish to eat. In the distance, he could hear sea lions barking as the males defended their territory or fought over the females.

"So peaceful," he thought. "If only we could live like this. One island after another, no cares, just us and the sea and the boat. Enjoy the moment he thought, it will be over too soon.

He finished the last of his coffee and looked at the water as it rippled around the stern of the boat. On impulse he slipped off his shorts, stepped to the ladder on the starboard side and eased into the water. It was cool— probably 65°, but it felt refreshing. He drifted free from the boat for a moment, letting the sea rinse perspiration from the previous day and evening from his body. He quickly climbed back on board, shivering from the cold.

He went below to get a towel. Juliana stirred in the

bunk. He gave her a wet, salty kiss, and brought her a cup of coffee. "Ready for breakfast?"

"In a few minutes," she said. "I just want to lie here and enjoy the coffee."

He went in the galley and started cutting up a green pepper and onion for an omelet. Juliana got out of bed as he worked. He watched as she climbed down from the bunk and went into the head, her back to him, her black hair hanging down to just above her shoulders, the curve of her waist, her hips, thighs, her trim calves. As the door closed, he experienced a moment of arousal before returning to the chore at hand.

Stirring the omelet, he thought about Juliana and how fortunate it was that they had met and fallen in love. How lucky he was to have someone who not only loved him, but put up with him, his work and frequent travel and, at the same time, meant so much to him in every way.

After breakfast, they took the inflatable to the boat landing and tied it off. They climbed the landing ladder that led up to the platform where supplies could be unloaded for the Park Service Ranger. On the way in, Kevin again thought about what he'd seen, the two guys with backpacks. His instinct told him something was wrong.

"It seems strange," he said. "There was something furtive about the whole thing. I wonder what they were up to."

They walked up the trail to the Ranger's cabin, but no one was there. Wildflowers were abundant following the winter rains. All around them on the hillside the coreopsis were blooming, large bright yellow blossoms on plants that otherwise looked dead. Other plants added shades of purple, blue, white and yellow.

They followed a trail that led around the crest of the island. From it they could look down into the cove and see their boat at anchor. After walking a short distance, Kevin noticed a short piece of yellow line tied around a branch at the side of the trail.

He stopped to examine it. It was new—no signs of weathering. It hadn't been blown there by the wind. It'd been tied there deliberately—that much was certain. He looked around. To his left there were some fresh skid marks, as if someone had slipped while trying to climb up the steep hill. He looked up the hillside, saw more footprints. He pictured someone coming down in the darkness, losing their footing and slipping.

"Wait here a minute," he said.

He climbed the hillside. Up one hundred feet or so above the trail there was a dense clump of brush. Two olive green backpacks had been pushed under the branches. He pulled one out carefully and unzipped it. Inside there were several packages wrapped in clear plastic and sealed. They were electronic devices of some sort, integrated circuits, circuit boards, other components he did not recognize. They were compact and ruggedized, like part of an aircraft, not like a computer or commercial electronic device. There was also a plastic envelope that had folded drawings and some kind of a manual. It was all sealed. He did not try to open it. In one corner he could make out the partial words "U.S. AIR FORC." The other backpack had similar components. It had a round chassis of die cast aluminum. The round shape seemed to imply that it was intended to fit inside a cylinder of some sort, possibly a missile.

Kevin sensed that something was very wrong. He picked up both backpacks and went back down to where Juliana waited on the trail. He described what he'd found.

"I want to hide these somewhere else," he said. "Then I think we should go back to the boat and radio the Coast Guard."

"Why not take them back with us?"

"Because I think someone is going to show up here looking for these, and I don't think we should be in the vicinity when they arrive."

Kevin untied the piece of yellow line. "Let's go back to the Ranger's cabin."

Part way back he stopped and retied the piece of yellow line on a bush. "That ought to add a little confusion."

They walked quickly to the Ranger's house, looking for someplace to hide the backpacks. The place was neat and orderly. Everything was locked up. Not far from the house there was a small aluminum rowboat, turned upside down.

"This will have to do." He slid the two backpacks under the boat, trying not to disturb anything. When he was done, he looked around. You couldn't tell it had been moved.

"Okay, I think we should go back to the boat and get out of here before we have visitors."

"You're really concerned aren't you?" Juliana said. "What do you think is going on?"

"I think someone has stolen some parts of something important, maybe a missile, and they stashed them here so someone could pick them up in a boat."

Kevin led the way back down the trail to the landing. As he untied the inflatable, he told Juliana his plan. "First thing, help me hoist the inflatable on board. Then you start the engine while I raise the anchor. Once we are clear, take us out of the cove and head east, back towards the mainland. As soon as you can clear the island, turn north so we get behind it. I don't want to be visible to anyone coming into the cove."

"What are you going to be doing?"

"I'm going to get on the radio and call the Coast Guard. Keep a watch and let me know if you see any boats approaching."

When the boat was underway and rounding the island, Kevin went below and turned on the VHF radio.

"Coast Guard, this is Whiskey Charlie Echo 8456. Over."

"Whiskey Charlie, this is the United States Coast Guard San Diego. Do you have an emergency? Over."

"Coast Guard San Diego—this is Whiskey Charlie. No emergencies, can we go to channel 21 alpha? Over."

"Whiskey Charlie, San Diego Coast Guard. Go to channel 21 alpha. Coast Guard San Diego. Out."

Kevin changed channels and called the Coast Guard back.

"Whiskey Charlie, this is the U.S. Coast Guard San Diego, how can we help?"

"I need to talk to someone about a national security matter."

"Whiskey Charlie, what is your current position?"

"My position is 33°, 28 minutes north, 119°, 02 minutes west. Over."

"Whiskey Charlie, stand by."

The radio went silent. Kevin poked his head out of the cabin to see where they were. The boat was rising and falling as it headed into the swells of the sea coming around the island. They were approaching the backside of the island. The radio crackled to life.

"Whiskey Charlie Echo 8456, this is United States Coast Guard, San Diego. Over."

"Coast Guard, Whiskey Charlie. Go ahead."

"Lieutenant Mason, Maritime Defense Zone Rep San Diego. How can I help you? Over."

"You have my location. There is a package of materials that pertain to national security, in a place where they do not belong. I'm hesitant to give details, since other vessels could be monitoring radio traffic. I'm requesting that you dispatch a rotary wing aircraft to my location, and I will advise how they can recover the materials. Over."

"Whiskey Charlie, can you give further details?"

"The materials appear to be some type of sophisticated aircraft avionics. There are both hardware and documents. Over."

"Whiskey Charlie, we're taking your information under advisement. Can you stand by? Over."

"Affirmative. I will remain in the vicinity. I have

reason to believe that a vessel might be coming along to collect these materials. Over."

"Message understood. Please stand by. We appreciate your concerns. U.S. Coast Guard San Diego. Out."

Kevin went up into the cockpit. Juliana had brought the boat around to the opposite side of the island.

"Good job," Kevin said. "I could be wrong, but I'm hoping anyone coming will be approaching from the opposite direction. Let's slow down to about three knots, just enough to make headway, until we see if the Coast Guard is going to do anything."

Minutes passed. The radio was silent, except for a container ship calling Los Angeles Harbor for a pilot. After ten minutes Kevin heard the Coast Guard calling.

"U.S. Coast Guard, Whiskey Charlie. Go ahead."

"Whiskey Charlie, we are dispatching a helicopter from Los Angeles base to your location. It should be there in about fifteen minutes. Do you copy? Over."

"I copy. When I have a visual on your aircraft I will hold a red flare for identification. Can your aircraft communicate on this channel? Over."

"Affirmative. Aircraft has VHF channel 21 alpha. Over."

"Advise aircraft that my current position is three miles north of the position where I first contacted you. Over."

"Roger that. U.S. Coast Guard San Diego. Out."

The radio went silent. Kevin opened the emergency locker and got out a red flare. He went back to the cockpit to watch for an orange and white Coast Guard helicopter.

"What are you thinking?" Juliana said.

"A lot of boats have radio direction finders. If anyone was monitoring all this Coast Guard chatter, they could figure out our general location. I'm hoping that being behind the island might confuse the issue."

Kevin heard the helicopter before he saw it. He

went below and brought a hand-held VHF radio into the cockpit. It was only five watts and had limited range, unlikely to be monitored by other vessels.

The helicopter came directly toward them, but Kevin ignited the flare anyway, and held it until the helicopter hovered a short distance away.

"Coast Guard aircraft, Whiskey Charlie Echo 8456. Do you copy?"

"Whiskey Charlie, Coast Guard 256. We copy skipper. I understand you have information for us."

Kevin could hear the pilot's voice mingled with the sound of the helicopter's powerful engine.

"You need to proceed south about four miles. Above the cove on the south side of the island is the Ranger's house. It is unoccupied. Behind it there is a flat spot where you can land. Also near the west side of the house there is an old aluminum rowboat, upside down. There are two olive green backpacks under the rowboat. They contain the materials you are seeking. We'll standby until you confirm that you have the materials. Whiskey Charlie out."

"Whiskey Charlie, Coast Guard 256. We are on our way."

The helicopter rose quickly and accelerated south in the direction of the island, where it dropped out of sight. A short time later it reappeared overhead.

"Whiskey Charlie, Coast Guard 256. We have the materials. Over."

"Very good. We are departing. It will take us five to six hours to reach port. Please advise that I will contact the Coast Guard when we reach the mainland. Also, you may want to maintain some surveillance of vessels going to the island for the next few days. Whiskey Charlie out."

The helicopter rose swiftly and soon was out of sight.

"That was exciting," Juliana said. "So much for our relaxing trip to Santa Barbara Island. I presume we're not spending another night at the island."

"No, I think we should get out of here in case someone comes looking for those backpacks."

❧

Kevin raised the sails and Juliana set course for Marina del Rey. She noticed some ominous clouds building in their wake. There was a fresh breeze from the northwest and *Seascape* was soon making five knots for the mainland. No suspicious vessels showed on the radar.

"We may be in for some weather," she said, eyeing the dark clouds astern. "Do we need to shorten sail?"

"I think we'll be okay, but keep an eye on things. I want to take a quick shower, then I'll fix some lunch and relieve you at the helm. You can read, shower, nap, or do whatever you like during the afternoon. It will be dark by the time we reach the Marina."

"Sounds good, especially the read, shower, nap, part. I'll probably do all three."

"In the morning, I'll come to the Marina and file a report with the Coast Guard station. It'll be interesting to see what they have to say."

Kevin went below, made a few notes in his log book before showering. He let the water run, no need to conserve it now on the homeward leg of the trip. The warm water was relaxing and felt good. He realized he was tired, probably stressed over dealing with the Coast Guard and worried about what might happen.

There was a sudden crash and Kevin was thrown against the side of the shower. He heard the sail slam back against the sheet. At the same time, Juliana let out a screech.

He pushed the shower curtain aside and stuck his head out.

"Are you okay? What was that?"

"I'm okay, but we took a big wave broadside and

I'm all wet."

"Hang on, I'll be there in a minute."

He dried off, threw on some clothes and his foul weather jacket and returned to the cockpit, where Juliana sat shivering.

He could see that in a short period of time the weather had changed dramatically. Four to five foot swells were racing down the Santa Barbara Channel and into the San Pedro Channel. The wind had risen to twenty knots.

"Julie, you need to steer for a couple minutes more. I'm going to furl the jib and shorten the mainsail with a reef. Then you can go below and dry off." He went below and returned with two harnesses and safety lines.

"Put this on and clip it to the rail," he said.

When the jib was furled, Kevin had Juliana turn the boat to ease the pressure on the mainsail. He went on deck to the base of the mast and lowered the sail to the first reefing point. The sail whipped violently about his head as he told himself to stay calm, get the job done.

Another large wave hit the boat broadside and Kevin grabbed the mast for support. His mouth was dry and he just hung on for a minute or two, watching the sail.

"Be careful there," Juliana yelled. "Are you all right?"

"I'm okay," he said. He had the first reef line tied and worked his way to the end of the boom to tie the second.

That done, he jumped back down in the cockpit and took the wheel, bringing the boat back on course. The wind was now twenty-five knots, gusting to thirty, and *Seascape* was heeled over, but riding better now and doing almost seven knots.

"We're okay now," he said. "You can go below and change. Take a shower and warm up. I'll be fine here."

"Do we need the storm sails?" Juliana asked.

"I don't think so, not unless it really starts blowing."

After Juliana went below, Kevin looked at the sails, made a few adjustments, and checked the wind again. It had steadied at twenty-five knots. The first drops of rain began to splatter on the boat. Kevin pulled the hatch cover closed to keep the rain from falling into the cabin. In minutes it was pouring and visibility dropped to a few hundred feet.

The wind blew fiercely, whistling through the rigging and making the shrouds vibrate and hum. Every fifth or tenth wave slammed into the port side of the boat, dumping spray on the deck and up onto the sail and over Kevin, crouched behind the wheel. Once he was satisfied about the trim of the boat, Kevin stopped worrying and relaxed. It was exhilarating to see the churning wake behind *Seascape* as she ticked off the miles to Marina del Rey.

Kevin sat hunkered down in the cockpit, water dripping from his hat, and kept *Seascape* on course. The boat was sailing fine, not bothered by the sudden squall. Sitting there, Kevin thought about the ocean. One minute, calm, peaceful, a sparkling blue expanse of beautiful water. But, he knew, the sea bided its time. When conditions were right, it would rise up. The blue water would turn into ugly greenish gray, topped with whitecaps. This was especially true of the giant storms that arose in Alaskan waters. They would move south, driving huge waves before them. In the south, the wind would funnel down between the mainland and the Channel Islands, building in intensity and forming huge swells that would hammer the coastal beaches and make entry into the affected harbors dangerous in the extreme.

Yes, he thought, that is the sea, beautiful, but unpredictable. You could never let down your guard.

The wind finally began to ease as they approached Marina del Rey. They entered the harbor as the sun slowly slipped below the horizon.

After the rain stopped and the waves subsided, the

wind dried off the deck, leaving a white residue of salt everywhere on the boat.

In the morning, Kevin went to the Marina del Rey Coast Guard station. After identifying himself he was interviewed by two officers. He described seeing the boat come into Santa Barbara Island, two men going ashore and dropping off the two backpacks, and then leaving, the boat departing with no running lights.

"So you just saw two men?"

"Yes, there were two that came ashore. There may have been more in the boat; I couldn't tell. As soon as the two returned, they hoisted the inflatable on board and the boat took off."

Kevin described the boat and men as best he could, including the direction it had taken when it left the island. He asked about the contents of the backpacks. "Was it important?"

"We think so," was the reply. "The materials you found have been turned over to the Navy for evaluation. That's all we can say at the moment. If you think of anything else, please give us a call. In the meantime, we would appreciate it if you did not discuss this matter with anyone, particularly not with the news media."

"Certainly," Kevin told the officer. "If you need anything further, here's my card. I'll be happy to cooperate in any way possible."

After being awake half the night, Kevin finally fell asleep. He'd gained no new insights. He wished he'd paid more attention to the boat, but at the time its arrival only seemed curious, not important. It wasn't until later that he thought it might be significant.

A few days later he thought about calling the Coast Guard to see if they had learned anything else. But then he got busy preparing for his trip to Washington and forgot. He was soon to learn that the incident was not only very important, it almost got him killed.

MOUNTAIN RETREAT

After meeting with Kidd and Taylor, Kevin and Juliana took precautions. Her office was the R&D Corporation in Santa Monica. She usually took the bus, but because of what happened, Kevin insisted on driving her to work each day and picking her up after work. After dropping her off, he drove to his office downtown, varying the route and times.

At first, she appreciated his concern and thought nothing of it. On the third day, she asked "Have the police contacted you? Any word on the kidnappers?"

"Nothing definite yet. They may have a lead on the car. Apparently there was a woman in the car behind you who saw you jump out. She was alarmed and called 911. She only got part of the license number."

"What do they say about us? Are we safe at home now, or should we go back to the hotel? Is there still something we should be worried about?"

"They think we're probably okay. They're keeping a watch on the house to be sure."

"What? You mean to say we have cops watching us at night? Why didn't you tell me?"

"I didn't want you to worry."

"I worry less when I know what's going on. How long is this supposed to last?"

"I don't know—I suppose until some arrests are made."

In succeeding days, Kevin noticed Juliana looking outside through the curtains. Once she called him to the window.

"Look—see that car? I've seen it come by before.

It's not a police car. Should we call somebody?"

"No," Kevin said. "They're using unmarked cars to keep an eye on our house. Don't worry, come to bed."

However, as the days passed Juliana became more preoccupied and even, Kevin thought, slightly paranoid. It began to affect Kevin also, to the point that he imagined cars following him on the freeway. It also bothered him not being able to tell Juliana all he knew, especially about his contact with the CIA. He wanted to say something, but he concluded that this was a case where the less she knew, the better. Still, after two weeks he decided to call Kidd.

"This uncertainty and surveillance is really bothering my wife, and it's getting to me also. We'd like to leave town for a week, let things settle down. That okay with you?"

"Where are you thinking of going?"

"My boss has a cabin at Lake Arrowhead. He said we could use it for a week."

"Just make sure your boss understands that he is not to disclose your location in case someone calls claiming they have to reach you because of an emergency or some other excuse."

"I can do that. I'll think of some reason why we need privacy."

"Good. Also, check in with us, just so we know you're okay. You know the protocol. If we have any news, I'll make sure you're informed. When you leave to go to the mountains, depart early in the morning. Don't tell anyone where you're going."

Kevin and Juliana arrived at Lake Arrowhead at noon. The cabin was on a hillside facing the lake. Inside, the walls were knotty pine with an exposed beam ceiling. There was a fireplace with a pile of firewood in the living room. Juliana took Kevin's arm and led him out to sit in two chairs on the porch.

"Look at the lake; isn't this beautiful? I'm so glad we came. It was really getting on my nerves staying in the house. You haven't said much, but I could tell it was bothering you also."

"I keep thinking about poor Bob Beske. What a shame. Think about his family, how hard it must be for them. He mentioned he was married, but I don't know about kids. I hardly had a conversation with him when this all happened. Afterwards I don't remember a thing."

"I don't think you ever told me why you were meeting with him in the first place. Was he a client?"

"No, not a client. He was an investigator, following up on the Santa Barbara Island incident. The Coast Guard thinks those items we found were stolen from San Nicolas Island and could be parts from a new drone the Navy is testing."

"Drones? What is so special about drones? I thought they were used as practice targets for planes and ships."

"You're right. In the 1960s, the Navy launched target drones from Point Mugu out into the Pacific Missile Range where ships shot them down while testing *Terrier* and *Tartar* ship-to-air missiles. The tests were monitored from San Nicolas Island, so it has been involved for many years. But drones have also been used for surveillance. Since the incident on Santa Barbara Island I've been trying to learn more about drones, or unmanned air vehicles, UAVs, as they are now called."

"What have you found out?"

"The technology changed around 1980 when the Israeli Air Force used drones to observe enemy positions and report back. The early ones were small, resembling model airplanes that carried cameras and were launched by hand. In the 1970s and 1980s, Israel developed two larger drones called the *Scout* and the *Pioneer*. During the first Gulf War the U.S. acquired Israeli drones and used them to monitor the Iraqis They proved so valuable that the U.S. started developing improved versions that could fly higher and stay up longer. A lot of money—billions of dollars—

has been poured into drone research. This led to the *Predator*, a UAV used in the Bosnian war during 1992 to 1995. The next step was to arm the drones with cameras and missiles and send them out on hunter-killer missions."

"I remember reading about this in the paper. Cheaper than planes, no pilots at risk."

"Right. This technology is obviously of great interest to certain Middle Eastern countries."

"Knowing that, I can imagine why the parts we found could be so valuable," Juliana said.

"Yes."

"So you're saying that we've upset the plan of some international spy ring?"

"I don't know for sure. But it looks that way."

"Oh my God, Kevin, that sounds terrible. What will we do?"

"We're going to let law enforcement take care of it and not worry anymore. Once the bad guys figure out that we don't have their stuff, they'll forget about us."

"It's getting cool; let's go inside and light a fire in the fireplace. I think I'm ready for a glass of wine."

In the morning they took a walk down to the lake and sat on an empty dock, watching a mother mallard with six young ducklings swimming in a line behind her. Kevin put his arm around Juliana. She involuntarily shuddered.

"Julie, what's the matter?"

"I'm sorry. I was looking at the lake, just daydreaming, and when you put your arm around my shoulders I immediately remembered the kidnapper doing that."

"Julie, I understand, I don't blame you, it was a terrible ordeal. Now you're fine, you're safe, nothing's going to happen. Try to put it out of your mind if you can."

"There's something else, something I'd totally forgotten until just now, something very scary."

"What?"

"They knew where I worked. They had to know

something about my job. They knew where we lived, and they must know about your job. What is going on?"

"How do you know this?"

"In the car, the guy in the backseat said that I worked at 'that think tank where they do secret stuff.' We were driving into Santa Monica so he could only be referring to R&D. I guess I just blanked out on it; I was so relieved after getting away, and then finding that you were okay, or I would have mentioned it to the police.

The week went quickly. As the days passed, Kevin could see Juliana's old personality start to emerge as her fears and paranoia lessened. They took walks by the lake, went into town for dinner, sat by the fireplace reading. At night she curled up with him more closely than usual, but slept through the night, not once getting up to go look out through the curtains as she'd done before.

Kevin, on the other hand, did not sleep well. He frequently found himself lying awake, agonizing over what he might have done differently. Juliana's revelation—that the kidnappers knew where she worked—bothered him, but he said nothing to her.

In the middle of the week, he slipped away from Juliana for half an hour to call his contact. The report was "no new information." On Friday, he called again, because he'd promised to be back at work on Monday. This time the report was, "Okay to return on Sunday. Check in on Monday for details."

"I called the authorities," he told Juliana. "They said it was okay for us to come home."

"Did they say why?"

"They wouldn't say," he said. "But it sounds like they're making progress. I don't know about you, but I'm ready to go home."

෨

Monday morning, Kevin called Charles Kidd and asked for an update.

"You'll be happy to know that we found Bob Beske's body. He was buried in a shallow grave not far from the cabin. As sad as the whole thing is, the fact that his body was found gives some comfort and sense of closure to his family. The car that belonged to Juliana's kidnappers was abandoned and set on fire on a side street in Sylmar. At least one of the kidnappers has been identified and a warrant issued for his arrest. It was the man who was in the backseat with Juliana. He has several prior arrests for assault and burglary. We believe the kidnappers fled the state, probably going to Mexico. Unfortunately, we're still missing the link or connection between the kidnappers, Beske's murder, and your kidnapping. Given where we are, I don't think there's any need for further surveillance of your home. However, if I were you, I would continue to be observant and vary your routines as we discussed."

"Also, I heard back from the Coast Guard," Kidd said. "I called to see if anyone had shown up looking for those backpacks."

"Since we hadn't heard, I assumed nothing happened," Kevin said.

"It sounds like the Coast Guard screwed up," Kidd said. "I understand they pulled into the cove and anchored the cutter right there in plain sight. They put one guy on shore to watch that place where you marked the spot. He left an inflatable tied to the landing dock. In the middle of the night a power boat—about thirty-five feet long—pulled in slowly, long enough to look around, then turned and headed back out to sea. The cutter's skipper was below getting coffee and came topside just as the other boat left. He couldn't leave without his guy on shore, so at first he decided it probably wasn't anything. Then he decided that wasn't smart, so he called the guy on the island to come back. By the time he returned, maybe half an hour had passed. When they finally hit the high seas and switched on the radar, no vessels showed up. I figure that at thirty knots, that boat had enough time to haul ass down to Catalina and hide behind the island where the radar wouldn't pick it up. Anyway, they went out, looked around for a while, and then went back to the island. They stayed there on and off for five days, but no one else showed up except for a couple of swordfish boats that put in for the night."

"We can probably conclude that the bad guys know that the stuff is not on the island now," Kevin said.

"So it would seem."

"What about the guy who used to work on San Nicolas?"

"He also has disappeared. His apartment was cleaned out, looks like he planned to get out of town."

"Another dead end."

"It looks that way."

"But what about the drone parts? Any further information on who wanted them?"

"No, we're still working on that. But I will say that we've learned of some other incidents that are tied to this. It now appears that this is a large, well-coordinated effort, bigger than we first imagined."

"There's one other new thing. In the mountains, Juliana suddenly recalled that the kidnappers knew where she worked and that R&D Corporation did classified work. Do you think there could be any connection? It bothers the shit out of me that they seem to know so much about us."

"I don't know," Kidd replied. "But that seems more than coincidental. I'll keep it in mind."

"I want to help; what can I do?"

"That's generous of you. One thing you can do is keep me informed about your travels. Your company has projects overseas. We have a special interest in the Middle East, which should come as no surprise to you. It's likely there is a connection from there to Bob Beske, but we don't know what it is."

"You'll let me know what kind of information is of interest?"

"Yes—when you know you have a trip planned, get back to me. We'll go over a list of topics. They will probably seem very mundane to you, but surprisingly, out of a lot of innocuous details, our experts are able to assemble a jig-saw puzzle that many times is surprisingly accurate. That brings up another thought: the next time you're going to Washington, let me know. I think it would be useful to have you visit Langley for additional briefings concerning overseas contacts and, most importantly, how to stay out of trouble."

After hanging up the phone, Kidd thought about what Juliana had said. Maybe it was nothing, maybe something. His judgment told him he needed to check it out. He made a mental note to give her a call.

LOVERS

The new Denver International Airport was a big project that would last for years. In 1983, winning that contract became the sole preoccupation of Al Gardner, a senior business development officer for Consolidated. Al was a tall jovial man, ex-Navy. He was a politician in a sense; he made it his business to know everyone in the mayor's office, anyone connected with the airport board, and everyone remotely connected to them. He was everywhere, laying the groundwork, making friendships, gathering intelligence, identifying the small nuances that would be key to writing a winning proposal.

He was also in touch with the competitors, telling them it was going to be a complex project, the city kept changing its mind, the job would be beset by bureaucracy, and he was probably going to end up recommending a "no-bid." Many of their competitors regarded him as affable, talkative, but shallow. To underestimate Al, Kevin knew, would be a big mistake.

While Al was engaged in these pre-proposal activities, he was accomplishing another very important task: sizing up the competition. The Pearson Corporation was Denver-based and had the strongest team. Al set about convincing Pearson that he had a stronger team and then planted the seed that, combined, the two firms would be unbeatable. He initiated the first steps to formulate a joint venture to bid on the project. The joint venture would be overseen by an executive committee comprised of senior management from both companies, led, of course, by Al.

As the due date for the airport proposal neared, Kevin

joined a team of people who were working on it in a rented office in Washington, D.C. Called the "DIA War Room," the office was spartan. It had computers, printers, shelves of documents, and the walls were covered with schedules, flowcharts, and timelines.

Kevin had earned a degree in civil engineering and a MBA from UC Berkeley. After graduation he went to work for Consolidated Engineers and Constructors. In Denver his job was to write and edit technical sections of the proposal, describing how runways would be built and how the new terminal and auxiliary buildings would be constructed. The new airport was to replace Denver's old Stapleton Airport. It was to be located on a large, fifty square mile site about twenty-five miles from downtown Denver. The proposal for such a complex project would ultimately require six four-inch-thick, three-ring binders.

There were about two dozen people in the room on a blustery spring day, as Kevin put the finishing touches on his write-ups. He was tired; the twelve-hour days were beginning to tell. He was fed up with the crummy hotel where he was staying. Most of all, he wanted to get back to the field and check on the progress of other jobs under construction.

Lost in thought, he paused, pen in hand, and stared across the room. On the other side of the room, a dark-haired woman was looking directly at him. Embarrassed, she dropped her eyes as soon as she saw him looking at her. Kevin kept looking at her, thinking that she was the most beautiful woman he'd ever seen. She was part of the graphic design team assembling artwork for the proposal. He'd seen her in the war room on several previous occasions, but hadn't paid attention because he was so preoccupied with getting the job done so he could return to Los Angeles.

His first thought was, where did she come from? He remembered she'd been in and out of the room during the past week as the proposal work entered its final stages.

He looked up again, saw her looking at him. This time she didn't look down. Instead, she smiled, gave a little movement of her head in acknowledgment, and returned to her work. Her eyes were dark brown. Medium length black hair framed a classic face. Her complexion was fair, a pale cream color. She wore a short-sleeved white sweater and blue jeans. He judged her height to be about five and a half feet. She had a trim, athletic, well-proportioned body, graceful, a ballet in motion when walking.

Whatever Kevin had been working on was temporarily forgotten. He put his pen down, leaned back, stretched, and got up. He walked over to the coffee machine and poured himself another cup of coffee—his third that morning. While stirring his coffee, he glanced over at the woman who was busy with her computer. He walked over, stood next to her, and looked at the monitor.

"Nice job," he said. "Can I bring you a cup of coffee?"

She looked up. "Oh, hi. Thanks Kevin, but I'm drinking tea."

Kevin was so taken aback that she knew his name that he was speechless for a moment. She extended her hand to him in greeting, saying, "I'm Juliana. Maybe you don't remember, but we met before at a pre-proposal meeting in L.A. I guess I should say that we didn't exactly meet formally, but you were introduced to the team."

"I'm sorry," Kevin said. "I'm embarrassed to admit I don't remember. There was so much going on then and the main thing I remember was hoping I didn't get tapped to come to Washington and be stuck in a hotel for two weeks working on this proposal."

Juliana laughed. "Well, guess what? Here you are. You have to make the best of it. Are we almost done?"

"I think so." He hesitated a moment, not wanting to end the conversation. "Do you have any plans for lunch?"

"I thought I'd sit here and eat my yogurt," she said, smiling. "Do you have something better in mind?"

"There's a place nearby on the Potomac River. I need some fresh air, a few minutes to step back from the writing and clear my mind. I feel like I'm bogged down, if you know what I mean."

"I guess the yogurt will keep."

"Great. Meet me outside at 11:30. It's not far; we can walk or take a cab."

It was a beautiful day, so they decided to walk.

"How did you get involved in this project?" Kevin asked.

"I work for a temp agency. My boss is friends with the head of your proposals group. When they get overwhelmed, we get called in to help. This the first time I've ever worked on a proposal so big and so technical. Most of my experience has been on sales brochures and a few proposals for school projects. What about you?"

"I'm normally in the field, managing construction projects. But every now and then the field guys get called in to help with the technical sections of proposals."

"So you're based in L.A?" She asked.

"Yes, I spend most of my time there when I'm in the office, but usually I'm in the field somewhere on a job."

"In California?"

"At the moment. But it could be anywhere. We have projects all over the U.S. and overseas. I do a lot of traveling. What about you?"

"I live in Santa Monica. I don't normally do any traveling. This has been exciting for me—to visit Washington. Every day after work I've gone somewhere to see the sights. On the weekends, I visited museums. The Smithsonian is amazing, I could spend days there."

They approached the restaurant and Kevin suggested sitting outside where they could see the river.

After they were seated, Kevin watched two people in kayaks come down the river.

"Look at the kayaks," he said to Juliana. "That makes me homesick—I'd like to be out on the water."

"Are you a kayaker?"

"Yes and no. I have a kayak, but mostly I'm a sailor. I have a twenty-five foot sloop in Marina del Rey and live in an apartment nearby. I love to swim and surf. I enjoy the harbor scene and spend weekends on my boat when I can. I had a fantasy that I'd sail it to wherever my next job was and live on it, but that hasn't worked out. So the boat mostly stays in Marina del Rey while I do the traveling. What about you?"

"I haven't done much sailing, but I love the ocean. I took some oceanography classes in college. My apartment in Santa Monica is about three blocks from the beach. I like to run on the beach—and swim, once the water warms up."

The waiter came and they ordered.

"Just a salad for me," she said. "I think I'll have the shrimp Louie and iced tea."

"I'll have crab cakes. They have to be good here, right at Chesapeake Bay."

During lunch Kevin found himself stealing glances at Juliana as she told him about her job and the various places she'd been visiting during her time in Washington.

My God, she's beautiful, he thought to himself. He mentally kicked himself for not noticing her sooner. How could he have been so stupid, so engrossed in work? He wanted to invite her to dinner, but worried about coming on too strong, especially with someone he'd just met.

"Do you know anything about the Kennedy Center," she was asking. The question snapped him back to reality.

"Yes," he said, "they have plays, concerts and other performances. Have you been there?"

"No, I haven't, but I'd love to go. I heard it's really hard to get tickets."

"Let me check," he said. "I don't know what's playing there tonight, but if I can get tickets, would you be interested?"

"I don't want to put you to any trouble," she said.

"I'll just make a few calls," Kevin said. "No trouble, I'll let you know what happens."

Back in the war room, Kevin put in a call to Al Gardner in the downtown D.C. office. "Hi Al, it's Kevin. I need a favor."

"How's the proposal coming, Kevin?"

"Good Al, we're almost there. Listen, this is important. A big favor."

"What's the problem?"

"No problem. It's just that I need two tickets to the Kennedy Center for the performance tonight. Good seats."

"Sounds serious, Kevin. Who is she?"

"Don't laugh, Al. This *is* serious. I know it sounds crazy, but today I met the woman I'm going to marry."

‰

Juliana checked herself in the mirror. She worried that her best dress wasn't formal enough for the Kennedy Center. When she'd packed for the trip to Washington she'd never anticipated any formal evenings. Kevin told her they were going to see "Frank Sinatra in Concert," and not to worry about what she was wearing. "For that program, you'll see everything from casual to black-tie."

She liked him—he was unlike other men she'd dated. He had an ability to bury himself in his work, ignoring the rest of the world. He'd failed to notice her for over a week, although she subtly tried to get his attention. On the other hand, he had a charming sense of humor and was good-looking. There was something about him that attracted her. She couldn't put her finger on what it was; she only knew that her feelings about Kevin were different from anything she had experienced before.

The Kennedy Center was sold out. Al had pulled some serious strings to get the tickets. In the cab afterwards, Kevin asked, "How'd you like the show?"

"It was wonderful. Frank Sinatra still has it, doesn't he?"

"Yes, it's kind of amazing, because he was a star in my mother's time."

"What kind of music do you like, Kevin?"

"I'm not much for classical music. I guess you could say I identify with soft rock. You know, bands like Fleetwood Mac, the Righteous Brothers, and the Eagles."

She tilted her head and smiled at him. "You go for that peaceful easy feeling, huh?"

Kevin was at a loss for words. Around Juliana, his feelings were anything but peaceful and easy. More like "on fire." Before he could say anything, she said, "I like the Eagles also. Too bad they broke up. Thanks again for the evening. It was wonderful."

At her hotel, Kevin jumped out of the cab and walked around to open her door.

"Good night, Juliana."

She smiled, a Mona Lisa smile that had many interpretations. "Good night Kevin. See you tomorrow."

Then she was gone.

After dropping her off at her hotel, Kevin didn't feel like going to bed. At his hotel he went to the bar for a nightcap. His concerns for the proposal he was working on were gone at this point as he thought about her. When he finally went to bed, he lay awake for a while, trying to imagine what it would be like if she was there with him. A few miles away, in another hotel, Juliana likewise went to bed but didn't fall asleep immediately, her first impressions of Kevin keeping her awake.

Kevin saw Juliana in the office the next day. As noon

approached, he looked up and saw her looking at him. He gave her a quick smile before returning to the document he was working on.

Once Kevin was back at work, Juliana stole another glance at him, trying to decide what about him attracted her. His hair was sandy-brown, cut short. He was wearing a navy-blue turtle neck sweater, tan slacks, and brown loafers. He looked to be about six feet tall, broad shoulders, slim, a muscular 180 pounds—an athlete's build. But it was more than that—some quality she couldn't put her finger on.

She put aside the work she was doing. A few minutes later she was at his desk with her carton of yogurt.

"Want to share this with me? It's a nice day outside, we could take a walk."

"I don't know about that yogurt," he said, "but a walk sounds good. And I've got an apple for lunch."

Springtime in Washington: trees were in bloom and people were out walking, enjoying the fresh air. Kevin and Juliana approached a park where several couples embraced on the grass, deep in conversation. They watched two squirrels chase each other up a tree.

They entered the park and found a bench to sit on. She ate her yogurt while he ate his apple. When done, he threw the core to an inquisitive squirrel.

"It looks like I'll be finished by this weekend," she said. "I'm flying home Friday afternoon. What about you?"

"I'm probably stuck here until the middle of next week. Would you like to hang around an extra day, maybe go to the Baltimore Orioles game on Saturday? The betting is that they'll win the league and be in the '83 World Series."

"Sounds tempting but I can't. I've got to get home, do some chores to get ready for my next project. How about a rain check, maybe go to a Dodgers' game after you return instead?"

"Are you a Dodgers fan?"

"Not really. But I like sports, and I've never been to the Dodgers' ballpark."

"Okay, you're on. I'll call you when I get back."

After Juliana left, the days seemed to go slowly. Kevin went to the Orioles game by himself, but the whole time he hardly watched the game, thinking about Juliana.

When he returned home, he waited a day, and then called her and made a date to go to the ballgame the next Saturday. The following week he took her out to dinner on the Santa Monica pier, and a few days later they went to a concert at the Hollywood Bowl. That evening, when he dropped her at her apartment and started to walk away, she grabbed him and kissed him on the cheek before hurrying inside.

Except for those times when he was away on a trip, they saw each other every week. As the spring turned to summer and the weather grew warm, they went to the beach or went day-sailing in Kevin's boat. A strong emotional attachment developed between them and they grew closer.

One evening, as they sat on Kevin's boat waiting for the sunset, Kevin said, "You told me you are a seventh generation Californian or was it eighth? How did this come about?"

"I'm named after my great-great grandmother, Maria Juliana Linares, who was born in Sinaloa, Mexico in 1771. She came to California as part of the de Anza expedition in 1775 when she was four years old. That trip must have been an adventure for a young girl, but it was more of a challenge for her pregnant mother. On the trail, she experienced early labor pains, but they went away. A month later, the pains were real. She was frightened, because another birth occurring shortly before the expedition departed resulted in the death of the mother.

Labor began and she gave birth to a boy named Salvador on December 25, 1775. He was born in a dusty tent in the Anza Borrego Desert at a place known today as Coyote Creek. Salvador became known as the "Christmas Day Baby." He was the fourth child in the family. When the baby popped out into the world on that cold December day, his first sensations, no doubt, were that it was damn cold and it smelled like a stable, with all the cattle, mules, and horses nearby. Young Juliana, my namesake, now had a little baby to help care for, so the trip became even more interesting for her."

"Amazing that you are a seventh or eighth generation Californian," Kevin said. "Please go on with your story. What happened after the baby was born?"

"In celebration of the successful birth, Captain de Anza issued brandy to the soldiers of the expedition. Fray Pedro Font, the spiritual leader of the expedition, charged with converting the heathens to Catholicism, complained to de Anza. Font thought it would lead to drunkenness. Anza replied that it was necessary for morale, since two previous pregnancies had ended in miscarriages."

"He was obviously an astute leader," Kevin remarked. "That reminds me—a little more wine? I see your glass is nearly empty. If you'd warned me, I could have brought some brandy for us."

He refilled both their glasses. "Please continue. I feel like I'm in the presence of a real pioneer."

"What I found interesting was, at that time, the country itself was being born. George Washington was not yet forty-three years old, the Boston tea party happened two years earlier, and the battle of Lexington and Concord took place eight months previously on April 19, 1775. While the expedition struggled across the desert, two thousand five hundred miles to the east the siege of Boston was going on in December of that year.

"While the British were preoccupied with their independent and increasingly restless colonists on the East

Coast of America, my Spanish ancestors were quietly going about settling the entire West Coast of America and claiming an area much larger—and hopefully more valuable—than the thirteen colonies.

"The other amazing thing was that de Anza brought the entire group of several hundred colonists to new homes in San Francisco without the loss of a single life while on the trail."

"How did you end up in Southern California?"

"My ancestors settled in Northern California. Several generations passed and then they started marrying gringos and moving south. My mom met my dad in Los Angeles. He was from the Midwest originally, but settled here after he got out of the Navy."

"So, what about you?" Juliana asked. "Are you one of those rare persons, a native Californian?"

"I was born here, but like you, I'm descended from immigrants. Mine came from Europe. After the French Revolution, the idea of freedom spread to other European countries. The German Confederation consisted of thirty-seven independent states plus Austria, Prussia and Bavaria being two of the most powerful. Bavaria took on the role of exerting power in the southern states to counter-balance Prussian power in the north and Austria in the south. A new Bavarian Constitution was drafted in 1818 to guarantee religious freedom. By 1837, it began to unravel, and Protestants were harried and oppressed."

"Impressive, Kevin. I was never very good at European history. But what about your ancestors?"

"I'm coming to them. Besides religious oppression, the economy was bad. Immigrants left Bavaria to seek jobs, to escape from wars and military service, and to find greater religious freedom. Wilhelm Jaeger, my great-great-grandfather was one of these immigrants. Around five million Germans—many artisans or skilled craftsman—immigrated to the United States during the 19th century, settling mostly in the East and Midwest.

"When Wilhelm was nine years old, the family came to the United States, where his name was changed to William Hunter. The family settled in Marietta, Ohio, and became successful farmers. The next generation continued the farming tradition. An exception occurred in the third generation; a son named George became a Baptist preacher in Nebraska. He married a woman who was the daughter of a missionary who'd served in India and Burma. They had four children, one who was destined to become my father. My grandfather died of heart failure and my father had to drop out of high school and work full-time to support the family."

"Are you sure you're not one of those Prussians? I thought the Bavarians were easy going?"

"I'm easy going, you know that. I admit I can be a little determined at times, but that's probably from my mother's side of the family.

"My mother's family was English or Welsh; I don't know where they originated or what brought them to settle in the Midwest. My other grandfather, Byron Riley, was born in 1882 in Illinois, one of four children. His father was killed in a hunting accident when Byron was five years old. When Byron was fifteen he lied about his age and enlisted in the Army. In 1898 when he was sixteen, his unit was sent to Cuba when the Spanish-American war broke out, then back to the Philippines with Admiral Dewey to battle the Spanish fleet.

"My other grandmother, Hannah Thomas, was the daughter of a soldier. She was born in 1888 in an Army guard house in Fort Bridger, Wyoming territory, where her father was stationed. He died when Hannah was eight years old, so her mother did laundry for the soldiers to support Hannah and her sister.

"She told me many interesting stories about Wyoming before it became a state. One day while her mother was hoeing weeds in the garden, an Indian came into their cabin, picked up her baby sister Rose and a freshly baked loaf of bread, and carried both out of the house. Waving her hoe, Hannah's mother chased the Indian until he dropped Rose and fled with the bread.

"In 1906 Hannah was at Fort Sheridan, Illinois, when she met that 'little, feisty, snot-nosed Corporal Riley.' They were married by a Justice of the Peace, when she was eighteen. Over the next two decades, Hannah gave birth to nine children. The first daughter, my mother, was born in 1917, just before Byron left for France to take part in World War I. He did not see his daughter until 1919, after the end of the war. My parents met when my mother's family moved to California. They were married in 1949. So there you have it, Julie. We're just a couple of immigrant kids in the new world."

"Interesting that we have something in common—grandmothers who were pioneers," she said.

"It's time to watch the sun," Kevin said. "If you look carefully, as it sinks into the horizon, you'll see a green flash."

"I've heard that story before," she said, "but, honestly, I've never seen it."

Kevin put his arm around her and they sat silently as the sun disappeared.

"There, did you see it?"

"No, did you?'

"Truthfully, no. But I have in the past."

He leaned in and kissed her. She put her arms around him and kissed him back.

"Hmm," he said, "I saw a flash then."

"Liar. Your eyes were closed."

After they had known each other for six months, Kevin knew for sure he was in love. He'd never known another woman like her. It seemed that they had so much in common. Money wasn't a big deal with her; she wanted to travel, she had a good sense of humor. When he teased her, she teased back, never got offended. She was a talented artist, and art—along with music—was so foreign to his experience and ability that he marveled at what she could do with a few brush strokes. There also was the issue of her Spanish ancestors. They'd been tough, willing to strike out in an unknown land, daring much to create new homes and lives, as had his ancestors. They were survivors. Only by knowing their roots is it possible to understand how Juliana and Kevin were able to respond to future dangers. They'd inherited this toughness. They too were survivors.

Kevin and Juliana became closer emotionally, more intimate, hugging, kissing, but never going beyond that.

One night he brought her back to her apartment after dinner. As he started to leave, she called him back.

"Come stay a while," she said. "It was a wonderful dinner. Thank you so much. Would you like a glass of wine before you go?"

Kevin sat on the couch while she went in to the kitchen and poured two glasses. When she returned, they toasted. She spoke a little more about the restaurant, the service, how much she'd enjoyed the salmon. She set her glass down and looked at Kevin, her dark eyes focused on him. She put her head back and closed her eyes.

He leaned over and gave her a quick kiss on the lips. She put her arms around him and pulled him closer, kissing him passionately, her tongue seeking his. She fell backwards on the couch and pulled him on top of her. He was moved to say something, but all he could think of to say was, "You're beautiful, you know." After he said it, he thought it sounded dopey.

"That's nice," she said, looking at him and smiling. "I hope you're not just saying that to take advantage of me." Then she closed her eyes and squeezed him in a tight embrace so he could feel the warmth of her legs and groin pressed against him.

Slowly he undid the top button of her blouse, and

the second one exposing her bra and the tops of her breasts. He started to push her bra up, but she placed her hand on top of his, stopping him.

"Wait. I'm sorry, it's my fault. I let myself go and I shouldn't have. I have some bad memories from a previous relationship, something that happened to me long ago. It has nothing to do with you. I need a little more time"

"It's okay,' he said. "My fault, I got carried away."

"I understand," she said. "Sometimes it's hard."

"Yes, that's certainly true," he said, smiling.

"No, that's not what I meant," she said, laughing. "I meant it's hard to stop when you care about someone."

"I know. I don't want you to get the wrong idea about me. I care a lot for you. That's the most important thing." Kevin sat up, picked up his glass and took the last swallow.

Juliana also sat up, adjusting her blouse, and put her hand on his. "Thanks for understanding."

He kissed her lightly on the cheek. "I'd better be going. I've got a busy day tomorrow." He stood and walked to the door. Juliana got up from the couch and met him at the door. She took hold of his shirt with both hands and undid the top button.

"What about you, can I kiss your chest?"

He laughed. "You can kiss any part of me you want."

She had a funny look on her face when she let go of his shirt.

Kevin opened the door and stepped out. "Good night, Julia. I'll call you tomorrow."

She stood in the doorway and watched him drive off.

Driving home, Kevin ached. The emotional state he'd reached was not going away. His erection was painful. He thought about his comment, and laughed to himself. Maybe she was shocked. She could have taken that comment several different ways.

Kevin had to go to San Francisco on business, so it was a week before he could see Juliana again. Upon his return, he called to invite her out to dinner but she countered.

"Come here for dinner. I feel like cooking. Maybe some pasta, if that's okay."

Juliana met him at the door with a glass of Chianti. "The secret of good pasta is to drink wine beforehand," she said. "Enough wine and any pasta tastes good."

"Are you having some?"

"Oh, yes, you know the saying, 'I always use wine when I'm cooking—sometimes I even put it in the food.'"

"Need any help?"

"No, go sit down and relax. I'll join you in a minute."

Kevin watched her while she stood at the stove stirring sauce. She wore a short sleeve white blouse and black slacks. She was barefoot. The blouse had a scoop neck, and when he walked in he could see the tops of her breasts as she handed him a glass of wine.

After a few minutes, she came out of the kitchen holding a spoonful of sauce. "Here, taste this. It's not too hot."

Juliana leaned over and brought the spoon to his lips. In that position, Kevin looked down her blouse. Her breasts were full, cream-colored, tantalizingly close.

"What do you think?"

"Umm good," Kevin replied, a little hesitant as he tried to focus his thoughts on the sauce.

Juliana stood up, smiling. "Good. Glad you like it. We'll eat soon. Some more wine for you?"

As she stood, Kevin noticed her nipples standing out against the thin fabric of her blouse. She turned abruptly and returned to the kitchen.

Dinner was exquisite. Juliana had candles and fresh flowers on the table. She served the pasta with a sauce that had Italian sausage, green peppers, mushrooms, and onions, topped with grated parmesan cheese. The first course was tropical salad. For dessert, she served tiramisu.

"I'm sorry about the tiramisu," she said after dinner as Kevin dried dishes for her.

"Why?"

"I bought it. I was going to try to make it, but I just ran out of time. When we're done cleaning up, would you like an espresso?"

"No, just a little more Chianti."

"Okay, go sit down, and I'll bring it to you."

Kevin sat on the couch and she joined him a minute later with two glasses of Chianti and one of the candles from dinner. She placed the candle on the coffee table, switched off the light, and snuggled up against him.

"So how was your trip to San Francisco?"

"Fine. The truth of the matter is, I wasn't focused one hundred percent on the project."

"Why was that?"

"I was thinking of you, Julie. I couldn't get my mind off you."

"That's nice. Good to know I have that effect on you."

"If only you knew."

He leaned over, put his arm around her, and kissed her. She responded immediately, with that nervous way her tongue flicked around his mouth as if she couldn't get enough. Kevin eased her over on her back while kissing her. She pulled him on top of her while their lips were locked together. Kevin kissed her on each eyelid, on her neck. He reached down and slid her blouse up, exposing her bare stomach and her bra. He kissed her on her stomach and then kissed her bra. His lips could feel her nipples through the soft fabric.

As in a dream she heard him say "Julie, Julie." Her mind drifted to some distant place. His presence comforted her and she wanted more, wanted to feel his warmth next to her.

"Wait," she said.

She pushed him away and sat upright, pulling her blouse over her head and tossing it on the floor. Kevin found himself kissing her everywhere as she clung to his head, stroking his hair. He desired her and knew he was fast losing control. He slid her bra up, freeing her breasts then kissing them. Juliana released his head, unhooked her bra, and let it fall to the floor. She pulled Kevin's head to her breasts, greedy for more kisses, losing herself in an exquisite feeling, some pent-up emotion that she couldn't explain. After a few moments the feeling became so intense she no longer could stand it. She pulled his mouth back to her lips and kissed him deeply again. She was breathing fast and her face was flushed.

"Now you," she said breathlessly. She jerked his shirt buttons undone and as he removed it, she lay back down, undid her slacks and slid them over her hips.

"I don't want to be the only one just wearing underwear, so why don't you get rid of those pants."

Kevin stripped off his pants and they lay together on the couch in a close embrace. Feeling her warmth and soft skin fully aroused him. His touch sought her sensitive places.

Lying next to him, she squeezed him close, running her hands up his back and through his hair. She gave up trying to hold in her feelings, unable to ignore the aching longing she felt.

"I want you to kiss me here," she said, pushing his head down while he held her breasts.

She was moist and he could smell her scent and taste her moistness. Juliana moaned softly, raising her hips and pulling his head hard against her.

He felt her thighs squeeze tight against his head as he kissed her while continuing to caress her breasts. Her hips rose and fell and she moaned as her orgasm swept over her.

He slid back up on top of her and kissed her lips as

he stroked her hair.

"Oh my God," she said, kissing him back, "oh my, my."

"You are fast," he said. "You didn't waste any time. No bad memories?"

"Oh no. How are you?"

"Don't worry about me."

"But aren't you frustrated?" she said. She could feel his hardness pressing against her stomach.

"I'll get over it."

She pushed him off to one side, reaching over and took hold of him. "It would be a shame to waste this," she said, stroking him gently. He lay there, eyes closed, not saying anything, his mind drifting to some distant place, carried away by the pleasure of her caresses.

Later, frustrations gone, he curled around her in a tight embrace.

"You are everything to me," he said. "I hope you know that, know how much I love you."

"Will you stay? I don't want you to leave, I don't want to be alone tonight."

"Yes, of course."

She turned over and kissed him.

"I love you."

They fell asleep in each other's arms.

Kevin was late to work the next morning. He'd awoken late, had to rush back to his apartment to change clothes. Juliana was tied up at work but he called her that evening, telling her how much he loved her. The next day he had to go to San Diego for two days of meetings. As soon as he returned, he called Juliana.

"Have you eaten?" she asked.

"No, I just got back."

"Come over and I'll fix something easy for us."

When Kevin arrived, Juliana greeted him, an apron tied around her waist. Good smells wafted from the kitchen.

"Hi," he said, taking her in his arms and kissing her. "I've missed you."

"I missed you too."

His arms were around her, holding her close.

She pulled away. "Just a minute," she said, "the stove."

She went into the kitchen and turned off the stove, returned to the living room, where Kevin had taken a seat on the couch. She removed her apron, tossed it aside, and sat down beside him. After a passionate embrace, she stood and took him by the hand. "Come with me."

She led him into her bedroom and removed his shirt and tie. Clothes were flung everywhere as they tumbled together on the bed, Juliana rolling over on her back, pulling Kevin against her, wrapping her legs tightly around him.

Dinner was forgotten.

The following week, Kevin bought an engagement ring.

He picked Juliana up after work and drove to the beach. He'd told her he was in the mood for a walk. He led her down to the water's edge. There he took both of her hands and asked her to marry him.

"When?" she said.

"Soon. As soon as possible," he replied, slipping the ring on her finger.

They set a date in August for the ceremony. They planned a small intimate wedding with Kevin's parents, his sister, and Juliana's mother along with a few close friends. The wedding was held at the Wayfarers Chapel in Palos Verdes. From there, Kevin and Juliana could look out over the Pacific Ocean and see Catalina Island in the distance, where they would spend their honeymoon.

NEW LIVES

Married life agreed with Kevin. It seemed that he and Juliana were perfectly matched. They were devoted to each other, but with differences. Kevin tended to keep things to himself, partly due to his upbringing, and partly due to his job. More and more, Consolidated was involved in designing, constructing, and in some cases operating and maintaining government facilities. Many of these involved classified projects and he had to get a security clearance.

Juliana learned of it when neighbors told her that an FBI agent had been asking questions about Kevin—questions such as, "Was he loyal to the United States? Did he have any bad habits?"

She was shocked about this and brought it up with Kevin.

"Don't worry, it's routine. Tell your friends that I'm not a criminal, just getting a security clearance for my job."

As the projects became more complex, Kevin said less and less about them to Juliana.

Still, on many occasions, when Kevin traveled to job sites, Juliana was able to go along and, in some cases, tour the work. She had enough flexibility in her own job that she could take time off to accompany him. They made trips to Germany, Japan, and once to Scandinavia.

Work was now going on at the new Denver International Airport, as well as other airports in the U.S. and abroad. Initially Kevin thought that they might have to move to Denver, but someone else was appointed to that position.

Kevin had started out as a project manager in the firm, but had been promoted several times and now had the title of "Senior Associate." His time was divided between managing increasingly larger and more complex projects, and business development.

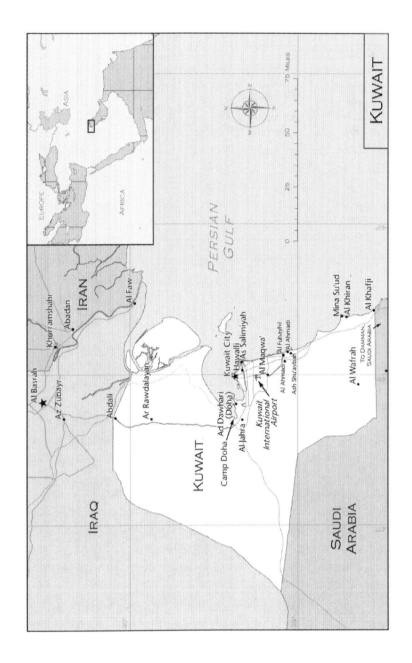

After getting married, he and Juliana moved into Kevin's apartment, which was larger than Juliana's. They started looking at buying a home. Housing costs in Southern California were rising, so in 1985 they found a three-bedroom house in West Los Angeles. It was halfway between Juliana's office and Kevin's. The price was good for that time as it needed work, but Kevin planned to use his construction contacts to renovate the house, with Juliana and him doing part of the work.

In 1986, after buying the house, Consolidated had a very good year and Kevin received a large bonus. He sold his twenty-five-foot sloop and bought a thirty-three-foot cutter-rigged sailboat. Part of the justification, he told Juliana, was that they could live on the boat while their house was being renovated.

Kevin loved the boat, which he named *Seascape*. Once the house renovation was complete, he turned his attention to the boat, working in his spare time to outfit the boat for longer trips. He added the latest navigation instrumentation, a new radar, a high-powered single sideband radio, and extra batteries and solar panels. With these improvements he planned to introduce Juliana to offshore cruising. He promised her that they'd take a vacation on the boat once he finished all his projects. Unfortunately, work intervened and the promised voyage kept getting delayed, although they were able to get away for short weekend trips.

In the decade following Kevin and Juliana's marriage, events occurred in the Middle East that would ultimately affect their lives in ways they could not have anticipated. Unrest stemmed from the assassination of Anwar Sadat, president of Egypt, the Soviet invasion of Afghanistan, the war in Lebanon, the destruction of the Beirut Marine Barracks by an Iranian suicide bomber, the Iran-Iraq war, and the Civil War in South Yemen. These conflicts and others, stirred the region and gave rise to a new generation of terrorists and suicide bombers.

❧

Near the end of 1989, increasingly ominous intelligence reports were coming from the Middle East. The Iraq-Iran war had ended in a truce with neither side a clear winner. In a sense, Iraq was the loser because it incurred a huge international debt during the war. With oil exports and economic development crippled, Iraq was thought to be casting covetous eyes on Kuwait, its small, rich neighbor to the south.

Consolidated had offices and ongoing projects in the Middle East. Because of its positioning and local knowledge, the company was a likely candidate to support an American build-up in this sensitive area.

One morning, Kevin called home shortly after going to his office. Juliana answered the phone.

"Hi. I wanted to catch you before you went to work. Some big developments are in the wind. I may have to go to Washington tomorrow. I wanted to let you know so you could clear our calendar if necessary. I know you were planning something, but I couldn't remember what."

"No problem. It was an art exhibit. I may go alone. How long will you be gone?"

"I don't know yet. We have a big meeting coming up in ten minutes where I expect to learn more."

"Okay, go to your meeting and we'll talk later."

As Kevin said goodbye, she interrupted. "Before you hang up and head off for your meeting, I want to leave you with an image."

"Oh," he said, "what image?"

"I'm standing here dripping wet and stark naked," she replied. "I just stepped out of the shower when you called."

"Great," he said. "Now I've got to go to this important meeting and try to concentrate on business when all I'm going to be able to think about is you standing there, wet hair and all, holding a towel in one hand and the phone in the other."

"Bye," she said. "Have fun at your meeting."

The next morning, Kevin was on a plane headed to Washington D.C. High-level sources in the Department of Defense were looking for "informal expressions of interest" in creating a logistics base in the Middle East. It was to be capable of rapid expansion as a forward operating base in the event of an "emergency." The "expression of interest" was to be followed by a statement of qualifications. The location was unspecified, but rumors placed it in Kuwait or Qatar. These locations, adjacent to the Persian Gulf, suggested that Iran might be the source of concerns. This assumption later proved to be incorrect.

A team was mobilized to prepare the qualification documents. Kevin returned to Los Angeles where he was able to work on the proposal from his home base. This task was completed in several weeks. After the documents were submitted, nothing happened. As usual with the government, it was "hurry up and wait."

Meanwhile, Consolidated received a contract to provide construction management services for the expansion of Kuwait University. One of Kevin's colleagues, John Remington, was selected to be the design manager. He traveled to Kuwait City with his wife and an international team of engineers and construction managers to oversee the work.

As the summer approached, Kevin once again brought up the idea of a sailing vacation. The boat was finally ready; Juliana was eager to go; his work schedule was the problem.

In July, Kevin received word that he had to go to Saudi Arabia and Kuwait. The purpose of the trip was twofold. First, to collect information related to the

Department of Defense "expression of interest," which at last had emerged as a formal request for proposals. Also, to meet with Kuwaiti University officials concerning their project.

After learning of this new assignment, he discussed the trip with Juliana.

"I've got to go to Saudi Arabia when the desert is at its hottest, and no wives allowed."

"What do you mean," she exclaimed, hands on her hips, "no wives allowed?"

"The Saudis have very strict rules on women. You can't appear in public in a dress that shows your legs or arms. Your hair and face have to be covered in public. You can't drive a car. You can't walk into a restaurant or bar by yourself. So, if you went, you'd sit in a hotel room all day—not something you'd want to do.

"What's your itinerary?"

"I fly to Frankfurt, change planes, fly to King Fahd International Airport at Damman, Saudi Arabia. I'll be at our office in al-Khobar for a couple of days, fly to Kuwait City for another couple of days, and home. I shouldn't be gone for more than a week."

"What about that vacation that you've been talking about for two years?"

"I know, I know. I think we can still do it. I'll talk to the boss and make sure it's okay. I'll need a couple of days to write reports and get over jet lag when I get back. Then we can provision the boat and take off. I know a nice little island in Baja California we can visit. In August, the fishing and diving should be great."

As he flew east, Kevin was unaware of ominous developments that were occurring and the possible threat to Kuwait.

Something was happening in southern Iraq. U.S.

intelligence detected construction of SCUD missile launch sites near the border with Jordan. These posed a clear threat and warning to Israel. Beginning in July, spy satellites revealed Iraqi armored divisions moving towards the Kuwait border with more than thirty thousand personnel. More data kept coming in from the KH-11 spy satellite orbiting Kuwait. Near the end of July, its photographs showed Iraqi trucks hauling ammunition and other supplies to Iraqi troops on Kuwait's northern border. Later satellite photos showed one hundred thousand troops in position along the Kuwait border. The CIA presented this top secret information to President Bush, but his civilian advisers convinced the president that Saddam was bluffing and no action was taken. On the morning of August 1, the CIA predicted that there was a seventy percent chance that Kuwait would be invaded in the next twenty-four hours.

Kevin knew nothing of this.

After the long flight, including a four hour layover in Frankfurt, Kevin was exhausted. The elapsed time was twenty-six hours. He wanted to call Juliana, but al-Khobar was eleven hours ahead of California, so he had to wait until 5 p.m. local time to give her a wake-up call in Los Angeles.

"Hi love, it's me. I just wanted you to know I arrived okay. I miss you already."

"Thanks for calling," a sleepy voice replied. "Will you call again from Kuwait?"

"Yes, I'll do that, and I'll let you know when I'm on my way home."

"Okay, thanks, be careful. Love you lots."

Kevin hung up the phone. He wanted to go to bed, but it was too early. Somehow he had to force himself to stay up until at least 10 p.m., or he'd be wide awake in the middle of the night. He went to dinner in the hotel restaurant, came back to his room and watched a movie until he couldn't keep his eyes open any longer.

The next morning he met with representatives of the

Saudi Consolidated Electric Company, one of the firm's clients. The following day it was with Resource Sciences of Arabia, a joint venture. This company would be an important participant in any future projects in the Middle East.

Dammam to Kuwait city was about two hundred fifty miles by road along the Gulf. It was a short airplane flight, but Kevin decided to go by land to get a feel for the countryside and arranged for a driver to take him. By road, the trip would take about five hours.

The first portion of the trip passed through undeveloped desert. Near the border town of al-Khafji, the road veered back to the Gulf and Kevin could see a beautiful, empty beach. Kuwait City was at the head of the Gulf. He made a mental note that the port facilities would be logical for bringing in supplies by sea.

The driver dropped Kevin at his hotel. He said he was available to stay, if Kevin wanted to drive back.

"Thanks, but I think I'll fly. I've got a tight schedule on the return. But thanks for the offer."

That evening Kevin had dinner with Don Swanke, the project manager, and John Remington, who was in charge of design. They discussed how the project at Kuwait University was going. Don was happy with his team of Americans, British expatriates, and several Indian engineers. Both men were accompanied by their wives, Brenda and Judy. Several other staff members had wives and children with them. The Kuwaitis were much more tolerant of foreigners than the Saudis.

"We have a good group; everyone gets along well, and the contractor is doing a good job," Don said. "We have no complaints."

"That's good to hear," Kevin replied. "Tomorrow I'd like to come out to the job site and pay a courtesy call on the client. After that, let's arrange lunch for your team so I can meet them and thank them for the good job they're doing."

"Anything else you want to do while you're here?" John asked.

"Maybe if you've got time you could show me around the city a bit. Suppose you wanted to build a big warehouse complex with access to the port. Where would you find an area to do that?"

"Anything specific in mind?" Don asked.

"No, we've had some inquiries, so I thought I'd see what might be available."

"In other words, you can't talk about it."

"In other words, I can't talk about what John's not going to show me."

"I got it," John said. "You look tired. Sleep well and I'll pick you up at 9 a.m. tomorrow."

෨

The next morning, John drove Kevin north around the city towards al-Jahra. At one point, they were on Doha Road.

"Somewhere out here might meet your requirements," he said. "As you can see, lots of open land and close access to the port and the airport."

That night John and Kevin had dinner at the hotel.

"Thanks for showing me around," Kevin said.

"You're more than welcome. Do you want to stay another day or two? I know some places where we can go snorkeling."

"Unfortunately, I've been traveling a lot, and I promised Juliana a vacation when I returned. I've an early flight. No need to worry about me. I'll just grab a taxi to the airport."

"What do you hear in the States about Saddam Hussein?" John asked. "He's quoted here with claims that the Kuwaitis are stealing his oil by slant drilling. It's also well known that he owes a lot of money to Kuwait for financing his war with Iran."

"I don't know much," Kevin replied. "The papers

have reported Hussein's saber rattling, but so far I don't think anyone at a high level takes him seriously. After eight years of war with Iran, I can't imagine the Iraqis want to start another one."

"Let's hope so. This is a nice little country with nice people, but in a hell of a location. Here we sit, surrounded by—in a clockwise direction—Saudi Arabia, Iraq, and Iran. By any measure, this is a nasty little corner of the world."

"Stay in touch. If I get any indication things are getting bad, I'll call you. If necessary, grab the guys and go south into Saudi Arabia. Leave the computers, equipment, and everything else behind if you have to get out in a hurry."

❧

Before going to bed Kevin put through a call to Juliana at her office.

"Hi Julie, I'm glad I caught you. I was afraid you might be going out to lunch. It's just noon there, right?

"Yes. I stayed here in the office with a sandwich. I'm working on my résumé."

"Your résumé? What's up with that? Are there problems at work?"

"No problems. But I've heard about a new opportunity. One of my girlfriends told me that the R&D Corporation in Santa Monica is looking for people to work on a new global climate change research project and I'm thinking of applying. It would be a perfect fit for the classes I had at UCLA. I'm sure there are many new developments in this field, but I have the basics of physical oceanography, climate change modeling, and remote sensing methods. This would be much more challenging than what I'm currently doing, and definitely would have better pay and benefits."

"Sounds exciting," Kevin said. "Is there a

deadline?"

"I have a week to submit my résumé. That would give you time to look it over. If they like it, I'll be invited for an interview. Speaking of looking over my résumé, when will you be home? And how is the trip going?"

"Actually, that's why I called. Mostly to tell you that I love you and miss you, but also to say I'm scheduled to get out of here early in the morning. I'll call you from the airport to let you know I'm on my way. When I get home I want to hear more about the R&D position. I think it would be a wonderful opportunity for you. I know the R&D Corporation and it would be a great place to work. I'll say goodbye for now because it's late and I need to get packed and hit the sack."

Goodbye, love," Juliana said. "Travel safe."

In the morning Kevin was late—literally running for the gate to make his flight—so he failed to call Juliana. Looking back, he was lucky he'd made the flight. He could have called during his layover at King Fahd airport, but didn't. So it wasn't until driving home after landing in the Los Angeles airport late on August 2, that he heard that Iraq had invaded Kuwait. In the previous twenty-four hours most of the Kuwaiti military forces had been defeated or scattered and Iraq was in control of the country. It was hard to imagine the situation there changing so quickly. While he and John were driving around the City, Iraqi forces were massing a few miles beyond the border, getting ready to pounce on Kuwait at 2 a.m. the next day.

When he drove in the driveway, Juliana came running out to greet him.

"Thank God you're okay. Why didn't you call? When I didn't hear from you, and then I heard about the invasion, I was worried sick. The Iraqis are taking over the whole country. They are killing people or throwing them in prison. People are running out into the desert, trying to escape. It sounds terrible!"

"Julie, I'm so sorry. I was running late and had no

time to phone you from Kuwait. I didn't hear about the invasion until I landed in L.A. and started driving home. Anyway, I'm okay, but I've got to find out about John and our crew there. I hope they got out in time."

❧

In the office the next day, everyone was talking about the invasion of Kuwait. The first thing Kevin did was to ask Holly to call Don and John at their apartments in Kuwait City.

"I tried to put a call through. But no luck. The phone service to Kuwait has been cut off. No one has been able to make calls."

Kevin compiled a list of project staff and dependents working on the Kuwait University project. This was forwarded to the State Department where diplomatic efforts were underway to remove noncombatants from Kuwait.

That night, Kevin and Juliana watched the television news reports. The Kuwaiti military forces had not been on alert and were totally taken by surprise. The fighting was vicious and brief and they were soon overrun. A few surviving aircraft were flown out to Saudi Arabia or Bahrain. Dasman Palace, home of the Emir of Kuwait, was captured after bitter fighting. Meanwhile, the Emir had managed to flee into the Saudi desert and avoid capture. Kuwait University was overrun and occupied by Iraqi troops. Portions of the University were converted into a prison where Kuwaitis were held. Many were tortured and some were executed. The invasion was quickly condemned by the United Nations Security Council, which passed a resolution ordering the Iraqis to withdraw. It was ignored and the Iraqis began systematically looting the country.

Two days passed and there was still no word about the situation of Don, John, their wives, and the rest of the team in Kuwait City.

On the third day, Holly rushed into Kevin's office waving a fax.

"They're all okay, she said. "They've been hiding out in the apartment building. They still have all their utilities—even cable TV where they've been watching CNN to see what's going on. Any foreigners appearing on the streets are immediately arrested. But the Indian engineers on our team are able to come and go freely, and they've been able to pick up some food and bring it back to our guys hiding in the apartment."

This was indeed good news. Kevin immediately responded and asked if there was any possibility that they could leave the city. John replied that some people had taken cars and headed off into the desert, but he did not know if they had reached safety. At this point he judged it to be impossible because there were Iraqi soldiers and checkpoints at every corner of the city. Kevin asked that he send in a daily report and advised that the State Department had been informed of the situation.

After three days, there were no further fax messages and the line went dead. The State Department was monitoring the situation and putting pressure on Iraq to release the hostages. There was nothing else that could be done from Los Angeles. Kevin decided that he and Juliana would go ahead and take the vacation they'd planned.

ISLA SAN MARTIN

"The boat has fuel and water and except for provisions, we're ready to go," Kevin announced. He and Juliana went to the supermarket and bought supplies for two weeks. Produce and fresh fruit along with bread and other perishable commodities were stored in two small hammocks, one that swung in the galley and another that hung over their bunk. Everything else went into lockers or the refrigerator.

They left Marina del Rey at 5 a.m. and sailed directly to Pyramid Cove on the east end of San Clemente Island. They anchored, had an early dinner, and were soon asleep, tired from all the last minute preparations and from the first long day at sea. The next day was pleasant, diving and relaxing, with the boat riding gently at anchor on the west side of the cove.

Early the following morning, Kevin checked the weather once again. Now the report mentioned thunderstorm activity that had been upgraded to a tropical depression and given a formal name—*Fifteen-E*. It was moving west-northwestward where it appeared that it might strengthen into a tropical storm and possibly a hurricane.

"Hey Julie," he called, "come here and listen to this weather report and tell me what you think."

"The west coast of Africa is the source of most Atlantic hurricanes and many Pacific hurricanes as well," she said. "They begin with a tropical wave, a low pressure area that moves from east to west across the tropics, causing areas of cloudiness and thunderstorms. They're generally carried westward by the prevailing easterly winds along the tropics and subtropics near the equator. This one seems to be moving in our direction."

"So what does that mean?"

"Maybe nothing," she replied. "It depends on what

happens next. We'll need to keep an eye on it."

In the morning Kevin went on deck and was surprised to see a power boat anchored some distance away. It was different in that it had no outriggers or obvious fishing gear, unusual for a pleasure boat in Pyramid Cove. No one was visible on deck. He gave it no further thought as he prepared *Seascape* for departure.

After breakfast, they were underway on a course to the southeast. Once past China Point at the end of the island, they picked up a breeze and Kevin went forward to raise the mainsail. As he did, he heard the high-pitched sound of a jet engine approaching from the west. Looking in that direction, he saw a slim, fast-moving object flying at low altitude directly toward the island. In a few seconds it disappeared from view. A moment later he heard a large explosion.

"What was that? Juliana asked.

"I don't know," Kevin replied." It looked like some kind of a rocket. Maybe a missile test. Whatever it was, it was going like a bat out of hell."

As he looked back at the island, a cloud of smoke rose in the distance.

"I'm glad we're on our way out of here. I wouldn't want to be anchored if that thing went off course."

The sea was calm and the wind favorable, as Kevin set a course to the next destination. They'd been sailing for fifteen minutes or so when Juliana noticed the boat.

"There's another boat," she said, pointing to the port side. In the distance, traveling on a parallel course, Kevin recognized the boat he'd seen earlier in Pyramid Cove. It was moving fast and soon was out of sight.

In the early afternoon, Kevin went below to take a nap, leaving Juliana at the helm.

He was sound asleep, dreaming that he was in the

water, swimming with a school of dolphins. He awoke abruptly at Juliana's touch.

"Kevin, I think you better get up. There's a boat behind us, and it seems to be coming fast, on the same heading as us."

"Okay. Let's see who's coming."

He climbed the companionway and stepped into the cockpit. In the distance he saw the boat. From the bow wave it was moving fast. It was white with an orange stripe.

"It's the Coast Guard," he said. "I wonder what they want? I better turn on the radio. Take the helm again for me, would you?"

Kevin went below and switched on the VHF radio to Channel 16. He had no sooner done so when the radio came to life.

"Sailing vessel heading 110°, this is United States Coast Guard cutter *Narwhal*. We request permission to board you for a safety inspection."

"Coast Guard, this is *Seascape.* We copy. You're welcome to come aboard. We're under sail with limited ability to maneuver. We will maintain course and speed while you come alongside."

"Roger, skipper. Thank you for your cooperation. Please stand by."

Kevin returned to the cockpit. The Coast Guard vessel could be clearly seen now. It took up station about five hundred yards astern, slowing to three knots to match the sailboat's speed.

"Kevin, shouldn't we drop the sail and heave to?" Juliana asked.

"Hell, no. Safety inspection? Bullshit. They're probably looking for drugs, but why stop us? We're headed in the wrong direction for smuggling. If we dropped the sails and lost maneuverability, they might run into us. They'll launch an inflatable and come visit. It will give them some practice."

Back on the cutter, there was a lot of movement and activity. It looked like the crew was having some trouble getting their inflatable launched.

"Take the wheel Juliana. I thought of something else." He went back below to the radio.

"*Narwhal,* this is *Seascape*. Over."

"Go ahead, *Seascape,* this is *Narwhal.*"

"I'm just confirming that we have the boarding ladder in place for your inspection. Also, one question: you wouldn't have any extra ice you could spare, would you?"

Kevin could hear muted laughter in the background on the Coast Guard vessel. After a moment, the radioman came back on.

"Sorry, skipper, we can't help you there. We've been out two weeks and our ice maker broke."

"Okay, no problem. *Seascape* clear." He returned to the cockpit, smiling to himself.

The Coast Guard inflatable was finally in the water. Three seamen got in it and it accelerated toward them, slowing to come alongside. With Juliana steering, Kevin held a line from the inflatable and two Coast Guard sailors climbed aboard, one male, one female. The third sailor remained in the inflatable, pulling away about twenty yards, but remaining on a parallel course. All were armed with automatic pistols.

"Skipper, I'm Lieutenant Todd Scott, and this is Boatswain's Mate Michelle Brown. Thank you for your cooperation. We'd just like to check a few things and then you can be on your way. Where are you from?"

"We're out of Marina del Rey headed to San Martin Island for a little diving."

"We'd like to see your ship's documents and take a look below if you don't mind."

"Feel free," Kevin said. "The paperwork is on the table in the galley, and if you want to check the flares, lifejackets and fire extinguishers, I'll be glad to show them to you."

"Thank you, sir. Perhaps you and I can do that while Boatswain's Mate Brown makes a note of the contact information for your crew."

"That's fine," Kevin said. "My crew is my wife, or on any given day I'm the crew. It just depends on who is doing what. There are just the two of us on board."

The Coast Guard officer looked over the ship's documents and barely glanced at the lifejackets and flares. He seemed more interested in the food stored aboard, the fishing tackle, and dive gear. After making some notes on a form he asked Kevin if the boat had a plaque regarding no discharge of oil or wastes overboard.

"Yes sir," Kevin said. "They're right here by the engine." He lifted the compartment lid to show the two plaques mounted there.

"What were you doing at San Clemente?"

"Just resting. We had a long sail down from Marina del Rey the day before yesterday."

"Do you have a video camera on board?"

"No, nothing like that. Why do you ask?"

"Did you photograph the island?"

"No, we were tired and went to bed pretty early."

"There was a missile test, and we don't want any photographs floating around."

"We heard it come in as we were leaving," Kevin said. But that was it. I was busy getting the sails up. What was it, if you can say?"

"It was a Tomahawk cruise missile, fired at a target on the island. It was launched by a submarine five hundred nautical miles west of here."

"Wow. That's pretty amazing. Do they ever miss?"

"I can't comment on that."

"What about that power boat that was in the Cove?"

"Power boat?"

"Yes, there was another boat there. It came in after we did and left after us. We saw it pass us at a high rate of speed this morning, headed southeast."

"The only report we had was for a sailboat. Did you get a name?"

"No, I never saw a name. It was a cabin cruiser, but didn't look like a sport fisher. And it was fast."

Lieutenant Scott jotted a few notes and returned to the cockpit.

"All set, Brown?"

"Yes sir."

"Okay, I guess we're good to go. Turning to Kevin, he said, "You're going to San Martín, right? Enjoy yourself. It sounds like fun, but be careful there. We've had some reports of boats—fast *pangas*—coming in at night, dropping off drugs. Someone then comes out from San Quintin, picks them up, brings them north. If you see any suspicious looking boats, I'd clear out, give them a wide berth."

"We'll do that," Kevin said. "Meanwhile, we hope you get that icemaker fixed."

The Lieutenant said a few words into a hand-held radio he had pulled from his belt, and the inflatable accelerated back to *Seascape* to pick up Scott and Brown.

Before boarding, Scott shook Kevin's and Juliana's hands. "Thank you again for your cooperation. Have a safe trip home."

The inflatable returned to the cutter. When it was back on board, the Coast Guard vessel made a U-turn and headed back north. "That's weird," Kevin said.

"What?"

"Why they came all way out here to look at us, when we're heading south? We're going the wrong way to be smuggling, so it made no sense. Then the Lieutenant asked me about cameras. That noise we heard was a cruise missile test. He wanted to know if we were photographing it. He didn't even know about the other boat."

"What do you think about his warning? He seemed worried about San Martín."

"I don't know. It's always been deserted when I've

been there, except during lobster season. The lobster fishermen come out from the *Cooperativo* on the mainland. They stay during the week and go home on weekends to sell their catch. They're nice, hard-working guys."

The wind picked up a few hours after the Coast Guard inspection and *Seascape* was making five knots. At 5 o'clock Kevin announced "happy hour" and went below to the gallery to make some margaritas. They sat in the cockpit nestled together, his arm around her. They were all alone on the sea—no other boats, not a bird in sight, the sails firm and their course steady towards the distant island that was their destination.

The wind was perfect and the *Seascape* sliced through the water effortlessly with all three sails set. Kevin loved to go out on the bowsprit and watch the bow wave as the boat raced along. Sometimes dolphins came and surfed along the bow wave, cutting in and out and effortlessly keeping up with the speeding boat. He would look down at them, knowing they were watching him. Some elemental communication took place—he was never sure what it was, but he knew that if he left the bowsprit the dolphins would lose interest and would veer away.

Kevin turned to the stern and looked at the wake of the boat flowing away into the distance behind them. The sun was a red ball, slowly sinking towards the distant horizon. The sea was smooth with a low swell coming down-sea behind them.

"I could go on like this forever," he said, kissing Juliana on the cheek. "If only we could shed our jobs and responsibilities and just keep sailing—Cabo San Lucas, Puerto Vallarta, on south to Costa Rica and the Panama Canal, or maybe to Cabo and then head west to catch the trades and sail to Hawaii."

Juliana laughed. "We could do it, my love. The problem is you. You're too caught up in your job and career."

Kevin shrugged, stood up for a few moments to

check the waters ahead, before sitting down again with her.

"I suppose you're right, but someday I may surprise you. At the moment, we've got the rest of this week to look forward to, so I don't want to think about business at all."

Juliana laughed. "So does that mean you're going to stay off the single sideband radio for the rest of the trip, no more checking in? I know you're worried about your crew in Kuwait."

Kevin didn't reply. They both knew he'd be on the radio once a day, making certain his projects were okay, seeing if there was any new word from Kuwait, and letting someone know where the boat was and that they were okay.

The sun was nearing the horizon. "Time to start dinner," Kevin said. "You've got the helm while I go below to cook. Watch for the green flash at sunset."

After dinner, Kevin cleaned up the dishes. "You take the first watch. Wake me up at midnight and I'll take it until dawn. We should reach the island a little before noon if this wind holds. We're lucky, we could not have asked for better conditions."

When everything was put away, Kevin took a last look around. The moon was just edging up and the first stars were out.

"If you see any other boats, wake me up," he said. "The radar is set for six miles. Every now and then take a look just to be sure. Sometimes the Mexican fishing boats don't have regulation lights. I don't think we'll see any this far offshore, but you never know."

"I want to check the weather," Juliana said.

"Good idea. Go ahead."

A few minutes later she was back. "That storm is now Tropical Depression *Lowell*. At the moment it's three hundred miles south of Acapulco. Usually if these storms develop into a hurricane, they head west to Hawaii. To stay safe we'll need to keep checking."

꙽

Juliana shined a light on her wrist watch. Almost 11 p.m. One more hour to go. She sat bundled up in the cockpit, wearing a life vest over her down jacket, with a safety line attached to the rail. She was stiff and drowsy from sitting there hour after hour. Every once in a while she stood and stretched and looked at the sea around them. There were no lights. Behind the boat, the wake reflected silver in the moonlight. It always surprised her how well you could see at night on the sea, with just the light of the stars and moon. Ahead of the boat, the light eventually faded into total darkness and gave the appearance of sailing into a black void. At first that bothered her, but now she was used to it. She had a small transistor radio that picked up music from some distant Mexican radio station. She turned it on again, to help her stay awake for the rest of her watch.

When her watch was over, she went below to wake Kevin. He woke instantly, climbing out of bed, putting on his clothes, lighting the galley stove to make a thermos of coffee. When she got into it, the bed was still warm from his body. As she fell asleep, she wished that he was there with her.

Kevin woke her with a kiss at dawn. "Time to get up, my love. The wind has dropped a little but we're still making good time. Get something to eat. There's still some coffee if you want it. I'm going to take a nap for a couple of hours. You should start seeing the island in about three hours. Wake me when we're a couple of miles out, sooner if you see any other boats or if the wind shifts."

Juliana took her seat in the cockpit. The boat sailed smoothly on course to a distant spot in the ocean that Kevin had marked on the chart. She glanced at the log book that he meticulously maintained, saw that nothing out of the ordinary had occurred during his watch, but he'd added a note to check on the *Lowell* storm. Before settling down she looked at the compass, the sails, the wind direction, and the autopilot. All was in order. She got out the book she'd been reading.

The boat continued on a southeast heading, sailing downwind and down-seas as the sun slowly climbed above the horizon. The boat was steered by a wind vane that required no power to hold a course. Juliana stood and stretched. In the distance she could see a faint smudge on the horizon, the first sight of mainland Mexico.

San Martin Island, not yet visible, was a small, low island, originally a volcano, located about six nautical miles west of the mainland and San Quintin Bay. A low-lying finger of land in the shape of the letter C curled around the east side of the island and made a protected anchorage, known as *Caleta* Hassler, or Hassler's Cove. That was their destination. There, Kevin promised, they could snorkel and see lots of fish. He hoped to spear a yellowtail or two for their barbecue.

Juliana read her book, looking up occasionally to check for other vessels and to make sure *Seascape* was still on course. After two more hours, she saw the low silhouette of the island dead ahead. As usual, Kevin's navigation had been perfect. She waited another hour, wanting to let him sleep as long as possible, and then woke him.

"Steer for the north end of the island," he said. "When we come even with that point, I'll bring in the staysail and jib. When we're around the point, you start the engine and I'll drop the main and get the anchor ready. We want to go in and anchor behind the island in about six fathoms of water."

Entering the cove, Kevin saw the mystery boat from San Clemente Island. It left as they were anchoring. As it pulled out, Kevin saw someone at the helm looking at him with binoculars. With a roar of powerful diesels it accelerated out of the cove and disappeared around the island, headed south.

Juliana backed down on the anchor and Kevin felt

the chain stiffen as the anchor grabbed.

"We're good," he yelled at her. She shut down the engine and turned off the instruments.

"We're here," Kevin said, as he returned to the cockpit and gave Juliana a hug. "Good job. What do you think of this place?"

Juliana surveyed the shore. There were no trees, but she could see cactus of some type growing on the rocky hillside. In the distance, the shell of an old sailboat was anchored. It had no masts and was covered with a canvas tarp. The shore had half a dozen dilapidated shacks. Otherwise the island appeared to be deserted.

"It's not exactly a garden spot," she said, "but I'll take your word that the diving will be great."

"Time to find out," he said. "I'm going to launch the inflatable, and we'll take a look. We don't have to go far—it's just over there at the end of that little point of land."

He launched the dinghy and Juliana helped lower the outboard motor. She went below to put on her wetsuit. When Kevin came back on board, she was standing in the companionway, pulling on her wetsuit, which was up to her waist.

He looked at her for a long moment, her nakedness causing an instant arousal. "God you're beautiful," he said, as he stepped close and cupped her bare breasts with his hands.

"Oh, stop that. Help me get this thing zipped up."

It was a short distance to the point, so Kevin rowed the dinghy and dropped anchor near the edge of the spit of land. He and Juliana slipped into the water and swam to the point. The water was crystal-clear. Baitfish, sand bass, sheepshead and other species were abundant.

"Take a look around here. I'm going to go around the point and make a couple of dives on the face where it drops off into deeper water." He swam away.

As Juliana watched, two large fish swam lazily by,

seemingly unconcerned by her presence. He should have stayed here, she thought, those were yellowtail. After a quarter of an hour, she started feeling chilled, so she swam back to the dinghy and got out of the water. Another ten minutes passed and she saw Kevin coming back. He was on his back kicking, his spear gun held vertically. As he approached, she saw that he was towing a large fish. He reached the dinghy and handed her the spear gun.

"We eat tonight," he said, grinning up at her. "Help me get this baby in the dinghy." Together they hoisted a thirty-pound yellowtail into the inflatable.

"I was lucky. On my second dive down the face, three of these swam by. I froze, and the third one was curious and came closer for a look. My shot hit him in the spine and stoned him. After that, there was no fight left in him. You look cold—are you ready to go back to the boat?"

"Yes—I'm dying for a hot shower."

While Juliana showered, Kevin took the yellowtail on the foredeck to clean. He'd gutted the fish and was taking off the first fillets when a *panga* with two Mexican fishermen came around the point and headed toward *Seascape.*

The fishermen waved a friendly greeting as the *panga* pulled alongside where Kevin was working.

"Que tal, señores," Kevin said.

"Hola amigo, you like the *langosta?"* One of the fishermen reached into a large box in the *panga* and pulled out a live lobster.

"Bueno," Kevin said *"cuantos son?"*

One fisherman stood up, holding onto *Seascape's* rail and looked at the fish Kevin was cleaning. *"Tiene pescado?"* he asked.

"Si," Kevin replied. *"Quieres* yellowtail?"

"Ah, si, es Jurel, pescado muy bueno. Jellotail is veree good!"

"Momentito." Kevin handed him one entire side of

the fish in a plastic bag. *"Para ustedes,"* he said, "for you."

The fisherman took the bag with obvious pleasure. *"Muchas gracias,"* he said. He tossed the lobster onto the deck by Kevin and motioned to the other fisherman to get another one out of their catch box and toss it to Kevin. *"Bastante?"* he asked.

"Si," Kevin replied. *"Es solamente yo y mi esposa. Mira, le gusta cerveza?"*

"Si."

"Momentito." Kevin picked up the two lobsters and went below, tossing them in the galley sink. He returned with two cans of beer and handed them to the fisherman.

"Muchas gracias," they said. *"Mira, en la tarde,* later, you come shore, visit, okay? We show island."

"Okay," Kevin said, *"muchas gracias."*

The *panga* pulled away and went to the hulk anchored in the cove. The lobster men unloaded their catch into some boxes and covered it back up with the canvas tarp. They went ashore.

About the time Kevin finished cleaning the yellowtail, Juliana came on deck.

"What was that all about? I heard you speaking Spanish."

"A couple of local lobster fishermen stopped by. They were friendly. I traded some yellowtail for two lobsters. They invited us to come ashore later for a tour of the island."

"You think it's safe?"

"Yeah, I think so. These guys are just hard-working fishermen."

That afternoon they took the inflatable and went ashore. Juliana was also fluent in Spanish, and they soon learned the story of Miguel and José, the two lobstermen. They lived on the mainland, near San Quintin. They belonged to the local fishing *Cooperativo* and came out to San Martin on Monday to set their lobster traps. They camped out on the island all week and returned to the mainland on the weekend to deliver their catch. It was a hard life.

Miguel explained that the abandoned shacks had once belonged to abalone divers. The abalone were fished to extinction and the island was abandoned. Only recently had the island been opened up for lobster fishing. The *Cooperativo* observed a rigid season and catch limits. With a permit, Mexico allowed sport fishing by foreigners, but lobsters were off limits.

Miguel and José took them on a hike to explore the island. Cactus with vicious thorns grew on the sides of the slope. Near the top they saw a cave and volcanic tubes in the old lava flow. There was no water to be found on the island.

Back on the beach, Kevin and Juliana prepared to return to their boat. Juliana asked Miguel if anyone else ever came to the island.

"*Si.* Other lobstermen from the *Cooperativo* come but they took this week off. Sometimes we see boats from the U.S. stopping here for the night on the way south to Cabo San Lucas. Also, sometimes the Mexican Navy comes. They look for the *narcos*, the drug traffickers. They're very bad men. We stay away from them. Usually, they come at night and drop their packages for someone else to pick up. This narcotics is *muy malo*, very bad business."

"What about that boat that left just as we arrived? Did you talk to them?"

Miguel shook his head. "No like talk. *No bueno. Tienen pistolas automáticos. Son Chinos*—Chinese."

After returning to the boat, Juliana checked the weather report again. *Lowell* was moving slowly northwest. It had been upgraded to a tropical storm and was now two hundred seventy-five miles southwest of Puerto Vallarta.

"The *Lowell* storm is growing and headed in our direction," she told Kevin. "Nothing to worry about yet, but we need to keep checking the reports."

The next day was a lazy one. Kevin went diving early in the morning and speared another yellowtail. In the afternoon he worked on the boat, checking fuel and engine oil, charging the batteries and inspecting all the lines and rigging. Juliana cleaned up the galley and squared away the interior of the boat, stowing things that had been tossed haphazardly during the previous night's cruising.

"I think we should plan to pull out of here tomorrow," Kevin said. "From here it's about 30 nautical miles south to Punta Baja and Isla San Geronimo. San Geronimo is a little uninhabited island with lots of sea lions, harbor seals and elephant seals. I'd like to show it to you. There's a place to anchor on the east side, or we can anchor at Punta Baja. A lot of surfers go there."

"Sounds good. After that, what's your plan?

"From San Geronimo it's an overnight run of about one hundred-twenty nautical miles back north to Todos Santos islands. Then it's another five nautical miles into Hotel Coral, a new hotel and marina just north of Ensenada. We'll get a slip in the marina and stay on the boat, but we get full use of the hotel's facilities. You can sit in a hot tub and look out over the Pacific."

"A hot tub? You're going to spoil me with luxury. I may not want to get back on the boat."

"We'll have some time there. If we leave late afternoon, we can be at the Coronado Islands at day break the next day and then go on into San Diego and clear customs that afternoon. From San Diego, my thought is to sail northwest to Avalon, spend the night on Catalina, and head directly back to Marina del Rey. Weather permitting, this would put us home on Sunday, eight days from now. We'll have a day to recover before going back to work.

"If you agree, I'll start fixing dinner. You can get a pot of water boiling for the lobsters while I rig up the barbecue to cook some yellowtail fillets."

When the food was cooked, they sat in the cockpit eating and drinking a French white burgundy Kevin had been saving for a special occasion. The first stars were out. It was cool but not uncomfortable.

"I'm proud of you," she said. "The whole day passed and you haven't brought up work. You were on the radio. Anything new about Kuwait?"

"Saddam announced that Iraq had annexed Kuwait as a new province. Sanctions are being discussed. Action is almost certain to follow. It doesn't look good. Enough of that." Kevin held his glass up to Juliana's. "Here's to you, my love. Wonderful being here with you. I'm so fortunate that we met."

"And here's to more sailing," Juliana said. "I could really get used to this life, lobster and fresh fish every night, dining by the stars, and..."

"And what?" he asked.

"...and you in bed with me, all cuddly and warm. I don't like the part of sleeping alone while you're on watch."

Following dinner, when Juliana went below, Kevin dipped a bucket of sea water and washed the dishes, then rinsed them with fresh water. As he dried and put them away, he glanced forward as Juliana climbed into the Pullman berth. She was nude. She leaned out of the bunk with an impish grin. "Hurry," she said, "it's chilly here without you."

The next morning Kevin was awakened by the sound of a powerful engine coming into the cove. He stepped to the hatch and saw a Mexican Navy patrol boat passing by, headed towards the beach. It stopped, anchored, and launched an inflatable boat. Six armed soldiers went ashore. Kevin could see them conversing with Miguel and

José. He went below and called Juliana.

"The Mexican Navy just arrived. It looks like they're planning to stay for a while. Let's pull anchor and get out of here. Don't go rushing around on deck or be conspicuous. We'll have breakfast later, when we're underway. I'm glad I put the dinghy on board yesterday afternoon. As soon as you're dressed, come up and start the engine, and I'll hoist the anchor. Turn us around and take us out of the harbor, nice and easy, about three knots. We'll run on the engine until we get clear of the island and I put up the sails."

Despite Kevin's misgivings, the Mexican Navy remained on the island, and he and Juliana sailed away unbothered. Kevin took the boat clear of the island and turned south towards Punta Baja and Isla San Geronimo. After the first hour the sea became rougher, with *Seascape* plunging her bow into the swells and every now and then taking green water over the foredeck. The wind had shifted. Kevin was forced to tack west, away from the coast to make any headway.

"Maybe we should get on the radio and check the weather again," Juliana said, becoming nervous as the sea grew rougher.

"Go ahead."

"It's still a tropical storm," she reported moments later. "It's headed west, so we shouldn't have any problems."

At noon they sighted San Geronimo and turned into Bahia Rosario. Once in the bay behind the island the sea seemed to settle down. Kevin dropped the anchor. He started to launch the dinghy, but thought better of it and decided to wait until morning.

By 4 p.m. the wind had risen and the seas behind the anchorage were increasing. When Kevin looked to the south he could see high, dark clouds building. He went below and turned on the radio to check the weather again.

When he returned on deck Juliana could tell he was

concerned. "What's the matter?" she asked.

"They've upgraded *Lowell* to a Category One hurricane with seventy-five mile-per-hour winds. It's turned more to the north. It's a couple of hundred miles southwest of Cabo San Lucas. I'm not comfortable being here. Just to the south of us is the Sacramento reef. This bay has lots of shallows and rocks. If we move to Punto Baja, we'll have no protection at all from a south swell. I'm thinking that we should get the hell out of here."

He started the engine. "You take the helm while I pull the anchor. Once it's clear, back us out of here. Try to angle to the port side, because the wind is going to push us to the starboard, and I saw rocks there when we came in."

Kevin went to the bow and started hoisting the anchor, holding onto the forestay as *Seascape* bucked in the south swell.

"Anchor's up," he shouted to Juliana. She backed the boat clear, reversed, and turned north to clear the island.

Once past the island, Kevin raised the mainsail, tied one reef in it, and headed west towards the open ocean. The wind increased as they got clear of the harbor. He wanted to get at least ten miles offshore in deeper water before turning north, so there was less chance of being blown ashore in an emergency.

A heavy swell was running, coming up from the hurricane in the south. The waves collided with the predominant southerly current, producing confused seas that rocked the boat first one way and then another. The wind gusted and moaned as it strained the rigging.

Juliana grabbed Kevin's arm and hung on tight. Are we going to be okay?" she asked. "I'm frightened. I don't want to be out here in the middle of a hurricane."

"Don't worry, Julie, we'll be fine. After another hour or so we'll head north and run before the storm. We'll have a smoother ride once we do that."

When Kevin judged that they'd gone far enough, he

had Juliana swing the boat into the wind so he could drop the mainsail and unfurl the staysail. He turned the boat and ran before the wind. With the swell aft and a thirty knot following wind, the small staysail drove the boat at six knots. The wind noise disappeared, and the boat settled down.

To the south, the sky was an ugly black and gray. Off to the west, the setting sun was blood orange as it sank in the horizon.

"Julie, why don't you go below and make a couple of sandwiches and a pot of coffee. It's going to be a long night."

While waiting for Juliana to return with the coffee, Kevin thought about sailing and especially about the sea. There was always something interesting. Sometimes it was the birds, far from land or diving on a vast school of bait, or, it might be a distant whale, spouting and then diving. Or, of course, the weather. It was never entirely predictable, no matter who did the forecasts. He thought of the sea as devious. It would lull you into complacency, unless you were careful. Inexperienced boaters could look across the channel and see Catalina Island on a nice clear day. They would jump in their small, ill-equipped vessels and halfway across find the weather had suddenly changed. There they would be, no working radio, unsure of what direction to go, being battered by waves, maybe the boat capsizing and tossing them into the cold Pacific.

Respect, he thought. You always had to respect the sea. Respect it and be prepared for the worst it could throw at you.

They made good time running before the storm. On the way north up the coast of Baja California, they passed Punta Colnett, ran into fog in the early morning hours off of Punta Santo Tomas, and reached Todos Los Santos

Islands late in the morning. From there it was a short run into the Hotel Coral marina, where they secured a slip and Juliana got her wish of sitting in a hot tub, sipping a margarita, and watching the sunset over the blue Pacific Ocean.

"I'm sorry we missed San Geronimo, but I'm glad you decided to turn around. I was getting worried," Juliana said. "One thing we can expect is that with global warming, there will be more frequent hurricanes, and that they will pack more energy and be more destructive."

"Why is that?"

"Because the oceans have more heat content, and that warm water is what powers hurricanes."

"What did you think about San Martin?"

"I liked San Martin," she said, putting her head on Kevin's shoulder as they sat in the hot tub, her hand on his thigh. "Lobster dinner and you—quite a combination. By the way, did you sleep well that night?"

"Very well. But I'd like to practice some more. Are you ready to go back to the boat?"

She looked at him and gave him a quick kiss. "My, my," she said. "You are ready. Can I just finish my margarita?"

They rested the next day, preparing for another all-night run. They left the marina at 5 p.m. and arrived at South Coronado Island at daybreak the next day. From there they made their way into customs at San Diego Harbor.

After a night at a guest slip at the San Diego Yacht Club, they departed San Diego early and made the long run up to Avalon Harbor on Catalina Island where they spent Saturday night and had dinner ashore. While sightseeing in Avalon, Juliana bought Kevin a shirt at a store called Buoys and Gulls. From Avalon they left early the next morning and pulled into Marina del Rey at 2 p.m. They packed up their clothes and what remained of the yellowtail, and sat in the cockpit for a final margarita before heading home.

Kevin put his arm around her, ran his hand through her hair, gave her a hug. "Are you glad to be home?"

"Two things: I'm looking forward to a shower that's not rocking back and forth, and also I'm hoping to hear that I've got a new job. What about you?"

"I want John and our gang in Kuwait to be okay. Now that we're back in the U.S., I hope we'll have some news. I feel guilty not knowing what's happened to them. In reality, I don't think we could have done anything, but it still bothers me."

"I know you're worried. Remember, Saddam is holding a lot of people, not just Americans. Now that he's got Kuwait, I think he'll ease up, let the hostages go."

"I hope you're right. Listen, Julie, how do you feel after spending two weeks at sea? You've turned out to be a great sailor. Would you want to take another trip like this one, or maybe even a longer one?"

"I enjoyed it. I've always liked the ocean. Sailing seems to me to be so peaceful and relaxing. I didn't enjoy the fog, and there were a few times when the wind came up and I got a little nervous. Being at sea under varying conditions gave me new appreciation for the oceanography classes I took. It's made me think more about the risk of global warming. But *Seascape* is a great boat, rugged and durable. Above all, I have confidence in your ability to know when it's safe to go to sea and when we're better off staying in a harbor somewhere and waiting out the weather. I think for my next trip I'd like to visit Channel Islands, if we can find time to do that."

"That's a great idea," Kevin said. "We can plan a series of long weekend trips and hit all of the islands. One of my favorites is Santa Barbara Island. I'd love to take you there the next time we can get away for a few days. It's a beautiful and tranquil island. No hurricanes there, so it should be quiet and relaxing."

In his wildest dreams, Kevin could not have

imagined the adventures that would result from this seemingly innocuous statement.

HUMAN SHIELDS

The first thing Kevin did Monday morning when he reached the office was to inquire about the crew in Kuwait. Holly told them there had been no further contact. More than five thousand westerners and Japanese were in Iraq and Kuwait during the opening days of the invasion. The largest contingent was British, with around fourteen hundred hostages. The invasion took everyone by surprise. The American intelligence community issued warnings of the impending attack a few days before it happened, but they were ignored by the highest levels of government. In a small way, it was Pearl Harbor all over again.

Three weeks after the invasion, Hussein appeared on television with a British family that was being held hostage in Baghdad. He made a point of showing a young boy being held for "protection." This program sparked international outrage. In September, a month after the invasion, the State Department advised that American hostages were being held as "human shields" at various Iraqi military establishments to discourage attacks by "foreign powers."

In September, the Iraqis relented and released women and children. It was a big deal on the news. When John Remington's wife Judy returned, she came into the office and told how she, John, and other Americans had managed to hide out for more than a month after the invasion. They were rounded up and taken to Baghdad. She knew John had been taken to some critical Iraqi facility, but did not know where. As far as she knew, the American hostages were not being mistreated.

Also in September Juliana called Kevin at his office.

"Are you okay?" he asked. He could tell she was excited.

"Great news. I got the job at R&D. I start in two weeks, and I'll be part of their climate change team. It's a perfect job for me."

"That's wonderful. I'm thrilled that you finally heard from them. I'll be home in a couple of hours. Don't cook. Let's go out and celebrate. I want to hear all about it."

ೈ

Three months later, the other hostages were released. John arrived home on December 9, 1990. When he came back to the office, he told Kevin that he'd kept a journal hidden in the false bottom of his knapsack throughout the entire ordeal.

"You were lucky you left when you did, Kevin, otherwise you would have joined us as guests of Saddam."

"I couldn't believe it when I heard the news. I'd just been there with you and was driving home from the airport and heard about the invasion on the radio. We were all very worried until we got that first fax. The most important thing is that you and Judy and the rest of the gang are okay."

Kevin called Juliana from the office. "Do we have any plans for Saturday night?"

"Not that I know of, why? Are you planning something?"

"I spoke briefly with John Remington at the office today. He told me a little about their capture by the Iraqis. I'd like to invite them for dinner on Saturday. I want to hear the whole story, and I thought you might like to hear his wife's version as well."

"I'm so happy they're okay. By all means, have them over. You can barbeque, right?"

Kevin laughed. "Since it's December, it may be a little chilly for a barbeque, but I'll do whatever you want, my dear. You buy the steaks."

Saturday afternoon turned out to be a perfect Southern California day. The Remingtons joined Kevin and Juliana on their patio, where Kevin had prepared a pitcher of margaritas and Juliana set out chips and guacamole as snacks.

When everyone had drinks, Kevin asked John to tell them about their ordeal.

"Let's see, when were you there? As I recall you left on the morning of August 1. August 2 started out as a typical day. I got up at 5:30 a.m. as usual to go jogging.

"Anyway, what with being sleepy, the noise of the air conditioning, and just banging around, I didn't realize that the booms outside were artillery shells exploding downtown. As I headed for the door, Don called and said that the Embassy had called to advise that Iraq had invaded Kuwait. We were told to stay inside. We went upstairs to Don's apartment on the seventh floor to get a better view. There were a lot of tanks in front of the American Embassy. We could see Iraqi troops moving through the streets and hear small arms fire from a ferocious firefight a few blocks away. All in all, it was terrifying. We never knew when the bullets would come our way."

"Could you see the shooting?" Kevin asked. Were any Kuwaiti forces visible?"

"Not that we could see."

"What were you thinking, Judy?" Juliana asked. "It must have been terrifying."

"I guess my initial reaction was disbelief, as in 'this couldn't be happening.' At first I wasn't frightened, not until later that night when it sank in that it was for real and the Iraqis were not leaving."

"Fighting continued for the next several days," John said. "Some people said that the Iraqis wanted to make a 'statement,' and then would pull back. From our vantage point, we saw more and more troops coming in, so it didn't look like the Iraqis were planning to leave. One day, an artillery round hit one of the empty upper story apartments and exploded. The neighbors close by were knocked off their feet but not seriously hurt. The blast scared us all. At night, lying in bed, listening to the shell fire, was one of the worst things we had to endure. It was impossible to sleep. After a couple of days we had a meeting of all the employees who lived in the apartment complex and got organized regarding sharing of information and food."

"That must have been when you sent us the fax. We were really relieved to get that and know that you were okay."

"Yeah, we were okay for a while. We just laid low. After a little more than a month of hiding out in occupied Kuwait City, the cats came to get the mice. Someone called us to say that the building was swarming with Iraqi soldiers. We turned off the lights and stayed away from the windows. Next we heard voices speaking Arabic in the hall, and then the sound of doors being broken in. As we wondered what to do, it was all decided for us. The door crashed in, and a polite, well-dressed soldier in the uniform of a Republican Guard informed us that we were to pack a bag and come with him. We were being 'relocated' for our safety. The next thing Judy and I knew we were on a bus to Baghdad.

"As I sat on the bus, naturally I was concerned. I didn't think the world—especially the U.S.—would stand by while Kuwait was overrun and Saudi Arabia was threatened. I didn't like the idea of being stuck in Iraq when the U.S. decided to go after the bad guys, because I knew when that hammer fell, it would be a heavy blow. I didn't share these concerns with Judy; I tried to keep her from worrying too much."

"He didn't need to 'share his concerns' about what was going to happen," Judy said. "I had that figured out. I thought it would just be a matter of time. I was more worried about what the U.S. might do than the Iraqis. I was worried we'd somehow be caught in the middle."

John continued. "As our bus moved north, there

was a steady stream of military vehicles, trucks and so on, coming south from Iraq into Kuwait. Going in our direction north there were a lot of civilian vehicles, cars and trucks. As I sat there, absent-mindedly staring out the window, I saw a familiar-looking vehicle pass the bus, driven by an Iraqi soldier. I did a double-take—familiar vehicle? Hell, it was my car. They'd stolen it and were driving it north.

"Crossing the border into Iraq was another ordeal, mostly bureaucratic, as it turned out. I was taken into a room for interrogation. After a number of questions, I finally realized this was immigration and customs clearance! We were going through the procedure like we were a bunch of tourists. On the entry form, under the question 'Purpose of Entry,' I wrote a single word: HOSTAGE.

"On September 8, women and children were taken to the U.S. Embassy, Baghdad, where they were to be repatriated home. It was with relief but much sadness that I said goodbye to Judy and watched her leave the hotel."

"I was really torn up about leaving John but we knew it was best for both of us," Judy said. "He had reduced his belongings to a single back pack. He was physically in good shape, so if an escape opportunity arose, he was in a better position to take advantage of it by knowing that I was not still in Iraq. I didn't want to leave John, but all the other wives were leaving. We discussed it and decided that by leaving I could give a full report of what happened and who was being held captive. We hoped the publicity and international condemnation would force Saddam to release the men as well. Besides, I really didn't have a choice."

"Did you know what was going to happen to John?" Juliana asked.

"Rumors were rampant and indicated that we were to become human shields at critical Iraqi defense installations," John said. "One-by-one the Iraqis came, usually in the middle of the night, and moved people out to various locations. My turn came on September 11. Don, another American hostage, a German hostage, and I were driven north out of Baghdad in a beat up Toyota Land Cruiser with a maniacal Iraqi driver. Don and his wife Brenda were taken to a separate nuclear research facility, several kilometers away. The rest of us passed Mosul that evening and were eventually deposited at the site of a dam. Don and Brenda were later released early for health reasons.

"Other than cooking, reading, sleeping, and being human shields, there wasn't much we could do at the dam. We could jog outside, as long as we didn't go near any fences. One day the Iraqi propaganda people came in with a TV crew to film us—supposedly so we could make message tapes for our families. In mine, I referred to us as hostages, which did not make the Iraqis happy. About the time we got this place reasonably well cleaned up, they came and moved us inside the compound, into a small windowless room. We had to cook and wash dishes in the adjoining toilet. We were inside a walled enclosure. The wall had three strands of barbed wire on it. There were perimeter floodlights and guard towers, not all of which were manned at any one time. There was also a perimeter video camera system. Fortunately, the camera near our area that faced the Tigris River, our possible escape point, was inoperable—the wiring all pulled loose.

"A word about our guards. We called them 'minders,' or, for the really obnoxious ones, 'zookeepers.' Unfortunately, most were civilians who had been recruited from their regular jobs to keep an eye on us. Backing them up, if we got unruly, were the military with guns, but they tended to stay in the background. Some of our minders were embarrassed about their job; one got fed up with the process and resigned. We needled them in subtle ways.

"One hostage had a key-chain medallion with a colored picture of Saddam Hussein. We unhooked the pull ring from the overhead toilet tank chain and solemnly installed Mr. President in its place. Since the minders occasionally used our toilet, this bit of irreverence was discovered and they did not see the humor in it that we did.

"In mid-October, some of the hostages started getting messages from family members over the BBC. We had a short-wave radio and managed to convince the Iraqis to let us keep it. Eventually I also got some messages. They were a real boost to my spirits, coming at a good time, because in October I got very sick—sore throat, fever, chills. Didn't feel like eating, couldn't really sleep. The Iraqis brought in an elderly doctor who, after a painful examination that left me seeing stars, determined that I had an infected lymph node, to be treated by injections of penicillin in the buttocks twice a day with a god-awful horse syringe.

"How did you get a doctor? Kevin asked. Did the guards speak English? What about the doctor?"

"Some spoke better than others. We decided that they all understood some English, even if they acted like they didn't. After I got better I was moved again in the middle of the night to the Saad 16 Nuclear Research and Development Facility. Words cannot describe the depression and sense of loss I felt as we rolled up to the main gate. This was maximum security—solid walls fifteen feet high, with rolls of concertina wire on top, armed guards everywhere, closely spaced guard towers with heavy machine guns, manned twenty-four hours per day. It is about thirty kilometers deeper into Iraq and further down the Tigris than my previous location—too far from the border to make a run for it, even if you could get beyond the urban area and into the desert without getting caught.

"Here our movements were very restricted, but we could see a lot of the complex, although it was far too big to see it all. There was serious stuff happening there: lots of buildings with frangible panels to absorb explosive blasts, also a building surrounded by numerous steel masts for lightning protection. That could only mean something very explosive inside that the Iraqis wanted to protect. We often heard test firing of rocket motors, day and night, but usually at night.

"By early December we were all resigned to the fact that we'd spend Christmas and New Year's locked up. Hopefully, the invasion would come soon—everyone knew that it had to happen before the desert heated up. No one thought that Saddam would back down—he'd lose too much face at this point to pull out. He was probably ahead in the deal at that time, considering he had to pay the soldiers in any event, and the invasion didn't really cost that much. In return, Kuwait was stripped. I'm sure the Kuwait treasury was now in Baghdad. Of course, we know that all our vehicles were taken there, along with all of our equipment—computers and so on—that was at the University. The British hostages told me they watched as the Iraqis brought in big tractor-trailer rigs and loaded up furniture and appliances from all of the empty apartments after the hostages had been moved out. The trucks went to the port where the loot was loaded on Iraqi freighters. Thousands of tables, chairs, beds, air conditioning units, TV sets, stereos, on and on. Then they went in the buildings and ripped out toilets and plumbing fixtures; kitchen cabinets and fixtures—anything removable. They even took traffic signals and street lights. Would they trash a place they intended to keep? How does this look to the Arab world—plundering and petty thievery on a grand scale—not exactly the image of a heroic Arab liberator.

"Then, all of a sudden, it happened. One afternoon one of my group came running outside, shouting that it was announced on Iraqi TV that all hostages were to be released. It was a Friday, and that night we had a song fest in the rooms in celebration. One of the guys had a guitar and the rest improvised with various percussion devices (spoons, glasses, shoes, etc.) The wine was about half gone when Zorro and Fahdel, two of the zookeepers, came in. They listened for a few minutes and laughed at our craziness. When we finished the song, Zorro told me to get packed. I would be leaving for Baghdad at 4:30 in the morning to go home. Everyone went crazy, hugs and shouts. I was totally surprised. I thought the Brits and the Japanese would go first, if they released anyone.

"Sunday, December 9, 1990—I was finally home. I can't describe adequately what a wonderful feeling that was."

༺

The return of John and the other American hostages was a fine Christmas present for everyone. As for their work at the University, it would all have to be redone after Kuwait was liberated, due to the Iraqi looting. After they stripped the buildings of everything removable, they stationed troops in the empty buildings. Since there were no facilities, the troops did their business on the floor in one corner of the room—too lazy go outside and dig latrines.

In November 1990, the United Nations had authorized force if necessary to cause Iraq to withdraw its troops from Kuwait. The Iraqis were given until January 15 to withdraw. Meanwhile, shortly after the Iraqi invasion, the U.S. began funneling troops and equipment into Saudi Arabia in what was known as Operation Desert Shield. With the U.N. mandate, the U.S. began organizing an international coalition to enforce the U.N. resolution. In all, thirty-four countries agreed to participate with troops, equipment, supplies, or cash. Saudi Arabia and Kuwait each pledged $fifteen billion to the cost of the effort.

"Before long," Kevin told Juliana, "the Iraqis will be hot-footing it back to Iraq as fast as they'd come into Kuwait, with Coalition forces right behind them. We don't know when, but we know it's going to happen."

There was one other, final ironic note. Military intelligence sources did detailed debriefs of all the hostages. Many, including John, were experienced

age | **128**

architects, engineers, or construction workers. During their time as human shields, they observed the locations of power installations and other critical equipment at the facilities where they were being held. This information was added to the Air Force target list, further evidence that the human shield idea had hurt Hussein more than it helped.

Iraq ignored the U.N. resolution and did not withdraw its forces. The day after the U.N. deadline, Coalition forces launched a massive air attack on Iraq's military establishment, hitting locations in both Kuwait and Iraq. A little more than a month later, on February 24, Coalition ground forces attacked Iraqi forces in Kuwait and in Iraq. A strong force entered Kuwait from Saudi Arabia, while another force entered the Iraq desert, flanking and cutting off the Iraqi forces attempting to retreat from Kuwait. Deprived of air cover and having lost most of its vehicles, the Iraqi Army ceased to exist as an effective fighting force. After one hundred hours, Iraq agreed to a cease-fire. Coalition forces withdrew from Iraq and did not push on to Baghdad. Saddam Hussein was allowed to remain in power, but was required to submit to U.N. inspections and to destroy all "weapons of mass destruction." As time went on, he did neither, but instead brutally attacked Shia and Kurdish minorities in the country to quell any opposition to his reign.

After Operation Desert Storm liberated Kuwait, the U.S. moved to establish a forward operating base in Kuwait. The possible threat of future aggression in this critical region was recognized. Initially, the U.S. was provided several warehouses near the port in facilities leased by the Kuwait Ministry of Defense from the Kuwait Port Authority. The U.S. moved several armored and infantry divisions into Kuwait, along with their equipment, basing them in this facility. This base, which became known as Camp Doha, grew rapidly over the next several years.

Following the Coalition attack on Iraq, some left-wing Arabs condemned the U.S. and other Western nations, saying it was an attack on Arab nationalism. Ironically, in some quarters Saddam's brutality was ignored, and he was praised as an advocate for Arab independence. President Rafsanjani of Iran condemned the attack, calling it a "historical catastrophe," although privately Iran was delighted to see the Coalition weaken its bitter enemy, Iraq.

By summer 1991, the Middle East was in the news every day. Howard Clark, Kevin's boss, decided to spend an afternoon discussing the implications of the ongoing crisis for the company's business and projects there. He invited Kevin and several other key business development personnel to "brainstorm" what might develop.

"Here's what I'm interested in hearing," Howard said. "I'd like your ideas on 'targets of opportunity' in the Middle East—where our services might be required in the next five years, and how we should position ourselves. Also, the other side of the story—what areas will pose unacceptable risk, where we should stay away, or even pull out. Let's go around the table and see if we have any consensus. Kevin, you start."

"Iran is a threat," Kevin said. "It's still smarting under the economic sanctions we imposed following the 1981 hostage crisis. It suffered huge casualties during the Iran-Iraq war, which in part it blames the U.S. because we supported Iraq. During operation Desert Storm, the U.S. displayed a vast array of new weapons and methods that devastated the Iraqi military. There were satellite photos and surveillance, GPS tracking and guidance, electronic countermeasures that jammed Iraq radar, and missiles that were so effective in attacking Iraqi radar sites that the Iraqis were afraid to turn on their radars. The Coalition also had drones that were used to locate targets for the Marines and Navy ships in the Gulf.

"My point is, Iran must have watched the battle, with all its electronic listening capability, trying to learn as much as possible. Conclusion: we have to worry about Iran in the future, because the U.S. military will expand bases in the Middle East, in 'friendly' countries, such as Egypt, Kuwait, the UAE, and Saudi Arabia. We should position ourselves to be able to respond to opportunities."

"Very good, Kevin," said Frank Kaufman, a Department of Defense marketing specialist. "You're correct about the drones. I heard they were designed by Israel and we had at least one in the air continuously during the fighting in Iraq. There was one unique event. A drone flew over a large group of retreating Iraqi soldiers. When they saw it, they started waving white flags, their shirts, anything they could find. It was the first instance of a group of soldiers surrendering to a robot."

"I agree with Kevin's assessment as to the geography," said Paul Parunyan, a specialist in Middle East politics. We need to develop our qualifications in the areas where the government is likely to seek support. This will be for water treatment facilities, power plants, airports, logistics, and vehicle maintenance and repair. We should compile the experience we have, and then seek new projects to build on it. I don't think we can trust Saddam Hussein. He's been humiliated and has lost face—but he's still in power. I think we'll hear more from Iraq in the coming years."

At the conclusion of the meeting, Howard asked Kevin to stay behind for a few minutes.

"Okay, you've heard what the experts think," he said. "I want you to take a couple of hours each week and dig into this. Find out what the issues are, according to DOD. See if you can identify the players, the decision-makers. Who should we be meeting with?"

At home that night, Kevin told Juliana about the meeting. "Howard expects me to dig into this stuff, get up to speed. This seems like something a more senior person should do."

"Why do you say that?" she said. "You've been to Egypt and the Middle East, and you understand technology. This is an opportunity for you. You can do it; I know you can."

That night, Kevin lay awake for a while, thinking over what Howard had said, and also dwelling on Juliana's comments. He appreciated her support and confidence.

Much later, Juliana awoke. She lay still, not wanting to disturb Kevin, who was sleeping soundly. But still, some premonition, some unknown fear, haunted her. She feared this assignment would put Kevin at risk. It was hours before she finally fell asleep.

Kevin began digging into all the information he could find about the modern history of the Middle East, taking the end of World War I as a starting point. At that time, the victorious Allies drew lines on a map to create the modern states. These lines for the most part ignored age-old tribal and religious boundaries. With this background, he was better able to understand the conflicts that engulfed the region, from the various Arab-Israeli wars to the Iran-Iraq war. What he learned from all the publicly available information on Operation Desert Storm came as a surprise, as he later revealed to Howard.

"Tell me some of the things that surprised you," Howard said.

"The first thing was that in the summer of 1990 the CIA knew Iraq would invade Kuwait. Four days before the invasion it informed President Bush and his top security advisers. There were satellite photos that showed massive Iraqi troop buildup near the border with Kuwait. The pictures were so good they could tell the number of troops, tanks, and artillery. The president's advisers believed that this was 'posturing' by Iraq and the president listened to them and took no action.

"On August 1, the head of the CIA met again with White House staff and delivered even more alarming satellite photos. That afternoon, the CIA estimated there was a ninety percent certainty of an invasion within twelve hours. Three hours later, Iraq invaded."

"What about notifying Kuwait and Saudi Arabia?" Howard asked.

"I don't know if that was done. Or, if it was, it was ignored. I do know that Kuwait was caught flat-footed, totally unprepared.

"What I found especially interesting was the surveillance by satellites and drones. As many as four satellites were programmed to pass over the area. They covered a broad swath of territory, from Riyadh in Saudi Arabia to Baghdad. They spotted troop dispositions, a one hundred and eight-mile long defensive trench the Iraqis were building, the locations of supply depots, SCUD missile launchers, even individual tanks. They saw that the Iraqis had anchored several oil tankers in Kuwait Harbor, and determined that the Iraqis planned to flood the harbor with oil and set it on fire if a landing was attempted there.

"But the most fascinating thing was that the satellites also showed a constant flow of trucks entering Iraq from—of all places—Iran! Imagine that: their bitter enemy, now aiding them. The satellites also showed truck convoys moving from the Soviet Union through Iran and into Iraq. These brought weapons and munitions. The satellites also discovered that Iraq had positioned Soviet countermeasure equipment inside Kuwait, to jam communications and signals of any attacking force.

"In spite of these surveillance successes, there were a lot of problems. There were delays getting satellite images to the ground, processed, and into the hands of the field commanders. The second issue was coordinating requests for surveillance and sharing data between the Army, Air Force, Navy, and Marine Corps. They used several methods. Satellites were controlled from a base in the U.S. Data were transmitted back to ground stations, sometimes to stations in Germany, Greenland, or direct to Fort Belvoir or Langley in Washington D.C., or other classified locations."

"What are your thoughts on what we should do?" Howard asked.

"Over the next several years, I foresee DOD putting emphasis on improving ground facilities for rapid acquisition, processing, and distribution of satellite data and images to commanders in the field. It also seems highly probable that the use of drones will increase. If we can develop or acquire the expertise needed to assist in these areas, it might be a fruitful opportunity for new business."

"Very interesting," Howard said. "On the surface, it sounds far afield from our core strengths. But I'll pass your ideas on to the management committee. I know they are exploring some acquisition opportunities, so they may want to consider a firm with these capabilities. I think we'll be hearing more about this."

When Kevin told Juliana about his meeting with Howard, he was surprised by her reaction.

"I'm worried that this means you'll have to go back to the Middle East. The other night I had a weird premonition, and I couldn't get to sleep for the longest time."

"You're worrying about my travels now?"

"I can't help it. I think John and Judy were lucky. I keep reading about kidnappings, killings, and suicide bombers. That entire region is turning dangerous, especially for Americans."

"To set your mind at ease, I have no immediate travel plans for the Middle East. Howard asked a group of us to think about where new business opportunities might arise. He also asked us to think about places to avoid. Please don't worry."

Despite his assurances to Juliana, Kevin also had a sense of foreboding. His meeting with Howard did little to ease his concerns. There was more to come in the Middle East, and he was destined to play a role. What it was, he couldn't tell.

THE FARM

Early in 1996, Kevin learned that he had to go to Washington for a week to attend a series of meetings on the Pentagon renovation project. As requested, he called his CIA contact Charles Kidd in Los Angeles to let him know about the trip.

"Thanks for calling," Kidd said. "When are the meetings scheduled?"

"They'll be held starting Monday, two weeks from now."

"Can I put you on hold for a minute while I check on a few things?"

"No problem," Kevin replied.

After a few minutes Kidd came back on the line. "Would it be possible for you to schedule a week's vacation following your meetings?"

"Yes, I think I could do that." Kevin paused. He started to ask the obvious question, but thought better of it.

"When will your meetings conclude?"

"We should be done by Friday afternoon. Usually schedules are set so I can catch a redeye flight back to Los Angeles."

"Go ahead and make your hotel reservation as usual, planning to check out of your hotel on Friday afternoon. You should schedule your return flight as you usually do. However, we will change your ticket for a flight on the following Sunday, departing Dulles airport at 6 p.m. for Los Angeles. You will be picked up at your hotel at 5 p.m. Friday after your meetings are over. We'll take care of your accommodations and expenses for the next week. Your program will include some briefings and several days of training that you'll find informative."

"That sounds fine, but what should I tell my wife?"

"I suggest you let her know that your trip may be

extended to visit some Navy facilities at Norfolk, Virginia, and if that happens you'll be able to provide her with new contact information. You can stay in touch; that won't be a problem."

"Thanks," Kevin said. "That will help me. She's been on edge lately and worries when I'm away traveling."

"I can understand. As I said, it won't be a problem. But in the meantime you'd better think of something nice to do for her when you return."

✖

The day Kevin flew to Washington, Juliana was at work, engrossed in a report she was preparing about South Pacific islands threatened by rising sea levels, when her phone rang.

"Mrs. Hunter, my name is Charles Kidd. We haven't met, but I'm one of the government investigators following up on the Santa Barbara Island incident. I've met with Mr. Hunter, but I believe it would be useful to hear your version of what happened, if you're willing to meet. I'm happy to come to your office if that would be convenient."

"You said your name is Kidd?"

"Yes, Charles Kidd."

"Kevin mentioned your name, but hasn't said much other than that."

"In that regard he was acting on my request—to avoid worrying you unnecessarily. I will clear that up for you when we meet."

"Does Kevin know about this meeting?"

"Actually, no. I called his office, but he is out of town. All I need is 30 minutes of your time. We can meet in the lobby of your building."

"I have a report to finish; would 4:30 be okay?"

"Fine. Thanks. I'll see you at 4:30 p.m." There was a click and the line went dead.

Juliana slowly hung up the phone, wondering what this was about. She knew there was no way to reach Kevin, who was on a plane flying east. A meeting in the lobby seemed safe enough, as R&D had security guards and there was a visitor's conference room used by vendors and others for unofficial meetings.

When the receptionist called Juliana to tell her she had a visitor, she was not sure what to expect. In the lobby she found a tall man, muscular, dressed in a slightly rumpled business suit. He greeted her with a firm handshake as she led him to the conference room.

"Thank you for meeting with me, Mrs. Hunter," Kidd said, as he put away his CIA identification. I know from what Kevin has told me that you are a very courageous woman. I hope that will allow you to keep our discussion confidential."

"Lately I haven't been feeling very courageous," Juliana said, "and I sense Kevin has some worries he's not sharing with me. That also bothers me. But yes, I'll keep our meeting confidential."

"The first item is a very sensitive one for which I hope I can count on your understanding. Your husband has volunteered to work as an informant for the Agency. When he travels overseas, he lets us know if he sees or hears anything unusual, or if any suspicious person contacts him. He is not a spy. He offered to do this after Agent Beske was killed trying to protect him.

"At my request, Kevin agreed to not discuss this with you."

"Why?"

"We felt the disclosure might put you at risk. The situation is different now, since the attempted kidnapping and the revelation that the kidnappers knew you work here at R&D. This suggests that there may be a broader plot, and that you could be drawn into it unknowingly. Working here, directly or indirectly, you may have knowledge of classified research. I'm sure you would never willingly disclose what you know. We've learned that our enemies are insidious and often employ seemingly innocent measures to gain access to our defense technology and trade secrets. They try to strike up friendships or at worst, place people in compromising circumstances where they can then exert control on them. In the hopes of easing your concerns a bit without causing you more worry, I thought it might be helpful if we met. That's the end of my little spiel. Here's my card. If you get wind of anything that doesn't seem right, please call me immediately. Any questions?"

"Do you think Kevin and I are in any danger?"

"I can't say for sure. I think the kidnappers fled the country. Whoever's in charge is still unknown. The best advice is to not lay awake at night worrying, but remain vigilant."

"What should I tell Kevin?"

"I think I'll leave that up to you," Kidd said. "I would prefer that this meeting remain strictly between you and me. I think that telling Kevin that you know about our agreement might cause him to worry more. Anything else?"

"I'm glad you shared this with me," Juliana said. "I was worried about Kevin since there have been times when he seemed preoccupied, not his usual self, but now I think I understand. I'll call you if I sense anything amiss."

After Kidd left, Juliana had second thoughts, wondering if she should tell Kevin about meeting Kidd. She decided to wait.

Kevin's meetings in Washington went well. The discussions had to do with some final design changes for the new central heating and cooling plant to be constructed as part of the Pentagon renovation. The few remaining issues were resolved quickly so the construction procurement documents could be issued. Kevin asked around, but no one knew anything about acquisitions or new marketing initiatives.

Friday afternoon Kevin collected his bag from the hotel bellman and took a seat in the lobby. At 5 p.m. a man in a dark suit entered, holding a small sign with Kevin's name written on it.

Kevin stood as the man glanced around the lobby. "I'm Kevin Hunter," he said, as the man approached him.

"Good afternoon, Mr. Hunter. My name is George. I'm your driver tonight. Let me have your bag; the car is just outside."

George led Kevin outside to the end of the J.W. Marriott Hotel entrance drive. He opened the trunk of a nondescript black Dodge sedan, placed Kevin's bag in it, and opened the rear door for Kevin. As he walked up to the car, Kevin noticed that it had a Virginia license plate and a small antenna on the roof. Otherwise, there was nothing special about the car.

George pulled the car out into the Washington traffic. At the first stoplight he turned around to speak to Kevin. "It's about a two-hour drive to the Lodge. Friday night, so the traffic will be heavy until we get away from D.C. When we arrive, your host will join you for dinner. You'll find some mineral water there in the back seat pocket if you are thirsty. Also, let me know if the temperature is okay for you."

"I'm fine, George. Thanks for picking me up. You have lots of visitors come to the Lodge?"

"I don't really know, sir. This isn't my usual duty; I had to fill in for the regular driver."

Kevin was tempted to ask George about his "usual duties," but decided not to. Meanwhile, traffic was slow as George traveled on the downtown streets, passing the Smithsonian Museum campus and crossing the Potomac River. George turned south on Highway 395. On his right side, Kevin could see the Pentagon in the distance. A short while later, Kevin saw the signs for Highway 95 S. to

Richmond. Once on 95, Kevin felt the car accelerate. From the sound of its powerful engine, he concluded that it was not a stock model.

George was intent on his driving and did not seem inclined to conversation, so Kevin sat back and watched as the scenery flashed by. At one point he heard a low buzzing sound and watched George speak a few words into a microphone that hung on a hook under the dashboard.

☙

About 7:15 p.m. Kevin felt the car slow and then turn to the east on a side road leading into a wooded area. Once again George spoke softly in the microphone and hung it up.

"We have to pass through security here," George said. "You'll need your photo ID."

After passing through the checkpoint, George drove up to a two-story building. He stopped the car and opened Kevin's door.

"Welcome to the Lodge," he said. "It's not quite as nice as your last hotel, but I'm sure you'll find it comfortable."

Kevin looked around. Not seeing any sign on the building he said, "This is the Lodge?"

"That's what we call it," George said. "It's easier than trying to remember the building number, and everyone knows what you mean."

He led Kevin inside to a small desk occupied by a uniformed woman.

"This is Mr. Hunter, Corporal."

"Welcome Mr. Hunter. Here's your key. You're in room 202. Top of the stairs, turn left. You can't miss it. I'll notify your host that you've arrived."

Kevin picked up his bag and turned to thank George, but he'd already left the lobby. Kevin saw the lights of the car pulling away. He picked up his bag and went upstairs to his room.

Unlocking the door, he went inside and looked around. He had a queen-size bed, a desk, a closet, a small coffee maker with some packets of coffee, and a bathroom with a shower and tub. The desk was clean—no stationary, no guidebooks to local attractions, no phone directory. In fact, Kevin realized that there was no phone in the room.

He opened his suitcase and hung up his suit. He was in the process of putting away his shirts when someone knocked on the door. Kevin opened it to see a middle-aged man with a crew cut standing outside. He was casually dressed with slacks and a dark turtleneck sweater. He was about Kevin's height, slim and muscular.

"Good evening, Mr. Hunter," he said, extending his hand in greeting. "I'm Roy Jones. I'll be your host here at Camp Peary. I apologize for barging in on you like this. Do you need a few more minutes to freshen up? I can come back."

"No, no problem. Please come in. I'll just put these shirts in the drawer and then be ready to go."

"We have a short walk to the building next door for dinner. I'm sure you're hungry after the drive down from D.C. Did George take good care of you?"

"No complaints. I wasn't watching the speedometer, but I have a feeling that we made good time."

Roy laughed. "George knows the road. I imagine he was anxious to get home to his family, this being Friday night."

They entered the building next door and took a seat at a table in one corner of the room. It was a small dining room, with perhaps a dozen tables. At the opposite end of the room there were four men in uniform having dinner. They looked up briefly as Kevin and Roy entered, then returned to their meal. When Kevin and Roy took their seats, a waiter appeared with menus.

"Anything from the bar, gentlemen?" he asked.

Roy turned to Kevin. "Mr. Hunter?"

"A glass of white wine, whatever you're pouring

would be fine."

"Make that two," Roy said. He closed the menu and set it aside.

Kevin looked up from his menu. "You know what you're having? Any suggestions?"

"The New York steak. The chicken and salmon are okay, but you're safe with the steak. You won't starve here, but beyond that it's not gourmet dining."

The waiter returned with two glasses of wine, took their orders, and disappeared into the back of the building.

Roy held up his glass. "Here's to your health, Kevin. I want to thank you for your willingness to help us. My colleagues in Los Angeles told me a little about what you and your wife have gone through. I could understand perfectly if you said you wanted nothing more to do with us. The fact that you're here is commendable."

"I don't know if I can do much to help, but if I could in any way see justice done to whoever killed Bob Beske that would be enough reward for me."

"Let's put it this way: you're a professional, dealing in high technology facilities, many of them related to national defense. You travel a lot, domestically and overseas. You've already shown that you are observant and can think on your feet. These are all qualities that can help us. While we're waiting for the food to arrive, let me tell you a little about this place.

"During World War II the Navy took over this area—about 9,000 acres—to use as a training facility for Seabees. It was named Camp Peary at that time. Later on, special German POWs were held here—those captured from submarines and naval vessels. We wanted the German Navy to think they'd been lost at sea, since we also recovered some codebooks when those vessels sank. After the war, the Navy abandoned the space, but then changed its mind in 1951 and came back in. Today the Camp is referred to as an Armed Forces Experimental Training Activity. The area is used by various Department of

Defense organizations for training purposes."

"Do the users include the CIA?" Kevin asked.

"It is rumored that the CIA operates a training facility here, known only as the 'Farm.' As you might expect, such a facility, if it existed, would be for the purpose of training Agency personnel in threat recognition, weapons training, communications, foreign languages, surveillance, identification of chemical or biological weapons or other potential weapons of mass destruction, and special armaments or materials used in their fabrication, such as rockets and UAVs."

"Well," Kevin said, "If such a facility existed, I'm sure I would find it interesting."

The waiter returned with their food. "Another glass of wine, gentlemen?"

"Thanks, but not for me," Kevin said.

"Bring some coffee, if you would please," Roy asked.

As they ate, Roy continued his discussion. "We've planned a program of activities for you here that I think you'll find interesting. You have a top-secret DOD clearance, In addition, as is customary, the Agency did further investigations into your background. We've learned that in matters of national security we can't be too careful.

"At the end of the week, you'll be returned to Washington where you will spend two days at our Langley headquarters, in McLean, Virginia, for some additional briefings."

"Impressive," Kevin said. "Someone has gone to a lot of trouble. I'm grateful."

"I want to be clear that your involvement in this program is strictly voluntary. You can opt out now, tonight, or anytime later on. No one will criticize you if you decide to do that. George could take you back to Dulles Airport in the morning and you could be home tomorrow afternoon, if you so choose. However, if you decide to stay, there's a paper you will need to sign. We ask you to promise not to reveal to anyone the training you receive, the names of your instructors, or even the fact that you visited this rumored facility that does not exist.

"Enough conversation for me. I hope that your steak is okay. Tell me, how is the Pentagon renovation project coming along?"

"The steak is fine, in fact better than the room service sandwiches I was subsisting on earlier this week. As for the PENREN project, as we call it, it is moving along, with all the usual complications of trying to renovate an historical building, while at the same time maintaining operations within it. I'll give you one small example. DOD wants blast proof windows. If you've ever noticed, the original windows in the Pentagon are wood frame sliders. The replacement windows have to look exactly the same, but obviously will be made of very different materials and, I should mention, will cost a lot more."

When dinner was over Roy escorted Kevin back to the Lodge. He stopped at the desk where Kevin had checked in.

"Corporal, would you give Mr. Hunter his welcome packet please."

She handed Kevin a large manila envelope.

"Let's go up to your room so you can look over these materials. I'll try to answer any questions you might have."

In the room Kevin thumbed through the materials. There were three items: a legal document that committed him to not disclose any details of his visit under penalty of a ten thousand dollar fine and imprisonment; a schedule for the week's activities; and a booklet of notes pertaining to each class he would be attending.

He read quickly through the legal document, signed it and handed it back to Roy. "I'm in," he said simply. "What's next?"

"Get some rest," Roy said. "I'll meet you at 7 a.m. in the dining room next door, and then I'll take you to the building where you'll be spending most of the week. If you feel up to it, read over the notes for Monday's classes. Don't lose these materials, because at the end of the week you need to return them to me. Also, please no written notes. And, I assume you do not have a camera or tape recorder with you. If you do, please hand it over and the Corporal will hold it for you until you complete your visit."

"No, I don't have anything like that," Kevin said. "But I do have one question. I need to call my wife. Can that be arranged?"

"No problem. In the lobby there's a phone booth. It is unique in that while it looks like a pay phone, calls are free. Call your wife and give her the number you see written inside the phone booth. If she needs to reach you, she should call that number. The call will come through to the Corporal who will advise the caller that you are in a meeting. She will get a message to you so you can call back."

The classes were fascinating. Kevin found himself among a small group of "students" who ranged in age from twenty to fifty. Some were new Agency recruits, some were in Army or Navy uniform, and some were senior Agency personnel learning about new developments in the field.

The first day was spent on communications, surveillance, and counter-surveillance. Kevin was amazed to learn about the sensitivity of remote listening devices, those that could overhear a conversation from a distance of many yards, to micro-size "bugs" that could be planted almost anywhere to record or retransmit sound to another location. Each lecture was illustrated with case histories of Agency experiences. The classic case was the bugging of the new American Embassy building in Moscow. It was loaded with hundreds of bugs during construction. When they were detected, the six-story building was abandoned and stood unoccupied for ten years. Finally, it was torn apart brick by brick and rebuilt. Among the bugs was one implanted in the Great American Seal presented to the U.S. ambassador by a group of Russian school children. It contained a passive resonant cavity bug—one that had no electronic components and required no power. When a certain radio frequency was aimed at it from outside the building, the reflected signal would transmit room conversations. It was eventually discovered, purely by accident.

Other courses covered methods of surveillance—how to observe individuals or shipping or manufacturing processes—as well as how not to. Sometimes the best disguise was no disguise. In Kevin's profession, a man wearing a hard hat and an orange construction vest and carrying a clipboard would not rate a second glance around a construction site.

In the threat avoidance discussions, the key was to be observant and vigilant. As the instructor put it, "If you're in a crowd and some guy with a long robe and an explosive belt decides to give you a hug, you're going to die."

Examples were cited of assassins on motorcycles or bicycles, and bombs planted in cars—and where to check for them.

The recommendation was to be unpredictable, vary routines, never follow the same route at the same time, day after day, and always take careful note of your surroundings.

Each night Roy met Kevin for dinner to ask him how it was going, if he had any questions, or needed anything.

Back on the west coast, Saleh received an interesting call. A Mr. Wu wanted to meet with him to discuss an "international trade" assignment. Lunch in Santa Monica was proposed. Saleh, who could barely understand Mr. Wu's English, refused, saying he was very busy and they would have to meet in Beverly Hills. Wu readily agreed.

At lunch, after food was served and Wu told Saleh about the software company he was running in Santa Monica, Saleh became impatient. "What aspects of international trade interest you?" he said bluntly.

Mr. Wu smiled. "I foresee opportunities in flight control software," he said. "This is new technology in which there is great interest—global interest, I might add. I'm wondering if you might have access to sources of such technology."

Saleh was shocked but maintained his composure. How could this man, who could barely speak English, know about his deal with the Iranians?

"That's a very difficult question," he replied. "The research is very expensive."

"I'm sure," Mr. Wu said. "One has to be prepared to spend money to succeed in international trade."

"By flight control software, I assume you mean drones—UAVs."

"Yes, that is correct. But also UUVs—their underwater counterparts."

Saleh had a blank look on his face and said nothing. He wondered: UUVs—what in hell were they?

"It should not be difficult for you," Mr. Wu said. "There's quite a lot of information available in Santa Monica, at the R&D Corporation."

On Wednesday evening when they met, Roy was already in the dining room, sipping a martini. Kevin noticed the cocktail as he sat down at the table. "Rough day, Roy?"

"No. I'm just bracing myself for dinner. Tonight I'm going to have the salmon. I need some of that omega-3 or whatever it is you get from fish. So how's it going with you?"

"Fine," Kevin replied. "I have an entirely new perspective on what the Agency does to protect us. I suppose that most civilians—me included—have no concept of the continuous threats that our nation faces on a daily basis. Threats that are economic, or military, or simply irrational and based on jealousy or hate."

"You're right. I try not to think about the negatives, just concentrate on doing what I can. By the way, tomorrow will be a little different. I'm going to take you to our range. We have an ex-Marine gunnery sergeant who will show you a lot of different weapons—the types most commonly found in Third World countries, and those used by terrorists. The idea is to make you familiar with various weapons and what they can do, not to teach you to shoot. By the way, what experience do you have with firearms?"

"I was never in the military. But my dad had a handgun and a shotgun, and he taught my brothers and me gun safety and took us hunting—mostly rabbits. Later I hunted deer and antelope once, and wild pigs a couple of times. Most years I go quail hunting on a private ranch with some friends, but that's about it."

"Then you should find this interesting. Let's order. First thing is to find that waiter and get you a drink." After they ordered dinner, Roy asked about Juliana.

"Everything okay at home? Able to reach your wife?"

"Yes, thanks. She's busy with a big project at work, so she hasn't had time to think about missing me."

After the food arrived, Kevin asked Roy about his job.

"Maybe you can't or don't want to talk about what you do. If so, I understand. But I was wondering if you are stationed here at Camp Peary?"

"Yes. I'm part of the instructional staff. I work with new Agency recruits on physical training, conditioning, and some martial arts. We train people to avoid any physical situations. Any disturbance or altercation is likely to expose them or get them arrested—just what we don't want to happen. You can forget all that James Bond stuff you see in the movies. We want our operators to be unknown and unseen. But if, for some reason beyond their control, they find themselves in a situation, we try to give them knowledge of techniques that can help them escape or at least avoid injury."

When dinner was finished, Kevin asked what else was planned.

"Tomorrow afternoon will also be interesting for you. We have some streets—sort of a track—set up for defensive driving. The instructor will take you out and show you how to do a few basic maneuvers. After the demonstrations, he'll ask you to do them. If he thinks you're good enough, there may be a simulated attack where you'll need to use what you've learned.

"Friday morning you have some concluding classes, and then we'll meet for lunch. After lunch, George will drive you back to McLean, Virginia. We'll book you into the Ritz-Carlton in Tysons Corner, which is close to our headquarters in Langley. Someone will meet you there for dinner, and take you on tour on Saturday. There will be a final briefing on Sunday morning, and a ride back to Dulles Airport to catch your flight home."

"What can you tell me about Langley?"

"I think you'll find your tour of headquarters interesting. It's not open to the public. There are a lot of stories about it. During World War II, 'Wild Bill' Donovan, director of intelligence, proposed to President Roosevelt to create a central intelligence agency. President Truman killed the idea after the war but a few years later it came into being. Wild Bill was considered too wild to head it up, so Rear Admiral Roscoe Hillenkoetter became the director. In 1953, Alan Dulles, then director, pushed to build a headquarters building at Langley. It was constructed in 1959 to 1961, but after the Bay of Pigs fiasco in Cuba, Dulles was sacked and he never got to work in the new building he'd created."

Back in Beverly Hills, Saleh went into his study and made a long distance call. He waited impatiently for someone to answer.

"Are you still in Mexico?" he asked.

"Where else?"

"Get back here; I have a job for you."

"I need money."

"Don't tell me that. You botched the last job. I'm giving you another chance."

"What is it?"

"I want you to grab the woman when she leaves home in the morning to go to work. Don't lose her this time. Bring her to Vegas. You know where. You'll get your money there, but I'm not paying for damaged goods."

"When?"

"As soon as possible. You may have to watch the house a few mornings to get the timing right. Call me when you're on your way to Vegas with the passenger."

Saleh hung up the phone. They would take her to Leila's place. Take some pictures. Leila would like that. The pictures would ensure she cooperated.

On the long flight home to Los Angeles, Kevin thought about his experiences during the past week. He'd had a rare and privileged glimpse into the behind-the-scenes working of America's top secret spy agency. Kevin was flattered by the attention he received and the respect shown to him. He wondered if this could be a subtle recruitment campaign.

There'd been no overt offers or discussion of a job, however. Saturday he'd had lunch with Michael Keefe, an aviation consultant to the Agency. Keefe told him that he'd been asked to provide a short briefing on UAVs.

"I understand that you had something to do with recovering stolen drone components. That's all I know and I don't need to know more. I've been asked to let you know the role we are foreseeing for drones," Keefe said. "Initially, this technology was seen as a valuable tool for surveillance—watching troop movements in Bosnia, for example. We wanted to know what the Serbs were doing. Drones were a low cost way of doing that and we didn't run the risk of having aircraft shot down and pilots captured, held for ransom, or put on display and executed. This worked well, though a number of drones were shot down—the early ones were slow-moving, low-flying, easy targets at times.

"What happens if one gets shot down? Isn't there a risk that someone could try to copy the electronics?"

"When they go down, we try to recover them, or blow them up, but this wasn't always possible. Around the Middle East people have collected the pieces and no doubt sold or traded them to other powers—Iran being a likely candidate, or Pakistan, maybe North Korea."

"What do you do about that?" Kevin asked.

"We have to keep innovating, improving the design to stay ahead. It didn't take long before someone realized that while surveillance was fine, wouldn't it be cool if the drone could launch an attack if it saw the bad guys. The next step was to outfit a surveillance drone with a couple of missiles and a guidance system. Presto. At our China Lake test facility and in the field, this worked great. That success led to the next technological leap: bigger, faster drones with jam-proof guidance systems that can fly higher and further and carry more weapons.

"That's where we are today. Considerable research and testing is underway to extend the performance parameters even further. Military planners are envisioning a fleet of UAVs that can provide twenty-four-hour surveillance of huge swathes of the Pacific and Atlantic oceans.

"What about civilian applications?"

"It's obvious that civilian applications will follow. There will be small drones for police work, medium-sized drones for mapping, for crop management, pipeline and transmission line inspection, you name it.

"The bottom line is that we see drones as vital to national security and defense. Other nations will no doubt build them. We have to protect our technology, keep innovating, and stay in the forefront. We need better, jam- and interception-proof control, command, and guidance systems."

The final message Kevin received while at Langley was to just keep doing his job. If he found that he was going to travel overseas, to let them know. Depending on his destination, they may have a list of topics of interest that they'll pass on to him. If it turns out that he learns anything about one or more of these topics, of course they'd like to hear about it. He was instructed to not go out of his way—stick with his job, business as usual."

Juliana was waiting in terminal six at LAX when Kevin walked out of the American Airlines gate. She greeted him with a hug and a kiss. She hooked her arm in his as they walked out.

"I missed you," she said. "How was it? Was Norfolk interesting? That's a big Navy base. Did you get to go on any ships?"

"No," he said, "I just saw the inside of buildings, no ships. I didn't get to see the Atlantic Ocean, although it wasn't far away. Not too exciting—just a lot of meetings. I'm really glad to be home. And you—how is your big project going?"

"All finished," she said. "I'm thinking of taking a few days off. I want to go see the wildflowers. Care to join me?"

"Let me check tomorrow at the office. I'm afraid we're going to be really busy getting out the Pentagon documents, but I'll see."

"I understand, but please try to get away if you can."

"By the way, have you eaten? I'll be happy to fix you something when we get home."

"No, I ate on the plane. All I want when we get home is a glass of wine, a quick shower, and you in bed with me."

She snuggled next to him in the car, her breast pressed against his arm.

"Sounds good. Can I join you in the shower? I'll wash your back."

"Just my back?"

"You want a shampoo?"

"That wasn't what I was thinking."

"Maybe skip the wine, head directly to the shower?"

"Maybe skip the shower, head directly to bed?"

"You're so romantic."

Her laughter was music as he drove home.

WILDFLOWER

When Kevin returned to the office Monday morning, Holly greeted him with a cup of coffee and a folder with letters and memos.

"How was your vacation, boss?" she asked. "I hope you got some rest, because everyone in the world is after you now. I sorted your mail—this is the important stuff. There is another pile you can deal with later."

Kevin noticed a funny look on Holly's face when she asked about his vacation. Maybe she'd guessed it wasn't much of a vacation. No matter—Holly was great. She knew when to keep her mouth shut and never broached a confidence.

"Juliana was hoping I could take a few days off this week. She wants to go look at the wildflowers. Doesn't sound like that's possible."

"I wouldn't do it if I were you, Buster," Holly replied. "If word got out you were out sniffing flowers, there'd be some coronaries up on the fifth floor. No telling what might happen to you. I used up all my excuses as cover for you last week."

"Thanks, Holly. I figured as much. She'll probably enjoy going by herself. She likes to linger and I get impatient—you know the wildflowers are beautiful this time of year but how many times do you need to see a hillside covered with California poppies or purple lupine?"

It was a busy day and Kevin worked late, not getting home until 7 p.m. Juliana had dinner waiting.

"How are things at your work?" he asked, as he kissed her.

"There is a new scientific initiative we're undertaking for the Navy. The success of drone technology in the air has stimulated interest in doing the same thing underwater. Unmanned underwater vehicles—UUVs—can be used for underwater surveillance, tracking and/or targeting enemy vessels and for data collection and analysis. They could make measurements on underwater sound propagation in different climate situations—important information for anti-submarine warfare."

"Underwater drones? They must have limited range in the water."

"Yes and no. I was amazed to learn that last year a robotic underwater glider crossed the Atlantic Ocean. It retraced the path of Columbus's ship *Pinta*, collecting data as it went. The glider is unique in that it has no engine propelling it forward. It rides the ocean currents and makes a series of dives and ascents to collect data on ocean circulation and heat content. Descents involve pumping a small amount of water into the nose of the vehicle, causing it to sink until it descends to a depth of one hundred fifty to one hundred eighty meters over a long forward distance. After reaching a programmed depth, it reverses the process by pumping a small amount of water into the tail, causing it to glide upwards. The vehicle surfaces three times a day to check its location, transmit data, and download new piloting instructions from a satellite."

"Wow. That's pretty wild. Clever to use the ocean current as a propulsion system," Kevin said.

"How about you? Lots of work waiting for you, I suppose," she said. "That's a bad part of being away from the office. The work just piles up, doesn't it?"

"Yes. Holly is good though. She dumps as much of it off on other people as possible. But about tomorrow. There's no way I can get away. I hope you will go anyway and enjoy yourself. Take some pictures."

"Okay, as long as you don't mind, I think I'll drive up to Lancaster in the morning. I'm not sure where the best spots will be. I might go to the Poppy Reserve out on Lancaster Road. There are a lot of different places off of Highway 138 that can be reached by dirt roads. Or, I could go to the Poppy Reserve and then backtrack and take Munz road down to Elizabeth Lake. That might be the best overall. It's about a two hour drive to get there so I think I'll pack a lunch, leave early, and be back by dinnertime."

The man known only as Johnson was glad to be back in Southern California. He had not enjoyed his forced stay in Mexico. Of necessity he'd dumped his car in Sylmar. He was sure it had been ID'd when the woman jumped out and ran away. His partner Jim took a bus to Phoenix but Johnson chose Ensenada. He was tired of living in a cheap motel near Rosarita Beach. After Saleh's call, he took a bus to the border and crossed back into California. In San Diego he bought a beat-up used Chevrolet Sprint and headed north. His plan was to grab Juliana, take her to Las Vegas, collect his money, and then hole up for a while.

Early in the morning driving north on the 405 freeway, he thought about the woman, how she had not only made a laughingstock out of him, but also cost him his car and a lot of money besides.

He turned off the freeway and drove toward her house. It was a little before 7 a.m. as he slowly came down the street, trying to remember which house it was. At that moment he saw a woman come out of a house carrying a small backpack. She got in a blue Ford pickup parked in the driveway, backed out, and started down the street.

"Holy shit," he said aloud, "there goes the bitch. That pickup she's driving is a lot better vehicle than this piece of crap." He decided to follow her, thinking maybe she was on her way to work and he could grab her in a parking lot and also steal the truck. Instead of going downtown, the blue pickup turned east and entered the northbound 405 freeway. This was not the direction he wanted to go. If she stopped in the San Fernando Valley that would not be too much out of his way. Here again he was to be disappointed, for she continued north and transitioned to Highway 14 headed towards Lancaster. He looked at the gas gauge—there was a third of a tank, probably not a problem, depending on how far she went. Heading out to the desert might be better, he thought. Less chance anybody would be around to witness the theft. From Lancaster he could head north past Mohave and then cut over through Barstow and on to Las Vegas. Take a couple hours longer, but if he got her and a better vehicle it might be worth it.

Up ahead, Juliana was unaware of the white Chevrolet that doggedly followed a couple of car lengths behind. She listened to the news and the traffic reports and played some tapes with music by the Eagles and Pearl Jam. Traffic was heavy coming into town but light going north in her direction.

She passed Vasquez Rocks on the left. Palmdale was ahead, another twenty miles or so. In the right lane in front of her, an ancient Volkswagen made its way up the grade. She'd once had a car like that and the sight of it caused her to flash back to another trip she'd made one Christmas vacation while still in college. As she drove toward Lancaster, her mind drifted back to that other day, a different trip, an earlier time….

Her idea then was to retrace a portion of the route followed by her distant ancestors when the de Anza expedition came up from Mexico to colonize Alta California. She'd packed camping gear and headed south in her ancient VW to Borrego Springs. East of town she found the dirt road that led to Font's Point, named for the Padre who had accompanied de Anza. At the end of the road she climbed up to the point.

A vast panorama was spread out below. Immediately beneath where she stood was the Borrego Badlands, desolate brown hills cut by numerous rocky canyons and no sign of a living thing anywhere. In the distance, towards the southeast, she could make out the Salton Sea, and beyond that, somewhere in the haze, lay Mexico.

Juliana returned to Borrego Springs and drove north on DiGiorgio road. She urged her VW over the rocks and stones at the edge of a broad wash leading to Coyote Canyon and the headwaters of Coyote Creek. There, some miles ahead, the Anza party had camped on Christmas Eve in an area where water and fodder for their stock was plentiful. A baby was born there.

After seven miles she came to a place where the road crossed the stream. She got out and surveyed the stream. It was not a good place to get stuck. As far as she knew she was alone here in this desolate spot. She'd not seen any other vehicles or people. She removed her boots and waded into the stream. It was about eight inches deep, not moving fast. The bottom felt firm. She tossed her boots in the back of the VW and drove on until she could go no further in her car.

It took several hours of walking to reach the area where Anza had camped two centuries earlier. She wondered what it had been like in 1775, when the expedition passed through. She tried to imagine her namesake, 4-year-old Maria Juliana, walking through the rough desert terrain. Juliana was enchanted by this spot—a veritable oasis in the middle of the desert. Here the stream flowed cleanly. On impulse she removed her boots and clothes and sat down in a pool of cool water, splashing it over her head and face and letting it run down her back and chest. Refreshed, she climbed out and sat on a rock for a while before drying off and getting dressed again. Then she looked for a spot to camp for the night.

Going up the trail, Juliana saw small secretive birds flit away from her into bushes as she passed. There were scats from some animal by the side of the trail, probably one of the coyotes that gave the canyon its name. A solitary mourning dove, startled by her approach, flew swiftly away to a distant hillside. At one point along the trail she watched a large black tarantula walking up the hillside, looking for romance. Contrary to first impressions, the desert was full of life, especially here near water. Once away from the spring and stream, the terrain reverted to the harsh desert landscape marked by scattered boulders, spiny cholla, creosote bush, yuccas, and cat's claw acacia.

She remembered sleeping for a few hours and then awakening to the sound of a coyote howling in the distance. Another answered from the other side of the canyon. Juliana crawled out of her tent, stretched, and walked off to the side of her campsite. She squatted and urinated. "Marking my territory," she thought to herself, thinking of the coyotes roaming somewhere in the darkness.

The sky was inky black as only a desert night with no moon can be. She returned and crawled into her sleeping bag. Now wide awake, she lay on her back and looked out at the sky, full of more stars than it was possible to imagine, after living in the city. That night she watched a meteor streak across the sky and then another and another. She was enthralled by the spectacular sight of the Geminid meteor shower, and wondered if a meteor shower had occurred two centuries before. It would have been an auspicious omen for the new baby. After watching for a while, she once again fell asleep, alone in Coyote Canyon, with the coyotes keeping watch.

She was jarred back to the present by a horn honking, an irate driver flashing past her in a sports car. While day-dreaming, she'd edged into his lane. Before long she saw that she was approaching Lancaster. She'd made the trip in about an hour and a half. She thought about stopping to get some coffee, but decided against it. Better to get out to the viewing areas before it got too hot or the wind came up, causing the poppies to close their blossoms.

She turned off on Avenue K and followed the roads west and north to Lancaster Road where the Poppy Reserve was located. Leaving the populated area, she could see the hills in the distance were sprinkled with color. Along the road the countryside was flat with a sparse covering of sage, Russian thistle—better known as tumbleweed—junipers, and Joshua trees. She decided not to go to the Poppy Reserve, which would probably be crowded with people. Instead, she turned off the main road onto Munz Road and headed south to Lake Elizabeth, where she could hike in the foothills. As she prepared to turn, she noticed the white Chevrolet coming down the road behind her. After turning, she glanced in the rearview mirror and saw that the white Chevrolet also had turned.

She continued down Munz Road, looking at the wildflowers that dotted the hillsides. She crossed over the California aqueduct and as she drove she watched for a place to pull off the road and park so she could leave the truck and hike. After several miles, she found a perfect spot and pulled over. A footpath led up the hill. She picked up her backpack, locked the truck, and started up the hillside.

Glancing back at the road, she saw the Chevrolet approaching. It came even with her truck but continued on down the road. She turned and started walking up the hill, paying it no further attention. When she'd climbed for ten minutes or so she paused to catch her breath. She looked back the way she'd come.

To her surprise, the Chevrolet had turned around and was now parked by her truck. A man stood at the driver's side door of her vehicle, looking in. He turned and stared up the hill at her. He started walking up the trail in her direction.

Juliana watched him for a moment. On the low part of the trail he was moving fast, not running, but taking big steps. At this rate, he would soon overtake her. Something felt wrong to her. He didn't appear to be a wildflower enthusiast. He had no camera, no guidebooks, no water. As she watched, there was something vaguely familiar about him. At that moment, he glanced up, saw her watching, and grinned at her.

Recognition came as a shock. She remembered that grin from when she'd sat in the back of his car, after he'd pushed her in and slammed the door. A dozen thoughts raced through her mind: how was this possible? What was he doing here; how had he found her?

She dismissed these thoughts and began climbing the hill rapidly, looking back every now and then. At first, Johnson seemed to gain on her, but he started falling behind. Juliana was in good shape, but Johnson was a two packs of cigarettes a day guy and quickly became winded.

Juliana could tell he was tiring so she moved off the trail to the left and began scrambling up a granite outcropping. It was a nearly vertical climb requiring her to step from rock to rock, and in some places, literally crawl to get to the top of large boulders.

As Juliana scrambled up the rocky hillside, she felt a moment of panic. Her breathing was rapid, her mouth felt dry. Stepping up on a rock, her foot slipped and she skinned the inside of her calf. When she looked back down at Johnson, he seemed to be gaining.

She grabbed a better toehold and pulled herself up.

Her mind cleared as she recalled climbing to Font's Point in the Anza-Borrego desert. She forced herself to think of her ancestors crossing the badlands. If they could do that, day after day, she could do this. She paused, watching him. Johnson had stopped. He was breathing hard, his head down. Her panic gone and confidence restored, Juliana scrambled higher.

When Johnson reached the base of the outcropping, he sat down to catch his breath, his head hung low as he panted. He rose wearily and started to climb up after her.

Juliana was beginning to tire as well and realized that she couldn't keep climbing indefinitely. She made it up another fifty feet and clambered out on a flat ledge about four feet wide. She sat down with her back against the hillside to catch her breath. When she turned to resume her climb, she faced a sheer vertical wall, without any place to step and no hand holds. She would have to descend, move to her left, and resume the climb. But that meant descending towards Johnson. The very thought was revolting. She tried to stay calm, hold off fear. She saw some soft ball size loose stones lying on the ledge.

She peeked over the edge. Johnson was resting about twenty feet below her. He looked up and saw her watching.

"Nice day for a hike, isn't it. Why don't you come down, and we'll talk things over."

"I know who you are," Juliana shouted. "Get the hell out of here, or you are going to be very sorry you followed me."

"Yeah? And what you going to do? Keep climbing until you run out of mountain?"

"No. I'm going to kill you."

He sneered. "You and what army?" Johnson searched around for the next foothold to resume his climb. He failed to see Juliana pick up one of the loose stones. She heaved it straight down at him.

The rock struck him squarely on the top of the head. His arms flew out to each side and he did a perfect back dive from his position on the slope, hitting heavily on his back about ten feet down, and then rolling down another twenty feet where he lay without moving.

Juliana froze, aghast at what she'd done. Her initial thought was to scare him, but the throw had turned deadly. She sat still, watching him for any sign of movement, letting her breathing and heart rate slow down. Her first fear was that he was faking, trying to lure her within reach. But as she studied him, his position was very unnatural, one arm and one leg twisted in awkward positions. His head was bleeding.

She decided to scramble down before he revived. She climbed down, bypassing where he lay, and soon reached the trail. She ran down to her truck and quickly unlocked the door, while watching the trail. There was no sign of pursuit. From her position by the car she couldn't see the spot where he'd fallen.

Her first inclination was to jump in the truck and drive off, but she thought better of it. She scribbled down the license plate number of the white Chevy, all the time watching the trail. Still no sign of Johnson. She reached in her backpack and retrieved a folding knife. She stabbed the front tire of the Chevrolet, but the knife bounced off the hard rubber tread. The next time she took two hands and stabbed the sidewall. This time the knife penetrated and she could feel air escaping. She twisted the knife to enlarge the hole, and repeated the procedure on the other front tire.

She jumped in the pickup and turned it around. Still no sign of Johnson. As she swung back onto the road, she could see both front tires of the Chevrolet were flat. She drove as fast as possible back to Lancaster. When she got in the town, she pulled off the highway into the crowded parking lot of a shopping mall. She drank some water and tried to calm herself, then found a phone to call Kevin's office. Holly answered the phone.

"Holly, it's Juliana. Can you find Kevin? It's an emergency."

"Hi, Juliana. Are you okay? Kevin's here on the floor somewhere. Hang on, and I'll go find him."

"I'm okay. Just tell him something's come up, and I need to talk to him."

In a minute or so Kevin came on the line. "Julie, are you okay? Holly said there was an emergency. Where are you?"

"I'm in Lancaster. I'm okay, but I'm really frightened. You won't believe what's happened."

Juliana related the entire incident to Kevin.

"I can't believe this," he said. "Are you sure it was the same guy?"

"Absolutely. Kevin, I don't know what to do next," she added. "Should I go to the police here? I just want to get out of here and come home."

"Give me that license plate number and tell me approximately where the car is located," Kevin said. "I'm going to call the LAPD and report this and ask them to get the Lancaster PD to send somebody out to investigate. Can you stay where you are for ten or fifteen minutes while I make the call? Stay in the truck with the doors locked. Call me back in fifteen minutes."

Fifteen anxious minutes passed before Juliana called back. Kevin answered immediately.

"I spoke with Detective Mead of the LAPD. Lancaster is sending someone out. They'll pick up the car if it's still there, and they'll do a search for your attacker. LAPD is sending what info they have to Lancaster. Jesus Christ, we were told this guy was hiding out in Mexico; now he's back here trying to grab you! What in hell is going on?"

"What do they want me to do?"

"If you feel up to it, come on home. Drive carefully. You've been through a lot and are obviously stressed. If you don't feel like driving home, I'll come get you—your choice."

"I'll drive home. I want to get away from here; I'll be fine if I can get on the road."

"Come straight home, and I'll meet you there. LAPD is going to have someone watching the house for the next couple of days until they find Mr. Johnson. Are you sure you're okay to drive? Listen, I love you. Please be careful."

When Juliana drove in the driveway, Kevin was already home to meet her. He came out and greeted her and walked inside the house with her. She noticed a black and white LA police car parked across the street.

"How are you doing?" he asked, giving her a hug. "I can't imagine what this asshole was doing going after you."

"I don't know. All he said was that he wanted 'to talk things over.' I didn't believe that for a minute. I think he wanted to kill me. For some reason that I can't explain, he wasn't acting like he wanted to kidnap me. He could've hidden by the truck until I returned and grabbed me and forced me into his car if he wanted to kidnap me. But no, he waited until I got away from the road and came after me."

"Juliana, there is one thing we need to discuss."

"What's that?"

"How sure are you that you hit him with that rock?"

"Pretty sure. It was a lucky throw. I was hoping to scare him so he'd leave."

"So, you can't be absolutely sure you hit him?"

"No, I suppose not. Why?"

"Because I told Detective Mead of LAPD that the guy threatened you, you thought he was going to attack you, you threw a rock to scare him, and he fell down the hillside as a result. I didn't say that you hit him. Since there is reasonable doubt, I think we should stick with that story."

"It all happened so fast, I can't be sure. But I'll say this, I yelled at him. I said if he kept coming, I was going to kill him. You know what he said to me? 'You and what army?' That's when I pitched the stone and he went over backwards down the hill."

"Fine. I think that you should forget that you threatened him. If it comes up, just say that you panicked and tossed the stone."

"Enough of this."

"Are you hungry? Doesn't seem like you had time to eat anything."

"No, I'm not hungry. I ate an apple while driving back. But I'd like a drink, maybe something strong to make me relax—like scotch on the rocks."

"Scotch? You never drink scotch!"

"I know. But somehow it sounds good right now."

Kevin went to fix the drinks. While he was in the kitchen the phone rang. He answered it and spoke to the caller for about ten minutes. He finished pouring two glasses of Scotch whiskey and took them into the living room.

"Who was that?" Juliana asked

"That was the LAPD, Lieutenant Mead. Lancaster PD found the car, and they also found Johnson's body. They're going to write it up as an accidental death while hiking. They want to see you for an official statement tomorrow, since you witnessed the accident. They found information—I don't know if it was on him or in the car— that indicates he was headed to Las Vegas to see someone. LAPD is having Las Vegas follow up on this. Johnson had just bought the car the day before from some used-car lot in San Diego. The car was a real clunker—almost out of gas. They think he may have driven by the house in the morning, seen you leave, and then decided to follow you, and settle a score. At the same time, get a better vehicle. Probably, we'll never know what he was thinking. But, for sure, we won't have any more visits from Mr. Johnson."

SURVEILLANCE

The fact that Johnson had crawled out of the bushes somewhere and threatened Juliana again really bothered Kevin. His first call the next day was to Lieutenant Mead of LAPD.

"You had information Johnson had gone to Mexico to hide out," Kevin said. "But then he came back. What do you make of that? Any new information?"

"No new information. But I'll say that I'm surprised. I thought he'd be smarter than that."

"Let's assume he isn't smart, but is following orders. What then? How did you know he went to Mexico in the first place?"

"We had a tip. I don't know the details."

"More importantly, what's happening in the Beske investigation?"

"I don't know. Unfortunately we're not involved. It's Riverside County, not our jurisdiction. They're working with the FBI, as far as I know."

"Not your jurisdiction? Heck, as far as you know he could've been killed in a LAX parking lot," Kevin replied, trying to keep the anger he felt out of his voice.

"I know how you feel, Kevin. It's a terrible thing, and I'd like to know who is responsible as much as you do. But it's out of our hands. You might want to see if the guy in the Beaumont PD will give you a contact name in the FBI."

"One final question. What about Saleh, the Saudi guy who owns the Beaumont cabin? What's happening there?"

"I'm sorry, but I don't have any new information. We've been told to hold off on doing anything with him. It may be that Riverside or the Feds don't want to alarm him until they have something solid to go on. Believe me, if we get the word, we'll do all we can to help. But here again, there are jurisdictional issues, and we'll have to work with the Beverly Hills PD since that's where he lives."

Kevin was silent as he thought about what he'd heard. After a minute passed, Detective Mead asked if Kevin was still on the line.

"Yes, I'm sorry, I was just thinking about what you said. I sympathize with you. Dealing with these jurisdictional issues must be frustrating, to say the least. Thanks for taking time to talk with me. Please call if you learn anything more."

"I'll do that, Kevin. Sorry I don't have more for you. My regards to Mrs. Hunter."

Kevin's next call was to Charles Kidd. After telling him about Juliana's narrow escape, he asked if Kidd had any new information. He also had nothing new to report.

"We've given any information we had to the Feds. The Agency has no authority to meddle in domestic matters—that's FBI territory. They get real unhappy if we stick our noses into their business, so we've just got to go along. Frankly, they don't seem to have given this much of a priority. I'm not happy about it, but at the moment we can't bring any more pressure to bear. I'll touch base with the LAPD and see if they know anything more about Johnson."

"What would it take to bring more pressure?" Kevin asked.

"One thing that would definitely make a difference? If there was a link to national security."

"For example, if the Saudi guy was trying to pass drone secrets to some party in the Middle East?"

"Yeah, something like that."

"Beske was working on an angle like that, wasn't he?" Kevin asked.

"Officially, no comment. But it is an interesting speculation, especially if you knew someone who'd found some top-secret stolen drone parts, like maybe parts of the guidance system. Of course, that's all wild speculation, so please forget I ever mentioned it."

"Of course," Kevin said. "I didn't hear what you never mentioned."

"Changing the subject, how was your visit to the Farm?"

"As you should know, officially there is no place called the 'Farm,' so I couldn't have visited it. But I did have an interesting week's vacation between Norfolk and McLean, Virginia, and I learned a lot from some meetings I attended."

"Any changes in your outlook?" Kidd asked.

"I'll tell you what I told my host."

"What was that?"

"I'm in."

When Saleh hadn't heard from Johnson after five days, he began to suspect something had gone wrong. He tried calling, but his phone was no longer in service. He knew Johnson needed money, so something must have backfired or he would have been in touch. The next time Saleh had business in Los Angeles, he stopped by the County Department of Public Health and asked to look at the death records for the past month. There it was—deceased in Lancaster, California. Cause of death: accidental fall. Saleh was totally mystified. Why was the idiot climbing hills in Lancaster?

Here was another setback. He'd have to think of something to tell Wu. And, at the same time, find another way to get at the woman. He wondered if she'd been involved. If so, it was the second time she'd gotten the best of Johnson.

In Kevin's opinion, the police seemed to have dropped the investigation of Bob Beske's murder; either that or the trail had gone completely cold. When Kevin asked about the Saudi lawyer who supposedly owned the Beaumont cabin, detective Mead implied that they had no basis to charge him. Kevin sensed that there was more to it; there seemed to be a reluctance to confront this individual. Kevin had no "jurisdictional issues." He decided to see what he could find out.

From the Riverside County authorities it was a simple matter to track down the property ownership records. The property was owned by Ridley Trading Company, LLC, represented by Fahad A. Saleh, General Counsel. Kevin next learned that Mr. Saleh had an office address in Beverly Hills. One weekend he visited the office, carrying a clipboard and wearing a hard hat. He learned that the "office" was a virtual office. No one actually worked there. A receptionist took care of visitors and directed them to a waiting room or conference room for meetings with the building tenants. Several telephone operators kept busy answering phones, where they either took messages or forwarded calls to other locations.

By searching Beverly Hills social events in the Beverly Hills Library files of the *Los Angeles Times*, Kevin was able to come up with a good photograph of Saleh, dressed formally in a dark suit. His companion was a tall, dark haired, strikingly beautiful Middle Eastern woman. After finding the picture, the next thing he needed was a Beverly Hills address; this was obtained with surprising ease from a friendly clerk in the City Hall.

Why am I doing this, Kevin thought? What for? This is not my job; the police should be doing this. He did not tell Juliana about his investigation.

The more he thought about Bob Beske, the more determined he became. It seemed that Mr. Saleh had some sort of political immunity, or possibly the police were afraid of a legal backlash.

He started driving by the Beverly Hills address at random times, on his way to work or on the way home. One day he was rewarded by seeing a black Lincoln back out of the driveway. Kevin came close enough to memorize the license plate and then immediately turned a corner as the Lincoln disappeared in the distance.

On his way home from work the next day, he was surprised to spot the black Lincoln ahead of him, proceeding west on Olympic Blvd. At the Avenue of The Stars it turned right, entering the Century City office complex, where it turned into an underground parking structure.

Kevin made a note of the office tower address and went home.

Juliana greeted him at the door. Later he sat in the living room with a glass of wine, thinking about what to do next. It appeared that Mr. Saleh had an evening meeting with someone in Century City. Kevin decided to visit the building and see the list of tenants posted in the lobby.

He waited until the next weekend to make the visit. He was surprised to learn that the building on Century Park East Boulevard housed the corporate headquarters of Northrop Grumman Corporation.

Kevin called Kidd and asked for a meeting. Kidd selected a restaurant on the Santa Monica pier. They met at 11:30.

"Let's order and have lunch and then take a walk," Kidd said. "I don't have a lot of time, but I don't think we should talk in here."

After lunch they walked out to the end of the pier. When they reached the spot where there were no fishermen, Kidd stopped.

"What's on your mind, Kevin?"

"You know the guy that owned the Beaumont

cabin?"

"Yeah, he's a Saudi lawyer. So what?"

"I did some checking," Kevin said. "His office is a sham; it's one of those virtual offices where someone answers the phone but no one is ever there. That seems strange for big shot lawyer. Next, he's got a very nice house in Beverly Hills, I'd say in the $3-$5 million range, so somebody's making a lot of money. Most interesting, he goes in after hours and meets someone in Century City. Even stranger, his meetings are in the Northrop Grumman corporate headquarters but always after-hours, like at 6 p.m."

Kevin could tell he had Kidd's attention.

"Well, well, you've been busy haven't you! This is interesting news. I'll see what I can quietly find out. At some point we'll have to turn it over to the FBI, if there's anything there. I don't know if you should do anymore. You need to be very careful, you know. If there is a link, you don't want to end up like Beske. You know these guys make their own rules. They could swat you like a fly if there is a link as you suggest."

"I'll watch my back," Kevin said, "but I'm not stopping. I think there was a reason Johnson came back, and I don't want something like that to happen again."

"I'm worried, Kevin. You may be in over your head."

"Thanks for your concern. Do me a favor and call if you find out anything that would connect Northrop, a Saudi lawyer, and drones. And one more thing—Johnson was supposedly headed to Las Vegas. What's there that might be part of the puzzle?"

"Nothing that I can think of," Kidd replied. He paused, thinking for a minute. "Wait a minute, this is a remote chance but it might fit. There's Creech Air Force Base out at Indian Springs. It's about forty-five miles northwest of Vegas."

"What happens there?"

"It's all hush-hush, but I hear it's a drone control center. Using satellites for control, they can fly drones all over the world."

⚭

After talking to Kidd, Kevin was more determined than ever to find something—some bit of information that might spur an investigation into the activities of the mysterious Mr. Saleh. He could not take time off from work, but from his home in West Los Angeles he could drive through Beverly Hills on his way to and from his office in downtown Los Angeles.

He did this on random days. Some days it was impossible because he had meetings out of the office. In the mornings, at 7 a.m., the house was usually dark, no sign of the black Lincoln. Once or twice he saw it parked in the driveway, but was unable to stay and watch.

In the afternoons he left his office around 5 p.m. and passed by the Beverly Hills house at 5:30. If the car was out, he pulled around the corner or across the street and watched for a while before heading home. Days passed with nothing happening to reward his efforts.

Then, on a Friday evening, he saw the black Lincoln leaving as he approached the house. He followed at a discreet distance as the Lincoln once again drove to Century City and pulled up in front of the Northrop Grumman tower.

Kevin quickly turned into a driveway and pulled forward to a point where he could still see the Lincoln, but where he was off the street. As he watched, a man carrying a briefcase hurried out of the building and got into the Lincoln, which pulled away from the curb, drove north to Santa Monica Boulevard, and turned left. Kevin let several cars pass and then took up a position about four vehicles behind the Lincoln. It went west to the San Diego Freeway and headed north to the San Fernando Valley.

Kevin almost lost it in heavy traffic on Ventura Boulevard, but found it again as it slowed and turned into a driveway. He continued on past and saw that the Lincoln had entered the Star Light Motel. He went to the next intersection, made a quick U-turn, and drove slowly back. The passenger was standing outside the Lincoln, leaning in the open door, talking to Saleh. He closed the door, walked to one of the rooms that faced the courtyard, unlocked the door and entered. Kevin noticed that he no longer had the briefcase. Meanwhile, the Lincoln drove ahead on the U-shaped driveway and came back out to Ventura Boulevard headed east past Kevin's parked car.

Now he was faced with the decision—should he follow the Lincoln? He decided to stay where he was. Whoever was in the motel had no vehicle, so chances were that someone would come pick him up. There was also the chance that he would stay there all weekend, and Kevin couldn't do that.

After the Lincoln left, Kevin drove east on Ventura Boulevard to Encino, found a restaurant and ordered a drink and dinner. While waiting for the food to arrive, he called Juliana.

"Hi Julie. Something's come up and I've got to work late. Don't worry about dinner. I'll grab a sandwich here."

"How late will you be?" she asked.

"I'm not sure—just a couple of hours hopefully."

"Don't be too late."

"I love you. Don't wait up."

After eating, he drove back to Tarzana and drove by the motel. A dim sign on top of the office building was now illuminated with the words *Motor Hotel*. Over the end of the motel building, a neon sign glowed red in the shape of three hearts placed side-by-side. This made it easy to spot the entrance to the motel. He went around the block, returned, and drove slowly through the motel parking lot. The building was single story, a long row of about twenty-five ranch style units strung out in an L-shape around a central courtyard. The entrance was through a framed overhead structure that connected one end of the motel units to a separate building with a sign proclaiming "Office-register here (ring bell)."

The motel, of the type first constructed when Americans took to the highways after the war, was run-down and seedy. The driveway and parking area was cracked and had weeds growing through it in numerous spots. The exterior paint on the buildings was faded and peeling. There were pickup trucks parked by three of the units, otherwise the place looked deserted. He left by the back driveway to avoid passing by the office again.

He parked on a side street about a half-block away from the motel with the car pulled over under a dense group of eucalyptus trees. He slouched down in the front seat. It was doubtful that anyone passing on the road could see him sitting in the car.

Minutes stretched into hours and Kevin found himself getting sleepy. Shouldn't have had that drink, he thought; should have had the restaurant fix me some coffee to go. He thought about getting out of the car, taking a walk, stretching his legs, but gave up the idea when he realized the indoor light would come on and someone might wonder what he was doing, sitting there in the dark car.

Suddenly, he came on full alert. A black Lincoln had passed the motel and then stopped abruptly. It backed up to a position in front of the red neon hearts and then turned into the motel driveway. Kevin started his car and pulled out into Ventura Boulevard and drove slowly past the motel. He could see the Lincoln parked at the end of the lot, away from the other vehicles. Two people—a man and a woman—got out of the car and walked quickly to the unit where the passenger had entered. He turned off his headlights and stopped. He saw them knock on the door. As they stood there under the overhead light, Kevin recognized Saleh, carrying a briefcase. The woman was tall, wearing a miniskirt that revealed shapely legs. The door opened, and they both entered the room.

Kevin made a quick U-turn and returned to the spot where he'd parked previously. After nearly ten minutes, Saleh came out of the room alone. He no longer had the briefcase. He got in the Lincoln and drove away.

Kevin decided to wait a while longer, although he was not sure it would accomplish anything. He gave himself until 10 p.m. If he stayed longer, Juliana would begin to worry. She might call the office and find out that he wasn't answering his phone, and then she'd worry more. He did not want that to happen.

A few minutes before 10 p.m. a taxi entered the motel courtyard. It sat there, engine idling. Kevin quickly got out of his car and walked up to Ventura Boulevard. He crossed the street and turned right towards the motel entrance. He walked along the street to a point where he had a good view of the motel courtyard. At that moment, a woman came out of the motel room. She had long dark hair; it had been done up in some manner previously but now hung freely to her shoulders. He had a brief glimpse of her face under the courtyard light before she entered the taxi. She was very attractive, dark makeup on her eyes. She appeared to be of Middle Eastern descent, possibly Egyptian. When she stooped to enter the cab, the short jacket she was wearing fell open, revealing a shear, low-cut blouse. She looked in his direction. Kevin quickly turned away and kept walking.

The taxi exited the motel and went west on Ventura Boulevard, away from him. Once it was out of sight, Kevin turned and retraced his steps until he could read the number of the motel door, then he returned to his car and drove home.

Kevin walked into the dark house quietly so as not to wake Juliana. He headed straight to the bathroom, washed his face, brushed his teeth, and undressed.

When he got in bed, Juliana was half awake. She rolled over and kissed him.

"Why can't you get your work done in eight hours like everyone else," she said. "I don't like to go to bed alone on Friday nights."

"Something urgent came up," he said. "I'm sorry to be so late." He kissed her.

She placed her hand on his crotch, holding him.

"Something is coming up now," she said, teasing him.

He kissed her. She sat up in bed and removed the thin nightgown she was wearing. In the semi-dark room he could see the silhouette of her breasts outlined as she pulled the nightgown over her head.

He pulled her back down and rolled over on top of her. He could tell she was ready. As he entered her, an image of the dark-eyed Egyptian woman flashed into his mind. He opened his eyes and saw Juliana's face beneath him. Her eyes were closed, her hair spread out like a halo around her head on the white pillowcase. He dismissed the thought of the other woman, ashamed that it had even occurred to him at that moment.

"I love you," Juliana was saying, as she arched her hips and held him tightly against her.

"Don't ever change," he said, kissing her again and again.

Afterwards, Kevin lay there awake for a while, thinking about Saleh, the man from Northrop, and the woman. He was certain she was a prostitute. Something had gone on with the briefcase. Possibly papers were switched or copied. What role did the woman play? Was she part of the payment, or was she a spy?

❧

The next day, as Kevin drove to his office, he found he couldn't get the Egyptian woman out of his mind. He kept thinking that he'd seen her somewhere before. As he drove into the parking structure at his office in downtown Los Angeles, he suddenly remembered the photograph of Saleh he'd found in the Beverly Hills library files. In the photograph, there was a woman. When Kevin got to his office, he opened a file cabinet where he kept a folder with notes and addresses. He pulled out the photograph. He couldn't be certain but the woman he'd seen leaving the motel in Tarzana looked very much like the woman in the photograph.

During his lunch hour, Kevin closed the door to his office, wrote up some notes, including the black Lincoln's license number, Saleh's address, the motel address and room number, and a copy of the photograph. He called the Agency number and left a message for Charles Kidd to contact him.

Kidd returned his call about 2 o'clock in the afternoon.

"I've some new information for you," Kevin said. "When could we meet for a few minutes?"

"How about 5:30 p.m. in the Pershing Square garage?"

"That will work. Where will I find you?"

"Come to the car wash. I'll be somewhere around there watching for you. We can take a short walk in the park."

"See you then," Kevin said.

Later that afternoon, Kevin walked into the Pershing Square garage, made his way to the car wash, and looked around. There was no sign of Kidd. He waited a few moments, wondering if he should look elsewhere, when suddenly Kidd appeared at his side.

"How are you Kevin? I assume you want to meet because you have some more information about our Saudi friend."

"And why would you think that?" Kevin said.

"It's just that I've decided that you can be a very determined person, when you set your mind to something."

Kevin laughed. "Some would say stubborn."

Kidd frowned. "Some might say a trouble maker. Let's take a walk. We can go up to the park and count the panhandlers."

They went upstairs and strolled through the park. As they walked Kevin slipped an envelope out of his jacket pocket and handed it to Kidd.

"I'm hoping that you can find this useful," he said. "There is a photograph of Mr. Saleh with a woman, and I doubt that it's his wife. I can't be sure but I think there's a good chance that she is the same woman that he delivered to a motel in Tarzana, to rendezvous with his contact from Northrop. She spent a couple of hours in the room, then called a taxi and left. Meanwhile, there was a briefcase shuffle between Saleh and the Northrop guy. You'll also find the address of the motel and the room number where this all occurred. I'm hoping that with the resources at your disposal you can use this information to determine what's going on."

"Kevin, you know this is a kind of thing that we're not supposed to get involved in, nor should you. But I'll tell you what, I'll see what I can do, if you promise me to back off and stay away from this guy."

"I don't know that there's much else I could do in any event. Also, I've got some key project work coming up and I'm going to be traveling, so I won't be around to do much in any case."

"I'll see what I can find out. If I learn anything useful I'll get back to you in a few days."

The week went by and one afternoon Holly stuck her head

into Kevin's office. "A Mr. Kidd is on the line for you," she said. "I asked him what it was about, and he said that your car was ready for the car wash. Do you want to talk to this guy?"

"Yes, go ahead and put the call through."

"Hi, Kevin. Can we meet today at 5:30 in the Pershing Square garage? "

"Yes. I'll see you there." The line went dead.

When Kevin arrived at the car wash he saw Kidd standing off to one side waiting for him.

"Let's take a walk. I don't have a lot of time. I just want to let you know that I followed up on your request. Fortunately, there's a guy in LAPD who owed me a favor. That plus some work by our international guys found out some interesting things. First, the woman, who goes by the name of Leila el-Masry, is an exotic dancer in Las Vegas. I suspect, for the right price, she will do some private dancing in your bed. She has one prior arrest for prostitution. She was part of that famous Las Vegas madam's stable of high-priced call girls. Now she dances occasionally at the Ali Baba restaurant. Saleh visits Las Vegas on a regular basis, but never stays very long. The room at the Star Light motel has been booked a number of times for one night by a man named Tom Bradley who always pays cash in advance. This gentleman is white, and most definitely is not the former mayor of Los Angeles, so I doubt that Bradley is his real name. Especially interesting is the fact that Mr. Saleh is a good customer of Al Baraka Islamic bank. He regularly withdraws large sums from the bank, but is not known to make deposits. The bank is headquartered in Saudi Arabia but has a significant presence in fifteen other countries including Pakistan, Jordan, Kuwait, and others."

"This is all very interesting," Kevin said, "but is it enough to get any action?"

"Not yet. Your Mr. Saleh is very careful. But somehow he doesn't pass the smell test."

"What else can you do?"

"As I told you," Kidd replied, "we're not empowered to undertake domestic surveillance."

"Yeah, I know. But doesn't this look like international espionage? Surely that justifies some concern. Get someone in Vegas who could find out who visits the dancer? Like, does she hang out with any Air Force guys? And I'm sure you can take a look at suspicious international banking transactions. It would be interesting to find out where the money comes from that ends up in Saleh's account, hypothetically speaking, of course."

"Kevin, you can be a real pain in the ass, hypothetically speaking. But I'll see what we can do. There is enough here that we're thinking about pursuing two avenues. The first is trying to establish who his connection is at Northrop Grumman. Secondly, we want to learn more about his circle of friends in Las Vegas. I'll keep you posted, but please forget I ever mentioned these plans."

"Thanks" Kevin replied. "By the way, I'm going to be out of town for eight or nine days. I'm going to Johnston Island."

"Johnston Island? That's out in the Pacific, right?"

"Yes—about seven hundred and fifty nautical miles west of Honolulu."

"What's out there?"

"It's an atoll that has four islands. Johnston Island, where I'm headed, is the largest. There's also Sand Island and two other small man-made islands. It's where the Department of Defense is destroying stocks of nerve gas and other chemical weapons. We have a contract to provide operations and maintenance support services there. I'll be looking at an emergency generator replacement project. So, I'll be out of action during that time. I'll check in with you when I get back."

Saleh had an informant in the American Express travel office who alerted him whenever a travel itinerary in Kevin's name came up. When he learned that Kevin was going to Hawaii, it meant two things: Kevin's guard would be down, and his wife would be home alone in Los Angeles. Here were two chances to find a way to apply pressure on Juliana so she would reveal what R&D was doing in its highly secret underwater drone research program. Saleh sensed that Mr. Wu was more interested in UUVs than UAVs and would offer additional money if he saw some proof that Saleh could deliver.

Knowing he had to act quickly, Saleh made two phone calls. The first was to a Saudi named Omar in Honolulu. The second was to a lowlife named Robinson who lived in South Los Angeles. Robinson was out on probation, instead of being in jail, thanks to Saleh. It was time to return the favor. He listened carefully to Saleh's instructions and took down Kevin and Juliana's address.

JOHNSTON ISLAND

Kevin walked off the plane in the Honolulu airport and headed for the main terminal, his bag slung over his shoulder. The warm, humid air with its smell of tropical flowers was refreshing after the stale odor of the plane. He took the escalator down to baggage claim, went outside the terminal, and flagged a cab.

A half hour later he was creeping through the Waikiki traffic on his way to his hotel. In the morning, he would return to the airport to catch a military flight to Johnston Island. He was looking forward to his visit there.

Johnston was a low, flat island surrounded by a reef, sunken remnants of an ancient volcano. During World War II, Consolidated constructed an airfield and port there as a forward base for operations against the Japanese. After the war, the island was used for nuclear weapons testing. In the 1960s, Thor ballistic missiles were launched from the island. They carried nuclear warheads to heights of one hundred to four hundred kilometers into the atmosphere as part of a U.S. test program.

After the nuclear test program ended, the Department of Defense constructed a facility on the island to "demilitarize" nerve gas and other chemical weapons. The facility, known as the Johnston Atoll Chemical Agent Disposal System, was the first U.S. chemical munitions disposal facility. In 1990, Johnston Island began operations, processing the first group of chemical weapons brought by ship from Japan, Okinawa, the Solomon Islands, and Germany. On the island, rigid safeguards were enforced. A special airtight building was constructed with filtered ventilation and airlock doors. In the event of a release, a siren sounded and all employees were supposed to enter the building and remain there until safe to exit.

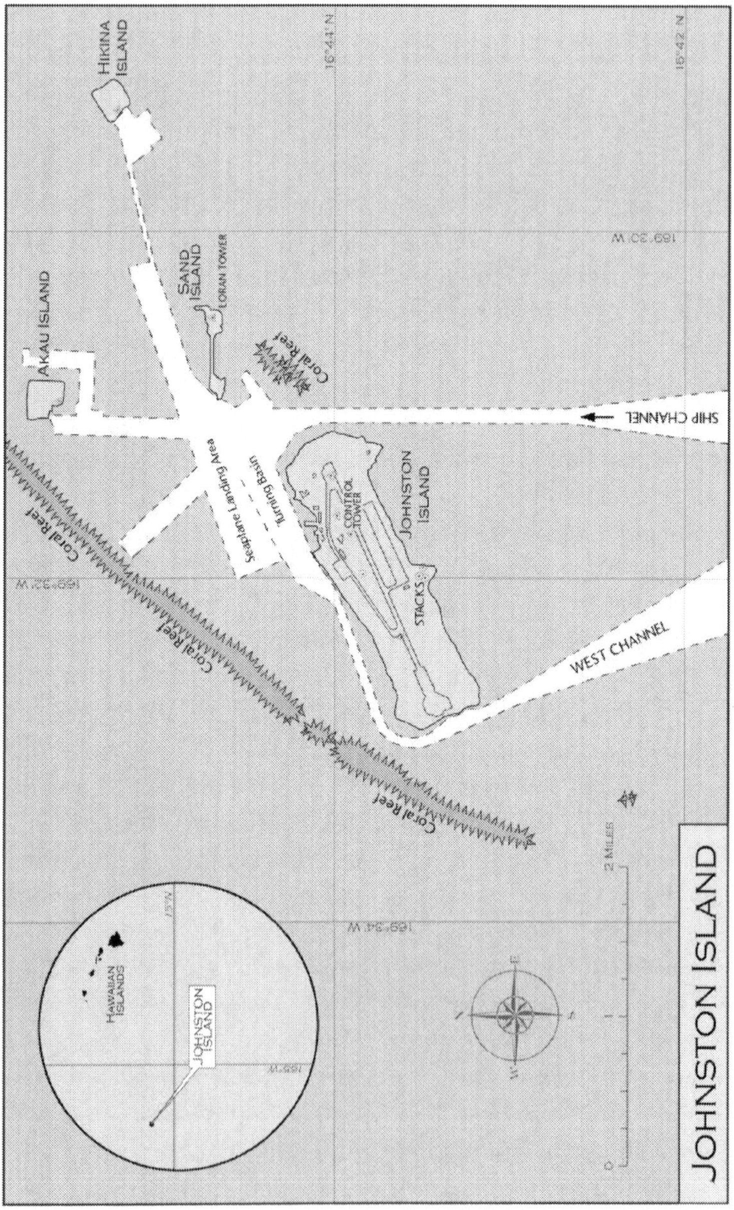
JOHNSTON ISLAND
HIKINA ISLAND
SAND ISLAND
LORAN TOWER
AKAU ISLAND
Coral Reef
Coral Reef
Coral Reef
Coral Reef
SHIP CHANNEL
Seaplane Landing Area
Turning Basin
JOHNSTON ISLAND
CONTROL TOWER
STACKS
WEST CHANNEL
16°44' N
16°42' N
169°30' W
169°32' W
169°34' W
0
1
2 MILES
HAWAIIAN ISLANDS
JOHNSTON ISLAND

Those who worked in the facility where the actual decommissioning of weapons took place received training in the use of nerve gas antidotes. They carried or had nearby access to hypodermic syringes with the antidote. In the event of a release within the facility, they had at most a few minutes to inject themselves or face an agonizing death.

Kevin's trip there in 1998 was to meet with the maintenance personnel to review the requirements for modification to the island's power plant. An additional emergency generator was needed. A loss of power could be critical. Without power, the ventilation systems shut down. There were special interlocks and safety systems that were triggered by loss of power. Emergency generators were tested monthly. In a recent test, a problem occurred when one of the emergency generators failed to start.

Kevin checked into the Prince Kuhio Hilton Hotel on Kuhio Street, took a quick shower, changed to slacks and a sport shirt, and left the hotel. He walked through the throngs of tourists in Waikiki to the Moana Surfrider Hotel, a favorite spot that he tried to visit whenever he came to Hawaii.

The Moana courtyard was crowded, but a table cleared as he approached and he grabbed it. He loved sitting outside under the huge Banyan tree, with the beach a few steps away. When the waitress came, he ordered a mai tai. The beach was thronged with people wading, surfing, or taking rides in a large catamaran that departed from the beach directly in front of the hotel. White pigeons fluttered in the courtyard, seeking crumbs on the pavement or flying to the tree to observe. Hawaiian music played in the background. As Kevin watched, a beach boy blew a note on a conch horn, signaling the return of the catamaran.

As he stared out at the crowded beach, his thoughts drifted to Juliana, wondering what she was doing, wishing she was here with him. He recalled several years ago when he and Juliana had spent three romantic days at the hotel.

They'd arrived on a late flight, picked up a rental car, and made it to the lei stands just as they were closing, and he bought her a pikake lei. Once checked in at the hotel, they enjoyed a quick drink in the courtyard bar, went to the room, took a fast shower together, and fell into bed.

Kevin's reverie was interrupted as a woman came in from the beach, carrying her sandals. She had short dark hair, a knee length skirt, a low-cut short sleeved white blouse, and a pearl necklace with an ivory pendant in the shape of a dolphin. She hesitated, looking around for an empty table, and caught Kevin glancing at her.

"Pardon me," she said, smiling at him. "What is that you're drinking?"

"A mai tai," he replied. "This place is famous for them. Whenever I'm in Honolulu I come here just for the mai tais."

"I guess I'll have to try one," she said, "if I can find a table somewhere."

"You're welcome to join me if you'd like." Kevin pulled out a chair and pointed to it. "I'm not staying long and you can have this table. If you have time, you'll want to have dinner here."

"I don't want to intrude," she said, "it looked like you were deep in thought."

"You're not intruding. I just arrived after a long flight and I guess I'm tired. Please feel free."

She sat down, and extended her hand. "I'm Sofia." Her hand was warm, her grip firm.

"Kevin. Pleased to meet you. Here comes the waitress. Do you want to try a mai tai?"

After the waitress took the order, Sofia turned to Kevin. "Thanks for sharing your table. This is a lovely spot. I can see why you like to come here. Are you vacationing?"

"No, on a business trip, unfortunately, just passing through. I'm leaving tomorrow. How about you?"

Sofia paused, looked away, and sighed. "I've

always wanted to come to Hawaii. For one reason or another, we were never able to find the time. After my husband died, I decided I would come anyway. Maybe that was a mistake. It's no fun being in such a beautiful place alone, nothing but memories to keep you company."

Kevin noticed that she spoke with a faint accent. "Where's your home?"

"I live in Florence. Most Italians go to Spain or the Mediterranean or Yugoslavia. But I always wanted to visit Hawaii."

"I'm sorry about your husband," Kevin said. "It must be hard."

Sofia's drink arrived. She picked up the glass and turned to Kevin, "Cheers."

"Enough about me. What kind of business are you in?"

Kevin hesitated a moment, then said "Construction. I work for a company that does engineering and construction, mostly public works. Nothing very exciting."

"But you get to travel, it would appear."

"Yes," he replied. "Probably too much. More than I'd like to do, in any case. After a while it gets old. One hotel after another, crummy hotel food, not enough exercise, not sleeping well. There have been times when I've woken up and for a moment couldn't remember where I was. Or, I'd return to the parking lot, trying to recall what color rental car I had. White? Or was that yesterday, in the last city I was in?"

She laughed. "You make it sound terrible. I think I'd enjoy the freedom, seeing new places, meeting interesting people."

"I guess I'm jaded. You're right. Travel does have its moments."

"See," she said. "Otherwise, I would not have known about mai tais!"

The waitress appeared at their table. "Another round?"

"Not for me," Kevin said. "I think I'm ready to crash. Bring the check if you would please."

"Let me pay," Sofia offered, "since you were kind enough to share your table."

"That's all right. My pleasure. I hope you enjoy your evening here."

The waitress returned with the check and Kevin paid the bill.

"I don't want to sit here alone," Sofia said. "I think I'll go back to my hotel also. I hope I can find it. I walked down the beach until I saw this place but didn't pay any attention to the streets."

"Where are you staying?"

"The Prince Kuhio."

Kevin looked at her, silent alarm bells going off in his head. "Small world. That's where I'm staying. I'll be happy to show you the way—it's not far."

On the way back to the hotel, Kevin pointed out the International Marketplace. "There's an interesting place to visit, if you want some souvenirs for your friends in Florence. You can take the bus everywhere here—it's very easy. You'll find better prices if you get away from Waikiki. The hotel can direct you to the Ala Moana shopping center, for example."

In the hotel lobby Sofia took his hand. "How about a quick nightcap in the bar here," she said. "It's my turn to buy."

Kevin withdrew his hand.

"Thanks, it's tempting, but I've got an early flight and have some reports to read. Very nice meeting you. Enjoy your stay here."

He left her as she turned to go into the hotel bar. At the elevator he punched the button for the sixth floor. When he got off, he quickly went down the hall to the stairs and walked down to the fifth floor where his room was located. Passing the elevator bank on the fifth floor, he saw that one was going up. It stopped at the sixth floor. He quickly went to his room and locked the door.

Kevin stripped to his shorts and got in bed. He lay there, wide awake, thinking of Sofia. The invitation was clear; she'd done everything short of propositioning him. But something was wrong. She wasn't just trying to pick him up. First, there was her accent, then her story. It was all bogus, had to be. Something was going on.

Sofia sat at a table in the far corner of the bar. After a few minutes a dark complexioned man entered. He stood by the bar for a few minutes, checking out the occupants. He saw Sofia and came over and sat down at her table. "Well," he said, "What happened?"

"He was tired and went to bed."

"That's it? You couldn't lean over and show him those tits of yours, put your hand on his leg, invite him for a nightcap?"

"I tried. He wasn't interested. He made it very clear."

"You're slipping, my dear. I'm surprised."

"Shut up and get me a drink."

The man got up, went to the bar, and returned with two scotch and waters.

"He's somewhere up on the sixth floor," he said. "I took the next elevator right after him, but when I got there he was already in his room. No one was in the hall, so I don't know what room. Otherwise, you could go up there and knock on his door, see if you could change his mind."

"I'm done with this guy. He's not going to tumble. I think we should get out of here, just in case he starts wondering. He's flying out in the morning."

"Okay. Give me back the camera."

The woman dug in her purse and pulled out a miniature camera.

"Did you take any pictures in the bar?"

"No. It was really crowded. I forgot."

The man shook his head in disgust. "C'mon, we're outta here."

§

Juliana was watching the late news on television when the phone rang.

"Hello," She answered.

"May I speak to Kevin?"

Juliana did not recognize the voice. "Who's calling?"

"This is Sofia. Maybe I have the wrong number." The caller hung up.

Juliana stared at the phone for a moment, then put the phone back on the receiver. She removed her food from the microwave and poured herself a glass of white wine. She went to her desk and got Kevin's itinerary. She called the Prince Kuhio Hotel.

A sleepy Kevin answered the phone.

"Hi love," Juliana said. "What are you doing?"

"Actually, I was sound asleep. Been a long day."

"I can imagine," Juliana said dryly. "Who is Sofia?"

"What?"

"Who is Sofia? She just called here for you."

"Juliana, this is bullshit. Something's going on."

"I can't imagine what," she replied, her sarcasm clear over the phone connection.

"Listen," he said. "I went to the Moana to have a quick drink before hitting the sack. One mai tai in our favorite bar. The place was packed. A woman walked in off the beach and asked what kind of drink I was having. I told her. She thanked me and looked around for a table but there weren't any, so I told her she could join me, because I was planning to leave shortly and she could have the table.

"She sat down and told me her name was Sofia, she was from Italy, her husband had recently died, and she'd made the trip to Hawaii because it was something they'd always wanted to do. All very proper so far."

"Yes, I can imagine," Juliana said.

"Julie, please, let me finish."

"Go ahead."

"I excused myself to walk back to the hotel and then she gave me a song and dance about not knowing how to get back to her hotel, and—you guessed it—she says she's staying at the Prince Kuhio. That's when I really got concerned. In the hotel lobby she invited me for a nightcap in the hotel bar. I said no thanks and goodbye and that was it."

"Why did you give her your home phone number?"

"Juliana, please believe me. I did not give her my home phone number. I didn't tell her anything except my first name. Something is seriously wrong here. Think about it—why would I give her my home phone if I had something to hide? Do you remember what happened the last time you got a strange phone call? You should leave the house right now. Go to one of your friends for the next couple of nights. In the morning, call the telephone company and change our phone number. Call me later and let me know where you are."

After Saleh's call, Robinson drove by the Hunter's house and saw that some lights were on. It was still early. He decided to return after midnight. When he came back, the house was dark. He went around to the rear. Using a slender piece of spring steel, he opened the rear door latch, which Juliana had forgotten to bolt. The house was still. He crept quietly from room to room, saving the master bedroom for the last. The bedroom door was closed. He opened it slowly, trying to avoid any sound. Once open a few inches, he looked in. The bed was made, the room empty. No one home. He left by the back door.

He returned the next day, and watched the house for a while. There was no sign of any occupant. That night he slipped in the back door once again and found everything undisturbed. After the third day, he concluded that no one was at home. He called Saleh to report what he had learned.

"She should be there," Saleh said. "Her husband is away and traveling alone."

"Maybe she's got a boyfriend."

"No, I don't think so. Go back there and keep an eye on the house for a couple more days. Grab her if she shows up."

"Yeah, right," Robinson said. "If the neighbors see me hanging around there anymore somebody's going to get suspicious. If I get busted, the cops will want to know why I'm there. What'll I say, 'My lawyer sent me?' Shit man, get real."

Saleh hung up the phone in frustration.

In the morning, Kevin took a cab to Hickam Air Force Base, where he boarded an Air Mobility Command flight to Johnston Atoll. On the flight out, Kevin couldn't get last night's encounter off his mind. Juliana was fine; she'd left the house and planned to spend the next several days at her girlfriend's house. Their home phone was disconnected, although it would take two days for a new number to become operational.

Kevin looked out the window. Nothing but blue ocean below, and a few scattered clouds. His mind kept turning over questions. What was with this 'Sofia' or whatever her real name was? He'd asked the desk; there was no one with a first name of Sofia checked into the hotel. That wasn't conclusive—she could've been registered under her husband's name, but it seemed to indicate she'd accompanied him back to the hotel, hoping to get invited to his room. But why? Not money, as he had little cash. Possibly to compromise him? Make him subject to future blackmail, or could it be something to do with the drones?

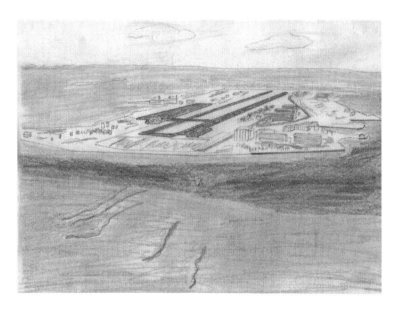

From the air, Johnston Island was an oblong-shaped atoll surrounded by a ring of white where waves broke on the distant encircling reef. Besides the main island, there were three additional small islands in the lagoon.

The plane made a smooth landing and taxied to a stop in front of a hangar. Kevin stepped out of the plane and was met by Brad Avery, the company's project manager on the island.

"Welcome to Johnston, Kevin," Brad said.

"I've got you fixed up in one of the guest cottages. I'll take you there so you can dump your stuff and then we'll have a little tour of the island. It won't take long. There's not a whole lot to see, but you'll want to visit our National Forest and then maybe take a swim."

"The National Forest?"

"Yes, trees are scarce on the island, so it's special to

those of us who are castaways here on the atoll. Six months staring at an empty ocean and gooney birds does strange things to some people's minds."

Brad drove up to Kevin's cottage. Hundreds of beautiful white birds perched on the roofs of nearby structures, or swooped gracefully through the sky overhead.

"Those birds are beautiful," Kevin said. "I thought gooney birds were albatrosses?"

"You're right," Brad replied. "Those are fairy terns. We get visited by a variety of seabirds, and "gooney" is a generic name for anything that flies."

Kevin dumped his bag in the room and returned to Brad's car. They drove to the base, visiting the shops, power plant, water plant, and other buildings. Brad pointed out a tall imposing structure with only a single door and no windows.

"That's where the nasty stuff is. You don't want to go in there. Actually, in spite of all the initial worries, we've had a good safety record with no major incidents. I've heard that DOD is considering closing this facility and moving the operation to Tooele Army Depot in Utah. It can be done just as safely there at one-tenth the cost, since everything we use has to come here by plane or ship. There's no corner hardware store here if you run out of something."

"How safe is this place? What I mean is, you've got all this nerve gas here. Suppose some bad guys decided they wanted to fly in here one dark night, steal a few canisters, take them somewhere, put them in a drone and spray the shit over New York or London?"

"I suppose anything is possible," Brad said, "if you're crazy enough to try. We have a contingent of Marines here to keep an eye on things and maintain order. Uncle Sam watches all of our Pacific possessions. No more Pearl Harbor surprises. Any unauthorized aircraft approaching this place would scramble fighter jets at

Hickam Air Force base on Oahu. And as for an unauthorized ship, unless it was a submarine, it wouldn't get a hundred miles from here before it was blown out of the water. I can't imagine anybody hijacking this stuff. Unless they were scientists, they'd probably kill themselves just trying to transport it. Why do you ask?"

"No special reason," Kevin said. "Just wondering. Iraq used chemical weapons in the conflict with Iran. You know the rumors. Israel has nuclear weapons, so now Iraq wants them. Israel says no dice and blows up Iraqi nuclear installations. Then the Iranians say they are going to develop 'peaceful atomic energy,' and the Israelis start shaking their heads, saying 'no way will they let that happen.' The Iranians probably have chemical weapons, but can you imagine what it would be like if the Ayatollahs had a nuclear bomb?"

"Yeah, the world is a screwed up place right now. We're done with the tour. How about a swim before dinner?"

"Great, I'd like that. I brought my goggles. Do I need anything else?"

"Nope. Get your suit and we'll go. There's a nice place out by the Commander's residence. She's off island now, so we can use her backyard as a launch spot."

Brad drove to a point on the island where the Commander had a small house that looked out over the Pacific.

"See that buoy out there," he said. "That marks the ship channel. From here it's about a half-mile swim. We'll pass over a reef where you'll see a nice assortment of reef fish, and if we're lucky, my favorite moray eel who hangs out there in his hole. Okay for you?"

"Sounds wonderful," Kevin said. "You lead the way."

Brad waded in, Kevin following. The water was warm, the sea calm. Inside the lagoon it was almost like swimming in a pool. As promised, the water was full of brightly colored reef fish, parrotfish, box fish, yellow tang, Moorish idols, blue crevalle and others. As they approached the ship channel, Brad stopped and got Kevin's attention.

"Mister moray is right down there below you, if you want to take a look," he said. "He's friendly as long as you don't get too close."

Kevin dove. About ten feet below the surface he saw a small cave in the coral. A large moray eel watched his descent. The eel's head and about six inches of his body protruded from the cave. It was the largest moray he'd ever seen. Kevin returned to the surface.

"I don't think you'd want to stick your hand in his hole," he said.

They swam to the buoy and then returned to shore, where they climbed out of the water and dried off.

"Let me show you around the Commander's place," Brad said. "She's got a great view of the ocean from her patio."

They walked behind the house. The patio was bordered by a sea wall that dropped directly into dark blue water. There was a gas-fired barbecue and some tables sitting in the patio.

"We've had some nice parties here. The Commander likes to barbecue. After dinner she entertains her guests by inviting the sharks to feed on the leftovers."

"There are sharks here?" Kevin asked.

"Let me show you." Brad walked over to the edge of the patio near the seawall and stomped on the concrete floor with his sandal three times. "Take a look," he said, pointing over the seawall.

Kevin watched. A moment or two passed and then two dark shapes emerged from the depths. They were black tip reef sharks, five or six feet long. They circled lazily for a few minutes and then disappeared once again in the depths.

"That's surprising," Kevin said. "You didn't tell me

about the sharks."

"Not to worry. They're spoiled. Unless you smell like barbecue they're not interested."

On the way back to the cottage Brad showed Kevin the island's recreational center. Employees could check out scuba gear, kayaks, or windsurfing equipment to use in the lagoon.

Kevin glanced at the lagoon. "Is there a way to get in here from the open ocean?"

"You could come in through the ship channel. That's how we get supplies. Why? Are you still worried about someone trying to steal nerve gas?"

"No, just curious. How safe is it in the lagoon?"

"What do you mean, safe? From weather, or from something else?"

"I guess I was thinking about sharks."

"We don't think it's dangerous. We caution people to be careful, use common sense. Several years ago we lost one windsurfer. Someone found his board floating on its side, the sail in the water. His body was never found, so shark attack was considered, but there was no evidence. He could've had a heart attack, or got caught in a wind gust where something hit his head. I doubt we'll ever know."

Over dinner Brad and Kevin talked about the emergency generator project. Kevin said that he would be working on the proposal as soon as he returned to Los Angeles.

"I think you have all the pertinent information," Brad said. "But let me know if you need any other drawings or information. I think it's pretty straightforward. Once we get the equipment, our guys can do the installation and startup testing—it shouldn't be a problem."

The flight back to Honolulu was scheduled to leave early the next morning, so Kevin had a drink in the bar with Brad and then walked back to his cottage. There was a warm breeze and the sky was full of stars. The island was quiet except for the distant hum of the motors that operated the main ventilation system.

Once in bed, he was tired but didn't fall asleep immediately. He kept thinking about the encounter in Honolulu. What could have been behind it? Brad was adamant that no one would be stupid enough to steal any of the chemical warfare agents they were processing. If they did, they wouldn't get far.

In the middle of the night he awoke. Something was banging outside his window. He looked out. The moon was up and the wind was blowing, causing a branch of the tree next to the cottage to rub on the window frame. He crawled back in bed, trying to remember the dream he was having when he heard the noise. In the dream, four windsurfers in black wetsuits were approaching the plant from the lagoon. Three were men and the fourth was the woman called Sophia. He pushed the thought of windsurfers, sharks, the giant moray eels from his mind and managed to get back to sleep.

At 0700 hours, he was at the airfield waiting to board a flight back to Oahu. After landing at Hickam, Kevin caught a shuttle over to the Honolulu International Airport and boarded an American Airlines flight for the mainland. Flying back to L.A. from Honolulu, Kevin wrote up a trip report on his laptop. When that was done, he started reading a novel. He read for a few pages and then set it aside. He couldn't get what had happened at the Moana out of his mind. It didn't seem possible that this was a random occurrence. He must've been targeted. Someone knew about his travel plans. They would have had to follow him from the airport, unless they knew about his hotel booking in advance. Either way, why him? It made no sense. The theft of the drone parts, his kidnapping, the threats to Juliana, a mysterious contact at Northrop Grumman, a wealthy Saudi, and now this woman in Honolulu—they all seemed to be part of something. But, try as he might, he could not see how the pieces of the puzzle fit together.

෨

Juliana met him at the gate at LAX. He was glad to see her waiting for him. He gave her a quick kiss and looked around. There was a crush of people, mostly vacationers returning from Honolulu, dressed casually, many wearing leis. He saw no familiar faces.

"Let's get out of here," he said, taking her arm as they turned towards the terminal exit. "Were there many people waiting for this flight with you?"

"I didn't notice," Juliana replied. "Traffic was heavy so I was running a little late. I worried that your plane had already landed."

"Did you see anyone that looked vaguely familiar, or out of place?"

"No. What's this all about?"

"I'm still bothered about what happened in Honolulu. Somebody had to know about my travel plans. If so, they probably knew about this flight. By the way, where have you been staying?"

"I went to my friend Carol Pangburn's house in Inglewood. But she was expecting company, so after four days I went home. I've been careful, but everything's been quiet at the house. No more calls from your friend Sofia."

"Hey, Julie, don't joke about this. I told you I'd never seen this woman before and I have no idea why she approached me. It worries me. I don't think it was random. The fact that she knew our home phone really bothers me."

"You're sure you didn't tell her, or maybe give her your business card?"

"I didn't give her my business card. Anyway it doesn't have our home phone on it."

"Maybe she called the office?"

"The office would not give out my home phone—of that I'm sure. But I'll check with Holly in any case."

"So, what are you thinking?"

"I'm concerned that someone is still interested in me. Make that *us*. Why, I don't know."

"You're being paranoid; it's not like you."

"Maybe so. But I hate the thought that something's going to happen whenever I go on a trip and leave you alone. You know, Motorola has just come out with a new mobile phone. I'm going to get you one. I want you to keep it with you at all times. Don't give the number to anyone. Keep it for emergencies or if you need to reach me urgently."

"Now I feel like I'm being paranoid."

"Why?"

"When I came home from Carol's I had a strange feeling, like maybe someone had been in our house."

"Was anything missing?"

"Not that I could tell. It was just a feeling. For one thing, our bedroom door was open when I returned, but I thought I'd closed it when I left the house. It's probably nothing, just my imagination."

Saleh paced nervously in his home office in Beverly Hills, waiting for a phone call. For the fifth or sixth time he looked at his watch. There was three hours time difference between California and Hawaii, but even so the call was two hours late. He got angrier by the minute as he waited. He had a lot of things to take care of, and not much time to get them done. There were several bank visits to be made, other pressing matters to be taken care of. He had a sense of walls closing in on him, panic starting to build.

The phone rang.

"Yes?" He said.

"It's Omar."

"I know who it is. What happened?"

"She followed the guy to a bar and had a drink with him."

"Then what?"

"She came back to the hotel with him, but he wasn't interested."

"That's it? She couldn't get into his room?"

"No she got cold feet. She thought maybe he was on to her."

"Did she get a picture or anything?"

"No. She had the camera, but she said she forgot."

"Idiots! You couldn't do this simple job? What about in the morning?"

"He left early. He didn't go to the International airport. It turned out he had a military flight."

"So, you screwed up twice," Saleh said. "I can't believe it."

"Wait, there was one other thing," Omar said.

"What was that?"

"Sofia called the home number, spoke with his wife. He'll have some explaining to do when he gets home."

"Oh, great, brilliant. That's a big help. Now he's going to wonder what's going on. He's not stupid, you know. Listen, I've got to go," Saleh said, as he slammed the phone down.

Time was short. Saleh was deeply frustrated. He realized that the stupid woman calling from Honolulu probably spooked Juliana, causing her to leave home. He decided he had a few more days to make arrangements. The best he could do now was to tell Wu he'd located a potential informant, and leave it up to Wu to decide how to proceed. No telling what might happen when Kevin returned. But it was no longer safe to stay in California.

MISSING PERSON

Saleh was in the den of his Beverly Hills home, burning documents in the fireplace. When it burned down he pulled more papers from a box and threw them in. As the fire flared up, he returned to a nearby chair and took another sip of tea. He considered his options. He hated the prospect of another meeting with the Iranians. If he gave them the materials he had stashed in a Beverly Hills bank safe deposit box, he would lose all leverage he had to protect himself. Once they had his materials, he doubted they'd pay him the balance of the money they owed him. More likely they'd kill him.

Then there was Mr. Wu. He was friendly and eager, not demanding and strident like the Iranians. As the fire died down on the last of his papers, he decided to call Wu.

"I have some information for you," he said. "Some technical details on guidance systems and flight operating performance parameters. The materials are extensive but I'm prepared to give you some samples to evaluate, if you still agree to the terms we discussed.

"Very interesting," Wu said. "If the material is what you say it is, there will be no problem. But I am not the person to make that decision."

"I'm going away for a while. Can you set up a meeting for me in Europe?"

"I think the person you need to convince is in Pakistan. Can you go to Karachi?"

"Yes, I can. But if your agent in Karachi approves, does he have the authority to complete the transaction? I will not take the materials with me. They are in a secure location. When my agent knows payment has been received and I have provided certain confirmations, you will be contacted with instructions for collecting the materials."

"I see," Mr. Wu said. "You're being cautious."

"I've something else for you to demonstrate my good faith. There is a woman at R&D Corporation who is deeply involved in the UUV research that interests you. Due to travel and other commitments I don't have time to follow up with her. I suggest you find an excuse to meet her, establish a professional relationship, and see where that leads. Her name is Juliana Hunter and she lives in West Los Angeles."

"Also very interesting," Wu repeated. "Thank you. I look forward to meeting Mrs. Hunter. Can I have twenty-four hours to make arrangements for your meeting in Karachi?"

"Yes, of course. But call me as soon as possible, because I have to arrange my other appointments."

Saleh was pleased with himself. The Chinese were accommodating and much easier to deal with than the Iranians. But he was not misled by Mr. Wu's soft-spoken and polite demeanor. It would be interesting to see how they handled Mrs. Hunter.

He went into his bedroom to sort out clothes he was taking with him on his trip. The rest he'd toss or put into storage. His phone rang. Without answering he looked at the caller's number and knew it was Leila calling from Las Vegas. He turned the phone off and continued with his packing.

Back in his office after returning from Johnston Atoll, Kevin was busy catching up on work and filing trip reports. There was pressure to get a proposal ready for the work that needed to be done to replace the emergency generator on the island. It was several days before he'd had a chance to call Kidd to set up a meeting.

"Welcome back," Kidd said, when Kevin finally made contact. "How was your trip to the islands?"

"It was interesting. But something happened that we need to discuss."

"I can't meet today. How about tomorrow afternoon?"

"Okay. Where and what time?"

"Let's say 5 p.m. at MacArthur Park by the boat rental stand."

"Fine. See you then."

Kevin started to ask if Kidd had any new information, but the line was dead.

It had been years since Kevin had visited MacArthur Park. He recalled taking Juliana there one weekend before they were married. They rented one of the paddleboats and paddled around the lake with a bottle of wine and some cheese and crackers.

In the 1990s the park was home to prostitutes and drug traders. The gangs would fight each other and sold "protection" to the street vendors who tried to make a living in the vicinity of the park. The "Picture Man," a street vendor who worked the park for decades with his Polaroid camera, snapping pictures of park visitors, told how the gangs charged him $20 a week for "rent."

The following afternoon Kevin decided to leave his car at the office and walk to the park. It straddled Wilshire Boulevard, about a dozen blocks east of Kevin's office. He kept an old denim jacket in his office for visits to construction sites. He removed his tie, put on the denim jacket and a hard hat, and walked east on Wilshire Boulevard. This simple change of dress guaranteed his anonymity and was better protection than a bulletproof vest. The whores would ignore him and any gang members automatically avoided anyone who appeared to be associated with the city bureaucracy.

Entering the park, he saw some family groups sitting on the lawn, young children kicking a ball around. In the distance a group of young Hispanics stood clustered under some trees, keeping an eye on anyone entering the park. As he made his way towards the boathouse, Kevin spotted the Picture Man posing a couple in a romantic shot with the lake in the background.

Approaching the boathouse, Kevin looked around but there was no sign of Kidd. As he walked closer, he passed a homeless man slouched on a bench, his head down. He had on a dirty Dodgers baseball hat, a tattered overcoat, and worn tennis shoes tied with string. Kevin glanced at him but kept walking. As he passed the bum, the man spoke to him in a low voice.

"You have any spare change, Sonny?" The bum raised his head and Kevin realized it was Kidd.

"Let's take a walk," Kidd said. "It would look funny for you to sit here and talk to me on this bench. We can go hang out by the tamale stand across the street. You can buy me a tamale if you want."

"That's quite a get up," Kevin said. "Did you wear it just for me?"

"No—it was just a practice run. I figure if it worked for you, it would be okay for a little assignment I've got coming up. I don't have a lot of time. What's on your mind?"

Kevin told Kidd about what happened in Honolulu. "You know, I'm by nature a friendly guy. So at first I didn't think anything about this woman wandering into the Moana courtyard. I know how it is when you're traveling alone. But somewhere during our conversation, things didn't seem right. It's hard to explain; maybe you'd call it instinct or sixth sense. Then, when by remarkable coincidence, this woman claimed to be staying in my hotel, alarm bells started ringing. When I found out she'd called Juliana I really got concerned. That meant she had to have all my travel itinerary, home phone, and God knows what other personal information. I immediately suspected a link to the kidnappers. I told Juliana to get out of the house and go stay with a friend."

They came to the corner of Alvarado and Wilshire

Boulevard, waiting to cross the street. Kevin paused, watching Kidd's face for reaction. Kidd waited until they started across.

"Two things occur to me," he said. First, someone wanted to get you in a compromising situation, get some pictures of you banging this Sofia. They could hold that over your head, try to force you to help them. The second possibility? They were interested in what you know about Johnston Atoll."

"But why? There's no connection with drones. Johnston isn't involved in flight testing."

"I know that," Kidd replied. "But that stuff they are processing there. It's really nasty, isn't it? Let's suppose someone figured out how to snatch a couple of canisters, load one on a drone, and fly it into Wall Street or the White House, for example. That would attract some attention, wouldn't it? These guys, the fanatics that want to take over the world, they need money. If they pull off something big that makes headlines around the globe, all the crazies will get excited and send them money."

"It's an interesting thought," Kevin said. "But Johnston is an island in the middle of the Pacific, eight hundred miles from anywhere. I asked the guys there about security. It's hard to imagine someone could sneak in and grab something, even less likely they could get away with it."

"So we are back to square one," Kidd said. "The compromise angle seems to be most likely. You were smart to keep your pants zipped."

"You don't know my wife," Kevin said. "I'm not perfect, but I love her and she means the world to me."

"Could we get a couple of those tamales?" Kidd said. "I hear they're really good and I didn't have lunch today."

"Okay. Go find a table and I'll get a couple. You want something to drink?"

"Just water."

Kevin bought a chicken and cheese and a green corn tamale and carried them back to the table where Kidd sat.

"Take your pick. This place is amazing. They have a dozen different types of tamales, some even with fruit."

"I'll take the green corn," Kidd said. "Remember this place. Come by here after work sometime and pick up a bag of tamales to take home for dinner. Your wife would probably like that."

"I'm sure she would. So tell me, have you learned anything new?"

"Yes and no," Kidd replied. "Most amazing, our Saudi friend has vanished, seemingly just disappeared off the face of the earth. It turns out that the big fancy house in Beverly Hills is now for lease, and is being handled by a property management firm. Likewise, the law office is closed, no forwarding address. The bank account is still open, but has been drained of most of its funds. There was a series of cash withdrawals, and some transfers to a bank in the Cayman Islands."

Kidd paused, thinking for a moment or two. "You know, people don't just 'disappear.' No, that's not exactly correct," he said. "Things disappear—boats and aircraft, particularly. In any given year, small boats and an occasional large one will simply disappear, usually swallowed up by the ocean. For a large vessel to disappear without a radio message or wreckage left behind, the usual explanation is a rogue wave. A vessel that had the misfortune to be in the locale where a freak wave suddenly rose up eighty or one-hundred feet before crashing down on its deck could be broken in two and sent to the bottom in minutes.

"But people, that's a different story. People almost always are found, if they lived in a civilized part of the world. In the Sudan, or parts of Africa. it's not so. You could go missing there and never be found."

Kidd took another bite. "These are really good,

aren't they? How's yours?"

"About Saleh. His disappearance is unusual. According to my sources, he was seen one day, April 29 in fact. Several people saw him on the 29th; the waiter, where he had dinner in the hotel restaurant; the doorman, who Saleh asked where the nearest pharmacy was located; and a clerk in the Rite Aid drugstore three blocks from the Beverly Wilshire hotel. He left the hotel at around 8 p.m., and the next day, gone without a trace.

"These days it is hard to disappear with all the electronic leashes that are attached to people. His clothes and all his belongings, so far as is known, were there in his room, waiting for his return. His rental car sat in the hotel parking garage until finally reclaimed by the rental company. There have been no charges to his credit cards. He simply vanished."

"Do you think you'll be able to find him?"

"I don't know. All I can say is that we'll keep looking.

"On another front, you'll be happy to know that we are getting some help. After you and I talked about Las Vegas and its proximity to Creech Air Force Base, I remembered an old friend of mine who works in Quantico, Virginia, at the headquarters of the U.S. Air Force Office of Special Investigations, OSI. It turns out that any threats to our drone technology are taken very seriously by OSI. They have offices at airbases all over the world including Jordan, Iraq, Saudi Arabia, Yemen and other Mideast locations. They have a group at Creech Air Force Base, called 'Detachment 202.' They said they will follow up on our lead in Las Vegas. As far as I know that bird hasn't flown her nest."

"So you think Saleh has gone back to Saudi Arabia?"

"Somewhere in the Middle East, but probably not Saudi Arabia. It is eighty-five to ninety percent Sunni Muslims and ten to fifteen percent Shia Muslims; the Shias are discriminated against and are second-class citizens. Iran, on the other hand is the opposite: ninety percent Shia and about nine percent Sunni. When you understand this, a lot becomes clear. The Saudi Shias don't like the way the Kingdom cozies up to the decadent West. They do like how Iran's Mullahs came to power, got rid of the west-leaning Shah, and have created a theocracy that pays strict observance to religious laws.

"So it makes sense that Saleh would link up with Iran. He may be some sort of middle man, funneling money from Saudi to those in Iran who want to spread the faith."

"What about Iraq?"

"Iraq is about two-thirds Shia and one third Sunni, so that is a possibility. Historically, the Sunni minority controlled the country. One of the reasons Iraq invaded Iran was the fear that the Mullahs would try to spread their revolution to Iraq and encourage the Iraqi Shias to revolt. I'm sure that Saddam Hussein also wanted to displace Iran as a Middle East power. Instead, look what happened. Iraq lost the war with Iran, and then got the shit kicked out of them when they invaded Kuwait.

"By the way, Iran has a long history with drones. As early as 1981 they built prototypes of a small drone designed to provide surveillance of Iraqi Army positions. The first one was called the *Mohajer-1*. It could stay aloft for an hour or so and had a range of about fifty km. In the 1990s, some of these were flown in Afghanistan to monitor the fighting there.

"Iran claims to be making more advanced versions, and this is of concern to us. We know that they can make the flight platform. The more difficult part is all the command, control and surveillance electronics. That is where the U.S. is clearly way ahead, and presumably that is the technology they'd like to acquire."

"So what's next?"

"Hell if I know. I think we just have to be patient and see what turns up. Maybe the Detachment 202 guys will come up with something in Las Vegas. So far we haven't been able to identify Saleh's Northrop connection, and it would be nice if the woman would lead us to him. The other angle is Saleh himself. We'll be monitoring his credit card transactions. So far he's shown himself to be very careful, though we might get lucky if he makes a mistake. Then we'll at least know what part of the world he's in. Finally, we have some assets in the Middle East. I wish I could say that we had some in Iran. We used to, but we were lucky to get them out in one piece when those radical students took over our embassy and held most of the staff hostage.

"I've got to go. It's been good talking to you, and I wish I had more positive results to report. We'll just have to be patient and see what develops. Meanwhile you should get home to your wife and stay out of trouble. If any future business trips come up, let me know. If you're worried about anything, contact me."

"Okay, I guess I'll see you when I see you."

As Kidd walked away, he turned and waved at Kevin. "Thanks for the tamale."

Kevin returned to his office. He answered a few phone calls and finished some correspondence he'd been working on, but found it hard to concentrate.

Saleh's disappearance really bothered him. All the time he'd spent—locating Saleh, discovering a connection to Northrop Grumman—it was wasted effort. The U.S. authorities were too slow to act, and the wily Saudi slipped away. It was maddening. In his heart, he knew Saleh was responsible for Beske's death. With Saleh gone, it also left unanswered just how broad the conspiracy was to steal U.S. secrets. Did it end with his fleeing the country, or was he just part of something bigger? Finally, what if Kidd was wrong about Saleh fleeing to the Middle East? Suppose he was still in the U.S. and was still pissed off that Kevin had ruined his plans to steal American secrets? Worse yet, what if he'd somehow found out about Kevin's surveillance?

Something tipped him off, otherwise why would he have abandoned the elaborate front he'd created in Beverly Hills? If he connected Kevin to that, there would be ample cause for revenge. The uncertainty left Kevin with an uneasy feeling.

The last hope had to be the woman in Las Vegas. Kidd said he had an Air Force contact in Las Vegas. It had better be a good one, Kevin thought.

LAS VEGAS

The airman went to his quarters on base, changed into civilian clothes, and left the base after dark. Past the gate, he kept checking his rearview mirror, but no cars followed him onto Highway 95. Reassured, he accelerated the Corvette, maintaining a steady seventy mph for Las Vegas. He was thinking about what lay ahead. Just thinking about her got him excited.

He failed to notice the black sedan sitting back from the highway on a dirt road. As he passed, the waiting car started up and slowly pulled forward onto the highway. Directly ahead there was a bend in the road. The airman's car made the turn and passed out of sight. The black sedan turned on its headlights and slowly moved up to a position far enough behind the Corvette to not be obvious, but close enough to maintain visual contact.

There were two OSI agents inside the car. They had been alerted to the airman's departure by the security officer at the gate. This is not the first time the white Corvette had made a run into Las Vegas on a Friday night.

"What do you think, Mike?" the agent riding shotgun asked the driver. "Will he go to Ali Baba or straight to the Green Valley Ranch?"

Mike looked at his watch. "It's still early. I think he'll go to Ali Baba, get a couple of drinks and something to eat. She has to finish her routine, then they'll hightail it over to the ranch."

"Nice car, a room in a fancy resort hotel, I wonder how he does it on airman's pay?"

"You think he's getting some help, some financial aid, sort of like a scholarship?" Mike said sarcastically.

"Unfortunately I think he's getting paid for services rendered, and I don't mean banging the dancer. Somehow he is bringing stuff out of the base, we don't know what—

or how—yet."

At the restaurant, the airman turned into a nearby shopping center and parked. The black sedan continued ahead on Eastern Avenue, then circled back to park where the two agents could watch the Corvette. One left the car, returning shortly with two cups of coffee. They settled down to watch.

Inside the Ali Baba, the airman found a table where he could view the dancers and ordered a beer and a kebab combo. When the food arrived, he ordered a second beer and waited for Leila to make her appearance. When she came on stage and started dancing, she spotted him. He'd stopped eating, just staring at her, mesmerized. She smiled provocatively at him, gave a few pelvic thrusts in his direction and then turned to face the rest of the audience to perform her routine.

As she danced, the airman picked at his food. He no longer felt like eating. It bothered him to see her performing like this in front of a crowd. He wanted the performance to be over so she could change and they would leave the restaurant and he would have her all to himself. As he watched, a man, obviously drunk, got up from his table, walked up to the stage and stuffed a twenty dollar bill in the waistband of Leila's costume. He lingered a moment, his hand moving down her leg. The airman stiffened, thinking of jumping from his chair, but Leila backed away and the drunk returned to his table. The airman relaxed. He hated this part, but had resigned himself to the fact that it was part of her job. He'd asked her about it one evening, but she had brushed off his concern, saying that while dancing, she thought only of her art and ignored the interruptions.

Outside in the parking lot, the two agents waited in their vehicle, a special camera ready for the moment when the airman would emerge from the restaurant. After several hours they saw the woman come out of a backdoor followed by the airman. They walked to his car. They came to the passenger side and he opened the door for her, then went around to the driver's side, got in, and drove out of the parking lot.

Mike started the car and drove slowly to the parking lot exit. "How are the pictures?" he asked.

"They're fine. You can see both faces clearly when he opened the car door for her."

"Okay. It looks like they're headed towards Green Valley Ranch. I'm guessing that he'll go to self-parking, and avoid the valet. Once I see him turn into the resort, I'm going straight to the entrance, let you off. Run inside and find a spot where you can get a picture of the two of them at the registration desk."

Mike dropped the other agent at the entrance to the hotel and circled back into the parking lot. In the distance he could see the airman and the dancer walking up to the hotel. He parked the car and waited. About fifteen minutes later, the other agent emerged from the hotel. Mike started the car and drove around to pick him up.

"Well, how did it go?"

"It could have been better," he said. "The airman came up to the desk by himself and picked up the keys. She stood off to one side not far from the elevator. I got a picture of him at the desk and then a picture of both of them as they entered the elevator. I don't think anybody saw anything, certainly not him. At this point I'm sure that all he was thinking of was getting her to the room so he could start undressing her."

"Yeah, you're probably right," Mike said. "I'd love to give him about a half an hour and then get a passkey and go into the room. I bet she'd be really working his skinny ass over. You know, he's kind of a weird guy. Maybe he likes to be tied up."

"Before this is over, he's going to be tied up, but not the way you're thinking. I wonder how he'll get along in a federal prison?"

"Are we going to hang around?"

"No, I don't think so. I want to go home, get some rest. My boys are in a soccer tournament tomorrow and it's going to be a long day. I don't think it makes any difference whether he stays in a hotel for a couple of hours or spends all night there. The point is we have proof that he picked up the babe and checked into the hotel with her. When he sees those pictures, I think he'll be ready to tell us anything we want to know."

❧

In the room Leila placed her purse on a nightstand by the bed and then closed the drapes while the airman went to the minibar.

"You want something to drink?" he said, pulling a small bottle of bourbon from the selection of miniatures in the refrigerator.

Leila went to the bathroom and returned after a few moments to the bedroom and turned off the overhead light. "No thanks," she said, "I'm fine, except my feet hurt."

She kicked off her shoes and turned to face the airman. Slowly and deliberately she removed her blouse and skirt until she stood in front of him in her bra and thong panties.

"Come to mama," she said, as she stood close to the airman and began unbuttoning his shirt. He drained the small bottle and tossed the empty on the bed. As she removed his shirt, he pushed her bra up, cupping her breasts in his hands. He felt all restraint slipping away. He smelled the faint odor of perspiration from her dancing, not quite masked by the perfume she'd put on. It made him want her all the more.

"Easy cowboy," she said, as she sat on the edge of the bed and began undoing his belt. "We're not in any hurry, we've got all night." The airman stepped out of his pants. Leila stood, hung his pants over a chair, and removed her bra. She stepped away from the airman and his eagerness, retrieved her purse, and pulled an envelope from it. She returned and stuffed the envelope into one of his pants pockets.

"Now that you got me all excited," she said, "I want to give you this before I forget about it. You've done such a good job that there's one more small request coming from my friend. I hope you'll take care of it."

She sat back down on the bed facing him, putting her arms around his waist. "Come here, honey." She knew then that he'd do anything she asked.

℘

Holly stuck her head in to Kevin's office. "That guy's on the phone for you."

"What guy might that be?"

"You know, the guy with the gravelly voice that always wants you to give him a call but never leaves a number."

"Oh yeah. He's an old college friend, always trying to get me to go somewhere."

"Yeah, right." Holly said. "I'll put him through." She closed his office door as she left.

"This is Kevin. How are you, Mr. Kidd."

"I'm okay. Do you guys have an office in Las Vegas?"

"Yes, we do. The group there specializes in leisure and entertainment projects."

"Can you get away for a day or so to investigate a leisure and entertainment project opportunity?"

"I'm sure I could do that sometime next week, would that work?"

"Great. How about Tuesday or Wednesday?"

"Wednesday would be best," Kevin said, after checking his calendar.

"Good. Get a flight and call me back with your flight number and arrival time. I'll be at the gate in

McCarran Airport and pick you up. Probably best if you spend the night and then get a flight back early in the morning."

"Are you going to give me a hint as to what this is all about?"

"The boys in detachment 202 have been checking out some leisure and entertainment projects. You'll find it interesting."

At dinner that evening Juliana told Kevin that R&D was sending her to a conference on climate change.

"When?"

"Next week for three days in Sacramento. I'll be part of a panel discussion on the models we're using to predict rising sea levels. Would you like to come along?"

"I'd like to, but I've got to go to Las Vegas for some meetings."

"How long will you be gone?"

"I'm flying there on Wednesday, spending the night, back in the office Thursday afternoon—a fast trip."

"Naturally you'll stay away from the roulette table and dancing girls."

"Of course."

When Kevin walked off the plane in Las Vegas he saw Kidd playing a slot machine not far from the gate. As he walked up, a bell started ringing and quarters spilled out of the machine.

"This must be your lucky day," he said to Kidd. "I guess we know who's buying lunch."

"Good to see you Kevin. Thanks for coming. Yeah, I'll buy lunch and dinner also. Let's grab a quick bite here. When we're done we're going on a short ride to visit my Air Force buddies."

After lunch they went out to the parking lot where Kidd had a rental car waiting. They drove from the airport to Las Vegas and then headed northwest on Highway 95.

"We're going up to Indian Springs, Nevada, home of Creech Air Force Base. It's about fifty miles, take us an hour or so to get there. We'll meet with OSI representatives who are going to fill us in on the results of some surveillance they've done on a certain unnamed airman. They suspect that he is somehow removing information concerning drone navigation and control and delivering it to that belly dancer we think is connected to our Saudi friend.

As they approached the Air Force Base, Kevin saw protesters outside at the edge of the highway. One prominent sign read DRONE ATTACKS KILL PEOPLE AND PEACE.

Kidd shook his head in disgust as they passed the crowd. "Don't those idiots have anything else to do besides stand out here in the sun and wave signs?" he said. "Obviously they haven't had any friends or relatives killed by a suicide bomber. They haven't seen what happens when somebody wearing an explosive belt walks into a crowded marketplace and kills a bunch of innocent civilians, mostly women and children."

They passed the protesters and turned onto the base. Up ahead was a tile roofed sentry post where Kidd checked in and got directions to the office where the meeting would take place. As they drove away from the sentry post, Kevin could see the tree-lined street had a series of fighter planes along one side, each mounted on a pillar as if it were taking off.

Kevin and Kidd were escorted into a conference room where Kidd was greeted by an Air Force officer. "Kevin, I'd like you to meet Lieutenant Mike Hardy. Mike, for your information, Kevin is a civilian who accidentally got involved in this matter. By his good judgment, the theft of some very important hardware was avoided. Somehow his identity was discovered by the bad guys and both he and his wife were kidnapped in separate incidents and are fortunate to still be with us. I think that is enough explanation of Kevin's motivation. However, there is an added fact that he is involved in a number of DOD construction projects, several overseas in sensitive areas, which gives him an opportunity to travel inconspicuously. He also has a top-secret DOD security clearance. Nonetheless, for the record we will not discuss any classified information during this meeting."

"Kevin, nice to meet you. Sorry to hear about the unpleasantness experienced by you and your wife. But from what Charlie has told me, your help has been very useful. I realize that you've probably been over this a dozen times, but if you wouldn't mind, I'd like you to go back to that day when you and your wife were on your boat at Santa Barbara Island. Tell me what you recall."

After Kevin finished his narrative, Kidd injected more. "Unfortunately that wasn't the end of the story. When Kevin managed to get away from the kidnappers, any sane person would've dropped the whole matter and laid low. In fact, I told him to do that. But he undertook a private surveillance effort that turned up the connection between your dancer in Las Vegas, a Saudi middle man who appears to be the paymaster, and possibly someone connected with Northrop Grumman. All this ties into drones, causing us to ask ourselves who might want to know more about U.S. drones? While one answer is probably, 'everybody,' there are a few candidates who stand out—Iranians, Pakistanis, Chinese, and al Qaeda and its terrorist offshoots. The bottom line is that we're pretty sure something's going on. We haven't been able to pin down the Northrop Grumman connection, and meanwhile the Saudi has closed up operations and decamped for parts unknown. But his girlfriend is still around and we're hopeful that she might be the connection that would lead us to him and possibly the Northrop guy. As you can see, we've got a lot of loose ends and no view of the big picture yet."

"Thanks to your tip we think we've identified another player in this drama," Mike said. "There was an incident that brought a young enlisted airman to our attention not long ago. He was seen off base talking to some of the protesters. One day he showed up with a brand-new white Corvette—a little above his pay grade. He's not a pilot, so he doesn't fly the birds. He's a clerk and an IT guy so he has access around the control room and equipment where the birds are flown. Some of the pilots have said that he asks a lot of questions. That in itself is not unusual because everyone is curious about the new technology and how a pilot sitting here in Nevada can fly an aircraft that is taking off and landing halfway around the world. We started paying a little attention to the guy and we found out he's pretty much of a loner, except that on Friday nights he likes to jump in his Corvette and go to Vegas. Here again that's not too unusual, although most of our folks don't have a lot to do with Las Vegas. But when Charlie told me that you might be interested in an exotic dancer here in Vegas, we did a little scouting and found that the airman had taken a liking to a certain belly dancer. This seemed more than coincidental. We did some of our own surveillance and found that once a month or so he goes into town and spends the night with her in a hotel.

"When you're concerned about people in positions involving classified information, any hint that they might be subject to bribery or blackmail becomes a big issue. Let's assume that he's getting paid off, either with money or the dancer's favors. If he is screwing her and he changes his mind, they've probably got compromising photographs that they'll use to keep him in line. But we're still left with the difficulty that we don't know what he's after, and if he's got anything, how does he get it off base?"

On the drive back, Kidd and Kevin discussed what they'd heard. It was gratifying to think that the Air Force had acted on their suspicions, but discouraging that not much was known.

"Why don't they just arrest that guy," Kevin said. "Put him in the slammer, tear apart his quarters and strip down that Corvette. They're bound to find something."

"They have to take it slowly," Kidd said. "Remember, the airman is just a pawn. If they move too quickly on him, whoever's directing the operation is likely to run. They don't catch him, there's nothing stopping him from laying low for a few months, recruiting another sympathetic insider, and getting back in business. These guys are pros, and they are relentless. You can feel sorry for the poor airman. It's just a matter time before the hammer falls."

Back in Las Vegas, Kidd turned the car into a casino entrance.

"What the hell is this?" Kevin asked.

"Why Kevin, I thought you were familiar with Las Vegas. This is the Luxor Hotel. Given all your experiences in Egypt, I thought you might like to stay in a pyramid. Here's the plan: We'll check in and get our rooms. I've set it up so you get the government rate. You can go to your room, take a rest, call your office, do your homework, or just take a nap. Meet me down in the lobby at 7 p.m. and we'll go to dinner. I hope you like Middle Eastern or Lebanese food. I'm pretty sure nobody there is going to recognize you and I sure as hell don't think anybody will recognize me, but we won't sit too close to the stage. At 9 o'clock our belly dancer comes on stage. It's a long shot, but I want to see if you recognize her.

At the Sacramento conference afternoon break Juliana was approached by a middle-aged oriental man.

"Mrs. Hunter, let me introduce myself. My name is Wu. I thoroughly enjoyed your comments on the modeling of deep ocean currents and upwelling." He handed her his business card.

"As you can see I'm involved in a software development company in Santa Monica. Could you spare five minutes for a few additional questions?"

Juliana read his card and hesitated a moment, looking at her watch before answering. "I'm not sure I could be much help."

Wu pointed to an empty table nearby. "Would you like tea or coffee?"

"No thank you, I'm fine."

They sat down.

"So I gather the purpose of your research is to try to improve these very important climate change models."

"Yes. We're trying to validate the predictive ability of the models. Unfortunately there are many people in the U.S. who don't believe that climate change is real or that it is influenced by human activities."

"Such as all the coal China is now burning?"

"Not only China, but the U.S. and India. But coal is only one of the sources of CO_2 we're concerned about and trying to model."

"So from your perspective, it's not just the ocean temperature increase that is important, but also changes to ocean currents that could result from thermal gradients in the sea."

"That's part of it. The phenomena are complicated and we're just beginning to learn about the interactions that occur." She looked at her watch. "You must excuse me, but I should be getting back to the meeting."

"I apologize for taking your time, Mrs. Hunter. I find your comments intriguing. Might I give you a call one day to come visit our office? We are a small company but we have some very bright people working on similar problems. You might find a visit interesting."

"Here's my card," Juliana said. "Feel free to give me a call. I'll see if we can find a time that works."

With that, Juliana returned to the meeting room. Mr. Wu remained seated at the table, staring at her card.

❧

It was midweek and the Ali Baba restaurant was not crowded. As they walked in Kidd pointed out the hookah lounge off to one side. "Hey look at that," he said. "You could go in there and smoke a pipe."

Kidd requested a table near the rear but with a good view of the stage. When the waiter came, Kidd told Kevin, "You're off duty, I'm driving. Go ahead and have a drink. Besides this is on me; I'm paying with my gambling winnings."

"I saw a lot of quarters come out of that slot machine," Kevin said, "but I'm afraid that will only pay for the drinks."

"Not to worry. As my former boss once told me, a government expense account is like a muscle. If you don't exercise it, it'll grow weak and you will lose it."

Kevin ordered white wine and Kidd had a martini, very dry.

Kidd ordered the food. He requested falafel and stuffed grape leaves as appetizers. For the main course he had chicken shawarma, a spicy, savory type of stew, while Kevin had lamb kabob.

After a leisurely meal, Kidd looked at his watch and then summoned the waiter. "Bring us two Araks," he said. Then in an aside to Kevin he said, "It's almost time for the show. You'll like the Arak, but drink it slowly."

Music started and all eyes turned to the stage. The lights dimmed and Leila came on stage and began dancing. Her dark black hair was pulled tight on the back of her head. A light gauze veil covered the lower part of her face. Around her neck was a necklace of pearls and beads. Her bra was two cups held by two thin straps over her shoulders with many dangling strings of beads on each side. More strings of beads adorned her shoulders like epaulets. Low on her hips she wore a tight pair of bikini pants with a draping half skirt in front and another half in back, but with no sides. The entire costume, including the beads and necklace, was in varying shades of lavender and purple with a gold fringe. A large jewel was fixed in her navel and she had multiple rings on her fingers. As she danced it was clear that she was a professional. Her motions were smooth and evocative. Seated close to the stage was a group of Japanese businessmen who gaped open-mouthed as she came to the edge of the stage directly opposite their table. Someone from an adjoining table came up to the stage and handed her a folded bill, which she stuck in her bra. Seeing this, one of the Japanese guests became emboldened and did likewise, much to the amusement of his colleagues.

Kidd leaned over to Kevin and quietly said "What do you think?"

"She's quite good, isn't she? Maybe that airman isn't as dumb as we think. But to be serious, I can't tell. There is a resemblance, but it was dark in that driveway, and I can't be sure."

At the finality of her act she removed her veil and pulled something from her hair, whatever it was that held up the long tresses. She did a deep bow to the audience, her long black hair flowing over her head and face, and when she stood up and looked at the audience with her hair hanging freely, Kevin knew.

Kidd sensed something. He leaned over to Kevin. "Well?"

"When she removed the veil and let her hair down, it hit me," he said. "I think it's the same person."

He watched her as she walked off the stage. At the last second before she went backstage, she turned and looked over her shoulder directly at Kevin.

In her dressing room, Leila went to the cupboard where she had hid her purse behind some cleaning supplies. She got out her cell phone and dialed a number.

Saleh answered. "I told you, don't call me at this number unless it's an emergency."

"Don't be a jerk," she said. "I know what you told me. I think I saw him—here in the club."

"Who? What are you talking about?"

"Your friend, the guy with the boat, the guy you told me about."

"The sailor? He's there?"

"He came in and watched the show with another guy. I'm sure it's the same man I saw on the street outside the motel that night. I'm worried. Why would they be here if they didn't know something? You've got to get me out of here."

"Don't panic, I'm sure it's nothing."

"That's easy for you to say. Where are you?"

"Never mind where I am. Don't worry, I'll see that you're taken care of."

"You'll take care of me, but you won't tell me where you are? You expect me to believe that? Give me some traveling money so I can get out of here. I don't think you should come here. I'll meet you somewhere."

"Calm down. Give me a day to set something up and I'll call you." The line went dead.

In exasperation Leila slammed her phone closed. "Bastard," she said. "He won't do anything."

Meanwhile, at Creech Air Force Base, Airman Foster was undergoing surveillance. Over the weekend a small camera had been placed in the ceiling where he worked. When the OSI agents reviewed the tapes, he could be seen connecting a small black object to one of the computers. In a matter of minutes, data was transferred and he removed the device and placed it in his sock. After leaving work, he was later observed hiding the object under the spare tire in his Corvette. On his next trip to Las Vegas, the agents planned to wait until he'd given the device to Leila, and then they would arrest the pair. Meanwhile, Air Force computer experts retrieved the device, downloaded the information it contained, erased the files, and replaced it in his car.

❦

In Los Angeles, Northrop Grumman security was working closely with the FBI to identify the employee who had been meeting with Saleh. The investigation focused on a naturalized U.S. citizen of Iranian descent who worked in the UAV guidance section. Rahmin Ahmadi was a MIT Ph.D., brilliant, unmarried, and with a penchant for the finer things in life. In a rare lapse of good judgment, he kept the photo of a dark-haired woman on his desk. When asked, he joked about his "old girlfriend from back home." In reality, the photograph had been given to him by Leila.

One afternoon his boss called him into his office.

"Rahmin, can you come up? I've got someone who wants to talk with you," he said.

As Rahmin waited for the elevator that would take him to his boss's office, he had a bad feeling about this meeting.

❦

On Thursday night, Leila called the airman.

"Are you coming tomorrow night?" she said, "I miss you. I want you in my bed all night long, and I don't mean sleeping."

The airman could hardly restrain himself. Just the sound of her voice on the phone aroused him.

"Yes, I'll be there. I can't wait to see you."

"You have another package for me?" she asked.

"Yes," he said. "And I've got a bottle of Champagne for us."

"How sweet of you," she said. Then she asked, "Do

you have any cash?"

He paused, surprised. Usually she gave him cash, once the "package" had been delivered and evaluated. "Why?"

"My sister is very sick, maybe dying, and I need to go see her this weekend. It would just be a loan for a few days. I get paid at the end of the month."

"I'm so sorry to hear that, Leila. Where is your sister?"

"She's in Indianapolis. I want to fly there on the weekend. I have to be back on Tuesday for my show."

"I can give you five hundred, will that help?"

"My darling, you're a lifesaver. That will be wonderful. I can't wait for the hours to pass until we're together tomorrow night."

After hanging up, Leila resumed packing. She had a large trash bag of things to throw away. Her costumes and other valuables she had crammed into two suitcases. She had booked a Saturday flight to Seattle. From there she planned to cross over to Vancouver. With this latest delivery from the airman, she had two "packages" for Saleh. That would be enough to make him come to Vancouver. Then she would make him take her somewhere where she'd be safe.

Rahmin's boss liked him. The MIT Ph.D. was quiet and reserved, but a hard worker who put in long hours on developing and improving guidance software. He could not imagine Rahmin being involved in anything illegal.

"Rahmin, thanks for coming up. This is George Brito, with Northrop security." He indicated a heavyset man who stood as Rahmin was escorted into the office by a secretary. "George, meet Rahmin Ahmadi." They shook hands.

"Please sit down. George has a couple of questions

for you."

"Of course," Rahmin said, trying to control his nervousness. His hands were tightly clenched in his lap. He looked at George, tried to smile, but the result was forced, more a grimace.

George was a Latino, with short cropped, gray-black hair. He was muscular, about six feet and a couple of inches. He spoke softly.

"Mr. Ahmadi, I understand you work in Division 400, where you are principal scientist working on guidance software and systems."

"That is correct."

"And you have been with the company for ten years."

"Yes, ever since I finished graduate school at MIT."

"How well do you know your coworkers?"

This question surprised him. Maybe there was something else they were concerned about. He relaxed. "Fairly well. I've no complaints about any of our group. It has been growing, so some people are new within the last two years."

"Do you get together socially with any of them?" Brito spoke softly, in a friendly manner. "You know, a drink after work, parties on the weekend, maybe taking in a ball game or something?"

"No," Rahmin said. "They all have families that keep them busy."

"What do you do in your spare time?"

"I guess I'm pretty boring. I read a lot. There is so much going on in my field it is hard to keep up. Otherwise, I like classical music. I go to the Music Center downtown once in a while."

"You live out in North Hollywood, right?"

"Yes." How did he know that? Rahmin wondered, starting to feel nervous again.

"You belong to any social groups or clubs out there?" Brito asked.

"No," Rahmin said, a trace of irritation creeping into his voice. "What is this about? Is something wrong?"

"I'm sorry to bother you with these questions," Brito said. "It's just routine. Our government contracts require that we do periodic random checks, so I just want to verify that you hadn't observed anything out of the ordinary in your department, anybody behaving differently, you know, maybe depressed, absent from work, that kind of thing?"

"No, absolutely not. We have a good team."

"Good, good. I'm glad to hear that. I think that about does it. Thanks for taking time to talk to me."

Rahmin stood to leave, but Brito remained seated.

"Oh, one more thing. Before you go, take a quick look at this." Brito pulled a photograph out of his jacket pocket and handed it to Rahmin. It was a photo of Saleh.

"Do you by any chance know this man?" Brito asked, watching Rahmin's reaction. Rahmin glanced at the picture, and quickly handed it back. Too quickly, Brito thought. He took the picture from Rahmin, holding it so it faced Rahmin. He noticed that Rahmin remained focused on the picture, not looking at him.

"No. I do not know this man."

"By any chance, have you seen him around, maybe with one of the guys in your department?"

"No. I'm certain he's never been around. We don't have visitors."

"Good, good," Brito said. "That clears that up. It's probably a case of mistaken identity. I'll pass that on and we'll consider the matter closed."

Rahmin opened the door to leave.

Brito got up from the chair and put the photo back in his pocket as Rahmin stood at the door, his hand on the doorknob.

"I'll be going now," Brito said. "I've got to return this photo to the FBI, tell them they need to look elsewhere."

Rahmin stepped out of the room and closed the door behind him.

Brito sat back down. "He's lying," he said. "I think we have a problem. Don't discuss this meeting with anyone. If Rahmin contacts you and wants to know what's going on, tell him it's just routine and you don't know anything more than he does. But let me know immediately if he fails to show up for work."

The airman went to the minibar and found two glasses. He popped the cork on the Champagne and filled the glasses. Leila had changed at the club. Her costume was in a small traveling bag she always used on the nights she danced. She kicked off her shoes and went into the bathroom.

The door was open and the airman watched her remove her skirt and blouse. Leila looked in the mirror and fiddled with her hair. When she walked out she was in her bra and panties. He was standing there holding the two glasses. She stood a few feet from him.

"Did you remember my loan?" she said.

"Of course."

She reached behind her back, undid her bra, stepped out of her panties, and tossed them on the bed. Leila moved closer, took the glass from him, and kissed his cheek. She saw he was aroused. She took his hand and held it on her breast, moved her other hand to his crotch.

"Want me to undress you honey?" she said.

At that moment the door opened and two uniformed men with guns drawn burst into the room.

"Freeze," they said.

Rahmin left work early. He drove by his apartment

building and circled the block before parking in the garage. Everything looked normal. He went to his apartment and unlocked the door. He went from room to room and saw that nothing had been disturbed. He sat down in the living room and stared out the window. He thought that the police might have been there waiting for him. He was sure they knew; but then again, maybe not. Maybe they were trying to frighten him, to see how he'd react. But they had Saleh's photograph. He wondered if they knew about the woman.

He got up and walked through the entire apartment again. What was there to find here? Nothing. His clothes, his books, his music. He kept no copies of anything from the office. It had all been handed over to Saleh. Saleh, who had told him about the Shia women and children being slaughtered by the American UAVs. Saleh who had said, "The Americans are waging war on Islam—the same Americans that you work for. How can you do this?" Saleh had asked him. "While others offer themselves as martyrs, you do the devil's work with our enemy."

He called Saleh on the secret number he'd been given. He'd memorized it—nothing written down. He had a very good memory.

The call went to voice mail and he left a message, letting Saleh know the authorities had his photograph. He said that security had come to talk to him, and he denied knowing Saleh. But they had your picture, I think they know…. He hung up the phone. He wondered if Saleh would call back. Probably not. He would go away, get the information in the right hands so they could strike back, defeat the American aggressors.

It was dark in the apartment. The sun had gone down as he sat there, thinking about Saleh, about his job, and about his family. They were all gone, his mother dead from cancer, his father and older brother killed in the war with Iraq.

Then there was a woman. Saleh had brought her to him. She was the only woman he'd ever known. She had given him unimaginable pleasures. He was torn with guilt, thinking about her and the things they'd done.

"These things are natural," she had said, "things lovers do." Still, he was tormented by the desire he felt to see her again, and the guilt he knew would follow.

Saleh would disappear. Of that, he was sure. With Saleh gone, the woman would be gone as well. He might as well recognize that he would never see her again.

At first the job had been easy. Then after a while, he started having trouble sleeping. Sometimes he thought about what he brought Saleh; other times, he lay awake all night thinking about the woman. Finally, he'd gotten some pills to help him sleep.

He got up from the couch and made a cup of tea. He drank it as he paced in the living room, pausing every now and then to look out the window at the street. It was quiet—no cars pulling up with flashing lights.

He knew what he had to do. A sense of peace flowed over his being as he undressed for bed. He crawled into bed naked. He took a pill and lay there, thinking about the woman, remembering how she had undressed and then undressed him and what followed. Thinking about her kept him awake. He took another pill. As he started to feel drowsy, he took three more. Three more after that. He finished the bottle and dropped it on the floor.

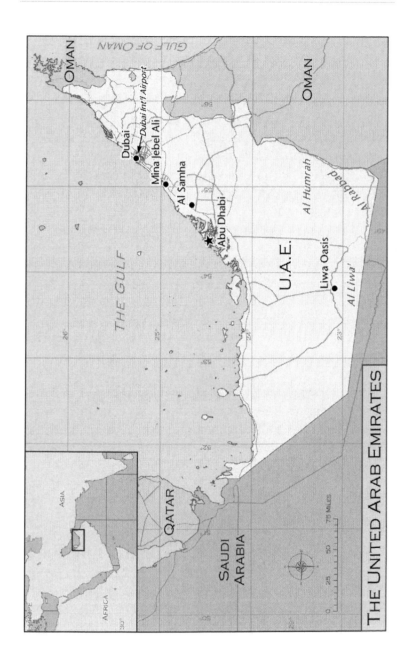

THE UNITED ARAB EMIRATES

THE MIDDLE EAST CAULDRON

For Kevin, things quieted down for a while as the new millennium approached There had been no more suspicious calls. The proposal for Johnston Atoll was finished and Kevin waited to see if it would be approved. Once the company had the order, the guys in the field could handle it. It didn't look like there would be any reason for him to return to Honolulu.

What was coming up was another trip to the Middle East. There was more work in Kuwait, a possible project with Saudi Consolidated Electric, and a new project in Dubai. Kevin had never been to the United Arab Emirates, so this sounded interesting. It was not far from Oman and the Strait of Hormuz. You could look across that narrow waterway and stare into Iran. It was a chokepoint for the Persian Gulf.

He left a message for Kidd to give him a call— nothing urgent, just another trip in the making. Kidd returned the call the next day.

"Can we meet later this week?"

"Sure. I suppose you'll want another tamale."

"Not this time. I'll give you a call in a few days."

When Kidd called back he told Kevin he'd pick him up at the office.

At 5 p.m. on the appointed day, Kidd was parked in a loading zone on Wilshire Boulevard in a black Mercury Sable. He was accompanied by another man. Kevin got in the back seat and Kidd swung the Mercury out into the traffic.

"Kevin—meet Don MacLane, one of my associates.

Don, meet Kevin."

Kevin reached over into the front seat and shook Don's hand.

"Pleased to meet you," he said.

"We're going to Lawry's Prime Rib on La Cienega, if that's okay with you Kevin."

"Sounds good," Kevin said. "That's a little fancier than Mama's Tamales."

"I thought you deserved it. I would've liked to take you to Perino's on Wilshire. It's not far from your office, but it has been closed for about ten years. Used to be my favorite spot for special occasions."

At the restaurant, Kidd handed the car keys to the valet and they went inside. He spoke a few quiet words to the hostess who immediately led them to a table in the back corner of the restaurant. When a waiter appeared, Kidd asked about drinks. Kevin ordered white wine, MacLane a Manhattan, and Kidd scotch on the rocks.

"Kevin, Don is one of our Middle East specialists. Would you mind telling him what the purpose of your trip is and where you'll be spending time? You don't need to go into any confidential business matters, just an overview of your itinerary."

"Sure. Kuwait City is my first stop. We have a project at Kuwait University that was interrupted by the Iraqi invasion and takeover of Kuwait. I've some meetings at the University, then I'll be visiting an Army site near the harbor. After the first Gulf War, the U.S. Army Central Command decided they needed a forward base in Kuwait, in case Iraq violated the cease-fire that ended the first Gulf War. The army took over a warehouse complex near the harbor and named it Camp Doha.

"My company is part of a joint venture that provides operations and maintenance support services for the Army at Camp Doha. We provide skilled civilians who repair and maintain the vehicles and perform other essential services so military personnel can focus on their mission.

I'll be there for a few days of briefings as we start to bring in additional personnel. By the way, it is a ten-year contract, so draw your own conclusions about peace in the region."

"We've heard about the buildup," Don said. "As you probably know, the President is very concerned about Iraq's capabilities to use weapons of mass destruction."

"What do you think?" Kevin asked.

"What I think doesn't matter," Don replied. "The Agency is pushing the idea that it's a problem. Saddam makes matters worse by refusing to allow inspections, so it looks like he's hiding something. But to those of us on the ground, it's all a bluff."

"Kevin, what about Dubai?" Kidd said.

"I'll be there for a couple of days. We're proposing on some interesting projects—a large tower complex and expansion of the Dubai International Airport."

"This interests us, especially if you could take off a couple days for sightseeing."

"I could probably arrange that. I've never been there before, so I don't know the country. Any particular sites I should see?"

"We'll get back to you with a list," Kidd said. There's someone we'd like you to meet. He's an associate of ours who's been traveling in India and Pakistan. We've had some unsettling news about him. We think it would be useful to have someone like yourself—an international businessman—meet him casually and see if he's okay. You know how it is—sometimes when you're overseas for a lengthy period of time all you can think about is getting home, getting back to all that is familiar, familiar foods, familiar customs, familiar languages. Chances are there are no problems, but we'd like your input."

"That's it?" Kevin asked. "I'm not a shrink."

"We know that," Don replied. "But you've recruited and hired people, and you've probably dealt with cases where someone has experienced burnout due to job pressure. We just want you to meet this man and then let us know what you think."

"How will I find this guy?"

"Let us know where you'll be staying and he'll contact you. His name is McKinsey."

❧

A few weeks after the Sacramento conference, Wu called Juliana, inviting her to visit his office. A date was arranged.

"Our business is very modest compared to R&D," Wu said, as he took Juliana on a tour. "Here we have a small library, in the next room is our sales office where we can demonstrate our software to potential buyers."

Next he led her to a door labeled "Lab" and punched in a code to unlock it. They entered a large room with about twenty workstations, each with a computer terminal and monitor, all state-of-the-art equipment.

"These are our programmers. About half are dedicated to developing new climate models, or to improving the existing ones. Would you like to see a demonstration?"

"Yes," Juliana said, "that would be great."

Wu pointed to a workstation occupied by a Chinese woman. "Miss Wong can show you one of our models."

Juliana watched the monitor display a three-dimensional image of a narrow channel between an island and a large landmass. As Wong entered different air temperatures, the water temperature shifted and arrows depicting current flow changed. The display was color-coded to indicate various temperatures and current speeds.

"Very impressive," Juliana said. There was something familiar about the island, but she did not ask Wu what it was. "Who are your clients for these models?"

"We think they will interest governments of those countries likely to be affected by rising sea levels. Also, we've had some inquiries from shipping companies, those with container ships and oil tankers. A favorable current can reduce transit time by hours or days in some cases, and that equates to faster turnaround for the shipping companies. Next, I'd like to show you our board room."

Wu led Juliana from the lab to another room. The walls were lined with the diplomas of the staff and various awards won by the company. A large table had two place settings and serving dishes containing a very elegant lunch.

"I hope you like Chinese food Mrs. Hunter. Will you join me in a light lunch? He pulled out a chair for Juliana and took a seat on the other side of the table.

"Mr. Wu, I wasn't expecting lunch. You've gone to too much trouble."

"No trouble—it's a very simple lunch. And you have to eat, correct?"

He poured Juliana a cup of tea and then served her a bowl of soup and a cold lobster salad. Once the food was served Wu told Juliana his goals for the company and its future growth.

"The big challenge we face is in finding capable, experienced, scientists and programmers. We want only the best. Of course, they are the hardest to find.

"I'm wondering, Mrs. Hunter, if you would have any interest in joining our team. I know we are small compared to R&D, but our salaries and benefits are among the best in our industry. Before you say no, let me ask you to think about one option where you can keep your present job and work part-time as a consultant for us, get to know us better."

"I don't think I could do that. My current job takes all my free time and then some. My husband already claims I have no time for him."

"You don't need to make a decision now, Mrs. Hunter. You can think about it."

"Thank you for the tour and lunch, Mr. Wu. Juliana glanced at her watch. "If you excuse me now, I need to get back to my office. I promise I'll think about what you've said."

"Of course. Thank you for coming. If you have any questions, please call me. By the way, our compensation for consultants is $1,000 per day. I thought it was important for you to know that."

Back in her office, Juliana ignored the project she'd been working on. She thought over Wu's offer, wondering what it all meant. He hardly knew her, other than from the conference he attended where she had taken part in a panel discussion. He had not asked her any questions about her education, experience, or qualifications—a strange approach for someone dedicated to building a staff of the best specialists that could be found. Then there was the computer model demonstration. Although the landmass and island were not identified, Juliana was almost certain that she was looking at current flow through the Taiwan Strait, the hundred mile wide channel that separated Taiwan from mainland China. Taiwan was not in much danger from rising sea levels, so it was curious that so much research effort was going into studying this critical waterway.

Alex McKinsey walked out of the darkened gate and down a side street lined with green mango trees. His long stride looked casual, but allowed him to move quickly along the street. He gave the impression of someone out taking an evening stroll.

McKinsey was a spy. He supposedly worked for the State Department in the Middle East. Actually, he was a statistician, and numbers were his game. All sorts of numbers and facts interested him, although none of them seemed to be associated with anything glamorous or exciting. Yet, these humdrum numbers—when compiled with thousands of other humdrum numbers—allowed the experts who fed on his information to paint remarkably accurate scenarios depicting the economy of those nations whose dictators and military governments were thought by some to be potential threats to world stability.

His great strength—besides a good memory, skill with languages, and an eye for detail—was that he didn't look like a spy. To an observer, he was just another American graduate student bumming around Pakistan, collecting data for a dissertation. He dressed in somewhat worn casual attire, spent time among the leftist students in universities, and demonstrated to everyone that he had no money. He was well-liked because he spoke openly and critically of Uncle Sam, American imperialism, and the need for self-determination.

He'd first come to New Delhi and spent several months leisurely traveling around India. While in New Delhi, he hired a car and driver one day and drove south two hundred kilometers to the town of Accra to visit the Taj Mahal. The road revealed the full complexity of the Indian countryside. The highway was shared between trucks loaded with cargo, some passenger cars, bullock-drawn carts, bicycles, and pedestrians.

After he finished his business in New Delhi, McKinsey looked into the best way to travel to Pakistan. His goal was to get to Karachi but he also wanted to spend some time in Hyderabad. He didn't want to fly because he could learn a lot more with time on the ground, interacting with local people. The most direct route was from Delhi southwest to Jodhpur then crossing the border to Hyderabad and on to Karachi. Unfortunately this direct route was destroyed during the Indo-Pakistani war of 1965 and now thirty-five years later still not reopened. Travel by bus was another alternative, but as bad as the crowded second-class Indian train system was, buses were even worse, with interminable stops, every seat taken, and people hanging on the luggage racks on top of the bus.

The next best alternative was to take a train northwest from New Delhi to Amritsar, which was close to the Pakistan border, with the major city of Lahore only forty-nine kilometers away. The method was to get a taxi at the train station, take it to the border, walk across the border and clear customs, take another taxi into Lahore, and then catch a train south at the Lahore station. The Karachi Express left Lahore at 4 p.m. and arrived in Karachi nineteen hours later, passing through Faisalabad and several other cities before reaching Hyderabad, and then continuing on to Karachi. From Faisalabad, the train traversed the edge of the great Thar Desert that straddled the border between Pakistan and India. It was the long way around, but it would have to do.

The purpose of McKinsey's work could be called "information gathering." That was basically what he tried to do. He was not interested in stealing secrets—this was a dangerous measure only used as a last resort. Actually, he simply discreetly acquired information that was readily available—people were only too glad to give it to him—and then passed it on to his contacts. He was certain that at some level in every country, its leaders were aware that such activities went on. Having to proceed in this way meant that the country seeking information had to be prepared to spend money to get and to analyze the data. Generally, the motivation was to learn what was going on more quickly than was otherwise possible, to get accurate information rather than what was passed by the censors, and to avoid embarrassing the government.

On a typical working night, McKinsey sat in a dingy hotel room with a pot of tea, meticulously preparing notes dealing with the movement of suspicious vessels in and out of the seaport. He collected the data by continuously sitting on a hill overlooking the port for three days and nights.

The results of his observations went into long talkative letters, addressed to a mythical friend in Cleveland. They were full of meaningless nonsense to throw potential censors off guard. Hidden in amongst this stuff were carefully disguised facts and data relevant to his assignment. Codes were never used. Not only were they awkward, subject to being broken, but they were a red flag that alerted officials and could bring about countermeasures. His letters and terse postcards were considered the safest means of conveying information.

When his work involved sensitive information, it was always transferred by word-of-mouth and personal contact. He made contact at a crowded spot in the city where surveillance was virtually impossible. He never kept notes on this type of information.

His third technique was to maintain a diary, in which he carefully recorded his travels. He'd learned that recollection of observations was easiest in a chronological context, in which the full extent of his mental associations could be employed to recall essential facts.

Arriving in Karachi, he checked into a cheap hotel near the water front. There he was able to meet seamen from many of the cargo ships that called at the port. They were always willing to talk about their destination and the cargos their vessels carried. On both sides of the port there were mangrove forests and shallow estuaries. Along the water front there were cafes with tables and benches where he could sit and drink a cup of tea while observing movements in and out of the port.

South of the port there was Manora Beach, located on a small island connected to the mainland by a sand spit. There were sandy beaches along the seaward edge. Nearby was an important Pakistani naval facility. Several wrecked ships were tossed up on the island. McKinsey could visit the area and be largely unnoticed among the other beachgoers. From the opposite side of the island, the movement of ships into and out of the harbor could be observed.

The Soviets had withdrawn from Afghanistan ten years earlier. It was known that the Mujahideen resistance fighters had received weapons provided by the U.S. and smuggled into the country by Pakistan. Peace had not come to Afghanistan; weapons and foreign fighters continued to flow into the country, with origins thought to be Saudi Arabia and Iran. McKinsey had seen evidence to confirm this as trucks left Karachi and headed north to Quetta.

McKinsey enjoyed his work. He considered it a constant challenge. After completing a year in Asia, he planned to return to the States for a Washington office job. Following this he expected a permanent assignment in one of the embassies where he would continue his profession from an office where he would review the field data collected by others doing what he did now.

His training had been superb, although in retrospect it seemed a little unnecessary. Still, it gave him a sense of confidence to think that, alone and unarmed—defenseless really—he was well qualified to take care of himself. The best weapon he had was a smooth proficiency with language. While English was widely spoken in both India and Pakistan, he'd learned Urdu. His instructors had seized upon his natural abilities and honed them to perfection. With subtle ease, he could joke in several dialects, as well as speak the classical language of an educated person. In a moment he could switch from an intellectual conversation with a professor to the vulgar language of the taxi drivers and pimps. Learning new words, inflections, anecdotes, was a constant hobby and amusement to him.

One evening when he was out walking, a car approached him slowly from the opposite direction as he walked down the street. It was the slowness—not typical of Pakistani drivers—that tipped him off. Two men in the car watched as he reached the corner of the street. When the car drew even with him on the opposite side of the street, McKinsey saw quick movement and a glimmer of metal in the car. Instinctively, he ducked around the corner, bumping his shoulder on the edge of the building. Two shots echoed out—sharp cracks, probably a small caliber revolver. One hit near his head and his face was stung with concrete dust and sand. He tore off down the street, running into the first alley he came to and jumping a fence into someone's yard. In the distance he heard the assassin's car accelerate into the night.

To avoid attracting attention he walked quietly through the yard and out into another street, then into another alley. His face hurt. When he rubbed it he saw blood on his hand.

Those bastards came close, he thought. *What tipped them off?* He looked cautiously out on the street. Crossing quickly, he calmly strolled into the center of a small park and splashed water on his face. He sat on a bench under a street lamp. Using his glasses as a mirror, he examined his face. There were some small scratches but bleeding had stopped. Thoughts raced through his mind. Had he blown his cover? Was it simply a terrorist movement, an anti-American action, or did someone suspect him? If so, he must be on to something big.

As he set out to leave the park, he noticed a pain in his right arm up near the shoulder. He remembered bumping into the building as he dodged the shots. He rubbed his shoulder, but the sharp aching sensation continued. He drew his arm over close to his face and when he saw a small bloody hole in his sleeve his reaction was disbelief. The bullet had entered the fleshy part of his arm, above the elbow. He pushed up his shirt sleeve. Blood oozed from a wound that seemed small and insignificant. He stuffed his handkerchief inside his shirt sleeve. Now what? He sat there for a few minutes, thinking about what to do. Probably not a good idea to go to the hotel. Also, probably not a good idea to sit here in plain sight. He stood and walked out of the park.

He paused for a second at the next corner, thinking he had to get himself under control in case they came back. He decided not to go back to the hotel, but to spend the night somewhere and then go to his contact to get medical help.

After walking for a while, his confidence was

completely back. His arm hurt but he could walk normally. He decided then that he must have been hit by a piece of the ricocheting bullet. He continued on until he reached another park. He found a bench where he could lie down. He listened for a while and then decided that no one was nearby and after a few moments fell soundly asleep.

In the morning the sounds of pedestrians and traffic woke him. The sun was just coming up and McKinsey thought the time to be about 6:30 a.m. He sat up and stretched, rubbing sleep from his eyes. The night had been warm, but his arm was stiff and sore. *Maybe I should've gone to the hotel*, he thought, as he staggered with nausea and dizziness from the sharp pain he felt in his arm. It took him nearly an hour to walk to his hotel. He let himself into the building, went quietly upstairs to his room. The lock had been forced. He quietly backed away from the door and left the building to locate a phone to call his Karachi contact.

His contact said that he would take him to a doctor and would have McKinsey's hotel checked and his possessions removed. "After the doctor takes care of your arm, you better go across to the Emirates and lay low for a while until things cool off here. I got word today that we've got a pretty complete picture of what's going on."

The contact took McKinsey to a doctor's office.

"Little hunting accident," said the contact. "My friend was too close and caught a ricochet."

The doctor was an American, an old hand who handled special problems for the embassy. He said nothing but slid McKinsey under an X-ray machine. When the pictures were finished he moved McKinsey onto an operating table and looked at the wound.

"Looks like part of a 22," he said. You're lucky it didn't break the bone. In the X-rays it looks like it's resting against your humorous. I'll probe for it, but we may end up leaving it there depending on what I can find."

The doctor injected a painkiller into the wound. The

pain was excruciating, causing McKinsey to cry out in agony.

After waiting the necessary time for the anesthesia to take effect, the doctor held McKinsey's arm with one hand and said, "Let's see if we can find that piece of lead." With brutal strength he jammed a probe into the wound. McKinsey thought that he'd never experienced such pain, certain it could get no worse. But it got worse and kept getting worse as the doctor scraped the probe along the side of the bone, trying to find the bullet.

"I got the damn thing," said the doctor, dropping a small piece of lead onto a tray. "My nurse will clean you up and bandage the wound. You'll need to watch it for a couple of days, make sure it doesn't get infected."

The contact took McKinsey to a different hotel near Karachi's Jinnah International Airport and gave him a ticket for Dubai.

"You may as well live in style for a while," he said. "Lay low and play the tourist. When you feel like traveling again, get in touch. Get a haircut, change your image, and keep off the streets."

McKinsey shrugged. "Okay with me. Keep me posted."

The next day, the contact met McKinsey in the hotel restaurant. "Here's your stuff from the hotel. We paid for the damaged door. We could tell that your visitors had looked over everything pretty carefully—not that there was much for them to look through. It looked like there was more than one person, and at least one stayed there for a while, waiting for your return. You were smart not to go back."

McKinsey smiled. "It's the first excitement in two years for me. Most of the time I wonder if anyone even reads the stuff I collect."

"They read it," said the contact. "You do a good job. But go easy now, get well, maybe make some connections in the university, but don't ask anybody any questions. Just listen and read, okay?"

"Yeah, I'll try for a while, until I get bored." McKinsey's suspicions had been somehow aroused. He thought maybe he had stumbled onto something important, and now the locals were trying to ease him out of the picture. "Who is going to do the follow-up here?" he asked.

The contact hesitated. "I don't know. I don't know who's available. Might have to wrap it up myself."

McKinsey nodded but said nothing. Inwardly he thought, *you son of a bitch. You're squeezing me out and taking on the whole show.*

The contact seemed to sense McKinsey's displeasure. "Look, it's nothing important. You've done a good job and you'll get credit. Besides, we don't have anybody in Dubai right now. By the way, when you get there, call the office. They want you to meet someone."

"What's that about?"

The contact shrugged his shoulders. "Who knows? I'm just relaying the message."

"One more thing, and this is important. I assume there was nothing in your hotel room that would lead back to you—no U.S. addresses, old letters, anything that they could use to trace you?"

"No, I don't think so. Why?"

Because when you go back to the States, you don't want to wake up one night with these guys knocking on your door."

The contact left, telling McKinsey he was going back to his office. That was untrue; in actuality he was on his way to meet a Pakistani woman who was a secretary in an import/export company that shipped goods in and out of the Karachi sea port. He was following up on one of McKinsey's leads.

Back in his room, McKinsey mulled it over, convinced there were plenty of people who could go to the United Arab Emirates. He'd said nothing, because there was nothing to do except what the contact told him to do.

What the hell, I might as well go to Dubai, he figured. *I could use a week off, take it easy for a while. I work hard enough for these bastards.*

He considered discussing his latest findings with the contact, something he had not yet reported. Then he decided, screw him. I'll pass this on later, let the office wonder why he didn't come up with it when he was here full-time. McKinsey'd had no briefings about Chinese-Pakistani collaboration, so maybe it was nothing. On the other hand, maybe it was big, really big. A Chinese vessel had come into port. Talking to dockworkers in a bar, he learned that the ship carried "aircraft parts." In reality it appeared that the Pakistanis were getting Chinese help building fighter jets, and maybe even Chinese drones. He knew that they'd asked for American drones but had been turned down.

In anticipation of his trip to the Middle East, Kevin spent several days in the library reading the latest news reports concerning the region. He formed several conclusions from his research.

Americans were welcomed in Kuwait where they were perceived as allies for rescuing the country from Iraq. In the Kingdom of Saudi Arabia, U.S. forces were tolerated. The Saudis wanted U.S. protection and the security it brought. They knew that Iraq had Scud missiles capable of reaching the Kingdom. On the other hand, they hated the western presence. One example, having female U.S. military personnel in the country grated on Saudi conservatives who feared it would trigger a feminist movement.

Iraq remained a powerful and destabilizing influence in the region. Iran continued its hate campaign against the U.S. and publicly vowed to annihilate Israel. Afghanistan had fallen into a destructive civil war following the ouster of the Soviet army. Now the country was largely controlled by the Taliban, composed in part of former Mujahideen fighters who had battled the Russians. Osama bin Laden, suspected of masterminding the bombing of U.S. embassies in Africa, was believed to be hiding in Afghanistan. In 1998, the U.S. had launched missile strikes on suspected al Qaeda bases, but with no results. The United Nations imposed an air embargo and economic sanctions, but Afghanistan claimed no knowledge of bin Laden's whereabouts.

Meanwhile, the U.S. had an uneasy partnership with Pakistan regarding efforts to stabilize the situation in Afghanistan. While on the surface Pakistan claimed to be denying support to the rebels, there was suspicion that the Pakistani Army tolerated their presence in the lawless border region of the country.

As the new millennium approached, there were abundant global concerns. There were also those who prophesied massive computer and electronics problems (the Y2K issue). Kevin did not believe this would be a problem. The political situation, however, seemed dire. Somewhere, somehow, more fighting was coming.

In the airport duty-free store Kevin bought a bottle of Crown Royal Canadian whiskey. From Los Angeles he flew to Amsterdam on KLM. The airline had a package deal that included an overnight stay in the city. He had dinner in an Indonesian restaurant near his hotel. Back in his room he got some ice and poured a drink of the Canadian whiskey, toasting Bill Ikeda, an old friend who had accompanied him on his first trip to Saudi Arabia.

In the morning Kevin continued his trip, arriving in Kuwait at noon. The University project was wrapping up. All evidence of the damage caused by the Iraqi invasion was gone and the campus was now a pristine showpiece.

Camp Doha had also changed. What previously had been a few warehouses was now a sprawling military complex. The joint venture was in the second year of its contract to maintain the Army's mechanized vehicles in a state of combat readiness.

As he walked around the facility and attended various meetings, Kevin had a sense of the tension that gripped the place. No one was saying anything, but he got the idea that if war came again to the Middle East, Camp Doha would be right in the middle of it. On his last night in Kuwait, before leaving for the airport, Kevin bought a plastic bottle of mouthwash. Saudi Arabia was strict about alcohol. He dumped the mouthwash into the toilet and transferred what was left of the Crown Royal into the other bottle, which was unlikely to be seized by the Saudi customs inspectors.

In comparison to Kuwait, al Khobar seemed remote and detached from any war fears. There was no visible U.S. military presence; most of the military was at bases in the north of Saudi Arabia. Kevin's meetings were concerned with a contract to provide additional American expertise to help expand a Saudi electric power network.

He had a ceremonial dinner with his client contacts at a fine restaurant in town. No alcohol was served. Only men were seated in the main dining room. In another section, screened off from public view by partitions, there was a family section where men sat with wives and children, the women clad in the traditional dress that left only their eyes exposed. Here, in the privacy of the room, they could uncover their faces to eat. As he left the restaurant, one family emerged. A woman looked at him, then quickly glanced away. In her dark eyes he sensed longing and suppressed passion. That night in his room he drank the last of the Crown Royal and fell asleep, dreaming that he was back in the restaurant and the woman looking at him was Juliana wearing a *burqa*.

৶

Dubai was a totally new experience for Kevin. On the taxi ride from the airport to the Hyatt Regency hotel, everywhere he looked there were towering cranes. It was amazing to think there could be so much construction going on concurrently in one city. The hotel had every amenity imaginable: shops, restaurants, even a cinema. His room looked out over the Gulf.

After checking in, Kevin went outside to look at the Gulf. The notorious Strait of Hormuz was a scant one hundred and twenty miles from where he stood. When things were calm, more than a dozen oil laden tankers passed through that 21 mile-wide channel every day, on average.

That night, after meeting with representatives of the airport board, Kevin received a long-distance call. Kevin recognized the gravelly voice of Kidd.

"My friend will be reaching out to you tomorrow," he said. "Can you be free to meet with him, maybe have lunch?"

"Yes, that's not a problem."

"Good. Tell him a little about our concerns, just the main points; no names."

"You mean our Saudi guy?"

"You got it. Safe trip home."

The line went dead. It was typical of Kidd. He was a man of few words, especially on the phone. Kevin wondered where he was when he placed the call. It was 9 p.m. in Dubai; that would make it 9 a.m. in Los Angeles.

Kevin slept in the next morning. It seemed his travels had caught up with him. In the middle of the night he'd woken from a bizarre dream. Whatever it was, the fright caused him to get out of bed and stand disoriented in the darkened room, trying to determine where he was. Back in Saudi Arabia? No, the room was unfamiliar. Kevin sat on the edge of the bed, feeling a mild panic as he tried to get oriented. Momentarily, he did not know what he was doing in this strange room. In the bathroom, he splashed some water on his face. Noticing his shaving kit, it all started to come back. He calmed down and returned to bed. Rattled by the experience, he couldn't sleep, lying there for a couple of hours, wondering what caused this strange blackout. He resisted calling Juliana, now at work, not wanting to bother her. Finally he drifted off to sleep.

The phone woke him in the morning. Groggily, he grabbed it and said "Hunter."

"Mr. Hunter, good morning. I hope I haven't woken you. My name is McKinsey. Would you have time to join me for lunch today?"

"Actually, I'm glad you called," Kevin said. "It appears I've overslept. In any event, I'm happy to meet you for lunch. Do you have a place in mind?"

"Your hotel restaurant—the poolside bar would be fine, if that's okay with you. It's more private than one of the fancy restaurants."

"Sure. How will I know you?"

"How about if I just have the desk call your room when I get there? That way you won't have to wait if I'm delayed."

"That's fine," Kevin said. "I've got some work to catch up on so I'll be here in the room."

"Many thanks. I'll see you at noon."

Kevin was greeted when he exited the elevator by a man about thirty years old. He wore a battered canvas hat, dark glasses, a sport shirt and cotton pants such as one might see in India. His face was tanned, almost dark and his hair and mustache were black. Overall, he had an Indo-European appearance, but might have been mistaken for an Egyptian or a Saudi. As they walked to the restaurant, Kevin noticed he seemed to be favoring his arm.

"Thanks for meeting with me," McKinsey said. "Is this your first time here in the UAE?"

"Yes. I'm surprised at the amount of building going on."

"There's a lot of money here. The Saudis and other Arabs like to vacation here because they have more freedom than back home. They bring their girlfriends and live it up."

"I've noticed they seem less strict here," Kevin replied. "What about you? Have you been here before?"

"Yes, briefly. The last four months I've been traveling around India and Pakistan. I work for the State Department and we make periodic in-country surveys, trying to keep up with how the local economies are doing, that kind of thing. And you?"

"I work for Consolidated Engineers and Constructors," Kevin replied. "We are a global engineering and construction company with projects in the Middle East. I'm here for a bunch of meetings—both project reviews and business development."

They found a table. McKinsey ordered a grilled cheese sandwich with French fries; Kevin had *dolma* and *falafel*.

"After traveling for a while you start missing the comfort foods, said McKinsey. "I've been a vegetarian now for so many weeks I never want to see another lentil the rest of my life."

Kevin laughed. "I haven't reached that point yet, although I was tempted to get a hamburger at Camp Doha. There is a place on the base called Uncle Frosty's Oasis where you can get hamburgers and hotdogs."

"Where are you based?" McKinsey asked.

The waiter arrived with their food. Kevin refrained from replying until he left. "Los Angeles is my main office. But we have offices in Washington D.C. and other U.S. locations, as well as a number in the Middle East."

"Do you go overseas often?"

"Too often, or so it seems. It depends on our projects and proposals. Maybe once a month."

"Always to the Middle East?"

"No. It could be anywhere—Asia, Europe, or South America. We don't have much in Africa, except for Egypt."

The conversation did not seem to be going anywhere. McKinsey seemed perfectly normal to Kevin; he couldn't fathom what Kidd's concerns were, or the purpose of the meeting. He decided to try for a more direct approach.

"I think we have some mutual acquaintances in L.A.," he said.

"Who might that be?" McKinsey asked.

"Names are MacLane and Kidd."

"That rings a bell," McKinsey replied. "How do you know them?"

"By accident, I interrupted an attempt to steal U.S. Air Force equipment, namely critical components of a new drone. The gentlemen I just mentioned are following up on this. A Saudi national may have been involved. He's mysteriously disappeared and we think he may have come to the Middle East. The evidence suggests Iran as a willing customer."

"Or Pakistan," McKinsey said. "We suspect a lot of weapons come in to Karachi by sea, and make their way overland through Quetta and into Kandahar in Afghanistan. The Pakistanis could stop this if they wanted to, but they look the other way. I'm not telling you anything you couldn't read in the newspapers. Also, it is known that Pakistan has asked Uncle Sam to give them drones so they can do a better job on the northern borders, and the U.S. said no, meaning, no way!"

"So what's next?" Kevin asked. "Are you going back to Pakistan and then to Afghanistan? I don't suppose there's any way you can get into Iran?"

"No, Iran's out of the question. I'll stay here for a

week or two, rest up. I don't plan to go back to Pakistan. I came close to getting killed there a week ago."

"What happened?"

"I don't know. I went out one night, minding my own business, and two guys in a car drove by and took a couple of pot shots at me. I was lucky they hit my arm and not my head. I didn't go back to my hotel room that night; good thing because it looked like they waited for me there. I got out of Dodge and here I am."

"Who do you think it was?"

"Most likely some goons from the Inter-Services Intelligence, Pakistan's version of the CIA. The ISI, as it's called, is thought to be the largest intelligence agency in the world. Most of the field personnel are ex-military.

"Maybe someone thought you were getting close to something," Kevin said.

"That seems unlikely. My stuff is pretty mundane for the most part. It's in the reports; your friends in L.A. can take a look at them." McKinsey paused.

"There's one thing that's not in the reports, something I only learned recently, when a Chinese vessel came into port. We think the Chinese are working with the Pakistanis to build fighter jets for the Air Force. There may be more. I picked up something that says they may provide the Pakistanis with drones—the Chinese version of the U.S. *Predator.* That may have gotten someone excited. I'm sure they don't want that known.

"You can pass this on to the boys in L.A. They may want to see if there is a Chinese connection, rather than an Iranian connection, with your Saudi guy."

"I will. It's a new angle. I don't know if anyone is thinking about the Chinese. If they are, they've not said anything to me."

"What are your plans for the rest of the day?"

"I've got a meeting this afternoon, and then a dinner tonight. How about you?"

"I'm going back to my room and sleep for about

twenty-four hours. But tomorrow, if you're interested, I could show you around the city, see a few sites."

"Thanks," Kevin said. "I'd like that. What time?"

"What if we meet here at 11 a.m. I'll call your room."

"That sounds good. See you then."

McKinsey pulled out his wallet, but Kevin waved him off.

"I've got lunch, don't worry about it."

"Thanks—in that case, I'll be on my way."

Kevin signaled the waiter and asked for the check, then looked around for McKinsey. He was nowhere to be seen.

ॐ

After a late, and seemingly endless, dinner with his Arab host, Kevin immediately went to bed. It seemed he'd just fallen to sleep when the phone rang. It was Kidd.

"Sorry to interrupt your beauty sleep," he said. "Did you connect with McKinsey?"

"Yes. Did you know he'd been shot? Somebody went after him in Pakistan."

"Yeah, I heard that. He's in Dubai for R&R. How'd he look?"

"He seemed okay. I could tell there was something wrong with his shoulder, but it was covered up. I'm going to meet him tomorrow. He's going to show me around the city."

"Be careful," Kidd said. "The reason I'm calling is we finally had a hit on one of Saleh's credit cards. He booked a flight from London to Dubai, scheduled to arrive yesterday afternoon. It was a one-way ticket. Maybe just a coincidence, but I don't believe in coincidences, so watch your backside."

"Christ," Kevin said. "That incident was almost three years ago. You think he is still interested in me? It makes no sense."

"So far, nothing makes sense," Kidd said. "All we know is that something is going on. Don't get careless."

"Okay, I won't. There was something else McKinsey told me. He said you'd be able to read his reports. He thinks there are arms coming into Karachi, being transshipped to Quetta, and then moved across the border into Afghanistan at Kandahar, with the Pakistanis looking the other way. He said there was one more thing that wasn't in his report—a Chinese connection. He found out the Chinese were working on fighter jets for the Pakistanis. But he thinks there is more. They may be intending to provide them with drones—a Chinese knockoff of a *Predator*. He suggested that you might want to consider a Saudi-China connection."

"Well, isn't that interesting," Kidd said. "A further complication. I don't know if there's anything to it, but I'll check around. Meanwhile get some rest and watch yourself.

"When are you heading home?"

"After tomorrow."

"Mission accomplished?"

"More or less."

"Travel safe. See you one of these days."

In the morning, Kevin got up, had breakfast, and went to a tourist shop next door to the hotel. There he bought a *galabea,* the traditional Arab men's dress, and a *shemagh* headscarf. When McKinsey called, Kevin emerged from the elevator wearing Arabic dress and dark sunglasses. He walked past McKinsey, who was watching the elevator door and failed to recognize him.

He returned and tapped McKinsey on the shoulder.

"Waiting for someone?" he said.

McKinsey looked him over. "Pretty good. A little

fancy if you want to be inconspicuous. You need a cheap one made of cotton, with some dirt and grease stains on it. Also, you need to lose those shoes, get some sandals.

"On second thought, not a good idea. Your feet will be white and clean—they'd stand out. You need to take some brown shoe polish and darken them up so you look like you've been here for all your life. And don't shave for about a week."

Kevin laughed. "This is the best I could do on short notice. I spoke to our friend in L.A. last night. I passed on your message about the Chinese. He said he'd look into it. The main reason he called, however, was because he thinks my Saudi friend may be here in Dubai. He cautioned us to be careful. It may just be a coincidence. But maybe not. You may not want to be seen with me."

"So that's why you went native."

"Yeah—sounds like I didn't do a very good job."

"It's better than walking around in a suit and tie. Let's get out of here. I want to take you for a quick look at the port, lunch, and then see some of the sights. Where we're going, I doubt that we'll run into your Saudi friend. I assume you don't speak Arabic?"

"Sorry, no."

"Not a problem. I'll do the talking."

They got into a taxi outside the hotel. McKinsey said a few words in Arabic and the taxi shot out into the main road. Kevin said nothing, watching the scenery go by.

In the taxi, McKinsey said, "We're going to take Al Khaleej Road southwest towards the port. We'll go through the Al Shindagha tunnel under Dubai Creek then go along the beachfront. Maybe it's not the same as your Southern California beaches, but you should find it interesting."

"Sounds great," Kevin said. "I've heard a lot about Dubai. I appreciate you taking the time to show me around."

"Do you like Middle Eastern food?"

"Yes, although most of my experience has been in

Egypt and Kuwait."

"Here most of the food is either Lebanese or Iranian, since they were the early immigrants. But there are plenty of places where you can get European or Indo-Pakistani dishes. If you're game, we'll have lunch at a place near the beach and have some falafel, kibbeh, baba ghanooj, and fish kebab—all in the Lebanese style."

"Where are we going?" Kevin asked.

"The restaurant is in the Dubai Marina Beach resort. It's a little rundown as a hotel but I like one of the restaurants there, called Al Qasr. It's good for Arabian and Lebanese food. If you go for belly dancing, it's a hotspot after 10 p.m."

The taxi dropped them at the resort and McKinsey asked for a table on the terrace with a view overlooking the gardens and pools.

Kevin studied the menu. "You were right, this place is pretty authentic. You can order lamb brains, lamb heart, or lamb liver, if you want to try something a little different."

After the waiter took their orders, McKinsey said, "If you don't mind, tell me more about this Saudi you're concerned about."

"We think he may be connected to the spy ring that was trying to steal drone components. I was at a meeting with an agent one night in the L.A. airport and somehow was drugged. He and I were kidnapped and taken out to a remote cabin. I survived and escaped, but he was killed. The same guys—at least we think they were connected—also tried to kidnap my wife. Why? That's the sixty-four thousand dollar question. Maybe they thought I still had the drone parts, or knew where they were, but they'd been picked up by the Coast Guard by then."

"Sounds like a real nice guy."

"We don't know for sure. It's all circumstantial at this point. But he definitely skipped town. His rented office is closed, he's gone, no forwarding address. And now he shows up in Dubai? Seems too much to be coincidental."

"When are you flying home?"

"Tomorrow morning."

"Just watch yourself tonight and go directly to the airport in the morning. Use the hotel limo, don't take a taxi."

"One more thing," Kevin said.

"What's that?"

"You startled me when you mentioned belly dancing at this place. My Saudi friend was connected with a belly dancer in Las Vegas. We think she was trading sex for secrets. Just before I left on this trip, I saw her in Las Vegas. The Air Force had her under surveillance and wanted to confirm her identity. As far as I know, by now she's in jail."

After lunch, McKinsey hailed another taxi and had the driver continue along the coast to Jumeira Beach Park. From there they turned left, passed another park, and then turned left again on Sheikh Zayed road, where traffic moved quickly.

"On weekends you see a lot fancy cars driving back to Saudi on this road," McKinsey said. "Wealthy Saudis come down here to spend time with their mistresses or the local hookers. So your Saudi friend may have connections here. "We're going to head back now because I want to show you the old part of town."

As they drove back towards the Creek, Kevin was impressed by two tall buildings.

"Are those the famous Emirate Towers?"

"Yes," McKinsey replied. "The tallest one is the business tower and is over three hundred fifty meters high, as I recall. The shorter one next door is a hotel. If the Emirates wanted to make a statement—they did it with the towers. And so I hear, there's more to come."

They stopped in the old part of the City and visited some *Souks*—open air markets, where you could buy almost anything, from textiles, to produce, spices, gold—even camels.

"This is where you should have bought that *galabea* you're wearing," McKinsey said. "It would have been a lot cheaper here."

They returned to the taxi and drove past the Juma Grand Mosque, with the tallest minaret in the City. It was built in the early 1900s as a school devoted to the study of the *Qur'an.* Later it was demolished, expanded, and rebuilt—several times. The taxi continued into the Bastikia quarter where McKinsey pointed out some of the old wind-tower houses. They were notable for the tall chimney-like structures that provided cooling by natural circulation of air.

"These were built a century ago and were homes of wealthy Persian merchants who came to the Emirates from southern Iran," he explained. "I suppose you've seen lots of cities and tall buildings, so I'm going to take you for a quick look at something you wouldn't expect to find in the desert—a wildlife and water bird sanctuary. Dubai lies in the migration path between Europe and Africa. If we're lucky, you might see some flamingos there. We can also see the Dubai camel race course if you want."

After a short visit to the wildlife sanctuary, McKinsey skipped the camel race course and told the driver to head back to town. The taxi circled, going back towards the Corniche and Kevin's hotel. A little further on the left he saw wharves where trading *dhows* tie up. The traditional boats were still in use, but now had motors instead of sails.

"Interesting contrast, isn't it," Kevin said, "to see these traditional boats reflected in high rise glass curtained towers."

"There is still a strong boating tradition here. On the waterfront we're passing there is an *Abra* station—*Abra* is

Arabic for water taxi. They take passengers across the Creek to the Bur Dubai area." Several boats waited for passengers. They were flat-bottomed, with an overhead awning for shade, and a bench on each side where passengers sat.

McKinsey directed the driver to turn right, heading back to the Corniche. The taxi made its way through a maze of narrow streets thronged with humanity, dressed in both western and traditional Arabic attire. McKinsey had the taxi pull over and stop a block short of the hotel. Kevin wondered, but said nothing. After the taxi departed, McKinsey said, "I thought it would be a good idea to have a look-see before we make our grand entrance. You dawdle here for a bit while I go take a look."

He returned shortly. "There's a car parked in the drive with two men in it and a third standing by the passenger door, watching people enter and leave the hotel. He is well-dressed and appears to be Saudi. The two guys in the car are definitely not tourists. They are bearded and ugly. We're going to go in a side door and make our way into the lobby to a place where you can look out and see if you can identify the guy. If he's the one you're worried about, go to your room, pack your stuff, and use your phone to check out. The hotel has a nice business center, right?"

"Yes, on the second floor."

"Okay, after you check out, go to the business center and wait. I'm going to point out Saleh and have the bellman hand him a note in Arabic from a 'friend' saying that you've left the hotel and gone to the police. I think that will spook him enough that he'll leave in a hurry, in which case I'm going to follow him and see where he goes. If he doesn't leave, I'll come find you and then we'll make a new plan. If I haven't returned in an hour, have the hotel shuttle take you to the airport. Get a taxi at the airport, leave, and check in at the Sheraton Dubai Creek Hotel. It's on Baniyas road, about two miles from the airport. I'll call you there tonight."

From a sheltered point inside the lobby, a quick look confirmed McKinsey's suspicion. Kevin immediately recognized Saleh. He nodded to McKinsey and left to go up to his room. He changed clothes and packed his carry-on bag. That done, he phoned the front desk and checked out, then went downstairs to locate the business center. After more than an hour McKinsey had not returned. Using the stairwell rather than the elevators, Kevin entered the lobby and looked around. Except for one or two people, it was empty. There was no sign of Saleh, the car, or the two men who were with him. Kevin asked the desk clerk for the shuttle to the airport, as suggested. He told the clerk he was going to Kuwait, but his real destination was Frankfurt and then Los Angeles.

From the airport he backtracked to the Sheraton where he got a room for one night and waited for McKinsey to call. He debated about ordering room service so as to not miss the call. As he looked at the room service menu, the phone rang.

"You okay?" McKinsey asked.

"Yes, I'm fine. I was careful, no one followed me. Where are you?"

"Actually, I'm at the airport. Your buddy is flying to Pakistan and I'm tagging along to see who he meets. Pass the word to Kidd when you see him."

"I will, but for Christ's sake is that smart, you going back to Karachi?"

"I'll be careful. From what you said, I expected Saleh to get on a boat and cross over to Iran. Instead he's going to Pakistan. Maybe he's got a Chinese connection after all. I want to see where he goes, then I'm coming home."

"Where is Saleh now?"

"He's down in the first class lounge having a drink. He seems nervous, keeps looking at his watch."

"McKinsey, be careful. That guy's a snake."

"I will. Got to go. They're calling the flight."

When Kevin returned from Dubai, Juliana told him about her meeting with Mr. Wu.

"Yes, I agree, that sounds very strange," Kevin said. "Especially since he didn't bother asking you about your experience or qualifications or even to see a résumé. There could be one explanation for modeling the Taiwan Strait."

"What would that be?" Juliana asked.

"Well, certainly a better understanding of that critical area would be of great interest to the Chinese Navy." One more thing, Julie. I strongly doubt that R&D would approve of you moonlighting in this sensitive area. Wouldn't this be viewed as a conflict of interest?"

SALEH

Fahad Saleh sat in the first class lounge of Pakistan International Airlines drinking mint tea and reflecting on his bad luck of the past three years. In the beginning, it was so promising. In Cairo, one of his Mideast clients had introduced him to a "scientist" very much interested in what the Americans were doing for flight control of their unmanned aerial vehicles.

It had seemed like a simple assignment. The scientist had a friend working for the Americans. He was in a position to steal some important aircraft components. A middle man was needed who could arrange their pickup and safe delivery to a transfer point in the Middle East.

"Why do you need me?" was Saleh's first question.

"There are several complications," the scientist said. "Travel to the U.S. is very difficult for me or any of my colleagues."

Of course, Saleh had already figured out that the "scientist" was Iranian, no doubt working for MOIS, the Ministry of Intelligence and Security, Iran's equivalent of the CIA.

"Then," the scientist added, "there is another complication."

"And what is that?" Saleh asked.

"The parts in question are on an island in the Pacific Ocean, near California."

Saleh was not a sailor, and knew next to nothing about boats. But he'd heard about smuggling operations that took place on the California coast—bringing in drugs, undocumented Mexicans and Central Americans, even Chinese aliens. He could find a solution to the boat problem. He told the scientist he'd think about it.

He returned to his office in California and began developing a plan. After some inquiries and research, he made another trip to Cairo for a second meeting with the scientist, who this time was accompanied by a second man, introduced as his "boss."

Saleh reported that the pickup of the parts was feasible and he could arrange for their delivery in Cairo. It would not be cheap, he added.

The Iranians ignored the question of cost and said that there was another part to the request. The hardware they were seeking was important, but there was also the issue of the control software and operating experience and testing.

At this point, the boss interrupted the conversation. "We need to be assured of your reliability," he said, looking Saleh straight in the eye.

"What you're about to hear must never be repeated"—he paused—"upon pain of death. No, I mean, painful death, if you understand my meaning. So we can part friends and end this meeting now, if you prefer."

"I am accustomed to maintaining client confidentiality," Saleh responded. "I assume you know this or you wouldn't be talking to me."

The boss nodded to the scientist, who continued.

"We also have the good fortune to have one of our scientists working for the American firm Northrop Grumman. He has been there ten years, has an impeccable reputation and excellent qualifications, and now wants to return home and help his homeland to defend against the threats we face from the Zionists and their American lackeys. You'll need to make contact with this man, gain his confidence, and collect the materials he will provide. He will need compensation for the risks he undertakes. You also need to take care of any personal requests he might have, incentives, so to speak. He is not married and lives alone. Although dedicated to his work, we suspect that there are times when he feels lonely. You may be able to help with this."

"Is that all?" Saleh said. He was wondering what

was wrong with these people, hiring him to babysit some introverted—or possibly perverted—Iranian scientist.

"Why doesn't he just grab the stuff, pack up, and leave?" he asked.

"I'm afraid it's not that simple. Security is very intense in the company due to the classified nature of his work. It will take a while for him to extract the information we need without detection. If he were to suddenly disappear, it would raise too much suspicion."

"Is that all?"

"No. There is one more task, but this may be beyond your capabilities, and if so we will understand. In Nevada there is an Air Force facility where UAV flight testing is conducted. We understand that flights in other parts of the world can be controlled from this facility."

"Don't tell me you have an Iranian in the U.S. Air Force?"

"No. That is the problem. We have no contacts there. There are lots of young American airmen there. They are not well paid, yet they live near Las Vegas, with all of its depravity and godlessness. Your task would be to recruit one of these men and obtain the information we need."

"This will take time," Saleh said, "and money."

The Iranian said nothing.

"A lot of money," Saleh said.

A month later Saleh returned to Cairo and presented an outline of his plan. He had a boat crew lined up. It was too risky to land on San Nicolas Island to get the parts, where the Navy maintained tight security. They would have to be transferred to a boat that would drop them on nearby Santa Barbara Island. It was not controlled by the military, and the parts could be inspected and picked up there. As for Northrop Grumman, he had established contact with their man there and was working on building trust and a friendship. He'd also traveled to Nevada and looked into Creech Air Force Base. It was a high-security facility out in the desert. He had a woman friend in Las Vegas who was tasked with "making friends" with some of the airmen.

"A woman?" exploded the scientist. "What have you told her?"

"Please be calm, I haven't told her anything except that I want her to make one of the airmen fall in love with her."

"Fall in love with her? Is that realistic?"

"Oh yes," Saleh replied. "She is very beautiful. The trick will be to find the right person, one who works in flight control."

"She is reliable?"

"She is Egyptian. She will do as I ask."

Next he presented a budget that totaled half a million U.S. dollars, with half paid upfront for expenses, for the boat crew, travel costs, and other items. He gave them wiring instructions for a bank account in the Cayman Islands. The balance of the money was to be paid in three installments, as each item they requested was delivered.

That had been the deal. Very straightforward until the meddlesome American interfered—and interfered, and interfered again.

When Saleh learned that he was in Dubai, it seemed the perfect opportunity to eliminate him once and for all. But somehow he'd slipped away. And now Leila was panicking and wanted money, Rahmin had been discovered, the Americans knew Saleh's identity, and the Iranians were insistent on seeing some results. He'd been able to explain away the failure at Santa Barbara Island— bad luck, the U.S. Coast Guard intercepted the smugglers. He made no mention of Kevin's involvement to the Iranians.

When they wanted their money back, he told them no. Most of it had gone for expenses, he said. He told them he would soon deliver the next package, they should be patient. He said he would reduce the fee at the end.

He held back delivering any of the materials Rahmin had provided, telling them "it was incomplete, he needed more time, he was working on the airman, some good stuff is coming through."

The Iranians became more strident; the threats became more direct and dire, and that made Saleh more determined to hang on to what he had as long as possible, considering it his insurance policy. He knew MOIS's reputation for assassinating dissidents and others who defied the regime.

At the same time he began to develop an intense dislike for the Iranians and their attitude towards him.

Then, out of the blue, he'd made contact with the Chinese. They were everywhere in California. Chinese came by the hundreds, setting up shell businesses or buying into existing ones, overpaying for expensive homes, sending pregnant wives and daughters to the U.S. so the children could be born in local hospitals and declared American citizens.

One thing led to another and now he was on his way to Karachi to meet with his Chinese buyer. The Chinese had agreed to pay a half a million dollars for two remaining items he promised the Iranians. In Karachi, he'd deliver samples. If they were approved, the money would be wired to his account and he would tell them how to pick up the rest of the materials in Los Angeles. He did not plan to return to California, and the Middle East was too close to Iran. His plan was to retire in Brazil. Too bad about Leila—but she could fend for herself. She was a survivor, he thought, as he walked down the corridor to board his flight to Karachi.

When McKinsey boarded the aircraft, he passed Saleh seated in first class. He was reading some notes scribbled in a small notebook, and did not look up as McKinsey passed in the throng of economy class passengers.

When the plane landed, McKinsey hurried to get through customs so he could catch up with Saleh and failed to notice an officer off to the side who paid him special attention as he went through immigration. He was photographed by a hidden camera as he passed the passport station.

Outside, in the arrival zone, he emerged just in time to see Saleh get into a Karachi Marriot shuttle. McKinsey got in a long line waiting for taxis. Twenty minutes later he was on his way to the Marriott hotel.

When McKinsey checked in, Saleh was nowhere to be seen. The desk clerk spoke poor English and either did not understand McKinsey when he asked if "my boss, Mr. Saleh has checked in," or possibly Saleh checked in under a different name. Karachi was an hour ahead of Dubai, it was late, and he was tired. He went to bed.

In the morning he went to the coffee shop, had breakfast, read several newspapers, and waited for Saleh to show. Being so focused on watching for Saleh and trying to appear inconspicuous, he failed to note a well-dressed Pakistani watching him. After an hour, the man left, but was replaced by a woman. Another hour passed and she left, as another nicely dressed man came in and took a seat where he could watch McKinsey.

A little before noon McKinsey saw an Asian businessman approach the desk and speak to the clerk. A few minutes later Saleh emerged from the elevator carrying a briefcase and escorted the Chinese gentleman into the restaurant. They ordered tea but no food. McKinsey loitered outside the restaurant, studying a menu. He was tempted to enter and order lunch, but it would have been too obvious. All he could tell, from where he stood, was that Saleh and the Chinese were discussing something in low tones.

McKinsey realized that he could not stand there and

study the menu any longer, so he gave it back to the hostess and went into the lobby where he could see anyone entering or leaving the restaurant.

After half an hour he saw the Chinese leaving with Saleh's briefcase. A few minutes later, Saleh went outside and departed in a taxi. McKinsey thought about following him, but decided that would be too obvious. Instead, he went to his room and placed a call to Kidd. He told him what he'd seen.

"What else do you want me to do?" he asked.

"Come home," Kidd replied. "I think you're in over your head there. A lot has happened here and we're about to shut down your friend's operation. Don't get in the middle of something."

McKinsey's feelings were hurt, but he said nothing about that.

"Okay chief, you've got it," he replied. "I'll fly out of here in the morning and see you in a couple of days."

Saleh completed his visit to a bank and returned to the hotel. Entering the lobby he saw two men at the desk speaking Farsi. He heard his name mentioned. He quickly ducked out of the hotel and went to a nearby café where he could watch the front entrance. After while the two Iranians came out and got in a car that held two other men. It took off in the direction of the airport.

Saleh returned to the hotel and asked the desk clerk if there were any messages.

"No, but two men were here earlier asking about you. They said that there was a problem with your flight and they were bringing you a replacement ticket."

"Thank you," Saleh said. "In that case I need to check out now. I'll have to meet them."

"Mr. Saleh, they said they'd return here this evening."

"I'm sure they would, but I hate to be a bother. I'll go see them at the office," he lied.

In the elevator, Saleh quickly reviewed his options. He had the Chinese initial payment. He could arrange a transfer by remote control from wherever he was. Flying to Brazil, or anywhere for that matter, did not seem like a good option at the moment. He needed time to make proper arrangements and get visas and at this point he did not think he had the time. As much as he hated to do it, he decided he would have to implement "Plan B," which was to travel by land. He would go to Quetta, and then cross over into Afghanistan. He had Saudi contacts in Kandahar. They were supporting a leader from Saudi Arabia whose mission was to drive the foreign devils from Afghanistan. Saleh would offer his services to find financial support for this man, who went by the name of Osama bin Laden.

McKinsey decided that for his last night in Pakistan he'd leave the hotel and find a traditional restaurant. He'd walked several blocks from the hotel when a taxi pulled up alongside. The driver rolled down the passenger side window.

"You need taxi, Mister?"

"No, I'm not going far, I'll walk. "

"You want beautiful girl, Mister?"

"No thanks."

McKinsey turned to go, unaware that two men had suddenly appeared behind him. Before he could do or say anything, one of the men hit him in the head with a piece of pipe. All went black. McKinsey did not feel himself being tossed in the back of the taxi.

Saleh left the hotel in a hurry, making certain he wasn't followed. He took a taxi to the train station, where he mingled with the teeming humanity sweltering inside the crowded station. There he boarded a rattletrap Pakistani train northwest to Quetta. He dumped his Western clothes and changed to traditional Arab dress. In Quetta he bribed his way onto a truck that was part of a convoy carrying supplies into Kandahar. They were destined for al Qaeda factions operating in the border area. It was there that Saleh hoped to meet bin Laden.

When McKinsey failed to return, and all contact with him was lost, the U.S. State Department made an official request for assistance to the Pakistani authorities. About two weeks later Kidd received a copy of a police report. McKinsey's body had been fished from a river. A mark on his head indicated he'd stumbled and fallen. Death was by drowning. The medical report indicated that he was intoxicated at the time.

Bin Laden refused to meet with Saleh. Many people came to see him, offering to help. He was only interested in fighters. Bin Laden did not value Saleh's fund-raising capabilities. "I have more money now than he can ever raise," was his comment.

It was quickly established that Saleh had no stomach for the hardships experienced by the Mujahideen. He languished in a small village near the border, where he tried to set up some smuggling ventures, but ended up being cheated by his Pakistani suppliers and then again by his Afghanistani customers, who always found some fault with the goods he shipped them.

THE UNTHINKABLE HAPPENED

In the United States' 2000 election, the Republicans recaptured the presidency. Former president Bill Clinton was ineligible to run again and the Democrats were damaged by the Clinton sex scandal. In a close race, Al Gore won the popular vote but a Supreme Court decision preventing a recount of Florida votes handed the election to George W. Bush. The Court's decision was widely condemned and damaged its reputation. It also set the stage for more than ten years of wars at a cost of billions of dollars and thousands of lives lost.

Within days after his inauguration in January 2001, President Bush met with his top security advisors to discuss a range of topics considered to be of concern to the U.S. Near the top of the list was the on-going conflict between Israel and Palestine. The decision was made to stay clear of it. Next, the discussion turned to Iraq. Bush had a strange fascination with Saddam Hussein. When the first Gulf War ended in 1991 with Saddam still in office, some critics accused Bush's father of "leaving the job unfinished." Whether this had any bearing on the younger Bush's subsequent actions has not been established.

In discussions with his advisors, Bush wanted to know if Saddam Hussein could be removed from office, in effect to "send a message" to North Korea and other small rogue nations that the U.S. was not going to stand by while they developed weapons of mass destruction. The consensus was that something could be done and Bush's directive was, "Find me a way to get this done."

In the months following his initial meeting with Juliana,

Mr. Wu subtly tried to build his friendship with her. He was unfailingly proper and polite, never pushy. He called from time to time, sometimes inviting her to lunch, other times offering her tickets to the theater or a Dodgers' baseball game. In his low-keyed way he learned when her birthday was and had an extravagant bouquet of flowers delivered to her office. For a while, he made no further mention of his interest in hiring her. Then, one day as she was leaving the office after work, she found him waiting outside for her. He asked if she had a few minutes to stop by his office, he had something to show her. The "something" was a formal employment contract that he wanted her to sign. When she demurred, his mood changed abruptly and he became insistent, telling her that she should consider the offer carefully and not miss an important opportunity to advance her career.

When she told Kevin about the incident, he downplayed it, remarking that he was not surprised that Wu was pushy and used to getting his way.

"Julie, you don't want to work for him. He sounds like a jerk. Just ignore him," was his advice.

Juliana did not sleep well. Thinking about Wu's reaction disturbed her. He had revealed another side to his personality that seemed so out of character it bothered her.

Kevin left early one Monday morning in September to fly to Chicago on business. Once he was out of the house Juliana decided to call Charles Kidd and ask his advice. He returned her call a few minutes after she left a message.

"Mrs. Hunter, good morning. No problems I hope."

"Thank you for returning my call. It's probably nothing, but I have this sense that something is not right. There's nothing I can point to specifically, but I'm bothered."

Juliana told Kidd about meeting Wu at the conference, his persistence in meeting with her, and his effort to recruit her.

"It could be nothing," Kidd said. "However, I agree

it sounds a little strange. He should know that by accepting his offer you could have a conflict of interest that would cost you your job. Let me make a few inquiries and I'll get back to you."

♋

Kevin's flight had been delayed and when he arrived in Chicago he was tired. He went directly to his hotel on East Wacker Street, a few blocks from where he'd be meeting in the morning. After checking in he called home. Juliana answered.

"Hi sweetheart, I'm just checking in to let you know I made it to Chicago."

"How was the flight?" she asked.

"Late, also crowded as usual. Otherwise okay. How are you? No mysterious phone calls or strange visitors?"

"No. All is well here. I'm just missing you."

"I'm missing you too."

"Hurry home then."

"I'll do my best. Love you lots. Gotta go now."

"Kevin, you're always in a hurry to hang up...."

"Sorry, I don't mean to be."

"I know, you've got stuff to do, things to get ready for tomorrow. Anyway, I love you too. Bye for now."

Kevin hung up. Afterwards, he realized he should have asked Juliana about her day. He knew she was nervous about a big project she was working on. He had time; he'd done all his preparations on the flight and was ready for the meeting.

He picked up the phone again and thought about calling her back, but instead dialed room service. He ordered a sandwich and a beer and watched the news for half an hour and then went to bed.

The next morning Kevin walked to the meeting of the corporate officers, enjoying the cool morning air along the Chicago riverfront. He entered the building and took the elevator to the sixth floor. As he walked into the office, he ran into Frank Walker and Ray Holder, two other executives.

Frank pointed to an adjoining room. "Coffee is in there."

"Good," Kevin replied. "That's what I need." He poured himself a cup and rejoined Frank and Ray.

"When did you arrive?"

"I've been here a few days," Frank said. "We're working on a big proposal for the Department of Transportation. How about you?"

"I came in last night from L.A. Every seat on the plane was full. Fortunately, I had an aisle seat; unfortunately, the middle seat was occupied by a five-year-old kid who couldn't sit still."

"I came from Washington," Ray said. "Meetings at the Pentagon on the PENREN project. We were discussing the renovation of Wedge 2, the next phase of the renovation. I was lucky; the plane was only half full."

"How is it going?" Frank asked Ray.

"As well as can be expected. The building is almost sixty years old, and DOD keeps changing requirements. It took sixteen months to build the Pentagon in 1944; it's probably going to take sixteen years to renovate it."

The conference room door swung open and the CEO, Bob Fishman stood there. He waved them into the room. "Come on in guys, it's 7:30, time to get started." Bob—known to the troops as "Big Bob," was heavyset, 300 pounds, 6 feet tall, ruddy faced. As Kevin, Frank, and Ray entered the room, they saw that Tom Jordan, the chief financial officer, was already seated, along with Robyn Grant, general counsel. Tom had a pile of computer printouts on the table in front of him. He looked up, but did not say anything nor did he smile. Kevin had never seen him smile, even when the financial numbers were very positive. Bob started talking as they took their seats.

"We've got a lot to do. Fiscal 2000 is over, dead

and gone. All that is left is for the accountants to wrap it up. We've got to plan for the new fiscal year. You've all submitted your plans; now we want to see how realistic you think they are, see what other new ideas you may have since the plans were submitted last July."

"Frank, let's start with you. How are we doing with DOT? The new transportation bill, it still hasn't passed. We need that, you know. What's going on with our lobbyist, that dip-shit woman? Is she really any good? She's a blonde, so that makes her suspect right from the start."

"Say what you want," Frank said. "She gets the job done. She's smart and capable."

"If you say so. Keep me posted on how that goes. By the way, did you see that article in *Engineering News Record* about the projected costs of repairing all the bridges in the fricking country? Billions of bucks to do the job."

"No," Frank said. "When did it come out?"

"You know how it goes; Congress probably won't appropriate any money until a bridge collapses somewhere. Just a minute, I'll get the article for you."

Bob walked out of the conference room. He was gone for about ten minutes. There were four clocks on the conference room wall. One showed Pacific time, one Rocky Mountain time, one Central time, one East Coast time. Central time was 8 a.m.

Ray looked at the clocks and said "What the hell happened to him? How long does it take to get a magazine?"

"Have you ever seen his desk?" Frank said. "He's probably forgotten which pile it's in."

At that moment Bob rushed back into the room.

"Hey guys, some asshole just flew a small plane into the World Trade Center. I've got a TV in my office, come take a look."

The group quickly exited the conference room and crowded around a small TV in Bob's office. CNN was showing the top of the North Tower of the World Trade

Center. A long plume of gray black smoke trailed from the building. The announcer was saying that the initial report of a small plane was incorrect and it was a commercial jet that had hit the building.

As the group looked on in shock, a newsflash interrupted the broadcast with a report that a second jet had struck the South Tower. It was 8:03 a.m. in Chicago, 9:03 a.m. in New York. The news went on to say that President George W. Bush, visiting an elementary school in Florida, was advised of the incident. Two Air National Guard F-15 fighter jets had been scrambled from Otis Air National Guard base to intercept any other planes headed to New York or possibly to the Capitol. The New York fire and police departments were rolling to the World Trade Center.

After watching for a while, Bob looked at his watch. "Jesus Christ," he said, "what the hell is happening? It's already 8:20. We can't do anything about whatever it is, so let's finish the meeting." After asking his secretary to keep an eye on the TV, he led everyone back into the conference room.

"Frank, tell us what you've got."

Frank pulled out his laptop and set it on the conference room table.

"Where do I plug this thing in?" he asked.

"There, under the table." Frank got down on his hands and knees to plug in the power cord. Kevin looked at the clock on the wall. It now read 8:40 a.m.

Frank resumed his seat at the table and turned on his computer, began fiddling with the mouse.

Bob's secretary came back into the room. "Another plane," she said. "It just hit the Pentagon. And people are jumping out of the World Trade Center windows. They think another plane has been hijacked and is headed to Washington D.C."

"Jesus," Bob said. "What about our guys? We've got sixty or eighty guys working in the Pentagon."

All thoughts of the business meeting, budgets,

annual plans, and marketing were forgotten. The group stood silent, listening as the news came in. Vice President Cheney entered an underground tunnel leading to a security bunker. The FAA directed all commercial flights to land immediately. International flights not yet in U.S. territory were told to turn around and go elsewhere. The White House and the Capitol were evacuated. President Bush was soon aloft in Air Force One, destination not disclosed. A minute before 10:00 A.M., New York time, the south tower collapsed. It appeared to fold into itself, in a slow avalanche of gray smoke, dust and structural materials. CNN announced that the Sears Tower in Chicago had been evacuated. A few minutes after 9:00 a.m. Chicago time word came that the fourth hijacked plane had crashed in a field in Pennsylvania. Apparently the passengers revolted and prevented the plane from reaching Washington. The dead included the crew of seven, the four hijackers, and thirty-three brave passengers who sacrificed their lives.

What is going on? Kevin thought. *This is worse than Pearl Harbor. We are in a goddamn war, but we don't know who to fight.*

Bob had the TV moved into the conference room and the group listened to the news updates and watched the horrifying images on the television. With the collapse of the WTC North Tower, it became known that hundreds of New York Fire Department personnel, police, and emergency medical technicians trying to fight fires and rescue people were in the building when it collapsed and most likely did not survive.

At noon, Bob had sandwiches brought into the conference room. No one felt like eating. The news seemed to go from bad to worse. At the Pentagon, fire crews were fighting fires. President Bush put the U.S. military on high alert on a global basis. The first suggestions that this attack was due to the Taliban or al Qaeda were broadcast.

After lunch the attendees began to make plans to return to their respective offices. Kevin, Frank, and Ray needed to go to Los Angeles. Kevin urged them to rent a car and drive. Ray claimed to have a special phone number for United Airlines and thought they could fly out in the morning. They decided to return to the hotel and meet for breakfast the next morning.

As soon as he reached the hotel, Kevin called home.

"Julie, it's me. I'm sure you've seen the news. Are you okay? What is happening there? What are you hearing?"

"Oh Kevin, it is terrible. All those poor people. Who could be responsible for something like this?"

"I don't know, but I'm sure we'll find out. We were just starting our meeting in Chicago and there was a little TV in Bob's office. He heard the first news flash and we came in to watch it and then saw the second plane hit. A half hour or so later we heard about the Pentagon and that was the end of the meeting. What about you?"

"I got up early and was making coffee. I had the radio on, not paying much attention, when the local news was interrupted with word of the first plane crash. Like everyone else, I was in shock when the second tower was hit, and then the Pentagon. I didn't know what else to do so I went to the office. Nothing much was accomplished; we just sat around dumbfounded by what was taking place. When I got home I stayed up half the night watching the television. Those images—so terrible. I'll never forget them.

"When can you come home? I'm worried about you. There are rumors Chicago might be attacked."

"We'll get out of here as soon as we can get a flight. Right now it looks like we're stuck here a few days."

"I heard on the news that the Los Angeles Airport is closed, and so is San Francisco," she said. "Planes are grounded. People everywhere are on edge. You should rent a car and get out of there."

In the morning at breakfast, Ray confessed to having no luck. United Airlines lost two planes to the hijackers. All flights were canceled. Frank reported there was an Amtrak train they could take, but no one wanted to do that. Kevin said that now there were no rental cars anywhere in Chicago—there'd been a huge exodus during the evening as other stranded passengers realized they were stuck.

There was nothing to do but stay in the hotel and try to conduct business by phone and fax. Ray said he would keep trying with United Airlines.

On the third day it became apparent that they were not going to get a flight. By then, people who had planned to fly to Chicago were driving in and rental cars became available. They rented a car and started driving west. By the time they reached Denver, United announced it would be flying again in the morning. They boarded a flight for Los Angeles at 8 a.m. After the plane took off, the pilot spoke to the passengers.

"If there's any funny stuff on this plane, I'll turn it upside down. Anyone out of their seats will experience serious injuries. Stay seated with your seatbelt on until we land. If you think this is a joke, think again. I'm not kidding. This baby will fly fine upside down."

Kevin went straight home from the airport to wait for Juliana to come home from work. He met her at the door when he heard her car drive up. She had two bags of groceries.

Kevin hugged her, groceries and all, and kissed her.

"You're back and okay," she said. "I'm so glad. How was the drive across country?"

"A little crazy with those two guys. We took turns driving, but it took a day and a night to get to Denver. We drove fast and got pulled over at night somewhere in the middle of Nebraska, but the cop let us off."

"Tell me all about it, but first let me put these things

in the kitchen."

While Juliana put the perishables in the refrigerator, Kevin poured two glasses of wine. They sat down in the living room.

"So you drove from Chicago to Denver?"

"Yes, Ray finally conceded we weren't going to get a flight anytime soon."

"You should have rented a car immediately."

"I know; I wanted to, but Ray kept thinking he could get us on a flight. You want to know something else ironic? Frank wanted to take a train. He checked into it, but we didn't want to get stuck on a train. The next day we heard the train had derailed somewhere—how was that for luck?"

"I'm still in shock over the attack. You have to wonder what could prompt anyone to commit suicide and take so many innocent people with him. Surely they had to know that they wouldn't just kill Americans."

"There were Muslims, Jews, Hindus, and other religions among the victims, as well as Arabs, and Asians. *Many* nationalities. It was more than an attack on America—it was an attack on the world."

ço

The U.S. lost no time in going after the terrorists. Within days the first Special Forces operatives were in Afghanistan and Pakistan, seeking out the training camps and the bases of the Taliban fighters and their al Qaeda operatives. Less than one month after the attack, the U.S. launched operation "Enduring Freedom" to drive the Taliban from power due to their support for al Qaeda.

Later, Osama bin Laden took credit for the attack, saying that he ordered the September 11 attacks because of injustices against the Lebanese and Palestinians committed by Israel and the United States.

He was rumored to be hiding in a cave in

Afghanistan, but initial efforts to locate and capture him were futile.

Meanwhile, U. S. forces under the leadership of General Tommy Franks continued to put pressure on the Taliban, driving them from Kabul and clearing other major cities. The remaining fighters retreated to small villages along the border with Pakistan where they went into hiding. Osama bin Laden was reported to be hiding in some remote caves at a place called Tora Bora.

With the Taliban supposedly on the run, Bush continued his secret planning to depose Saddam Hussein. General Franks was ordered to begin developing a plan to attack Iraq, stop Iraq's production of chemical and other weapons, and drive Saddam from power.

Military focus then shifted to Iraq, which had not attacked the U.S, while the job of rounding up Osama bin Laden, who *had* attacked the U.S., was left to the Afghanistan and Pakistani forces that were sympathetic to him.

Kidd called Juliana at her office.

"I hope you don't mind me calling you here. I didn't want to call the house and have your old man answer the phone. Here's what I learned about your Mr. Wu.

"In its infinite wisdom, the U.S. government encourages foreigners to make investments in United States businesses. This is called the EB-5 program. You can either create a new business, or purchase an existing business, or expand an existing business. The key is to create at least ten full-time jobs and make an investment of one million dollars in the business."

Kidd went on to explain that the government looks for individuals with extraordinary ability, professional experience, and multinational service as an executive. Applications are made to the U.S. Citizenship and

Immigration Services agency. If you qualify, this is a fast way to get a U.S. green card and, eventually, citizenship. Lots of Chinese have taken advantage of this program. They put their kids in U.S. schools. If their wives get pregnant and their kids are born here, they automatically become U.S. citizens.

"You found out that Wu is part of this program? So he's legitimate?" Juliana asked.

"Wu, full name Jin Wu, is a Chinese investor who bought Internet Innovations Inc., a software business in Santa Monica. He has been expanding the staff at the company. He also bought a home in Santa Monica," Kidd said.

"We know that many of the EB-5 participants are legitimate. They want to invest their money where they think it will be safe from expropriation by their government. Others are here at the request of their government. Their purpose is to establish what appears to be a legitimate business, but then use it as a front to acquire U.S. trade secrets, proprietary technology, or classified information."

"You're saying that he might not be legitimate. How would I know if he's spying?"

"There are several methods. The easiest ways to get information is under the guise of a price quote or purchase request, or by collecting marketing information. More sophisticated attempts involve agents trying to land a job in the target contractor's organization so they can steal information firsthand. An alternative is to establish relationships with critical employees and possibly compromise them so they can be coerced into giving up secrets. China is suspected as one of the key players these days.

"These type of cases fall under the Department of Justice with the Federal Bureau of Investigation responsible for determining if a crime has occurred. According to my contacts, Mr. Wu has been very careful, but he's done something that brought him to the attention of the Justice Department. I think you should discuss this with Kevin—but don't say I said so."

❧

In the months following 9/11, the U.S. news media began building a case for Iraq as an international rogue nation.

One day, Kidd called Kevin and invited him to lunch. They met at the Pacific Dining Car. Kidd was there waiting, sipping a scotch on the rocks.

"I'm buying," he said. "What will you have?"

Kevin hesitated. "Oh, what the hell. I can coast this afternoon—no deadlines. I'll have what you're having."

Kidd waved the waiter over and placed the order.

"I haven't talked to you in a while, so I thought I'd give you a call, catch up. Any trips planned?"

"Not at the moment. Since 9/11 I've been staying away from airplanes."

"That was a godawful mess, wasn't it? One of your projects got hit, I recall."

"Yes, they hit the part of the Pentagon we'd just renovated. It was strengthened and we hadn't moved all the tenants back in, otherwise the loss of life would have been much greater. As it was, one hundred twenty-five people died, many more injured. Now we have a new project—the *Phoenix Project*—to repair the damage within one year from 9/11.

When the waiter returned with Kevin's drink, Kidd ordered a steak sandwich.

"You need more time?" he asked Kevin.

"No, I'll have the veal marsala."

After the waiter left, Kevin raised his glass and toasted Kidd. "What have you been working on?"

"A lot of paperwork," Kidd said. "Analysis reports, studies, hypotheses, frankly, a lot of crap. Stuff for Conde, if you know who I mean."

"I know. She went to school across the bay from Berkeley. So is it good stuff?"

"As I said, it's a lot of crap. They're trying to build a case to take out Saddam, but there's nothing there. Buying uranium, getting steel pipes, it's all hearsay."

"So, you're saying there's nothing to it, no weapons of mass destruction, nothing like we read about in the papers or hear on Fox News?"

"That's right. That's the way it looks," replied Kidd.

"Jesus. That's a hell of a note. You know, I'm not surprised. When I read the accounts in the paper, they always seem to be hedging. It's always third-hand reports. Nobody has produced a smoking gun yet."

"Well, if Bush gets his way there will be plenty of smoking guns. You know the other thing that gets me?" Kidd continued. "There's no end game. We get rid of Saddam, then what? The Iraqis are going to love us? I don't think so. Americans do not understand that many Arabs view us as greedy and selfish, intent on imposing our decadent values and secularism on their world. Our politicians seem to think that if we go busting into Iraq, we'll be welcomed with open arms. Dream on. It sure as shit isn't going to happen."

"What are you going to do?"

"I don't know. Maybe it's time to retire, move on." Kidd paused, reflecting for a moment. "You know what's really sick?"

"I can think of lots of things, but tell me," Kevin said.

"We're screwing around with this stuff, trying to make something out of nothing. But what were we and the Feds doing before 9/11? We should have picked up on something, these foreigners coming in here to get pilots' licenses. For aliens to attend flight school here it would seem to be a domestic matter, wouldn't it? So why didn't someone pick up on this, especially since these guys were only interested in learning to *fly* and never spent any time learning to *land*. Don't you think that would be a clue to somebody that something was out of kilter? How could we let that happen?"

"Yeah, that seems inexcusable. I heard that they were mostly Saudis, citizens of our staunch ally in Saudi Arabia."

"Correct. But there were also two from the United Arab Emirates, a Lebanese, and an Egyptian, a veritable United Nations of assholes."

"There is another thing I wanted to ask you," Kevin said. "What about the Egyptian woman?"

"What about her? After she was arrested, she was tried for espionage and has been sentenced to five years in Carswell Federal Prison at Fort Worth, Texas. That's an all-woman prison with some bad actors. One of those Manson women is serving a long term there, and there's a woman who spied for Cuba, and a couple of others on death row. So our Egyptian friend is in good company."

"And what about the guy at Northrop Grumman?"

"I never told you? He was interviewed by Northrop Grumman security and must have panicked, because he committed suicide. Between him and Saleh they left enough tracks that we were able to penetrate what remained of Saleh's Los Angeles organization and recovered the stolen materials before they were handed over to the Chinese. Unfortunately, the identity of Saleh's Chinese contact is unknown. It is believed to be someone living in the West Los Angeles area. The FBI is working on uncovering the Chinese connection."

"Anything more on Beske? Anyway to tie Leila to him?"

"Nope. The consensus is that Saleh was the mastermind. The Air Force could not tie Leila definitively to Saleh, although it seems there was a connection. At this point, he's disappeared but remains the prime suspect. We'll get him eventually; something will turn up. What about you?" Kidd asked.

"Besides the Pentagon project, we're sending a lot of people to Kuwait. I get the feeling something big is going to break loose there before long."

Kidd pushed his plate aside and looked at his watch. "I've got to get back to the office. Good to talk to you. Let me know if you're planning any trips."

"One more thing," Kevin said. "I was at a meeting a while back and some guy heard that I worked on the Pentagon. He came up to me afterwards and asked if I thought it really happened. I asked him what he meant. He said, 'You know, the plane crash. Did that really happen?' I said, 'Yes of course, how could you imagine anything else? Don't you watch TV?' So he says, 'Yeah, I saw it on TV and it looked real to me, but there's this website on the internet that says DOD faked it because they wanted an excuse to invade Afghanistan and Iraq.' I was speechless. I really didn't know what to say. Finally, I told him that it was real, real people died, and anyone who would say it was a fake was a traitor and should go to jail. Then I walked away before I said something really nasty."

"Yeah, I know," Kidd said. "There are kooks that claim NASA faked the moon landing. How stupid can you be? Listen, I've got to go. Don't pay attention to idiots, including the one in the Oval Office."

"Thanks for lunch. I'll let you know, but I'm planning to stay close to home for a while."

In 2002, Kevin and other members of the PENREN project were invited to the dedication of the rebuilt Wedge 1. The ceremony took place on September 11, exactly one year after the terrorist attack. The building had been completely rebuilt and the occupants moved back in. A huge American flag was draped on the side of the building behind the outdoor stage. The Secretary of Defense and other dignitaries spoke and President Bush dedicated the facility.

Kevin was amazed at the security. Portable missile launchers were on the roof of the Pentagon. Tanks and armored vehicles patrolled nearby streets. Snipers were positioned on nearby rooftops, keeping an eye on things.

It was a moving, impressive ceremony that he would never forget.

That same year, the U.S began expanding Camp Doha in Kuwait, and building a coalition of forces to take on Iraq. In 2003, the U.S.-led coalition forces attacked Iraq to put an end to the "weapons of mass destruction" Saddam was assembling. The Iraqi forces were no match for the U.S.–British ground troops supported by massive air attacks and naval cruise missiles. The Iraqi forces were slaughtered and the war became a rout. Baghdad was taken and Saddam fled, later to be captured while hiding in a hole in the ground.

Teams of experts roamed the country, looking for the "weapons of mass destruction" that had led to the war in the first place. None were found. The entire premise of the war was found to be false. Iraq posed no threat to the U.S.

Meanwhile, Osama bin Laden, the man who had attacked the U.S., the most wanted man on earth, disappeared. From various hiding places he managed to issue periodic videos to prove he was still alive and to taunt his enemies. By this means he encouraged further suicide attacks against the Western nations who were "attacking Islam."

Following the September 11, 2001, attacks on the Pentagon and the World Trade Center, the Department of Defense expanded development and production of drones. One development was to modify the *Predator* drone by removing its camera array and replacing it with a multispectral targeting system and two Hellfire missiles, making drones deadly combat vehicles. In 2002, a *Predator* was used in Yemen to fire a Hellfire missile into a car. The vehicle was carrying Qaed Salim Sinan al-Harethi, the al Qaeda leader who masterminded the October 2000 attack on the *USS Cole*, in which seventeen U.S. sailors died and thirty-nine were injured.

Terrorists who had until this time used the ubiquitous cell phone with impunity to coordinate attacks, now faced a new danger. They could be tracked and targeted by a UAV that struck suddenly with deadly accuracy and no warning.

Saleh was desperate to leave Afghanistan, but through his contacts, he learned that Rahmin was dead and Leila was in jail. The whole scheme in Los Angeles had come unraveled and he was a wanted man. Even worse, the Iranians had learned of his double dealings with the Chinese and had issued a *fatwā* with a reward for his capture or proof of his death.

Saleh resigned himself to remaining where he was until things settled down. He felt safe in the village because the presence of al Qaeda fighters kept outsiders away. Life continued in this uncertain state until one afternoon, as he walked in the village past one of the houses occupied by al Qaeda, he heard an unusual buzzing sound. A few seconds later a Hellfire missile slammed into the house and exploded, killing him and the occupants of the house. The missile had been fired from a *Predator* UAV high overhead, that was controlled by a twenty-six-year-old airman based at Creech Air Force Base, halfway around the world.

With this and other demonstrations of the versatility and usefulness of UAVs, the Department of Defense launched a research and development program to expand them. Besides the MQ-1 *Predator* and the MQ-9 *Reaper*, UAVs with wing spans from four and a half feet to one hundred sixteen feet were developed. The RQ-11B *Raven* was a small, back-packable system that could be used by ground troops. At the other extreme, the RQ-4A *Global Hawk* built by Northrop Grumman had a range of over eight thousand miles at an altitude of sixty thousand feet and could remain airborne for up to thirty-two hours. The RQ-170 *Sentinel*, a "flying wing" type UAV developed by Lockheed Martin, was also known to exist.

A CHINA CONNECTION

Not surprisingly, the 9/11 attack heightened everyone's concern about terrorist activity. How could these foreigners come into the country, take flying lessons, and not raise some official questions? It was inevitable that concerns would grow, not only about embedded terrorists, but espionage as well. Juliana was beginning to wonder about Mr. Wu. She decided to ask Kevin for his opinion.

"Wu won't leave me alone. He was nice at first, but lately he keeps pestering me about coming to work for him. He got angry when I put him off. He's always asking questions about R&D's research programs. I think he's up to something. What should I do?"

"Let me talk to our security officer. He's the one we're supposed to report to if we're contacted by foreign nationals. He'll probably suggest that you contact the FBI."

As Kevin predicted, a meeting with the FBI was recommended, with the result that Juliana agreed to assist with the investigation of Wu. Agent Bob Fiske was assigned as her contact. She was given a small voice activated recording device that fit in a side pocket of the purse that hung by a strap from her shoulder. She practiced using it by recording conversations with Kevin at home, standing, sitting the purse on a table, and in other positions. Kevin was not happy with this plan.

"Julie, I worry about you meeting with this guy. Are you sure you want to do this?"

"Agent Fiske thinks it's the only way to find out if Wu is what he claims to be. The FBI hasn't said anything negative about him to me, but I have a feeling that they were already looking into his activities."

"Okay, but if you get even a hint of any danger, any suggestion of a threat, you need to quit and let the FBI deal with him."

"I will. You and I have had enough intrigue to last us for two lifetimes. But it really bothers me that foreigners can come into our country, enjoy our freedoms, and then take advantage. Fiske says they will be keeping an eye on him. I'm supposed to call if anything unusual happens."

Juliana called Wu and told him that she was interested in his offer, but first wanted to know more about what he expected. They met in his office. He requested that, as a first task, she prepare a one-hour seminar on key issues of modeling deep sea currents for presentation to his staff. Following that, she would meet periodically with his research team to review and critique the progress they were making. When she concurred, he gave her an employment agreement and had her sign it.

After meeting with Wu, Juliana turned the recording of the meeting and the contract over to Agent Fiske. He set up a meeting with the head of security at R&D and explained what Juliana would be doing. She was provided with a dossier of research findings marked "Confidential" to be used in preparing notes for the seminar. All of the information in the dossier was unclassified and in the public domain, while certain lesser known results and data were falsified. They would serve as "markers" if the information subsequently appeared in Chinese literature.

Wu was full of praise for her after she gave the seminar. She had a folder that contained her notes and the "classified" document. She left the folder in plain sight on her desk when she went to the rest room. She took her time, and when she returned she could tell that the document had been moved and probably copied.

During the next six months Juliana continued to provide "data" to Wu and to accept payments from him. The checks were deposited in a special bank account set up in her name by the FBI. Over time, Wu's requests became more specific. It became clear that he wanted to know the scope of R&D's classified underwater vehicle research program.

At first, Juliana balked at these requests and he began applying pressure, subtly threatening her. She pretended to give in and promised to get him "good stuff." To make it more convincing, she asked for more money because of the risks she was taking. Wu told her that he would consider her request if the information was good enough.

At some point, Wu became suspicious that she was leading him on and, worse yet, might be an informant.

Late one Friday afternoon, Wu called Juliana.

"Mrs. Hunter, are you free to come to a meeting tomorrow afternoon at my office?"

"Mr. Wu, it's Saturday, and I have plans." In reality, she had no special plans. Kevin was away traveling and she was apprehensive because she was alone.

"I'm sorry to trouble you, but it's very important. My boss in China will be here and he is anxious to meet you. You must change your plans. It will be a short meeting, no more than an hour, but I really need you to be there."

"What time is the meeting?"

"Be here at 5 o'clock."

Juliana hesitated, but ultimately agreed. She had never been to the office on Saturday. Meeting at that late hour was very unusual. After hours the building would likely be deserted.

The call from Wu was disturbing. He seemed tense. He spoke abruptly, not his usual diplomatic self. The time of the meeting was a total departure from practice. Wu was very methodical; he always followed a rigid schedule.

Juliana called agent Fiske at his FBI office. She explained that Wu asked her to come to the office on a Saturday for a "special" meeting. She was nervous about the meeting. Agent Fiske told her to go ahead with the meeting, promising to provide surveillance and backup.

At the meeting, Wu escorted her into the board

room where two other men were seated. They remained seated, a breach of manners that she immediately noted. She took a seat, hanging her purse over the back of the chair. Wu introduced a Mr. Wong as his boss from China. The third man, short and stocky with close-cropped hair, Juliana recognized as Xi, Wu's driver. Wong wasted no time in coming to the point. He told Juliana that they had determined that the information she has been providing was mostly worthless. She denied this and told them she had taken risks to get Wu what he requested. Wong interrupted her, accusing her of betraying them.

At this, Juliana panicked. She bolted from her chair, tried running out of the room. Xi grabbed her. He shoved his arms are under hers and locked his hands behind her neck. She couldn't move.

Wong stood and came around to face her. "If you are innocent," he said, "why would you run? Are you hiding something?"

He unbuttoned her blouse, ran his hands roughly over her breasts and up and down her back, and then lifted her skirt and ran his hands up and down her legs and in her underwear. He then looked at Wu and said, "Nothing here, she's clear."

Wu noticed that Juliana glanced at her purse. He picked it up and dumped the contents on the table. He found the recorder. Xi was momentarily distracted by the discovery and Juliana twisted free, kneeing him viciously in the groin. She tried to run but was grabbed by Wong and tossed to the floor.

Wu glared at her, dropped the recorder on the floor and smashed it with his heel.

"Mrs. Hunter, you disappoint me. You've caused me great inconvenience. I regret that our agreement has to end like this." He motioned to the men, "Get her up."

Wong and Xi pulled Juliana to her feet. Wu walked over to her and slapped her hard across the face. Her nose started bleeding.

"Take her out the back door. Put her in the car and get rid of her."

Juliana struggled to get free. "You bastard. You'll never get away with this," she shouted.

In a van outside on the street in front of the building, the FBI listened in, recording the conversation. There was a moment of panic when they realized Juliana was in danger and they needed to get to the back door. Fiske left two agents on the street and raced around to the alley.

Wong grabbed Juliana's neck and put pressure on her carotid artery as she struggled to break free. He and Xi dragged her out of the board room and through the laboratory to the back of the building. Juliana blacked out as they reached the rear entrance. Wong opened the door and looked out to the deserted alley.

He unlocked the car and opened the trunk. Xi held Juliana's slumped body by the shoulders and Wong picked up her feet. As they placed her in the trunk, FBI agents careened into the parking lot and arrested them.

Once the two Chinese were in handcuffs and sitting on the ground next to the rear of the building, Fiske checked Juliana. He noticed a bruise on her neck. She appeared to be breathing and had a strong pulse. To be on the safe side he called for an ambulance. He pulled her blouse together and buttoned it. She awoke groggy and grabbed his hands.

"It's okay, Juliana," he said. "You're safe now."

He and another agent lifted her out of the trunk and placed her on the back seat of Wu's car.

"Just rest here for a few minutes. An ambulance is on the way."

"What about Wu?"

"Don't worry, we had the front of the building covered. He's in handcuffs."

Afterwards, Agent Fiske apologized to Juliana. "We had a listening station set up and we heard most of what went on. We were a little slow reacting because we thought you'd be coming out the front door. You were very brave, you know, to do this. We think Wu is one cog in a larger machine. From his records, and with or without his help, we believe we'll be able to shut down a major spy ring."

AL QAEDA ATTACK IN SAUDI ARABIA

In May 2004, Kevin began to make arrangements for another trip to Saudi Arabia. The second Gulf War had reached the stage where Baghdad had been taken, Saddam Hussein had been captured in 2003, and a new provisional Iraqi constitution signed, but there were continuing skirmishes in various parts of the country. Al Qaeda had been pushed back from Afghanistan into the lawless regions on the Pakistani-Afghanistan border. Iraq was still in turmoil and the Saudis were expanding oil production to fill the gap caused by the drop in supplies due to the Gulf War and Iran sanctions.

In the background, Saudi Arabia chafed at the presence of the British, the Americans, and the other non-Muslims who had come to defend the Kingdom, liberate Kuwait, and depose Saddam Hussein. For decades Saudi Arabia had tolerated a small population of foreigners because they supplied the expertise and technical know-how to extract oil and design and build the infrastructure essential to the Saudi economy. That not only made the royal family rich, it was those revenues that enabled the Saud family to stay in power by ensuring that the population had adequate income for their needs. In addition, the Saudis were quick to silence anyone bold enough to dissent.

Still, there were elements in the society that bitterly resented the presence of foreigners. From time to time foreigners were attacked and sometimes killed. Ostensibly, foreign housing compounds and office facilities were under the protection of Saudi police and military personnel, but when incidents occurred, it seemed the Saudi response was so slow that the attackers inevitably faded into the desert and escaped.

Kevin was aware of the situation, but not overly

concerned. Al-Khobar was the home of many foreign companies affiliated with Saudi counterparts. The city seemed more accepting and progressive and had not experienced any major problems.

❧

"It's your buddy on the phone," Holly said, sticking her head into Kevin's office. "You want to talk to him?"

"Yes, put the call through, please."

Kevin picked up the phone. "Hunter."

"Hey Kevin, got a minute?" Kevin recognized Kidd's voice.

"Sure, what's up?"

"Have you heard the expression 'collateral damage' used in battlefield reports?"

"Yes—usually it refers to civilian casualties, right?"

"Correct. A couple of months ago we used a *Predator* to target a bad guy named Nek Muhammad Wazir. He supported Taliban and al Qaeda terrorists at a base in South Waziristan, Pakistan near the Afghan border. Afterwards, we always try to get local confirmation. In this case there was positive identification, not only of Wazir and a couple of his buddies, but also a civilian who happened to be nearby. Turns out he was a Saudi named Saleh. We did some further investigation and beyond a doubt that's our boy. Case closed."

"Any idea what he was doing there?" Kevin asked.

"The best guess is that's where he went after he double crossed the Iranians. McKinsey followed him back to Pakistan. I know, because he called me and asked me what to do. I told him he was in over his head and to get his ass out of there. Well, he didn't, and you know the rest."

"How sure are you that it was really Saleh?"

"Positive. There was a photo ID and we also found bank records and other information that confirmed. By the way, do you have any trips coming up?"

"Yes, as a matter fact. A quick one—just a couple of days—to Saudi Arabia. Why?"

"Nothing special. No request at this time. Just be careful. You never know… as you well know.

"I'll stay alert. It should be okay—the Saudis are our allies, right?" Kevin said, with a hint of sarcasm.

"One more thing," Kidd replied. "I just found out that by 2002, we knew of over thirty terrorist cells operating in twenty states across the U.S. They hid under fronts disguised as 'charitable,' 'research,' or 'civil rights' organizations, but are funded by al Qaeda, Hamas, the Islamic Jihad, the Muslim Brotherhood, Hezbollah, and other unsavory groups. Their goal is to establish relations within Muslim immigrant communities in the U.S. for recruitment purposes. That's a hell of a note, isn't it? You can guess what we're doing about it—nothing."

"Why do you always have to be the one to go to the Middle East?" Juliana asked Kevin as they ate dinner that evening. "I worry about you. You know what has happened in the past."

"I know," he replied, "but things are changing. The Saudis know they have to relax things a little just to keep their own citizens content. They know they can't let terrorists take root in the Kingdom or they will lose control."

"But the fact remains," Juliana said, "that Osama bin Laden is a Saudi and his family is there. Those pilots that attacked the World Trade Center and the Pentagon, most of them were Saudis."

"I know," Kevin replied. "I'll be careful. It's a short trip, in and out in a couple of days. I'll have a room at a hotel in the Oasis Compound where many foreigners live, including our office personnel. It's fenced, there is a checkpoint with two gates to pass through before entering, and there are armed guards. It's very secure."

"Is that supposed to make me feel better?" Juliana replied. "If it's so safe, why do they need armed guards and all that security?"

"That's so you won't worry," Kevin replied. "Can we change the subject? What are your plans while I'm gone?"

That night in bed as they were reading. Kevin dozed off and dropped his book. He awoke, picked up the book, and continued reading. The second time it happened he put the book down, switched off his light, leaned over and kissed Juliana's cheek, and closed his eyes.

Juliana read for a few minutes more and then put her book away and turned off her light.

She lay on her back for a while, wide awake unable to sleep. Kevin, who could fall asleep anywhere, anytime, in an instant, when he willed his body to do so, was already asleep.

Juliana rolled over and curled around his inert form. He came half awake and mumbled, "Good night, my love."

Juliana squeezed him in a tight embrace. "I have a bad feeling about this trip. Do you have to go?"

"It will be okay," he said. "Go to sleep and we'll discuss it in the morning."

Julia turned away, knowing Kevin would be back asleep in minutes. She also knew that they would not discuss the trip in the morning. His mind was made up. There was some compelling reason that made him feel the trip was necessary, and there was probably more to it than just a "simple marketing trip," as he had said. For several years now all had been quiet. His trips had been mostly domestic. There had been no further signs of the Egyptians or the others who'd been involved in the drone theft. Still she could not sleep, recalling her fears, remembering the kidnappers and what had happened.

❧

Four men sat around the table sipping coffee in a run-down house in a poor neighborhood on the outskirts of al-Khobar. The room was sparse—not much in the way of furniture and no decorations, no pictures on the wall. The window was covered with a heavy curtain. There was an array of weapons stacked in one corner—AK-47 semiautomatic rifles, a RPG7 rocket propelled grenade launcher, Markov 9 mm automatic pistols, and knives. A man known as Fawaz al-Nashimi, alias Turki bin Fuheid al-Mutairi, was speaking. In the room with al-Nashimi were Nimr al-Baqami, and two others. Al-Nashimi was describing a plan that had been hatched at an earlier meeting.

"We will make a diversionary attack on the al-Khobar Petroleum Centre at 6:45 in the morning. We will kill the guards and any foreign infidels going to work that morning. Next, we'll proceed to the Arab Petroleum Investments Corporation building. The compound is only half a kilometer away so we can hit it twenty to thirty minutes later.

"While the police are distracted by these attacks, we will launch the main attack at 7:30 at the residence compound where many foreign infidels live. Any questions?"

No one said anything.

"Fine. Look to your weapons and then get some sleep. We will leave the house at 6, after prayers.

"Allahu akbar"

Kevin had a busy morning in the office. At 11 a.m. he called Holly to come in and meet with him.

"I'm going to the Saudi Consulate this afternoon to get a new visa," he said. "My old one has expired. How are you coming with my itinerary?"

"Travel is working on your flights. You wanted to arrive on Friday, May 28. Unfortunately, there is something going on in Europe and the flights are full. The best we can do is get you out on May 31, unless you want to go through Paris and Cairo and change planes half a dozen times. You'd spend three days traveling."

"No," Kevin replied. "I want to take that direct flight on KLM to Amsterdam, spend the night, then fly direct to al-Khobar, two full days there, and then the same route home."

"Okay, I'll check, I'm pretty sure travel can do that. Then you would stay two nights at the Soha Towers Hotel in the Oasis Compound, June 1 and 2?"

"Probably three nights, June 1 to June 3, because I won't have any time for meetings on the first day."

"Okay. I'll get the hotel reserved. Travel already checked and they're not that busy."

"Fine. Also send an email to Frank Lloyd in the al-Khobar office. He's our marketing manager there. See if he could have dinner with me on that first night. He lives right there in the compound."

"Will do."

That evening, Kevin went over his travel plans with Juliana.

"I'm leaving on May 31 for Saudi. As I promised, I'm keeping the trip as short as possible. Only two days there and then I head home. I should be back on June 4, assuming the airlines stay on schedule."

"So you'll miss Memorial Day? You know we usually have a party then."

"I know. Instead, what if you and I take a week off, go to the island for a few days, just the two of us? The boat is ready; all we need are some groceries."

"I'd love it. Promise me that you'll really take the time off, and not have some 'emergency' when you get back."

"I promise. It's been a long winter. It'll be great to

go to the island. It should be beautiful—with all the rain, everything will be green."

ॐ

Early in the morning on May 29, terrorists struck at the al-Khobar Petroleum Centre. Three people were killed. The terrorists sped away before security forces could react.

A short time later, terrorists in a vehicle drove up to the gate of the Arab Petroleum Investments Corporation compound. One man jumped from the car and fired a rocket propelled grenade at the gatehouse, killing two security guards. There was more shooting. At that moment a car passed, carrying children on their way to school. A stray bullet hit the gas tank, causing it to explode, killing a ten-year old boy, son of an Egyptian employee. Next, a car arrived with a senior employee of British nationality. They fired on his car, wounding him. He was pulled from his car and tied to the back of their four-wheel vehicle, still alive. They raced off, dragging the unfortunate victim behind the vehicle until he fell off into the street. The terrorists shot their way through several police road blocks and made their way to the Oasis Compound.

At the Oasis Compound, al-Nashimi and his gang drove up to the security entrance. There was one car in front of them. As they waited, a school bus drove up behind them. There were two gates. The first gate opened, the car ahead entered, was inspected by the guards, and then the second gate opened and the car entered the compound.

The guards carelessly left the second gate open. Al-Nashimi shouted "open the sunroof." He drove straight through both gates. One of the terrorists popped up through the sunroof, killing the two armed security guards with automatic rifle fire, then emptied the clip at the school bus waiting to enter. Two children were killed and four were wounded. Al-Nashimi and his gang exited the vehicle and ran into one of the residential buildings. They broke down doors at random and executed any non-Muslim they encountered, either slitting their throats, or shooting them in the head. Frank Lloyd was sitting at his desk signing paychecks. He looked up at the intruders and was shot in the head by al-Nashimi.

৵

When Kevin entered the office on the morning of May 30, Holly grabbed him, went into his office with him, and closed the door.

"Did you hear the news about al-Khobar?" she asked.

"No," he said, "what's going on?"

"There were several terrorist attacks yesterday. Supposedly it was al Qaeda killing non-Muslims, but they managed to kill some Muslims and a bunch of kids. Also, I'm very sorry to report that Frank Lloyd was one of the victims."

"Oh shit," Kevin said. He slumped into his chair "I can't believe it. It's terrible. What happened?"

"Some terrorists shot their way into the compound. It seems that by the time the Saudis reacted, most of them had escaped. After their killing rampage, supposedly they went into the restaurant there and had breakfast. Meanwhile they booby-trapped the entrances to the compound and posted guards, keeping everyone remaining there hostage. After breakfast they went into another part of the compound and started killing Indians, because they were Hindus.

"It wasn't until 9:30 at night that the Saudis surrounded the compound. They rescued the children, but still have not been able to enter the compound because the terrorists inside say they will kill the hostages.

"Poor Frank! How terrible for his family. Has someone reached out to them to see what can be done to help?"

"I think that's in progress," Holly said.

"Thank god I didn't go earlier. I could've been right in the middle of that mess."

"I canceled your hotel and flights."

After canceling his trip, when Kevin arrived home from the office, he found Juliana in the kitchen fixing dinner.

He gave her a quick kiss and looked in the oven. "Something smells good. By the way, you'll be happy to know I'm not going to Saudi after all." Without further comment, he went to the cupboard and took out a bottle of Dewar's 12-year-old Scotch whiskey.

Juliana looked at him, saw something in his face, and turned off the stove.

"It must be important," she said, "since you went right for the scotch."

"What would you like?"

"Something tells me I should have something stronger than white wine," she said. "What about a martini?"

Kevin mixed her a martini and they clinked glasses. "Salud," he said.

They sat down in the living room.

"Now tell me."

"There was a terrorist attack in al-Khobar," he said. "They hit various locations including where I would have been staying, killing one of the guys I planned to meet. If the flights hadn't been full, I might have arrived in the middle of that."

"It's strange," Juliana said. "I had a bad feeling, a premonition, about this trip. That has never happened to me before. Why now, after all these trips?"

"I don't know. Sometimes it is better to be lucky than smart. I'm lucky the planes were full, lucky I didn't try to get smart, press the issue, and get there earlier."

"Kevin..." Juliana started to say something, then stopped.

"What?"

"No, it's probably crazy. I don't even want to think about it."

"Think about what?"

"Those Saudi terrorists. Is there any chance they knew about your trip and came looking for you?"

"No, I don't think so. This trip sort of came up at the last minute. Very few people knew I was going."

"Your Saudi client knew. Frank Lloyd knew. People in the hotel reservations knew. What if someone said something?"

"I suppose it's possible, but hard to imagine. It's been years since Saleh disappeared and now he and his cohorts are dead or in jail. At this point, why would anyone care? I think the attacks were aimed at causing trouble for the Saudis. The foreigners were just scapegoats."

"I hope you're right, God, I hope you're right. I'd finally reached the point where I don't have dreams about those guys anymore."

૭

Kevin later learned that during the Oasis attack, al-Nashami had the gall to call al-Jazeera television and had the station record an interview, in Italian, with an Italian hostage. After verifying that the interview had been recorded, he had al-Baqami kill the hapless Italian by shooting him in the head. The official report stated that early the next morning, Saudi Special Forces came in by helicopter, landed on the roof of the Soha Towers Hotel and searched for the terrorists. They freed the hostages and reportedly wounded and then captured Nimr al-Baqami. But by the time the Saudis finally acted, the other three terrorists had slipped away from the compound and disappeared. The Saudi government was widely criticized for its delayed and ineffectual response to the attacks. It was rumored that the Saudi government made a deal with the other three terrorists to flee to avoid their threat to blow up the hotel.

Later, more news filtered out from al-Khobar. There were wild rumors of other attacks at various locations in the city, at or near compounds holding foreign workers. Another dozen or so security and military personnel were reportedly killed or injured, and it was determined that these attacks were caused by the same terrorists as they fled the city. After the killings, al-Nashimi was interviewed by the *Voice of Jihad*, an on-line newsletter, where he described the attacks, stating that the brave Jihadists had defeated hundreds of cowardly Arab police and soldiers.

As a result of the attack, security at the Oasis Compound was increased with barricades, special lanes for entering and exiting, and additional Army personnel armed with machine guns. Of course, these efforts were of little consolation to the relatives of Frank Lloyd and the others who lost spouses or children during the vicious attacks.

A few months later, in Riyadh, terrorists kidnapped and held hostage an American engineer. This time the Saudi security forces had some of the terrorists' meeting places under surveillance. When al-Nashimi and another terrorist drove up, they were accosted by the Saudis. In the ensuing firefight, both were killed. Unfortunately, it was too late; they had beheaded the hostage earlier that day.

Kevin called Kidd to request a meeting. They agreed to meet for lunch at the usual spot, one of the back corner tables in the Pacific Dining Car. When Kevin arrived he found Kidd waiting. As Kevin took a seat, the waiter brought two scotch on the rocks to the table.

"It's been a while, young man. I hope all is well with you and your lovely bride. Here's to your health." They toasted.

"What about you? Any new projects?"

"Same old, same old. You know, more and more I'm thinking about retiring. I've got a few more years to put in, then I move to the backwoods of Virginia or someplace where I can be anonymous."

"You can't do that; you'll be missed."

"I don't think so. The Agency has changed. They don't like thinkers. Look at the mess we're in in the Middle East. The money we're spending on 'nation-building'— what a joke. We have no comprehension of the reality of the situation. Sunnis and Shias—they've hated each other for two thousand years. They'll keep fighting as long as there is one more of the other guys alive somewhere. Now that we stuck our nose into their affairs, we've become a convenient fall guy. The one thing both sides can agree on is to get rid of us."

"You're a thinker. That's all the more reason you should stay," Kevin said

"The sad thing is, we should've known better. We went into Afghanistan, we kicked ass, everybody was for it because we'd been brutally attacked and we chased out the Taliban. We were so close to being good guys. If we had just nailed Osama bin Laden there in Tora Bora, brought all the troops home, and told the Afghanistanis they could have their country back, we would've been looked up to throughout the world. We would've lived up to our American standards and democratic principles. But no, we had to go and invade Iraq, a country which we had no right to invade, and we also stayed in Afghanistan. How stupid could we be? The British tried it in 1838, and bled and bled. The Russians tried it in 1979, and bled for nine years and for what? There's nothing worthwhile there besides opium poppies. We've been there now for three years. Mark my words, we'll be there another ten before we finally wake up and get our asses out of there. Meanwhile, the Iraqis and the Afghanistanis that we tried to help will all end up hating our guts. And for every one of their young men and women we kill as 'terrorists,' five more will be motivated to take their place."

"That's a pretty pessimistic outlook. I hate to say it, but I think you're right."

"Consider this—we've failed to realize that the goal of the wacko Jihadists is a battle to the death. There can be no 'peace' talks, no compromises. I don't think we can kill enough radical Muslims to stop the movement. It will spread and continue until the world changes. Defeat the infidel nonbelievers—that's what draws poor and wealthy, uneducated and educated Muslims, to willingly commit martyrdom. You know what bin Laden said in an interview?

> *'The defeat of the USSR in Afghanistan was a great boost to Muslim jihad. It destroyed the myth that the superpowers were unbeatable.'*

"Of course, who helped the Mujahideen defeat the Russians? Us. I'm sorry; you shouldn't have got me started," Kidd said. "I don't mean to preach. I sound like the bitter, disillusioned old man that I am." He downed his drink.

"Why did you want to meet?" he continued. "Surely not to hear me vent like this."

"There was an attack in al-Khobar last week," Kevin replied. "Some Americans and other non-Arabs were killed. One of the victims worked for my company. Do you know anything about it?"

"I read the reports. I'm sorry about your guy. When I saw who he worked for, I thought you might know him. From what I've heard it didn't seem like the Saudis did much to prevent it. Why are you asking?"

"I was supposed to be there for some meetings. At the last minute I changed my flights, otherwise it could have been bad for me. I'm just wondering if there could be any connection, my going there and the attack, that is."

"I don't think so," Kidd said. "But I'll look into it, see what I can find out. You planning to go there now?"

"No. My wife would divorce me. We're taking care of business another way, letting our in-country partners handle the details. There seems to be no need for me to go there."

"Good. Give me a few days and I'll get back to you."

"One more thing. Frank. The guy who was killed—he was a good man. If there is anything I can do—you know, information-wise—I'd want to help out."

"I'll remember that and let you know."

A few days later Kidd got back to Kevin.

"I checked on a few things," he said. "First, the Egyptian dancer is safely tucked away in Carswell. She's been on her good behavior. Then, regarding Saleh, he appears to have been pretty much a lone wolf. No living relatives in the Kingdom. It seems his father was arrested by the Saudi authorities for 'blasphemy.' That's a catch-all that probably means he said something uncomplimentary about King Fahd or the royal family. His old man died in prison, supposedly of natural causes—congestive heart failure. That seems to be what radicalized Saleh. He started hanging out with some fringe element Saudi Shias, and then got cozy with some Iranian Shias. I think that's what led to the deal to steal the drone secrets. There wasn't much he could do directly to get even with the Saudis, but by helping Iran, he could strike a blow against Saudi Arabia and its patron, the 'Great Satan,' the good old U.S.A."

"So you don't see any link going back to Saleh or one of his friends?" Kevin asked.

"No. With Saleh's legal background and fluent English, I think the Iranians were impressed, thinking he could become a long-term asset for them. He must've had some help getting set up with the Beverly Hills address and office. He spent a couple of years making contacts and cultivating an image as a middle man for trade in the Middle East. So he wasn't thinking of the drone business as a one-shot deal. We'll never know for sure, but if he'd succeeded, I'll bet they'd task him to go after some nuclear secrets."

"So if there was a link, it would be to Iran?"

"That's my guess. It's all speculation. Bottom line, I don't think there was any connection between the al-Khobar attack and you. It was just some Saudi terrorists trying to stir up trouble for the royal family."

Somehow Kevin wasn't satisfied with Kidd's explanation. There were coincidences and there were coincidences. It was unsettling. He tried to put it out of his mind.

Kevin and Juliana had a Memorial Day party with some close friends, but for him, it was not enjoyable. He couldn't get the terrorist attacks out of his mind. As promised, he had a week's vacation and took Juliana sailing. He hoped the sea would distract him, help him forget and find peace. At Santa Barbara Island the weather suddenly turned foul and he cut the trip short. Staying at the island was no longer enjoyable—it brought back too many bad memories.

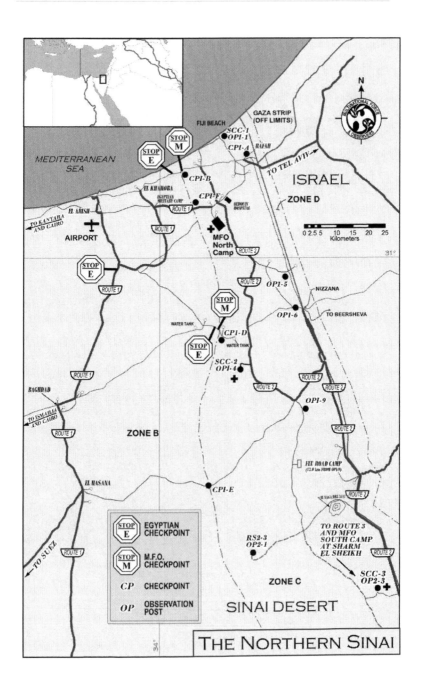

THE NORTHERN SINAI

SINAI JIHAD

One day in the spring of 2005, Kevin came home with a bouquet of roses for Juliana. She was immediately suspicious. "What have you done now? Why the flowers?"

"You don't think it's just because I love you?" he said.

"Well, it's not my birthday, not our anniversary, so, it makes me wonder." Juliana could tell by the look on his face that something was up.

He hesitated for a moment, thinking about how best to break the news.

"Julie, how would you like to see the pyramids?"

"Oh no. You promised me, no more trips to the Middle East."

"I know, but this is different. Egypt is a friendly country. Everything is calm and peaceful there. Tourism is a major source of income, so they are very protective of tourists. It's a good time to go. We can visit the pyramids, see the Sphinx, and go to the Cairo Museum, which is really an amazing place."

"Sounds nice, but what's the catch? What do you have to do in Egypt?"

"Do you remember me telling you about the MFO?"

"Vaguely," Juliana replied. "Something to do with the Egypt-Israeli war in 1978?"

"Yes. After the fighting ended, the parties met at Camp David in the U.S. to broker a peace treaty. One of the unusual outcomes was the formation of the Multinational Force and Observers, or MFO. It was created to ensure that the terms of the treaty were observed by both sides, make sure there were no violations. A headquarters organization was established in Rome. Eleven nations contributed troops, aircraft, weapons, and ships. The MFO took over two former Israeli airbases, one at al Gorah in the northern Sinai desert near the Mediterranean coast, and another in the south, at Sharm el Sheikh, near the Red Sea. It established thirty remote outposts along the length of the border between Egypt and Israel. Consolidated was hired to provide logistical support to the peacekeeping force. We formed a joint venture with an Egyptian company."

"Why do you have to go?"

"I have a meeting with one of our clients. I have to pay a courtesy call on our Egyptian partner in Cairo, who will no doubt take us out for a nice dinner, probably on a boat on the Nile. Then I have to go to the Sinai for a couple of days to meet with our client there. The contract is coming up for renewal and I need to make certain there are no performance deficiencies."

"What am I supposed to do while you're in the Sinai?

"We'll stay at the Mena House Hotel in Giza. It's a beautiful place, very secure and comfortable, within walking distance to the monuments. The main dining room has a spectacular view of the Pyramids. It's an historic place where Churchill, Roosevelt and Chiang Kai-Shek met in November 1943 for the Cairo conference during World War II. You'll love it."

Against her better judgement, Juliana had acquiesced when Kevin showed her pictures of Egyptian art and promised to take her to the pyramids. Arriving in the Cairo airport, they entered arrivals area. It was crowded, a surging mass wearing Arabic and Western attire. Outside, they grabbed a cab to take them to the hotel.

The Mena House was a short drive west of the city. Leaving Cairo they could see the tops of the pyramids dominating the skyline. It was dusk, and the pyramids were silhouetted against the sky, backlit by the setting sun.

"They are huge, aren't they?" Juliana said. "I've seen pictures, but they don't do justice to the real thing."

"Yes," Kevin said. "Just imagine them being built over four thousand years ago, thousands of laborers cutting limestone with crude tools and manhandling the blocks of stone up ramps. No cranes or vehicles in those days."

After checking, in they went to the bar for a nightcap. The corridors of the hotel were decorated with historic photographs and paintings.

"I'm glad we came," Juliana said. "It is a beautiful place. Just imagine, people living here, working here, building cities thousands of years before the first Englishman or Spaniard set foot in America. Our country is only five hundred years old, by comparison. I wonder what it will it be like, four thousand years from now?"

"You're forgetting the Native Americans. They were there long before your relatives and mine."

"True. But can you believe this ancient civilization? In some ways it seems so modern. The furniture, art, jewelry—they could grace a contemporary home."

"I know, and you, with your beauty, could be the wife of a pharaoh. How about finishing your drink so we can go to bed? Tomorrow will be a big day."

Kevin undressed quickly and got in bed while Juliana was in the bathroom. She emerged a few minutes later wearing a sheer white nightgown that contrasted with her dark hair. As she stood in the doorway, framed by the light behind, he stared at her in admiration.

"Julie—you're beautiful. Twenty years of marriage and I swear, you're more beautiful than when I met you. I don't tell you that often enough, I'm sure, but you are always on my mind. You need to know that."

Juliana crawled across the bed and kissed him. "I know that. And I love you too."

She knelt on the bed, reached behind, and pulled the nightgown over her head. She removed the clip holding her hair and it spilled down her back and over her shoulders, partially covering her breasts. At the sight of her with her arms raised, Kevin was fully aroused. He sat up and tenderly moved strands of hair to behind her ears, then put his arms around her and kissed her breasts.

"Come here under the covers."

She slid the covers aside and crawled on top of him. "How's this?" she said. She pressed her mouth on his, her legs tight against him.

The next day, Kevin and Juliana were taken on a tour of old Cairo and the old city marketplace. They returned to visit the Cairo Museum and had dinner in a floating restaurant on the Nile.

"Tomorrow we'll visit the pyramids," Kevin said. "I want to show you around. It's an easy walk from the hotel. The next day I'll be picked up for the trip to the Sinai. You'll be on your own for three days. The hotel can arrange guides and a driver if you want to go anywhere. Use them if you decide to make any excursions. If you want to go back to the pyramids to do some sketching or photographs, you can walk. You'll know your way around after we go tomorrow, and I don't think there's anything for you to worry about."

The next morning after breakfast they headed up Al Ahram road to the Great Pyramid, where they bought tickets to join a guided tour of the pyramid. Their group entered through the entrance made by grave robbers centuries before. They went down the descending corridor into the subterranean chamber, one hundred feet below the surface. The guide explained how the stone masons labored underground to carve out the chamber with hand tools. For some unexplained reason, it was never finished. Next, they went up to a chamber known as the Queen's Chamber and then further up through the Grand Gallery into the King's Chamber. Kevin marveled at the nine polished granite beams, each weighing more than forty tons, that made up the chamber ceiling.

In one corner of the chamber they examined the Pharaoh Khufu's sarcophagus, one corner chipped, the cover gone. Whatever happened to Khufu's mummy was an unsolved mystery. The Pharaoh behind this monument that stood for centuries as the world's tallest man-made structure, had disappeared. Only a small ivory statue bearing his image remained, on display in the Cairo Museum.

After the Great Pyramid, they walked to Khafre's pyramid, and on to Menkaure's pyramid. They visited some tombs that had been restored. In one of the tombs Juliana led Kevin to a dark corner away from the others in the group. She held him in a tight embrace.

"In a way it's creepy, being here in these tombs. They are all monuments to death, aren't they? Yet, in another sense, there is something erotic about being here, thinking about Cleopatra and thousands of years of Egyptian queens. Women had power in ancient Egypt— very different from other parts of the ancient world. Standing here in the darkness, I can identify with that, feel something of the ancient powers. Am I crazy or what?"

"No, you're not crazy. Egypt has worked its magic on visitors for centuries. Even Napoleon was affected when he was here. Please save your memory of that feeling until we get back to the hotel."

That night in bed, Kevin thought of ancient kings and pharaohs as he lay with Juliana. Moonlight came in the windows of their room, illuminating Juliana's face. He looked down at her luminescent eyes as she lay beneath him, her dark hair spread out as a halo around her head. Then his eyes closed as he lost himself in a precious moment of togetherness with her.

Juliana walked to the lobby when the car came to pick up Kevin. The uniformed driver had a hat with the MFO emblem on it.

She kissed Kevin goodbye and then turned to the driver. "Take good care of him for me."

"Yes ma'am. He'll be fine."

"Don't worry, Julie. Have fun and enjoy yourself, but you be carerful also. I'll call you when I get to North Camp, and I'll be back in three days. Love you."

He kissed her and got in the car in the front passenger seat. She watched the car until it pulled out of the hotel and disappeared down the road.

❧

Kidd was in his office in Los Angeles reading some reports when his secretary buzzed him.

"What is it?"

"You've got a call. A Lieutenant Hardy from Creech Air Force Base."

"Go ahead, put it through."

"Howdy Hardy, what's up? Did you hit a jackpot on one of those Las Vegas slot machines?"

"No, I wish it was something like that. Our bird has flown."

"What do you mean? That Egyptian? For Christ's sake, she was in Carswell, that federal prison for women in Fort Worth. How did she get out of there?"

"They have an adjoining low-security 'camp' where they keep low-risk inmates. She got a job there on good behavior. After settling in and behaving herself for a while, she just walked out. We think someone was waiting and picked her up on the outside. That afternoon a security camera in the DFW airport picked her up. She was with a Middle Eastern-appearing man. We don't know what flight she boarded yet, but I think we'll be able to figure it out. She was probably on a plane before she was missed at the camp."

"Is somebody working on this?"

"We've put the word out, so yes, somebody is

working on it. Given her background, it's probably not a real high priority."

"I understand. Let me know when you find out where she was headed. It may not matter, but there are a couple of people I should give a heads up. Thanks for getting in touch."

᠀

While Kevin was in the Sinai, Juliana arranged for a car and driver to take her to Khan el-Khalili, the famous shopping area in the Islamic district of Cairo. The driver found a place to park and guided her through the Bab al-Badistan gate and into the crowded narrow streets of the bazaar. People pushed by, and everywhere was the sound of vendors crying their wares in Arabic. Fragrant odors came from restaurants and food stalls. At one point they passed the al-Hussein mosque. Elsewhere, the guide pointed out a wall containing limestone blocks with hieroglyphics on them. "Those stones came from Giza," he said.

Juliana wanted to buy a souvenir for Kevin, something unique to remind him of their trip. As she walked through the streets jammed with people, merchants came out of their *souqs* holding colorful scarves, necklaces and other items they were eager to sell. Juliana soon learned that if she so much as looked at the salesman, he would follow her for a block, encouraging her to buy and lowering his prices as he followed her. When she paused in front of one store, a vendor rushed out of another shop waving some scarves. The first shopkeeper pushed the other salesman away and a fight broke out. Juliana's guide eased her away. As she left, there shouting and scuffling in the narrow street. It was unnerving. She felt like a target, standing out among the other passersby who wore Arab dress. She asked the driver to take her back to the Mena House.

❧

In the car, Kevin read his notes about the MFO. The Sinai desert had twice been a battleground between Egypt and Israel. On the eastern border it abutted a portion of the Gaza Strip, the nation of Israel, and further south, Jordan. When the MFO was established in 1981, the Sinai was divided into four zones. Zone A was on the west side, closest to Egypt. Zone B covered the vast central area of the Sinai Peninsula. Zone C was the area along the border with Israel. Zone D, a narrow strip on the Israeli side of the border, was monitored by Israel.

The drive coming from Cairo into the Suez was interesting. Crossing the desert, in the distance Kevin saw something moving—some type of a structure. Drawing closer, he realized that behind the sand dunes a large ship was headed north. Then, from a low rise, the Suez Canal suddenly appeared. Crossing into the Sinai, beyond el-Arish, the road passed along the coast, with the Mediterranean sparkling blue in the distance.

The trip to al-Gorah took five hours. Upon arriving at North Camp, Kevin checked into the VIP quarters. He had an hour to unpack and relax before the first of the series of meetings. While hanging up his clothes, he noticed a newspaper on the nightstand by the side of the bed. It was a copy of the *Sandpaper*, a newspaper printed on the base for MFO personnel. There was a small article on the front page announcing his visit to the base. He thought that was a nice touch.

About forty-five minutes after he arrived, there was a knock at the door. Dave Everly, Consolidated's site manager, greeted him. "Hi Kevin. Welcome to North Camp. How was the drive over from Cairo?"

"Just the way I like it—uneventful. The most interesting thing was the approach to the Suez Canal. You look out the car window and all you see is desert. As you get closer you see large objects moving across the sand. Suddenly you realize they are the masts and superstructure of large ships."

"It is amazing," Dave said. "When you think about it, the canal is a remarkable piece of engineering work, but also politically very significant, in that there's been a lot of fighting over it. If you're ready, we'll walk over and pay a courtesy call on the Force Commander, Maj. Gen. Tellefsen. He's a Norwegian, very well-liked and has done a good job here. After this meeting, I'd like to spend a little time with you to go over our plans for the next several days. We'll have dinner at eighteen hundred hours at the Multinational Dining Facility, our on-base restaurant."

Kevin asked the Force Commander if he was satisfied with Consolidated's performance under the terms of the contract, and was pleased to hear that there were no complaints. Performance reviews in all sectors were from "very good" to "excellent."

Back at the VIP quarters, Dave briefed Kevin on a series of meetings planned for the next day. In the morning they would visit some of the shops and base maintenance facilities where Kevin could get a firsthand look at the work being performed by Consolidated's personnel. Next, there would be a formal lunch with the Force Commander, followed by a series of office visits with key personnel including the Chief of Staff, Chief of Support, the Force Contracts Manager, and the Site Manager for Consolidated's Egyptian subcontractor.

The meetings all went well. Kevin was pleased to find that there were no performance or labor issues. In the various workshops he met technicians and maintenance personnel of all nationalities. A large number of the expatriates were British. From conversations and the attitudes of the people he met, Kevin could tell morale was high.

At the end of the day, Dave told Kevin that a small reception had been arranged in his honor.

"We're going over to the Globetrotters bar for happy hour," Dave said. "I don't know if you're aware of it, but a number of years ago Consolidated received permission from the Force Commander to renovate the old Israeli officer's club on-base. This was done with private funds. Over the years it has become quite an historic place. Besides having a great bar, you'll be impressed with the decorations. There are banners and plaques with the coat of arms of all the various military units that served the MFO over the years. Also, you'll find a number of historic photographs that are interesting. Since the company is buying drinks, we'll probably have a good turnout of people who would like to meet you. And if you like to play darts, there are several dartboards set up. It's a popular way to decide who pays for the next round."

The next morning Kevin met Dave for breakfast at the Multinational Dining Facility. At 0800 hours Kevin got in a MFO SUV with Dave to begin a visit to some of the remote outposts. He preferred to spend the day in the field, where they would cover a distance of about one hundred and fifty kilometers on rough roads. This was a better way to learn about the status and performance of the project rather than sitting in someone's air-conditioned office. Their travels would take them south on Route 2 to Observation Post 4, then further south to OP-9. From there, they would loop back north to OP-8, which was very close to the Israeli border. From OP-8 the road traveled along the border to a checkpoint by OP-6, also on the border. From there they would go on to OP-5, where they would swing northwest on Route 2 back to North Camp.

On the road through the desert there were signs marking areas where landmines or unexploded ordinance were a hazard. Every now and then they passed the burnt out hulk of a tank or armored personnel vehicle, relics of the bitter fighting that had taken place there during the 1973 Yom Kippur war. Incongruous among the other sights, he saw a single Bedouin with a small herd of goats, standing next to a crude hut constructed of brush. The Bedouin stood without moving, watching them pass.

There were no other vehicles to be seen. After driving about an hour, Dave turned off to the right.

"I want to show you some of the checkpoints," he said as they passed a solitary water tank surrounded by a fence. "This road leads to an Egyptian checkpoint. The MFO has its own checkpoint just inside the Zone C border, about four kilometers away. We're set up to monitor traffic on all the known roads."

"What about the open desert?" Kevin asked. "That Bedouin we passed wasn't on any road."

"The Bedouin go where they please," Dave replied.

"Isn't that dangerous?"

"For them, yes. Not so much for us. They wander around out there and every now and then someone will step on something they shouldn't. Kaboom! They get blown up. If they're lucky, they just lose a leg. Sometimes they get help in time; other times, we find a lot of goats and sheep milling around with no goatherd."

At the checkpoint a soldier stepped out and walked over to the car. He was a Fijian, about six feet-two, lean and muscular. He wore a dark green uniform and the distinctive red beret with the MFO pin on the front. He greeted Dave, and noted the time and license plate number of the MFO SUV they were driving.

"Get out and stretch your legs," Dave said. "I'll just be a minute."

While Dave was inside talking to a Fijian officer, Kevin surveyed the surrounding area. The road to the west leading to the Egyptian checkpoint was empty. It traversed dry, barren terrain. He looked out over the desert, and tried to imagine Egyptian tanks storming across this land, long trails of dust in their wake, trying to penetrate into Israel.

In a few minutes they were once again on their way.

"Nothing happening there," Dave said. "I always try to stop in and say hello, see if they're getting water deliveries on time or need anything. It's a hell of a job, being stuck out here. The Fijians are great—they are among the best conditioned, toughest troops in the MFO. They have been participating since 1982. They have three infantry companies with over three hundred personnel here in the desert. It must be a shock for the newcomers when they first arrive, so different from the islands where they live. But you could not find a prouder, more dedicated bunch of soldiers. They are English-speaking and their military is modeled after the British Army."

"Where to now?" Kevin asked.

"We're heading south down to OP-9. It is the southernmost post occupied by FIJIBATT. Further south, the posts are operated by the Colombian Battalion. Next I want to show you the Israeli border, then we'll stop and have lunch with the Fiji troops at OP-6. The Lieutenant there is a particular friend of mine."

OP-6 was surrounded by rolls of concertina wire. A

sentry at the gate waved them into the compound. Kevin noticed that everything was neat and orderly, the dirt driveway surfaced with gravel and the borders marked by white stones. High-intensity lights on tall poles illuminated the perimeter fence at night. He saw that one of the outbuildings housed a generator that supplied power to the post. There was a large storage tank that held non-potable water.

Inside the command center, Dave introduced Kevin to Lieutenant Joni Senibus, who was in charge of OP-6. The Lieutenant—tall, six feet 4, very handsome—was all muscle. He wore the distinctive FIJIBATT red beret. His hair was cut short and he had a neatly trimmed mustache. He was soft-spoken, obviously well-educated, speaking English with a faint British accent.

"Kevin is my boss in the States," Dave said. "He had some meetings here with the Force Commander and some of the supply and logistics personnel, but also wanted to visit some of the remote outposts. Of course, I told him he had to come to FIJIBATT, because your operation wins all the performance awards."

"You're most kind.

"Kevin, if I may use your first name, I will tell you frankly that I and the men here are very happy. Dave, as your company's representative, does a fine job. We never are lacking in the essentials—water, fuel for vehicles, diesel for our generator and, of course, food."

Dave laughed. "Thanks Lieutenant for the kind words. We do our best."

"Let me tell you about food," Lieutenant Senibus said. "Before joining MFO I served in Bosnia as part of the UN peacekeeping force. The food there was terrible. Here your company provides us with excellent rations. I confess, I don't know how you do it, here in this remote desert location! But we get fish, tropical fruits, coconuts, special items that make us feel like we're back home. It is a great boost for morale."

"How about if I show you around the outpost?"

The Lieutenant took Kevin and Dave to the troops' quarters, beds made, everything very neat. They visited the kitchen with its large refrigerator and freezer and the mess hall, where Kevin declined an offer of coffee.

Following this they visited the garage where two soldiers were working on a strange vehicle. It looked like a glorified dune buggy, except that it mounted a 50-caliber machine gun. The Lieutenant explained that this was a fast attack vehicle, nicknamed FAV.

Back in the command center, Kevin examined the maps on the wall, marked off in a grid. The locations of the main roads, checkpoints, water tanks, and other observation posts were noted. Significantly, every sixty or seventy kilometers there was a MFO ambulance facility.

"You have a lot of radios," Kevin noted.

"Yes, the Force Commander has direct links to the Egyptian and Israeli authorities. Any incursions in violation of the peace treaty are immediately reported. All of our aircraft and patrol vehicles as well as the observation posts and checkpoints are linked by VHF radios. We have a series of repeaters up and down the peninsula for relaying radio calls, and multiple frequencies for each remote outpost, for reporting fires or medical problems and there is an emergency band. Unfortunately, there are a number of locations in the desert where communications are interrupted by the terrain. We have these dead spots mapped, so our personnel are aware of them."

They returned to the Lieutenant's office. Dave excused himself momentarily to visit the head.

As Kevin and the Lieutenant sat discussing supply needs, there was a sudden loud explosion outside the building.

"Get down and stay down!" the Lieutenant shouted, as he grabbed his weapon and ran out the door. Outside Kevin could hear shouts and several short bursts of automatic rifle fire. It was quiet for a moment, then another loud explosion rattled the building. He could smell smoke; somewhere, part of the building was on fire. He crawled closer to the door, trying to see what was going on.

Lieutenant Senibus came running back into the room. "You okay?"

"I'm fine," Kevin said. "What happened?"

"Terrorists. One came walking in off the desert. He was dressed like a Bedouin, walking like he was feeble or ill. When he got close to the gate he set off a bomb concealed under his robe."

"Bad?"

"Very bad. Two of my fellows dead, two wounded. In all the confusion a second guy fired an RPG into your four-wheel-drive, fired on my men, and then disappeared back into the desert. I think he had help."

"What can I do?"

"Nothing. There was a small fire, but it's under control. I've called for a helicopter to transport the wounded. We're going into the desert and see if we can find the other terrorists. There will be aircraft looking for him or them as well. Sorry about your vehicle."

The Lieutenant paused as Dave hurried back into the room.

"Here's Dave. You both better come with us. I'll turn you two over to the squad at the next outpost, and they'll get you back to base. I don't think you should hang around here. Who knows, you may have been the target. Otherwise why attack us? Something is crazy."

They rushed outside. Two soldiers pulled up in the FAV. They wore full combat gear and had grim looks. Two others pulled up in a Humvee that bristled with antennas. The Lieutenant got in the front with the driver and motioned Kevin and Dave to get in the back with the second soldier.

As they roared out of the compound, Kevin saw the ruins of the gate and the destroyed sentry post. Two bodies covered by ponchos were laid out on the ground. The

Lieutenant turned around and spoke to Kevin. "They were good men. They both have families back home. Someone will pay for this."

The vehicle raced out of the compound, bouncing over the desert terrain. The Lieutenant talked to someone on the radio. It was impossible to hear what was said over the engine noise and the jarring of the vehicle. The soldiers stared out at the desert, looking for movement. No one spoke.

After about ten minutes the Humvee stopped abruptly. The Lieutenant jumped out, looking up at the approaching helicopter. He spoke to the two soldiers in the FAV. Within moments they were racing northeast across the open desert as the helicopter swept low over the Humvee and raced ahead of the FAV.

"With the helicopters spotting them, I think we'll get these guys," the Lieutenant said.

"Let's hope so," Kevin said, as the Humvee accelerated into a left turn, heading back to the highway. "But listen, your guys on the ground may need some reinforcements. Don't worry about taking Dave and me to the next outpost. Let's go ahead and finish the job. We'll stay out of your way and be fine."

The Lieutenant turned around and looked at Dave first and then Kevin. "You're sure?"

"Positive!"

"Okay, hang on." The Lieutenant leaned over to the driver and said something. The Humvee made a quick right turn back to the original heading and tore off across the desert. By now, the helicopter was out of sight. A faint dust cloud marked the path of the FAV. A few more minutes passed and the radio came to life. Over the jarring of the Humvee, Kevin heard part of the message.

"Lieutenant, this is Aero 12. We have two suspects in sight, traveling northeast on dirt bikes. Will approach and dust off…" The rest of the message was unintelligible.

"What did that mean?" Kevin asked.

"The pilot will overfly the suspects at a low altitude, stirring up so much dust and sand they'll have to either slow down or crash."

The FAV reported that they had the helicopter in sight.

Aero 12 reported, "Rider down. We're taking fire." A loud hammering sound came over the radio.

"Aero 12, report in," the Lieutenant said.

"This is Aero 12. We're fine. Suppressing fire was effective. Both suspects down. They're not going anywhere. We have the FAV in sight and will remain on station until the ground crew gives the all clear."

The Lieutenant said a few terse words to the driver. The Humvee turned once again to head back to the highway. He got back on the radio again. When he finished, he turned to Kevin and Dave in the back of the vehicle. "Everything's under control. I'm taking you to OP-5, and they will get you back to North Camp. I need to return to the outpost and take care of things. I want to meet the FAV crew and see what I can learn. We've got medical people coming in and also my boss, the MFO higher-ups, and someone from the Egyptian army. No doubt I'll be writing reports for the next three days. This is a big deal. Things are usually pretty quiet out here. We've had a few incidents, but not many. I'm just glad you're both okay."

"Lieutenant, Dave and I feel terrible about the loss of those two men. If we can do anything for their families, we'd like you to let us know."

"That's kind of you, Kevin. Let me think about what might be appropriate."

Juliana sat on a low wall near the tomb behind the Great Pyramid. As she was sketching the pyramid, she heard a loud noise in the distance, possibly an explosion. She paused in her work and looked around. Up on the nearby access road, where tourists had been walking, she saw that they had suddenly stopped and were looking back in the direction of the hotel. They started moving quickly, some running off the road in the direction of the middle pyramid. In minutes the road was deserted. She heard a siren approaching the plateau where the pyramids were located.

She closed her sketchbook and scrambled off the wall, going down an embankment into the Western Cemetery, where she crouched down behind some rubble and watched the road. All was still.

She thought about returning to the hotel, but decided the route back would leave her exposed to traffic on the side streets. While she was considering the alternatives, an Arab carrying a rifle appeared on the access road. He stopped, aimed, and fired a burst of three shots in the direction of the other side of the road.

While his attention was directed away from her, Juliana ran quickly behind a tomb and into a narrow passageway where she could not be seen from the road. Keeping low, she plunged deeper into the labyrinth of the cemetery, moving away from the Great Pyramid until she found an open tomb. She crawled through a low opening and into the dark interior. She crept carefully along the wall, feeling as she went, until she reached the farthest corner where there was an alcove with a low wall. This had once been a chapel housing items needed by the tomb owner in the afterlife.

Juliana crouched down in the alcove, the only sound now being her racing heart. Minutes passed. She heard voices outside, men speaking Arabic in low tones. A light flashed momentarily inside the tomb, but no one entered and the voices moved on. Silence returned.

She tried to get more comfortable, seated on the floor and leaning against the wall. On edge, nervous, she steeled herself to remain calm and wait as long as necessary.

೪

"Would you mind staying another day?" Dave asked, while he and Kevin were having breakfast at North Camp. "There's going to be a memorial service for the two guys that were killed."

"No, of course not, what time?"

"It will be here in the Force Theater at 0900."

"What are your plans for the day?"

"I've got to go out to OP-6 to see how the repairs are going. We've got crews there rebuilding the sentry post and cleaning up the mess."

"Anything more about the attack?"

"No one's claimed responsibility. Usually these things are done to try to stir problems between the Egyptians and the Israelis. The Palestinians in the Gaza Strip rely on smuggling from Egypt because the Israelis control the supply routes. Whenever someone in Gaza fires a rocket at Israel, they clamp down. It hurts the population more than the militants, which makes more enemies in the long run. Do you know what the main stuff is that they smuggle in?"

"No idea."

"Stuff like cement, cooking oil, fruit, medicine, and vegetables to feed the people. The Israelis have an embargo so that food and medicine are in short supply. Young people can't get jobs as there is no work and it's like living in a giant refugee camp. Of course, they probably smuggle weapons also, but the Egyptians keep a close watch out for weapons or materials that can be used to make weapons."

"Is there any solution?" Kevin asked. "Doesn't seem likely, does it?"

"I'm really pessimistic," Dave said. "I feel sorry for the Palestinians. They deserve a state. Most of them have lived there for centuries, long before the modern state of Israel existed. But the Israelis are intent on squeezing them out. They don't want a two-country solution. The

Palestinians respond with rocket attacks on Israeli civilians, which do no real damage, but harden Israeli attitudes and give support to the conservatives, who crack down more. Each Israeli repression creates another generation of young Palestinians determined to take revenge for the death of family members and friends. And so it goes—on and on, with no end in sight."

The Force Theater was full, standing room only, testament to the popularity of the FIJIBATT soldiers and the cohesiveness of the MFO in general. The Force Commander was present as was the FIJIBATT commander, the company commander, and the Lieutenant. In the front, by the altar, two pairs of boots, each with an inverted rifle topped by a helmet, stood as a reminder of the tragedy.

Chaplain Russell welcomed the attendees and gave the invocation prayer. One of the FIJIBATT soldiers read the Scripture in a deep solemn voice, *"I am the resurrection and the life. The one who believes in me will live, even though they die; and whoever lives by believing in me will never die."*

The eulogy of both men was presented by the company commander, followed by personal recollections and memories offered by several of the fallen soldiers' comrades. The Force Commander addressed the assembled troops, reminding them of the importance of the peacekeeping mission, and praising the dedication of the two fallen soldiers. He concluded by stating, "If our mission here succeeds in maintaining this fragile peace, countless thousands of lives will be saved and in that case the lives of Sgt. Nanuku and Specialist Satala will not have been given in vain."

Chaplain Russell added his reflections on duty, faith and the ever after. The first sergeant gave the last roll call, and FIJIBATT played taps, ending the somber ceremony.

Afterwards, Dave knocked on Kevin's door in the Base quarters. "There's something going on," he said. "It sounds bad. There have been a number of bombings in Cairo, and Alexandria. They hit the Cairo Museum and some hotels, as well as the new library at Alexandria."

"What hotels?" Kevin asked.

"There were several. I don't remember which ones, I wasn't paying that much attention, but they were tourist hotels. I think the Mena House was one, you know that hotel out by the pyramids."

"Yes, I know it," Kevin uttered, extremely upset. "That's bad. It's where Juliana is staying. Where's a phone?"

Kevin paced back and forth waiting for what seemed a long time before the hotel operator finally answered.

"I'd like to speak with Mrs. Hunter in room 125," he said impatiently.

Juliana answered the phone almost immediately.

"Julie, it's Kevin. I heard there was an attack on the hotel. Are you okay?"

"Yes I'm fine," she said, speaking rapidly, "but it was frightening, very scary."

"What happened?"

"Some guy rode up in front of the hotel on a bicycle. He apparently had some explosives. He must've been nervous or something, because when he sped up the driveway he fell off his bicycle. This alerted the security guards so when he started to detonate explosives, they shot him. The blast was far enough away from the front entrance that no serious damage was done and there were only minor injuries. At the time, I was up at the pyramids, sketching at a place behind the Great Pyramid. I heard the shots and explosion and then saw people start racing around. One guy had a gun and was shooting. I ducked down into the area behind the pyramid and ran into a tomb to hide. I waited there for about an hour until things quieted down. When I came out of the tomb there were police everywhere and they were clearing all of the visitors out of the pyramid sites. I returned to the hotel and have stayed here, hoping you would call."

"I was so worried. It sounds like there was a series of simultaneous attacks around Egypt. There was a bombing at one of the Sinai outposts where I was visiting and two soldiers were killed. Fortunately, the terrorists didn't make it inside the Outpost. I'm back at North Camp and will be returning to Cairo tomorrow. Sounds like you should stay close to the hotel and not venture off for any sightseeing trips. I'll give you a call when I leave for Cairo. I'll have the driver take me directly to the Mena House. We have a flight back to the U.S. the next day, so we'll get the hell out of here.

"I love you lots and I'm sorry you had this scare. Please be careful until I get there."

"You be careful also. Don't worry about me, I'm staying right here in the hotel. Love you."

Kevin met Dave for breakfast before leaving for the trip back to Cairo and asked if he had any word on the terrorists.

"No," Dave said. "Everything is hush-hush right now until the Force Commander has been briefed and decides what to tell the world. I'm sure they want to keep things quiet while they investigate the staff to make certain there was no collusion, no inside help. You know, we have a mixture here, mostly Egyptians, but a few Lebanese, Palestinians, and Jordanians. They all have been carefully screened and cleared, but you never know if maybe a bad actor slipped through."

"I was wondering," Kevin said, "how many people knew I was going to be here?"

"It's hard to say. You saw the announcement in the *Sandpaper*. I suppose one answer could be 'everyone on base,' but in reality most of the locals aren't interested in our visitors. We get lots of politicians from the MFO member countries who come out here on boondoggles so they can justify their travel expenses to Europe or somewhere more interesting. Why do you ask?"

"Maybe I'm paranoid. It's probably just a coincidence."

&

Kevin returned to Cairo without incident, he and Juliana flew home, and two days later he was back in his office. When Holly gave him his messages he saw that Kidd had called. He returned the call. Kidd answered his own line.

"This is Kevin. I thought you were going to retire."

"I am—one of these days. Right now, I can't afford to. I need a couple more years to get full benefits."

"I got a message that you called."

"Yes. Where were you? You didn't tell me you were taking another trip."

"I thought since you were going to retire you didn't care anymore."

"Yeah, I can see why you might have thought that. Where were you?

"I was in Egypt. We have a project supporting the MFO, so I went there for some meetings. We had some excitement."

"Oh? How's that?"

"There was a terrorist attack in one of the remote camps I was visiting, along with some attacks in Cairo, including one at the hotel where Juliana was staying."

"Jesus! Sorry to hear that. You both okay?"

"Yes, but two of the MFO soldiers were killed and several were injured."

"I don't know if there is any connection, but our Egyptian friend escaped from federal prison. When last seen she got on a flight in the Dallas-Fort Worth airport for Kuwait City. She was probably headed to Egypt. I really feel bad. I just left a message. I should've told your secretary to have you call me. Is anything known about the attackers?"

"I haven't heard yet. One blew himself up at the security checkpoint. At least two others, maybe more, ran off into the Sinai desert with some MFO troopers hot on their trail. They were tracked down and either killed or captured. I'll get a report and let you know."

"Do that. One more thing. When we last met after the al-Khobar attack, you said you wanted to help. Is that still the case, or have you had enough of us?"

"No. That's still the case. Maybe more so. I just don't know if I can be of any real help, but I'll try."

✎

Kevin called Dave a couple of weeks later. "What do you know about the Cairo attacks? Were they connected to the ones in the Sinai?"

"I don't know," Dave said. "The official version is that they were 'copycat' attacks, inspired by what happened in the Sinai. I can give you a summary of what happened in the Sinai. You can probably pull up the news release if you go to the MFO website, if you want to read more.

"Basically, it was determined that there were only three attackers. They were 'Sinai Jihadists,' some kind of nutty fringe group that wants to drive all foreigners out of the Sinai. Of the two that fled, one was killed in an exchange of gunfire with the MFO helicopter. The other was wounded but survived. Both were Egyptians."

"Was anyone else in MFO injured?"

"No. The news release reported that two MFO soldiers were killed. Otherwise, damage was minimal, and the MFO remains steadfast in its dedication to preserve the peace, etc., etc. What the news release doesn't say is that so far, no MFO staff member has been implicated in any way, so it appears to be a home-grown Egyptian plot. The dirt bikes the attackers rode had Egyptian licenses. The Egyptian State Security Investigations Service (SSI) has taken over the case and is using the information they collected to round up other suspected members of this radical Sinai group. So you can expect a big crackdown. I just hope they don't haul in any of our guys.

"Regarding the reasons for the attack, it was all the usual political hogwash, cleansing Egypt of the foreign infidels, they're all lackeys of Israel, you know, that stuff. The Lieutenant was in on the initial interview with the surviving terrorist, and he picked up one interesting comment. While he was spewing all his hate of the MFO, he singled out Americans. Why?"

"They are the worst of the bunch," he said. "They put my sister in prison."

The interrogation of the MFO attack survivor by the Egyptian special security forces in the Sinai was, as Dave predicted, harsh but effective. No MFO personnel were involved in the attack. Terrorists calling themselves the "Sinai Jihadists" recruited and radicalized a young Palestinian to wear an explosive vest. He was brought into the Sinai from Gaza by a tunnel under the border. In addition to a brief period of training, he was given doses of hashish to bolster his courage. The surviving terrorist, Samih el-Masry, also revealed the location of the training "camp," a ramshackle building in the al-Jura district of al-Arish. By the time the Egyptians raided this building, the other terrorists had left, but the police found traces of explosives, enough evidence to convict other members of the group, once they were found. Neighbors reported that there had been five men and a woman in the building. Three of the men were either dead or in custody, so the search narrowed to finding the remaining two men and woman. The neighbors also stated that the group had a blue

Fiat vehicle.

The car was spotted by an alert customs official at a checkpoint on the other side of the Suez Canal. The vehicle was impounded and the occupants detained. A search of the vehicle revealed weapons and ammunition.

The occupants were taken into custody and transported to Cairo. There, after a brief hearing in front of an administrative judge, they were sentenced to twenty years in prison. The woman was found to have forged identification documents and her real name was Leila el-Masry. After escaping from Carswell, she used forged documents to fly to Kuwait and then to Cairo. She had no place to stay in Cairo, so she joined her brother in the Sinai. Despite her protestations of innocence, she was sentenced along with the two men. After less than a month of freedom, she found herself once again in prison, this time in Egypt.

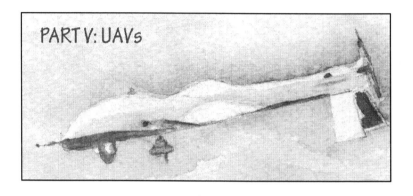

PART V: UAVs

QUAGMIRE

After the events of the last trip to Egypt, Juliana begged Kevin to promise he would not travel again to the Middle East. On the home front, Consolidated's government support contracts were rapidly expanding as the firm was called upon to design, build, and operate logistical facilities in Iraq and Afghanistan. There were power plants, water treatment facilities, and airports to be repaired, as well as barracks and supply bases to support the ever-growing numbers of U.S., British, and NATO troops in the two countries.

Following the election of Hamid Karzai as president of Afghanistan in 2004, the country held its first parliamentary elections in more than thirty years. Initially beaten back, the Taliban and al Qaeda fighters showed no sign of quitting. Suicide bombing attacks continued. NATO officially assumed responsibility for security throughout Afghanistan, with the U.S. providing the largest number of troops.

Kevin helped organize a special group within Consolidated to design barracks for Afghani troops. Rather than use American design standards, these facilities were planned to respect Afghanistan culture.

Meanwhile, in Iraq, the idea that the Iraqi population would welcome U.S. troops as liberators quickly faded. Bloody fighting continued at Fallujah, Mosul, and other locations. Insurgents made deadly use of discarded or captured Iraqi Army artillery rounds—IEDs— to create roadside bombs that were effective in blowing up U.S. and coalition military vehicles. As the number of fatalities and maiming of U.S. soldiers increased, these became a feared weapon in the hands of the insurgents.

Finally, near the end of 2005, U.S. President George W. Bush stated that the decision to invade Iraq in

2003 "was a result of faulty intelligence." He did not clarify whose intelligence was at fault.

On December 30, 2006, Saddam Hussein was executed. In 2007, the Iraq war troop "surge" was announced as a strategy to stabilize the country and eventually shift responsibility for internal security to the new Iraqi forces that were being trained by the U.S. During the conflict there was growing evidence of meddling by Iran and Iranian officials, and offices in the region were targeted by U.S. forces.

Top Iranian military officials were observed traveling unrestricted throughout Iraq. Iraq's porous Eastern border with Iran allowed the free flow of personnel and arms. In 2007, the U.S. military raided a so-called "Iranian liaison office" in the northern Iraq town of Irbil. Five Iranians were captured, along with computers and documents. They were imprisoned for two and a half years and then released.

In Afghanistan, the situation was no better. Despite attempts to train Afghani military and police forces, the country continued to experience unrest. There were several incidents where "friendly" Afghan soldiers or police turned their weapons on U.S. or NATO troops, killing or wounding them before being shot down. In September 2008, President George W. Bush sent additional troops to Afghanistan, replicating the "surge" strategy previously used in Iraq.

In January 2009, after President Barack Obama was elected, Kevin got a call from Kidd.

"How about lunch on Friday, the usual place. I've got somebody I want you to meet."

When Kevin walked back to Kidd's usual table, he was surprised to see a woman seated there with him.

She was petite, short dark hair tinged with gray.

The woman was conservatively dressed in a gray business suit. She had no makeup other than pale lipstick, but was attractive. Her facial features were classically proportioned and her eyes were dark brown. As Kevin slid into the seat next to her, she gave him an unsmiling, appraising look, and did not stand to greet him.

"Kevin Hunter, meet Col. Mary Minnick. Mary's going to take over some of my responsibilities when I retire. I've asked her to work with you. Mary is an Air Force Academy graduate, a pilot, and just retired from the Air Force to join us. Her specialty is UAVs, so you two have something in common. I told her how you and I first became acquainted."

"Hello Col. Minnick," Kevin said, shaking her hand. "It's a pleasure to meet you. I don't know if I can be of any help, but I'll do whatever I can." Kevin noted her handshake was firm and sensed a toughness beneath her apparent mild exterior.

"I'm pleased to meet you Mr. Hunter. Thank you for joining us."

"Let's order lunch and then Mary can fill you in on priorities."

Mary had iced tea while Kidd had ordered his usual scotch and rocks. Kevin ordered iced tea also.

"Kevin, you know the menu here, so what will you have? We've already ordered. Mary's having a seafood salad and I'm having my usual, the steak sandwich. Eat hearty, because Mary's buying."

Kevin looked at Mary, who simply nodded in confirmation as a waiter stood by, waiting for Kevin's order.

"The shrimp linguine for me."

When the waiter departed, Kevin turned to Mary. "I'm impressed that you attended the Air Force Academy. It wasn't so long ago that they started admitting women, as I recall. I can imagine that in the early days it was tough being in an all-male institution."

Mary smiled. "It had its challenges. I entered in 1980. We were the fifth class to have women. The previous classes had it harder than we did. By the time we got there they had at least removed the urinals and provided proper toilets."

"And you were a pilot?"

"Yes. I was in the 437th Airlift Wing, stationed at Charleston Air Force Base. We flew Boeing C-17 Globe Masters—amazing planes that could carry a couple of buses, a tank, or a hundred paratroopers. I flew some missions as part of Operation Enduring Freedom in Afghanistan after 9/11, and later in Operation Iraqi Freedom, the second Gulf War."

"Very impressive," Kevin said. "Were you ever stationed at Hickam Air Force Base in Oahu? I once took an Air Mobility Command flight to Johnston Island from there."

"No. Never had the good fortune to be stationed in Hawaii.

"I understand that you have projects and offices in the Middle East, particularly in Kuwait, the United Arab Emirates, and Oman," Mary said. "As you probably know, the Strait of Hormuz, the narrow waterway leading from the Persian Gulf into the Gulf of Oman, is an area of great concern to us and to the rest of the world. Around twenty percent of the world's petroleum passes through that narrow strait. On several occasions Iran has stated that it will close the strait to shipping and the U.S. has responded that this would be considered an act of war and we would use military force to reopen the strait."

"I remember that a U.S. vessel hit an Iranian mine in the waterway during the Iran-Iraq war in 1988," Kevin said. "This provoked a strong retaliation from the U.S."

"Yes. That was a frigate, the *Samuel B. Roberts.* Despite heavy damage, the crew kept it from sinking. More recently, Iranian speedboats came out and harassed U.S. vessels in the strait. No shots were fired but words have been exchanged and the rhetoric got hot once again. As a result, the U.S. sent several battle groups, including carriers, into the Persian Gulf as a show of force."

"I'm aware of the general situation," Kevin said. "Once, just for the hell of it, I went to Al Khasab on the Musandam Peninsula in Oman and looked out into the Gulf. It was kind of an eerie feeling, realizing that across that narrow strait I could see Iran, with all it had come to symbolize these days. But even so, I'm not sure if I can be of any real assistance."

"Sometimes small, seemingly trivial pieces of information can be combined to paint a bigger picture. We want to avoid surprises. Knowing that the normal patterns of trade, transportation, movement of people or other everyday matters have suddenly been modified could signal something important is in the works. If you get a sense that anything is out of the ordinary in your normal business dealings, we'd like to hear about it."

"Okay, that's not a problem," Kevin said.

"There is another subject that concerns us," Mary said. "It is Iran's UAVs. You've already had some experience with the extent to which Iran is willing to go to try to defeat our advanced capabilities. The Iranians first developed a primitive UAV during the Iran-Iraq war in the 1980s. This drone, called '*Mohajer*-Migrant,' was first used to survey and photograph Iraqi troop positions.

"After seeing the value of 'eyes in the sky,' Iran continued to improve it, developing *Mohajer-2,* capable of longer range and with an auto pilot so it could fly beyond the range limited by direct radio control. By now, as far as we know, the Iranians have version 4. We know it was used to observe action in Afghanistan. In addition, the Iranians gave or sold some to Hezbollah. Hezbollah flew one into Israeli airspace in 2004, but screwed up, lost control and it crashed in the sea. These are slow, relatively low-flying and with a maximum flight time about six to seven hours, and a range of one hundred miles. As far as we know, Iran does not have the capability yet to arm its UAVs with accurately guided missiles."

"I assume that one of our concerns is that Iran is moving ahead, trying to develop the advanced guidance technology to enable offensive capability," Kevin said.

"In terms of conventional liquid- and solid-fueled missiles, Iran is developing or has developed short and intermediate range missiles," Mary replied. "It obviously wants to be able to reach targets in Saudi Arabia, Israel, Iraq, Turkey—wherever unfriendly forces might have bases. To date we don't think these missiles are highly accurate, but that becomes less important if there are a lot of them, and even less important if they are nuclear tipped."

"In parallel, the Iranians are working hard to improve satellite communications and means to jam the satellite and GPS communications of their enemies," Kidd said. "They are also working on broadband radar capable of detecting stealthy aircraft."

Mary noticed that Kevin had hardly touched his food.

"I apologize if we've caused you to lose your appetite," she said.

"No, it's not that," Kevin said. "We hear bits and pieces of the news and tend to dismiss it. But when someone puts it all together—succinctly, as you've done, it's a little frightening. Obviously, there's no easy answer. Those 'hawks' who say we should attack Iran and destroy its nuclear capability have no idea what a mess that would create, do they? That was a problem with Iraq. We invaded, but there was no endgame, no plan for what to do after the Army and Navy did their job."

Kidd added, "We have to be alert; we have to be aware. One Pearl Harbor, one Twin Towers per century is enough—actually, is too much, really. We don't want any more surprises.

"Coming back to our concerns, the greatest

destabilizing force in the Middle East is Iran," Mary said. "They have their hand in everywhere they sense weakness in the local authorities. They support terrorists, particularly Hezbollah. We know they have an active UAV R&D program and are pushing ahead with their nuclear energy program. We don't want to help them by exporting critical components or technology.

"Another way the Iranians can copy our UAV technology is by getting one of our drones. The Serbs shot down a *Predator* over Bosnia in 1995. It was in that war that the significance of UAVs really became apparent. They could be used to avoid civilian casualties and to avoid loss or capture of pilots, plus they were much cheaper than modern aircraft. Dozens were next used in the Kosovo War in 1999—not only U.S., but British, French, and German UAVs were deployed, and over thirty were shot down or crashed, including four *Predators*. When that happens, we try to prevent them from ending up in the wrong hands. This is a big concern."

"Now Bush is out and Obama is in," Kevin said. "During the election campaign Obama said he wants to bring home the troops. Do you think he will, or will the Pentagon sway him to keep fighting in Iraq and Afghanistan?"

"In the campaign he said he would remove all combat troops from Iraq sixteen months after taking office. Our reading of the situation is that he is doing that. They're pulling back to Kuwait and then coming home. Of course, we'll still have a military presence there, training the Iraqi self-defense forces and protecting our embassy and other interests," Kidd said.

"Kevin, do you have projects there?" Mary asked.

"We've had or have several projects in Iraq. The major one is a global maintenance and repair contract to service, repair, and maintain military vehicles. Now that effort is directed at training the new Iraqi Army to maintain surplus U.S. military vehicles that have been donated to them. Another project we're doing, funded by USAID, is providing consulting services to Iraq's financial sector, trying to rebuild Iraq's economy through economic reform. I'm not involved in this project, but I know a few of the people. At one point Consolidated had a lot of people in Iraq, but now it's down to two or three hundred.

"We've also had projects in the Green Zone, the secure area of Baghdad where the U.S. and other embassies are located. The new Iraq government has facilities there also. It's a fortified area in the Karkh district of central Baghdad, near a bend in the Tigris River. It's surrounded by concrete blast walls and access is limited to a few guarded checkpoints. Security was formerly controlled by coalition troops, but full control has been turned over to Iraqi security forces. The other area where we had projects was at Baghdad International Airport. The airport was turned back to Iraqi civilian control five years ago. It used to be a harrowing experience to drive from the Green Zone to the airport, but I hear it's not so bad now. The commercial airlines are returning. Of course, there still are sporadic incidents of small arms fire at incoming aircraft."

"I'm familiar with the airport," Mary said. "We landed there a few times. Your projects are very interesting, Kevin. Charles tells me that you occasionally travel to the Middle East for meetings."

"Yes, I've done a lot of traveling there."

"Kevin lets us know when he's got trips coming up," Kidd said. "If you have any requests, he might be able to help."

"What about Afghanistan?" Mary asked. "I assume you have projects there also."

"Yes, similar to Iraq, we have a maintenance and operational support contract with the U.S. Army. We maintain and repair vehicles and other equipment, support base operations, and provide supplies and services. More recently we're rebuilding damaged Mine Resistant Ambush Protected vehicles—so-called MRAP vehicles—in

Afghanistan, rather than airlifting them back to Kuwait. This is saving the Army a lot of money. We also have another USAID contract called 'Stability in Key Areas' that funds local small infrastructure projects, trying to rebuild damaged communities."

"How safe is this work for your people?"

"Frankly, it's about as dangerous as it is for the military. I was surprised to learn that the number of civilian contractor personnel killed in Iraq and Afghanistan runs close to the number of military killed. In the first six months of this year, for the first time, more civilian contractor personnel were killed than soldiers. Our firm is fortunate in that it has not had a large number of deaths. Many of the other contractors have more personnel in harm's way, for example serving as security guards."

"How has this affected your ability to recruit people?"

"So far, we haven't had too much trouble. The pay is good. The challenge is finding people with the right skills—diesel mechanics, for example. We end up hiring a lot of ex-military because they know the equipment."

"Do you get involved in recruiting and hiring, Kevin?"

"Sometimes. Mostly in interviewing potential candidates who have applied to HR for the higher-level positions."

"I see. Hypothetically speaking, suppose we were able to recommend a highly qualified individual to you, do you think you could help him get a position in Afghanistan?"

"If he's had any experience with MRAP vehicles, for example, the answer would be definitely yes."

"I'll keep that in mind. You never know what might come up. One other thing," Mary said. "Would you like to make a quick visit to San Nicolas Island? This would be an opportunity to learn a little more about our drone concerns."

"Yes, I would like that."

"Charlie, I believe Mr. Hunter has the appropriate security clearances, does he not?"

"Yes."

"Good. Let me do some checking and I'll get back to you with a date. We'll drive up to Point Mugu and take a Navy plane over to the island from there."

On the appointed day, Mary picked Kevin up at his office at 6 a.m.

"I think we'll drive up the coast. It's a little longer but we'll be going against the rush hour traffic."

Once on Pacific Coast Highway, Mary asked, "What do you know about San Nicolas Island?"

"Not much. I know it's linked up with the China Lake Naval Ordinance Test Station and has been used to test antiaircraft missiles. As I understand it, they fly target drones out from Point Mugu and try to shoot them down out in the Pacific Missile Range. So I assume they have some pretty sophisticated tracking and telemetry systems."

"That's true," Mary said. "Although I don't know a lot about the full capabilities of the facilities, I know they have had a lot of historic 'firsts' with their test programs."

"Actually, I've been out to the island once in my boat."

"Oh? What for?"

"I was with a couple of guys on a diving trip. We were at Santa Barbara Island and decided to go out and see what the diving was like at San Nicolas. At that time, the island shoreline was divided into three zones. Two were off-limits, but the third one was open to civilian small craft as long as no tests were being conducted. You could anchor but not go ashore. From the sea, the island is not very impressive, sort of flat and ugly. It has none of the mountains or beauty of Santa Cruz or Catalina."

"How do you get permission?" Mary asked.

"I called ahead on the radio and they said it was clear. We anchored, did a little fishing, had dinner, and went to bed. In the morning, everyone got suited up to go diving. Just as we're getting in the water, a Navy patrol boat appeared and told us we had thirty minutes to leave the area, before the bombing started. We got everyone back on board, pulled the anchor, and got the hell out of there. On the way back to Santa Barbara Island I kept looking back, watching for aircraft or signs of an explosion, but nothing seemed to be happening."

"Santa Barbara Island is where you first got involved with Charlie, right?"

"Yes. And it's still one of my favorite places to go." Kevin looked out the window as they went through Malibu, passing Zuma beach.

"Can you see the island?"

"No. It's pretty hard to see from the mainland unless you're up higher and it's a clear day. But we should get a good look at it on the flight over from Point Mugu."

After checking into the base they sat in a waiting room at the airfield, where a C-440 aircraft would fly them out to San Nicolas. There was a group of contractor personnel also going out to the island.

"What about San Clemente Island? Ever been there?"

"In my boat, yes. I like going to Pyramid Cove on the east end of the island. Great spot for fishing and diving or just spending the night while fishing in the waters off of San Diego. Same deal there. Sometimes you can't stay, because the Navy SEALs are training or the Navy is bombing the island or shooting cruise missiles at it."

The flight to San Nicolas was a short one. After landing, Mary and Kevin were escorted into a briefing room that resembled a small theater. The walls were adorned with maps and photos of some of the tests performed at San Nicolas. There they were greeted by a tall dark-haired naval officer in a tan uniform.

"Good morning, I'm Lieutenant Commander Rob Mackey. And you must be Col. Minnick," he said, shaking hands with Mary.

"That's retired Col. Minnick," Mary said. "And this is Kevin Hunter."

The Lieutenant shook hands with Kevin.

"Welcome to San Nicolas or as we call it in the Navy, where everything has an acronym, 'SNI.' I understand that your purpose in being here is to get a briefing on what we view as threats to our unmanned air systems. I also understand that Mr. Hunter once had some first-hand experience with those threats—someone trying to steal some pretty critical guidance hardware. As a side note, we have a small but heavily armed security force that patrols the island. The loss of the hardware that Mr. Hunter providentially recovered was a matter of great embarrassment to the security folks. Changes were made as a result.

"Let me give you a brief overview first," Mackey said. "As you saw, we have a 10,000 foot runway. C-5 aircraft can land here. We have our own power plant and water plant, and are pretty much self-sufficient. We have missile launch capabilities, radar, telemetry, satellite communications, advanced optical tracking systems, and miss-distance indication and Doppler systems. In short, we can launch almost anything, track it, see how well it works, and in most cases recover it. That goes for missiles launched from China Lake, Vandenberg Air Force Base, or ships at sea. It applies to everything from backpack type drones to ICBMs."

"What are you doing with drones?" Kevin asked.

"Specifically, with UAVs, we were involved in the first cross-country flight of Northrop Grumman's *Global Hawk*, which flew across the U.S. from Patuxent River on the East Coast and landed at Point Mugu in California. We worked on integrating the *Predator* into fleet training exercises for reconnaissance tracking and attack, day or night. Between us and China Lake, we've tested just about every drone in DOD's inventory, including *Pioneer, Scan Eagle, Raven, Predator, Reaper, Fire Scout, Global Hawk,* and others.

"The engineers continue to innovate and then we test to see if the systems work as they are supposed to under realistic field conditions. Our primary goals are to improve accuracy, range, and flight ceiling of the drones, and making them jam proof. We did the first high-power GPS jamming tests on the *Reaper,* to reduce the likelihood that an enemy could take control. To sum it up, I'd say that loss of control is our number one concern. We don't want an enemy to be able to interfere with the flight, or to intercept the information the drone is sending back to us, as happened in Operation Enduring Freedom."

"Is this still a problem?"

"You'll be surprised to know that one of our biggest concerns is the damn smartphone," Mackey said. "To control a drone, you need to be able to sense direction, in other words, a compass; position, meaning a GPS; altitude, a pressure sensor; a gyroscope, to measure rotation; and three axis accelerometers to measure yaw, roll, and pitch. It used to be that this was a lot of expensive hardware. Today, thanks to the development of smartphones, all of this capability is integrated into a single chip that you can buy off the shelf for less than $20."

"Have you seen any evidence of smartphone technology being used in a UAV?" Mary asked.

"Not directly—yet," Mackey replied. "Don't get me wrong: it takes more than this to make a major weapon system. You also need an airframe, engine, and communication systems.

"But you can see where this is going. Just about any country with some halfway decent engineers can build some kind of a drone. They can experiment, test, try things out. I think it's just a matter of time before some Jihadist buys a 'hobby' drone, loads it with some explosives, and flies it over a wall, into a military compound, and detonates it. How do you defend against something like that?

"One final note: where does Apple make smartphones? In China. How 'smart' is that?"

On the flight back to the mainland, Mary fell asleep. Kevin looked out the window at the sea below. It was early afternoon and the wind had come up. The first traces of white caps could be seen. Santa Barbara Island was visible in the distance. He imagined himself in his boat, with the wind freshening and the boat heeling over, picking up speed.

Seeing the island reminded him of the fateful day when he and Juliana found the backpacks, and how that singular event had altered their lives.

He turned away from the window and his thoughts snapped back to reality. Lieutenant Mackey's presentation was sobering. The world, already a dangerous place, was becoming more so.

When Kevin returned home that evening, Juliana was quick to ask him about his trip. He'd told her he was going to San Nicolas Island to look at some potential projects. He'd been forthright in telling her that Col. Minnick was a woman, a former Air Force pilot.

"We drove up the coast to Point Mugu," he said, "and there the Navy flew us out to the island. On the flight back I had a good view of Santa Barbara Island. It made me want to get in the boat and go there."

"Did you and Col. Minnick stop for breakfast in Malibu, maybe a quick walk on the beach?"

Kevin looked at her, shook his head. "No, Julie, Col. Minnick is very professional—all business. And she drove. We didn't stop anywhere. We had coffee and a donut at the airfield in Point Mugu."

"You mean 'Mary,' right?" Juliana said. "Holly says she calls you all the time."

"Holly doesn't like her for some reason. Anyway, she doesn't call 'all the time' and the few times she's called, it's been on business. You don't need to worry about her."

"Is she married?"

"I assume so. She's never said and I've never asked. She never talks about personal matters, but I told her I was married."

"I'm sorry Kevin, it's just that sometimes I get funny feelings."

He gave her a hug. "That's okay. I understand."

"So what was San Nicolas like?"

"It has amazing facilities for missile testing and tracking. They perform tests in conjunction with Point Mugu and China Lake. A lot of it was over my head."

"Are you going to get a project there?"

"I don't know. This was a preliminary briefing. We'll see. Anything interesting on the news today?" Kevin asked.

"The U.K. is withdrawing the last of its troops from Iraq this month. What do you think that means?"

"President Obama said that the last of our combat troops will leave Iraq in August. Supposedly that means the war is over and with parliamentary elections scheduled for next year, Iraq is on its way to becoming an independent democratic nation. I'm skeptical. A lot will depend on whether the Iraqis can stem the violence and protect their cities from terrorists.

"Frankly, I think the entire Middle East is a powder keg. We're still battling al Qaeda in Afghanistan. Many of the jihadists there are not Afghanis, but have come to Afghanistan from other Arab countries to fight us and learn how to use weapons and make bombs when then they return home. The situation is very uncertain in my mind. It would just take a small spark to set the entire region ablaze."

ARAB SPRING

In December 2010, in the town of Sidi Bouzid, central Tunisia, an event occurred that went unnoticed by most of the world. At first.

An unemployed worker named Mohamed Bouaziz struggled to make a living selling fruit from a wheelbarrow in the city streets. He was frequently harassed by corrupt city officials who wanted bribes. On the fateful day, he was slapped by a woman official, his wheelbarrow load of fruit dumped in the street, and an electronic scale he used to weigh his produce was confiscated. When he went to the municipal authorities to get his scale back, he was denied. Distraught that he'd been unfairly robbed of the very means to earn his livelihood, he doused himself with gasoline and set himself on fire.

The Tunisian government's callous indifference to Bouaziz's plight captured the imagination of many other young Tunisians who were unable to get jobs and likewise suffered from government corruption. Riots began throughout Tunisia, with the result that President Zine El Abidine Ben Ali eventually fled the country. In the coming year, the first free elections in more than fifty years were held.

Following the Tunisian example, protests, riots, revolution, and in some cases, wars, occurred in other countries. Protests erupted in Algeria and Lebanon. In Yemen, long-time president Ali Abdullah Saleh was forced to resign and flee the country. He narrowly escaped death when explosives detonated inside the presidential compound.

The example of the Tunisian riots spread to twenty other Arab countries. There was widespread dissatisfaction with absolute rulers who had held power for decades, amassing wealth while ordinary people struggled to support their families. Corruption was rampant and ruling family members were favored, regardless of ability. In many countries, masses of educated young people could not find jobs. Rising food prices and shortages of essential goods were also a stimulus. The response varied from country to country, but began with protests including rallies, sit-ins, occupation of government buildings, additional self-immolations, and strikes. The government's reaction to protests varied, but when its response was violent, it had the effect of strengthening, rather than stopping, the protests.

One unique aspect of the protests was the widespread use of social media and the Internet to plan and coordinate protests and marches.

ॐ

One day in January 2011 when Kevin came home from the office, he found Juliana watching a newscast on television.

"Kevin, come here. I think you should see this."

The television cameras panned over an area Kevin recognized as Cairo. In the background he had a fleeting view of the Cairo Museum. Thousands of Egyptians were in Tahrir Square, taking part in a huge anti-Mubarak protest. As far as Kevin could tell, the protests were largely nonviolent, with speakers calling upon Mubarak to resign.

"That's a real mess," Kevin said, as they watched the images on television. "I don't think Mubarak will resign. I'm sure we'll see violence if this continues."

As Kevin suspected, the riots continued, spreading to Suez, Alexandria, and other cities in Egypt. The second day, government police and security forces were prepared and there were violent clashes with the protesters. Many were beaten and arrested. Police used tear gas to drive the protesters away from government buildings.

In Egypt, the labor movement was a catalyst for action, protesting poor working conditions and inadequate pay. The Egyptian government responded with riot police to break up strikes. The strikers were joined over succeeding weeks by college students and young workers who used social media, including setting up a Facebook page, to attract support for the protests. This culminated in the huge anti-Mubarak demonstrations in Tahrir Square in Cairo on January 25, 2011. In the midst of the riots a number of prisoners were either released or escaped from Egyptian prisons. After protests swelled and spread throughout the country, Egyptian President Hosni Mubarak resigned in February. Thus ended his thirty-year regime.

In Syria, protests led to the resignation of the cabinet, but President Bashar Assad remained obdurate and mobilized the Syrian army to put an end to the protests. Assad was a member of the Alawite sect, an offshoot of Shia Islam, in a country that consisted mostly of Sunni Muslims. Since he assumed the presidency, civil liberties had been tightly controlled. Dissidents were arrested, jailed, and frequently "disappeared." To maintain control, Assad staffed the military and the government bureaucracy with friends and relatives. The public sector was gradually "privatized," enriching his friends and relatives through patronage.

In response to Assad's violent suppression of the protests, some Syrian army personnel revolted. This led to the formation of the "Free Syrian Army" and the country slid into a brutal civil war.

As protests continued to grow in the Arab world, they spread to Libya and fighting occurred. Muammar Gaddafi was overthrown, ending his forty-two years in power. Under a United Nations resolution, a coalition of twenty-seven European and Arab nations intervened to protect civilian lives. Gaddafi attempted to move the government to his hometown of Sirte but the city was overrun and he was killed.

In Iraq, there were protests in Kurdistan. South Sudan agitated to secede. Protests erupted in other Arab countries considered less volatile. There were limited protests in Saudi Arabia, Jordan, Morocco, Kuwait, and Oman. The United Arab Emirates escaped; some agitators tried to organize protests, but the population was not interested. They had good jobs and good pay.

ॐ

One day Kevin got a call from Mary Minnick.

"Kevin, you're not going to believe this. Charlie set up a watch list with some peoples' names on it and said I was to immediately notify you if any of them came up. Well, one did—a woman. I don't know if it is important, but Leila el-Masry was among the prisoners who escaped from the Wadi el-Natrum prison near Cairo last January. She was listed in the Egyptian records as a 'person of interest' to the U.S. due to an outstanding InterPol warrant for her arrest for jailbreak. Over one thousand mostly political prisoners were helped to escape from Wadi and four other prisons by agents of Hamas, Hezbollah, the Muslim Brotherhood, and Sinai-based militants. With all the confusion in Egypt she could be anywhere. Also, I doubt that we'll have much success getting anyone there to take an interest in her, but I can make an effort."

"I don't know what to think," Kevin said. "She was linked to the Sinai attack five years ago. Her brother was one of the terrorists. He was captured and put on trial for the murder of the two MFO soldiers who died in the attack. The last I heard he was in prison, but I don't know if he was executed or is still in jail."

"Egypt has the death penalty for terrorist activities that result in someone being killed," Mary said. "From what I know, there are more than a thousand condemned prisoners on death rows in Egypt, but only ten or so are executed in any given year. They're all held in high-security prisons like Torah or Qena. So I'd say the chances are he's still alive. Your MFO contact might be able to find out."

"Could that woman still bear a grudge after all these years? If anything, you'd think she'd be focused on springing her brother from prison," Kevin said. "Who knows? I suppose anything is possible. I don't plan to return to Egypt anytime soon, and I doubt she'll try to return to the U.S., so I guess I'm not inclined to worry about her. Thanks for letting me know that she's on the loose. If you get any more information, I'd like to know."

With more militants converging on Syria and expanding into Somalia and Yemen, new threats emerged in both Iraq and Afghanistan. President Obama decided to increase the use of drones. Beginning in 2004, President Bush authorized drones to be used against al Qaeda in the Afghanistan/Pakistan border area. In all, about fifty drone attacks were made. They were successful, not only in killing al Qaeda and Taliban senior leaders, but in sowing confusion and demoralizing the command structure. It was believed that many of the strikes were launched from Shamsi Airfield in Pakistan, although both sides denied this. Shamsi was ideal—a remote, isolated location, about two hundred miles southwest of Quetta in Balochistan Province, where the al Qaeda leaders were believed to hide out.

Unfortunately, in November 2011, U.S. and NATO aircraft flying from Afghanistan attacked two Pakistani border posts, killing twenty-four Pakistani soldiers. It was a typical "fog of war" scenario. The U.S. claimed they were defending Afghani troops that had come under fire from the border area, while Pakistan claimed the border posts were just monitoring the area.

The Pakistan reaction was strong; the U.S. was given fifteen days to vacate Shamsi airfield, so the base was lost to U.S. use in December.

This did not slow down the U.S. drone attack. President Obama approved two to three times as many strikes as Bush did in his final year as president, when there were thirty-six reported attacks. Also, drones were now being used against targets in Somalia and Yemen as well as the Pakistan/Afghanistan border area. The ability to locate, identify, and confirm terrorist targets was critical.

Holly stuck her head in Kevin's door. He was busy working on a report, barely glancing up at the interruption. "I'm sorry to bother you. It's that Mary woman on the phone. Do you want to talk to her? I told her you were busy."

"Stall her for a minute while I finish this, and then put the call through."

When the phone rang Kevin picked up.

"Kevin, this is Mary. Your secretary said that you were busy, so I can call at another time if you prefer."

"No, go ahead. I need a break."

"You recall our discussion about recruitment?"

"Yes."

"I've come across someone I'd like you to consider. His name is Ahmad S. Maiwand. He is a U.S. citizen, born in New York to an American mother and Afghan father. His father was a professor at the University of Kabul. He came to Cornell as a visiting professor in 1978, and when the Russians invaded, he stayed here. While at Cornell he met and married his wife and they had one son, Ahmad, born in 1980. When the Russians left Afghanistan in 1989, the family returned and his father resumed his teaching position at the University in Kabul. Ahmad attended local schools there. In 1996, when the Taliban seized Kabul, professor Maiwand was able to get the family to France and then to return to the U.S., where they settled in Fremont, California. Ahmad was admitted to San Jose

State, got a bachelor's degree in mechanical engineering, and joined the U.S. Army reserve. From 2002 to 2006 he saw duty in Afghanistan. He is fluent in Pashto as well as English, and his language abilities made him invaluable. He received an honorable discharge in 2006 and went to work for the Caterpillar Company, diesel engine division, in Peoria, Illinois, up until last year."

"And now?" Kevin asked.

"Now he's interested in new challenges, where he might serve both his new adopted country and his ancestral homeland."

"I suppose you realize that our employees have to get a security clearance."

"Yes, of course. I would not be wasting your time if I thought there was even a remote chance of that becoming an issue."

"To put it rather bluntly, will Ahmad be on your payroll?"

"No. However, as with any person working overseas, we would imagine that he will want to keep his family informed of events in their former town, status of old family friends, and of course his own health and well-being. He would also provide you with any reports required by his work assignment."

"I think I understand," Kevin said.

Also, I believe that your vehicle maintenance contract is five years, of which two years has elapsed. So after three years Ahmad is likely to be released to pursue other interests. I believe that with the overseas experience he will have gained, he would be a shoo-in for a career position in the U.S. Foreign Service, if he were interested."

"I think we can find an opening," Kevin said. "He seems like an ideal candidate. Let me make a couple of calls and I'll get back to you."

"In the meantime, I took the liberty of collecting his documents for you. I'll courier over to your office his résumé, a copy of his discharge papers, university transcripts, and a letter of recommendation from his former employer."

"I assume he would be available for an interview."

"Yes, he's currently home with his family in Fremont. His contact information will be in the package I send you."

"Very good, Mary, thanks for thinking of us."

"You're more than welcome. Let me know how the interview goes."

❧

Kevin reviewed Mary's dossier on Ahmad Maiwand. He appeared to be exceptionally well-qualified. An interview was set up with Consolidated's Human Resources office of overseas employment. Kevin sat in on the interview, observing but saying little. When the interview was completed he asked Maiwand when he was returning home to Fremont.

"I have a flight to Oakland at 3 p.m."

"Fine," Kevin said. "I'll give you a lift to the airport."

"Sir, you needn't bother, I'll call a taxi."

"No, it's not a problem. I'm going that way anyway."

They were in Inglewood near LAX at noon, so Kevin detoured and took Maiwand to the Proud Bird restaurant for lunch.

"We have time before your flight, so I thought you might like to have lunch here. As you can see, it's sort of a historic place. Also I wanted to thank you personally for coming to Los Angeles to meet with us."

The waiter arrived and took their orders. After the waiter left, Kevin told Maiwand that he felt the interview went well and an offer of employment would be forthcoming.

"One thing I should warn you about. The security

clearance can take up to a month. We have a priority so we can get them as fast as two weeks, and with your military record, there shouldn't be any delays, but you never know. They have a big backlog of people requesting clearances. Don't worry if it takes a while."

"Thanks for warning me. I can understand why it would take longer—in certain cases."

After the food was served, Kevin asked, "How did you find life in Kabul, returning after an absence of many years. You had just finished high school when your family came back to the U.S., correct?"

"Yes, that's right. When I went back, some things were the same and others were very different. Life had been difficult for my father. First the Russians and then the Taliban. He is a peace-loving man who only wanted to be left alone so he could teach. My family still has some relatives in Kabul. When I visited them, they were surprised that I had joined the American Army. I think I was able to convince them that the Americans were not like the Russians, and their fight was with the Taliban and al Qaeda not with the Afghanistan people. They would help bring peace, so ordinary people could go about their lives without living in constant fear."

"Do you think that the Afghan people look upon Americans as enemies?" Kevin asked.

"Afghanistan has been invaded numerous times, most recently by the British, then the Russians, and now the U.S.," Maiwand said. "The people are very independent and have always united to drive out invaders. America is not seen as an 'invader' at the moment, but there are elements in the country that are trying to stir up the young men to repel the Americans and their foreign practices."

"As you know, we are there because the U.S was brutally attacked by terrorists hiding in Afghanistan. Our goal is to eliminate that threat, and not to take over Afghanistan."

"I know that and you know that. If America can

succeed in its goal of capturing bin Laden and driving out al Qaeda, and then leave Afghanistan on some preordained date, I think ordinary people will view America as a friend. Our challenge will be for Afghanistan to become strong enough to prevent the resurgence of the Taliban. Some things are beyond Afghanistan's control. Pakistan says one thing to the U.S. to get our generous financial support, says something else to the Afghanistan leadership, and meanwhile covertly supports Taliban and al Qaeda in the border areas between our countries. This is a very difficult problem, politically and militarily for the U.S."

"I think you summed up the situation accurately," Kevin said. "Let's hope the U.S. can act wisely with dignity and respect for your culture."

"In my experience, the American soldiers were dedicated and capable," Maiwand said. "For many, it was difficult, so far from home, in a culture they didn't understand. I think I was able to help by explaining some things to them."

Kevin looked at his watch. "I'd better get you to the airport."

As they walked to the car, Maiwand thanked Kevin for lunch. "Mr. Hunter, you may rely on me to perform my duties satisfactorily on your project."

"I understand."

"In addition," Maiwand added in a steely tone, "I'll be observant when not working. Who knows what I might stumble across."

Maiwand proved to be a model employee. In Kabul he quickly earned the acceptance of his fellow workers. On his days off, Maiwand dressed in the traditional attire of an Afghani workingman and wandered the streets, bazaars, and coffee shops of Kabul and its suburbs. He never asked questions; he simply listened. If asked, he said that he had recently returned to Afghanistan from Pakistan and he was trying to find a job as a mechanic.

His skills and diligence soon caught the eye of one

of the master sergeants who oversaw work on the motor pool. They struck up a friendship after he learned of Maiwand's previous service in Afghanistan. Occasionally, Maiwand was invited to accompany the troops on visits to outlying villages. There Maiwand mingled with the villagers and picked up bits of information and formed an assessment of the villagers' outlook, which he later shared with a squad leader. In this manner he was able to warn the troops of villages where they needed to be extra cautious.

Once a month or so he wrote to Kevin telling him about progress on the job, mentioning any issues that he saw developing regarding staffing or equipment needs. These were informal reports, since the project manager in Kabul made formal monthly reports to the Army's project manager who oversaw the program.

Invariably, Maiwand's letters would conclude with a phrase referring to Kevin's "sister." Since Kevin had no sister, this was puzzling, until Kevin happened to mention it to Mary one day when she called to ask how Maiwand was doing.

"Oh, that," she said. "I thought I told you. I'm the 'sister.' It's an Afghani custom to refer to family friends as sisters and brothers. If it's not too much trouble, you could just copy those parts of his letters and send them on to me."

One day as Kevin listened to the evening news on television, he heard of a successful drone strike in Surobi, a town about sixty kilometers from Kabul. A senior Taliban leader named Hajji Saifullah Haqqani and two associates had died in the strike. The man was reported to have been responsible for organizing several suicide bombings at U.S. military installations in Kabul.

As he listened to the report, something seemed to register with Kevin, but he couldn't recall what it was. He remembered that Surobi had been the site of several bitter battles with the Taliban, including one in 2008 when they ambushed a contingent of French and Afghan soldiers. After thinking for a few minutes, he gave up and promptly dismissed it from his mind.

The next day while sitting at his desk in his office, he remembered the broadcast and finally realized what had caught his attention. It was the name of the victim. Why would that seem familiar? Then he thought of Maiwand's letters. He went to his filing cabinet and got the folder with Maiwand's correspondence. He found what he was seeking in a letter dated a month earlier.

"Tell my sister…" The letter began and then went on to talk about food prices and other trivial matters. Near the end he wrote, "and by the way, I ran into our old friend Hajji Saifullah Haqqani. He has moved his business to the town of Surobi. He seems to like the new location."

Kevin knew enough about Maiwand and his family to know that a senior Taliban leader could not be an "old friend." The only conclusion was that he had passed on some critical information to Mary, it was somehow verified in the field, and the Agency had acted on it.

In other letters, Maiwand spoke of "persons of interest." In the guise of being interested in joining al Qaeda, he became aware of shadow groups that met outside Kabul. From them, he became convinced that bin Laden was no longer in Afghanistan, but was hiding somewhere in Pakistan. It was impossible to get close to bin Laden. The rumors said that he dealt only with a handful of trusted confidants and issued his orders via trusted couriers—never by telephone. No one knew who the couriers were, but there was someone who might know someone else who might know.

Maiwand forwarded all these names to Kevin's "sister" in the description of a fictional "family gathering." He never heard if this information was of any value, or even if it had been acted upon.

IRAN

After ten years as the world's most wanted man, Osama bin Laden was finally brought to justice. On May 2, 2011, the world was electrified by reports describing how an elite group of U.S. Navy SEALs stormed his hideout in Abbottabad, Pakistan, killed him, and escaped with his body and a treasure trove of al Qaeda computer files, flash drives, and other information.

During the attack, a RQ-170 UAV flying over the area transmitted live video back to American authorities watching in Washington.

Kevin saw the large black headlines on the front page of the *Los Angeles Times* when he went out in the morning to pick up the paper. *Finally*, he thought, remembering all of the victims in the Twin Towers, in the Pentagon, and in the four crashed aircraft. It was a bitter pill, thinking that all this time bin Laden had been living in comfort with his five wives in a compound less than a mile from the Pakistani Military Academy. There, he was tolerated, if not supported, by America's erstwhile ally in the fight against terrorism. Afterwards, it was revealed that the chief of ISI, the Pakistani Intelligence Service, knew he was there.

It was hoped that the death of bin Laden was a significant turning point in the war on terror. Events proved otherwise. The Taliban continued its campaign of assassinating prominent figures, among them President Karzai's half-brother and ex-President Rabbani, a go-between in talks with the Taliban. Around five hundred prisoners, most of them Taliban, broke out of prison in Kandahar.

In Iraq, al Qaeda continued to be a danger. Even more alarming was the stream of weapons and personnel flowing from Iran into Iraq. Iran-backed Shia extremist groups were growing and would soon be a serious threat. An extremist branch of al Qaeda had broken away to form what was known as the Islamic State of Iraq and Syria, or ISIS. ISIS's goal was getting rid of Shia Muslims—and U.S. and other Western forces. While Iran first denied involvement in Iraq, it later admitted that some of its top military commanders were there to give advice to the Iraqi Army, Hezbollah, and the Palestinian resistance movement. More and more, Iran appeared as a force to be reckoned with as it extended its influence and military force indirectly through the use of its cohorts.

In December 2011, Kevin heard reports that Iran had captured a U.S. drone that was flying in Afghanistan. He called Mary's office to set up a meeting.

"I heard on the news that the Iranians captured a U.S. drone," he said, when they met in the Los Angeles Central Library reading room. "Remembering our conversation, I thought I should give you a call. At first I heard that we lost control. Then I heard that it had crashed in Iran and the Iranians had it. What really happened?"

"It was the same type of drone that sent back the satellite videos of bin Laden's capture. It had been flying in Afghanistan near the Iranian border. It was captured near the city of Kashmar in Northeastern Iran. RQ-170s have been flying in Afghanistan for about three years. There is a rumor that its real purpose in Afghanistan was to search for clandestine Iranian nuclear facilities.

"The Iranians claim that they captured it intact by jamming its GPS flight control system and feeding it spurious signals, causing it to think it was landing on its home base, when actually it was landing in Iran. They say they will 'reverse engineer' it and make a flyable copy."

"Do you think that is possible?" Kevin asked.

"I don't know," Mary said. "But I know someone

who might know. Give me a few days and I'll set up a meeting."

❧

"Kevin, you wanted some background on why Iran would go to such lengths and risk to steal U.S. guidance technology," Mary said. "I've asked my colleague, Neil Brock, to give you a briefing on the Iranian threat as we perceive it today."

"The first thing to emphasize is that we should not underestimate Iran," Neil said. "The statements coming from there can lead one to believe that the country's rulers are totally irrational. That is not the case. Iran uses misinformation, exaggeration, and rantings, but behind it all is a realistic appraisal of Iran's situation. Iran's leaders recognize that in terms of the nuclear arms race, they are far behind. Israel has nuclear weapons and the capability to deploy them. If, in a few years, Iran could develop a fission bomb, it would face the threat of far more powerful Israeli thermonuclear weapons. One can be certain that Israel has every major Iranian city targeted if a retaliatory strike should ever be necessary.

"Iran's blustering and threat of developing nuclear weapons can be seen as a way to deter its enemies and to buy time to improve its defenses. At the same time, it has to walk a fine line and not provoke a preemptive attack by Israel or the U.S. Iran recognizes that it could never hope to defeat the U.S. in all-out war."

"Why is that?" Kevin asked.

"Consider Iran's forces. Its Air Force is outdated and would be quickly destroyed. It has no Navy to speak of and would be defeated in an offshore confrontation with the U.S. Navy. On the ground, most Iranian tanks are old versions dating from the Iran-Iraq conflict or earlier.

"So what is Iran doing, if not developing nuclear weapons?" Kevin asked.

"First, they're putting a lot of effort into developing short and medium-range missiles. The big weakness of their missiles is accuracy. They're working hard to improve guidance systems. Right now, Iran missiles can reach across the Gulf to many locations and to Israel and U.S. bases in the Middle East. Due to inaccuracy, the main impact would be psychological, but they likely would not do much damage.

"Second, they are developing fast, small surface boats and small submarines capable of operating in the shallow waters of the Gulf where the large U.S. submarines cannot operate. This gives them a means to attack U.S. vessels with torpedoes and guided missiles. They may also be developing unmanned underwater vehicles—UUVs, which could be another serious threat.

"Regarding air defense, Iran claims to have radar coverage of the entire country. They are developing new radar tracking and guidance systems that may be able to target 'stealth' aircraft. In addition, they are developing electronic jamming technology and the capability to disrupt GPS satellite signals. There is evidence that they have used a laser to 'blind' an observation satellite.

"Rather than investing in new aircraft for the Air Force, they are developing improved unmanned aerial vehicles—drones—that are less costly and more suited to the conflict Iran thinks it might have to face. Iran claims to have developed twenty types of UAVs, but we are certain that some of their claims are exaggerated. Their first and best known UAV is the *Mohajer* 'Immigrant' series with an estimated range of fifty kilometers and a fifteen thousand foot ceiling. They were first used in the 1980s for observation, and then later were armed with RPG's. Several crashed in Iraq, so you can assume we're familiar with their technology. They are reportedly working on larger UAVs that could be armed and used in combat. Here again, we have no firm evidence that these are real or just more propaganda.

"Then there's the Lockheed Martin RQ-170 '*Sentinel*' that the Iranians captured. They claimed to have 'reverse engineered' it, but from the photographs, some of our experts believe it to be a fiberglass fake.

"If I follow you," Kevin said, "Iran's strategy has two prongs: build defenses that would intimidate its enemies from attacking, while at the same time trying to improve its offensive capabilities as a deterrent against attack. The nuclear option could be a real goal, although pursuing it involves huge risks, or it could just be a bluff, a bargaining chip to wring concessions from Iran's enemies. In any case, high priority objectives are improved UAVs, better guidance systems, electronic jamming capability, and better air surveillance and interdiction systems."

Neil said, "That's a good summary. One other thing. Iran recognizes that if it attacks Israel or other Gulf states directly, it can expect swift and strong retaliation. So, instead, it has been arming Hezbollah and Hamas with rockets and missiles, letting them make the attacks. Iran can sit back and observe the response, study what countermeasures are employed. Some sources say Hezbollah has twenty thousand, maybe thirty thousand short-range rockets. We know that several thousand of them have been fired into Israel from southern Lebanon and Gaza. They haven't done much damage nor killed many people, but the psychological impact is huge. Israel is being forced to spend billions on missile defense systems, to protect against this onslaught of cheap rockets."

"What is your opinion about copying our advanced technology?" Kevin asked. "Are they capable of doing this, and if so, what do we do about it?"

"It is much more difficult than it might seem," Neil replied. "They certainly have the capability to copy the airframe and put a motor in it. That is not so different from the technology of their *Mohajer* UAV. Copying the satellite guidance technology will be much more difficult. Our newer birds receive guidance from encrypted signals sent by satellite. The signals were not encrypted on the earlier versions. We know it is possible to jam GPS signals. We don't depend on that."

"So what is the concern?"

"One worry? They might learn enough to take control of an armed drone in flight and redirect it to another target. Maybe an ally, a friendly nation, or someone who would react strongly to a perceived attack."

"What are your thoughts on how we might deal with that situation?" Kevin asked.

"We're developing special birds—homing pigeons we call them—to fly in sensitive border areas. They're designed to detect a jamming attempt.

"The jamming signal is relayed to our base for verification. If identified as real, the bird responds as if under the control of the jamming signal and initially changes course to follow the false signal. What is really happening is that it is locating the source of the jamming signal. Once it has a fix on the coordinates of the false signal's control system, it transmits the location to our base for verification and approval. This way we have the option to abort the mission, retake control, and fly the bird home if we want to.

"However, our plan is to release the bird to home in on the jamming station. It will follow the jamming signal straight back to where it originates and target it with 500 pounds of high explosive, then fly back to our base. The bad guys are left with the impression that their jamming went awry. We think that after a few applications of 'homing pigeon' they'll stop trying to take control of our birds."

"What happens now if the satellite link is lost?"

"The drone crashes. It will fly around for a while until it hits something or runs out of fuel. We have programs where the drone will circle automatically to reestablish the link. If after a certain time it fails to reestablish the link, it will return to home base and land by local line of sight control."

"In the best of all possible worlds, there is still a lot of uncertainty."

"That is correct."

"So, somehow, we need to get better information on Iranian technology and hardware, especially the new drones they are supposedly developing."

"That is also correct."

"I assume we have obtained a *Mohajer* and our experts know all about it," Kevin said.

"No comment on that. Bottom line, we need to get information on Iran's UAV research and development efforts. That's the hard part."

✎

A few weeks later Mary called and invited Kevin to lunch. They met at the Pacific Dining Car. Kevin asked Mary if she'd heard from Kidd.

"Yes, he calls from time to time. He seems to be enjoying retirement. I asked him if he missed working and he just laughed. He always asks about you and reminds me that I'm supposed to keep an eye on you. He's very protective of you, seems to feel that he's your godfather, or something like that."

"That is kind of him. Please give him my regards. What about you, how are you doing?"

"Fine. I finally feel I've been accepted by the old boys' network. They allowed me to make a trip to the Middle East—Abu Dhabi and Dubai specifically. This is highly confidential, but let me just say we have a few contacts on the other side of the Persian Gulf. As you can imagine, it is extremely difficult to get access to any information there, and even more difficult to get it out of the country. Any person with government connections cannot enter Iran, and if they manage to get into the country, they would be under constant surveillance."

"I know about that," Kevin said. "I also know that there are some American and other foreign journalists languishing in Iranian prisons accused of spying, so if you're suggesting I might make a trip to Tehran, the answer is a resounding no, with exclamation marks."

"I understand, and I agree with your assessment. I would not want you to place yourself in jeopardy. But there's someone who works for Consolidated who might be able to make such a trip. She was born in Tehran and is an American citizen. Her father died in the Iran-Iraq war and her mother is not in good health. We believe that she could obtain what is called a 'compassionate' or humanitarian visa to pay a short visit to her mother."

"And what would she have to do while in Tehran?"

"Visit her mother, take her to a local clinic for a full physical exam, get her some better medicine, give her some money, all things a dutiful daughter would do for an elderly, ill mother who is unable to travel."

"That's it?"

"Pretty much. Naturally she would want to go shopping to buy fresh bread and treats for her mother, buy a few postcards, and stop in a coffee shop, where she would be surprised to run into an old friend."

"And what would this 'old friend' do?"

"He would mention that he'd heard her mother had been ill and he would give her a small box of candy for her mother."

"And?"

"She would give the candy to her mother, after first removing a small flash drive that contains confidential information being sent to you by a former employee and one of your best friends from years ago. He wants to get out of Iran to go to work for Consolidated in the Middle East, but cannot write to you because of censorship and because it would jeopardize his present job."

"And what is really on the flash drive?"

"Some extremely detailed and important

information about Iran's UAV research program."

"So, let's suppose some Iranian customs official finds this and plugs it into a computer. My employee goes to jail or worse."

"No. While it looks like an ordinary flash drive, this one is very special. If an unauthorized user tries to access the file, it erases all information. It will appear to be empty. It takes a special computer program to extract the information."

"What is this employee's name?"

"Dori Tooran."

"You know, Mary, it is humiliating that you know more about my coworkers than I do. I've met her, but it never registered that she was Iranian. I can't commit to do something like this without talking to her. I will have to tell her enough that she understands the risks."

"Of course. I leave that to your judgment and discretion. But realize that if any of this gets back to Iran somehow, your 'old friend' could be in very serious danger."

"How do you suggest I approach this matter?"

"Meet with her, tell her that you've learned that her mother is ill, and because of her good work, the company is prepared to offer her a compassionate leave for two weeks and will pay her travel expenses. In return, you have a small favor to ask her. If she agrees, then you approve her travel request, charge it to division overhead, and there will be a supplementary change order to the Pentagon renovation project to cover it. Would that work for you?"

"I can arrange that. I'll have to think about how to handle it internally, but I think it will work. First I have to talk to her."

"Let me know how it goes."

When Kevin arrived home that night Juliana was sitting on

the couch with a glass of wine. He could tell something
was bothering her.

"How was lunch today?" she asked.

"Nothing special."

"Well, the Pacific Dining Car isn't exactly where
you go for a quick sandwich. How is your friend Mary
these days? Do you have lunch with her every week?"

"It was a business meeting. She called me. What's
the problem?"

"I called your office today and Holly answered. She
said you were out, so I told her, never mind, it isn't
important but then she said something. Don't go jumping
on her, because I'm sure it was accidental. I know she
doesn't like Mary. But she started to say something about
'government goons,' and then clammed up. So what is
going on? What did you and Mary talk about? Then I asked
Holly about the San Nicolas Island 'contract' and she said
there was no job at San Nicolas Island. You told me that
you were working on a proposal. Not true?"

"I can't talk about it."

"What do you mean, *you can't talk about it*? I'm
your wife!"

Kevin sat silent for a long minute.

"I suppose now is as good a time as any," he said.
"There's something I've been meaning to tell you for a
while now. Then something else would come up and I
worried about placing you in danger."

He paused. Juliana looked at him but said nothing,
waiting to hear what he had to say.

"The truth is that for the last fifteen years I've been
working with the CIA. Not as an employee, but as an
'unofficial resource.' When I travel overseas I visit places
of interest and let them know what I see, sometimes meet
with people. It started because of Beske. I felt bad that he
was killed trying to protect me. I wanted to help anyway I
could, and one thing led to another. Mr. Kidd was my first
contact. When he retired, Mary was his replacement. I

signed papers saying I would never discuss these activities with anyone."

"My God, Kevin, hasn't it been dangerous for you? For us?"

"Not really. I had some training; I've been careful. They've never asked me to do anything dangerous and they brief me about the places I'm traveling to."

"What about the Company? Your boss—do they know?"

"No."

"What about Holly?"

"No."

"Do they want you to make any more trips?"

"No. I told them I was not traveling overseas anymore."

"You mean it?"

"Yes."

"So what was this meeting about?"

"Iran is a serious threat. We need to know more about Iranian capabilities. An Iranian woman works for Consolidated and may go to Tehran to visit her sick mother. If she does, and if she's willing, I'm going to ask her to bring back some information for us."

"Won't that be dangerous for her?"

"Hopefully not. All she has to do is bring back a small flash drive when she returns."

"Kevin—tell me honestly—you're not going to Iran or anywhere near it are you?"

"No. No more travel to the Middle East."

"Will you continue doing things for the Agency?"

"Probably not. My value to them was to travel overseas as a businessman. Without traveling, there's little I can do for them in the future."

Juliana relaxed visibly, took hold of his hands. "I'm sure you've done enough. They get paid to take risks; it's their job."

"Juliana, you can't tell anyone about this. This has

to stay between you and me. Otherwise it could jeopardize our safety or the safety of the people in the field who might have met with me. Two have died already. You know about Beske. Another man I met in Dubai was subsequently killed in Pakistan. I don't want to frighten you, but please forget we had this discussion."

For a moment Juliana was silent, thinking back to her meeting with Kidd years ago. She wondered if she should tell Kevin that all along she'd known about his CIA involvement, but decided not to, not wanting to betray that Kidd had confided in her.

"Thanks for telling me, Kevin, it explains a lot. You could have told me—you should have known I would never tell anyone."

Kevin waited until Friday to have Holly call Dori Tooran and ask her to meet with him. He considered inviting her to lunch, but decided against it. He wanted the meeting to be as businesslike as possible.

He opened the door to her knock. The woman who stood there had dark hair. She was about five feet two, slender, dressed in grey slacks and a matching jacket. Greeting him, she appeared poised, confident, outgoing.

"Thank you for coming, Dori. Let me quickly set your mind at ease; there are no problems, your job is fine, and you do excellent work."

"Thank you for saying that. Frankly, I was little nervous. My project is winding down and no one has told me if I have a job after this."

"You certainly do," Kevin replied. "The reason for the meeting is that I've learned that your mother is ill. By coincidence, I need someone to pay a short visit to Tehran, so I thought you might be interested in checking up on her."

"That would be wonderful. I am worried about her.

When she calls me she says she's fine, but I can tell she's not."

"When was the last time you went to Tehran?"

"I went about five years ago."

"Any problems?"

"No, I stayed inside most of the time. When I had to go out I dressed appropriately, always wearing pants and covering my head. I never had any run-ins with the religious police, although I saw them arresting a woman because they thought her dress wasn't long enough. She was taken to the police station and beaten."

"Do you think you could return for short visit? I've heard there is such a thing as a 'compassionate visa' although I don't know if that's the correct term in Farsi."

"I'm pretty sure I can go back. I still have a valid Iranian passport."

"My thought is that we would give you two weeks leave and pay your plane fare. Would that be acceptable?"

"That would be very generous. I can't imagine any company doing that for me."

"Well, as I mentioned, there is one small job I need you to do while you're there. It would take an hour or two."

Dori stiffened. "What kind of a job?"

"Before we discuss that, I'm interested in your background. Tell me a little about yourself, how you became an engineer, and why did you come to the U.S? For starters, what was it like growing up in Tehran?"

"It was very different than America. We don't have the conveniences that Americans are used to. My brother and I lived with our mother in a small apartment. The building complex was more like an extended family. We knew all our neighbors. We would spend time in their houses and they would spend time in ours. I was the oldest, so many household responsibilities fell to me."

"No father?"

"He passed away when I was twelve."

"Sorry to hear that," Kevin said.

"On a typical school day I would get up at 5:30, fix myself some breakfast, take two bus rides and walk a mile or so to get to my school. Our schools were segregated— only girls at my school. We had to study very hard, going beyond what was in the textbooks that were provided. There was a lot of emphasis on getting good grades. You had to do more than just listen to the teacher.

"When school was over, once back home, I prepared the food for our dinner so it would be ready when my mother came home from her job. After dinner we could relax, maybe watch television for half an hour. Then it was homework every night.

"What did your mother do?"

"She was a secretary for a large corporation. She's retired now."

"Us getting an education was important to her. We went to school six days a week with Fridays off, the same as the work week. There wasn't much time left for a social life. On occasion I would get together with other girls who lived nearby and we would listen to music, or go to movies. I loved to see foreign films. In fact I saw 'Some Like it Hot' and that was one of the things that inspired me to come to America. I liked the images of the sunny areas and the beach.

"Also on Fridays we had chores, like washing and ironing clothes. Clothes were washed in a tub and hung on a clothesline outside to dry.

"In school I was very good in mathematics, so I decided to pursue that as my educational goal. In Iran we had to take competitive examinations, which determined at what level we would be placed in a university. These were national tests and the results were published in the newspaper for everyone to see. I was so nervous about the results that I didn't want to go out and buy a newspaper. I waited and hoped someone would call me and tell me that I had done okay.

"I was accepted to the University of Tehran. During

the first year I had to take required courses for an engineering major. Meanwhile, I was pursuing my dream of going to America. I applied to California State University at San Diego and was accepted, subject to demonstrating English proficiency. In those times, before the seizure of the American Embassy by the Iranian Revolutionary Guard, travel was easy. I went to the embassy to see about getting a visa to go to California. I showed them my acceptance papers from Cal State. At the embassy they said I could have a visa but I had to come back with my parents to get their approval. So I brought my mother and came back to the embassy and was able to get a visa."

"Why did you switch from math to engineering? Was your father an engineer?"

"No. I found that my engineering classes were more interesting. I'm not sure my mother fully understood what I was doing at the embassy. Either that or she did not think I would really go to America. With a visa in hand I made my plans. I knew no one in America, but there was the family of a friend of a friend who lived in San Diego and who agreed that I could stay with them for a couple of weeks until I got oriented and moved into the dormitory. Seventeen and a half years old, barely able to speak the language, and with eight hundred U.S. dollars in my pocket and with my suitcase of Iranian clothes, I flew to Los Angeles and then to San Diego.

"I shared a room in the dormitory with several other girls. I adjusted to the new experience of life in the U.S. When the seizure of the American Embassy happened, relations between Iran and America became very bad and communications were interrupted. I did not receive the money from home that I required for registration for the new semester. I didn't know what I was going to do. Fortunately, one of the faculty members found out about my problem and loaned me money so I could register. I eventually got my funds and was able to repay him.

"While at the University I was able to get jobs grading math papers and tutoring. Somehow I managed to get by on the little money that I was able to earn or get from home and graduated with my bachelor's degree in electrical engineering. After graduating I was fortunate to be able to get a job as a junior electrical engineer with a small San Diego firm. Several years later a friend told me Consolidated was hiring so I applied and was accepted. At that time I felt my career in my new country was launched."

"That's commendable," Kevin said. "It must've taken a lot of courage to do all that, come to a foreign country, all on your own, no friends, barely knowing the language."

"I didn't look at it that way. I wanted a career and wanted a life that didn't seem possible for me in Iran. I'd seen enough to know these things were possible in America."

"I assume you might want to take your mother to a good doctor or clinic while you're there, make sure she has the proper medicines, that sort of thing. With travel time, getting acclimated, lost time on weekends, you'd end up with about ten days to do what you need to do. Would that be adequate?"

"Yes, that would be wonderful. It's very thoughtful and generous of you. What can I do for you?"

"My job is very simple. I have an old friend in Tehran who used to work for Consolidated. His name is Ahmad Firouzi. He would like to leave Iran and come to work for us in the Middle East. But he works for the government and is worried that if he writes to me and sends his updated résumé and other paperwork, he could lose his job. I will ask him to give you a flash drive with this information, and you can bring it back to me."

"I'd be happy to help. I can understand his concerns. How will I find him?"

"You don't need to find him. You need every

minute you have to take care of your mother. I'll have him find you. The best thing would be if he could meet you in a coffee house or something similar near your mother's home. Is there such a place?"

"Yes, I know of one a few blocks away. I assume it's still there."

"Fine. You work on some dates for your trip, get your visa or whatever travel documents you need, and let Holly know. I think you should make the plane reservations yourself and pay for the tickets. Bring in the receipts and we will reimburse you. Keep track of your expenses in Tehran and we will reimburse those also. Leave your mother's address and phone number with Holly in case we need to reach you for some reason. Actually, it might be good for you to call in a couple of times to let us know how things are so we don't worry about you. And if you can get the name and address of the coffee shop, I'll get a message to Ahmad to look for you there at 3 p.m. on three successive days. That way, if you're busy on one of the chosen days, you don't need to worry about it, just go the next day."

"How will I know him?"

"He'll find you. I can't describe him exactly because I haven't seen him for years. But if a middle-aged Iranian man, very polite, approaches you and asks, 'How is your mother's health?' you can be sure it is him."

"Very well. And that's all I have to do? My mother will be so happy."

"Yes. That and take care of your mother—and yourself. Don't get in any trouble in Tehran. Keep reminding yourself that you're not in Los Angeles. If you have other questions, give me a call."

"Thank you Mr. Hunter."

Kevin stood and opened his office door for Dori. He shook her hand. "Thank you Dori, have a safe trip and stay in touch."

As she left, Kevin noted that she used a ruby red

lipstick.

ॐ

Dori's arrival in the Tehran International Airport brought back memories of her last trip to Iran. How happy she'd been to walk out and take a seat on the plane that was taking her back to the U.S.

This time the airport seemed even more oppressive. Before leaving the aircraft she'd wrapped the scarf around her head. She wore slacks and flat shoes. There were armed security guards everywhere and cameras scanning every part of the reception area. She passed through passport control where the officer asked her how long she planned to stay and the reason for her visit. She replied in Farsi. He stamped her passport and thrust it back to her, motioning the next person in line to step forward.

The custom inspector was surly and rude. He made her open her purse and hold it while he pawed through it. She'd had the foresight to remove a small wallet with her cash and credit cards and placed it in an inner pocket in her jacket. The official removed the case that held her eyeglasses, opened it, removed the glasses, felt around the lining of the case, and then dropped the case back in her purse without replacing the glasses.

He opened the side pockets of her carry-on bag, looked at each one, pulled out a pair of tennis shoes, removed her cosmetics case, and shook its contents on the table. He inspected each item, toothbrush, toothpaste, hairbrush, jamming each item back in the case. He opened a small jar of facial cream and smelled it, then replaced it.

In the main compartment of the suitcase he dug his hands into the bottom and probed each corner. He lifted off the top layer, some shirts, a sweater, and jeans, looking through her clothing until he found her lingerie. He rubbed the soft cloth between his fingers, giving her a malicious look that she ignored.

His inspection done, he pushed her still open bag to one side and signaled for the next passenger to approach.

Outside the airport Dori went to the taxi stand. The driver leaped out of the car and placed her bag in the trunk. She gave him her mother's address.

"How's business," she asked, just to make conversation. The driver was polite, very friendly.

"Terrible," he said. "The economy is no good here. If I could, I'd go to the UAE. There you can make good money with tourists. Here, no tourists. What about you? You're Iranian, but you're not Iranian. You're coming from America."

Dori was surprised. "America? Why would you say that?"

"Your clothes and your accent. You speak good Farsi, but I can hear English in your accent."

"You're right," Dori said, "I work in America, but my family is here. My mother is not well."

At her mother's apartment, Dori thanked the driver and paid him with Iranian currency.

In the apartment, Dori hugged her mother, trying to suppress the initial shock she felt at her mother's appearance. She'd lost weight, her hair was thin, entirely gray, and she moved hesitantly as she went into the small kitchen to make tea.

As they drank tea, Dori told her mother the latest news about her job, the apartment where she lived, and how her boss had paid for her trip to Iran.

Her mother found that unusual. "Are you seeing this man?"

"Oh no, nothing like that, *maman*. He is married. Besides, he's the big boss."

"No boyfriends, Dori?"

"No *maman*, no time for boyfriends. Don't worry about me. If I find a boyfriend, you'll be the first to know."

Dori found herself getting sleepy after the long flight and early morning arrival. She excused herself to take a nap. Her mother woke her up a few hours later for lunch. Dori could see that her mother had gone to a lot of trouble to fix a typical Iranian meal with rice, lamb, stuffed cabbage and squash, and other delicacies. While she enjoyed the meal, Dori noted that her mother picked at the food, eating hardly anything. In the morning she'd need to find a reputable clinic. She had no confidence in the family doctor her mother visited. Now in his eighties, he probably shouldn't be practicing medicine. But he was nearby, his fees were low, and he had few patients, so he had ample time to listen to all their complaints.

The clinic doctor who examined Dori's mother said that she appeared to be anemic and probably was suffering from arterial sclerosis and high blood pressure. He recommended an electrocardiogram and an ultrasound of her carotid arteries, plus additional blood work. At Dori's urging, the clinic was able to schedule the tests the next day.

Dori took her mother home and helped her to bed for a nap. It was 2:30 p.m. on the first of the three days she'd marked out to visit the coffee shop. She put on her headscarf and long overcoat and walked out of the apartment.

At the coffee shop, she opened the door and stood there for a moment, looking around. There were some small tables and a bar where several couples sat, sipping coffee. Iranian music played in the background.

She noticed a middle-aged man wearing slacks and a casual shirt. He walked over to her and said, "How is your mother's health?"

"Thank you for asking," Dori said. "She's not well. I took her to a clinic today and we need to go back tomorrow for more tests."

"I'm sorry to hear that. Do you have time to join me for coffee, or tea if you prefer?" He indicated a table. Dori followed him to the table and saw that he'd left his jacket hanging on a chair. "By the way, forgive my rudeness for not introducing myself. I'm Ahmad Firouzi."

The waiter came and Dori ordered tea.

"I can't stay long. I left my mother sleeping. She'll worry if she wakes up and I'm not there."

"I understand. I also have to get back to work."

The waiter brought Dori's tea and went back to the bar.

"With your permission I have a small gift for your mother. It's *baklava* from a very good bakery near here. Please take it with my compliments. And here's something for you." Ahmad handed her a tube of lipstick.

Dori was surprised, but took it and removed the cap. She saw that the color was ruby red. She looked up at Ahmad.

"I hope that's close to your color. It was the best I could do here in Tehran. Despite the economic sanctions, one can still find most things."

Dori was silent, holding the lipstick, looking at Ahmad.

"If you would be so kind, just give it to my friend in Los Angeles. He will put it to good use."

She suddenly understood. "Of course. You surprised me, I was expecting something else."

"I hope your mother's health improves. Ahmad placed some money on the table, then smiled and stood up, putting on his jacket. I'm sure your visit here is worth a hundred doctors. Have a safe trip home."

Then he was gone.

Dori lingered for a few more minutes, the *baklava* on the table, the lipstick clutched in her hand. She quickly thrust the lipstick in her pocket and left the coffee shop, carrying the *baklava*.

That night, after her mother had gone to bed, she tried the lipstick. It was very close to the color she used. She scrubbed her lips until all traces of it were gone. In Tehran, she never wore lipstick when she went out in public, although many women used makeup in defiance of the religious police.

She reminded herself to throw away her other lipstick. It might attract attention to go through customs with two tubes of lipstick of similar color. One never knew what the customs officials would do. It was safe to assume they were all corrupt. For that reason, she'd brought no valuables, no jewelry, no camera or anything they might find an excuse to confiscate.

ॐ

Dori once again sat in the lounge in the Tehran International Airport. Taking leave of her mother had been hard. Tears flowed, and her mother had said, "This is probably the last time we'll see each other."

Her mother was already looking better. She had medicine for her blood pressure and vitamins for her anemia. A follow-up at the clinic was arranged for a month following the first visits. The tests had shown some arterial blockage, a little more than average for her age. Surgery was not indicated, at least not until her general health improved. The clinic promised to send Dori copies of her mother's reports after the follow-up visit.

Meanwhile, now there was the ordeal of customs. Passport control had been easy. The official looked at the passport, looked at Dori, stamped it and waved her through.

They would be calling the flight soon. Dori waited until there was a crowd lined up for baggage inspection. This time she had placed her panties and bras on the top of the clothing in her carry-on. If she got one of the younger, more religious inspectors, she hoped that he would be embarrassed by the sight of her personal garments and might hasten her through the process.

At the table, she handed her purse to the inspector, greeting him in Farsi, trying to calm her nerves. He opened it, looked at her, pulled out her glass case, opened it, removed her glasses, put them back in the case, and replaced it in the purse.

He went to her carry-on, examined shoes, replaced them, and pulled out her cosmetic bag. He opened it, and stared at its contents for several seconds. Dori felt droplets of sweat forming in her armpits and between her breasts. She thought about her mother, to distract herself and keep her face neutral.

The inspector pulled the lipstick tube from the cosmetic case, removed the cap, put it back on, and replaced the cosmetic case. He unzipped the carry-on main compartment, saw Dorie's underwear, quickly zipped it up, and slid her bag down the table, waving her through. She looked at him demurely, her eyes downcast, caught his eye, and said "Allah is great."

She went into the boarding area to wait until her flight was called. A great sense of relief flooded over her. She could see the plane outside. Soon, assuming no mechanical delays or other holdups, she would be on her way home. As she waited for the boarding to begin, she kept glancing back to the customs area, half expecting to see some official come running in to pull her from the flight.

Once airborne, she finally relaxed. Her carry-on was under the seat in front of her. On a whim she reached down and retrieved her cosmetic case. She removed the lipstick and went to the restroom. Removing her blouse, she used some paper towels to wash and dry her armpits. She put her blouse back on and carefully applied lipstick before returning to her seat.

When Dori came in to Kevin's office, the first thing he said was, "How is your mother?"

"First, I can't thank you enough for arranging for me to go home." She gave Kevin a brief summary of what had transpired.

"I'm so glad I went. Her health has really declined since my last visit. But this new clinic will be good for her. Fortunately, she likes the doctor there, so I hope she'll follow up. The clinic is supposed to keep me posted."

"And the trip? All went well, no problems?"

"Yes. I met your friend Ahmad, and he seems to be a very nice man. I hope you will be able to find a position for him." Dori pulled the lipstick from her purse and handed it to Kevin. "He gave me this to give to you."

Kevin removed the cap briefly and replaced it. He could see she was wearing it.

"I hope you don't mind. I decided to try it. It seemed more my shade than yours."

Kevin laughed. "Touché. By now you've figured out there's more to this than lipstick, right?"

"Yes. I was nervous going through customs. But Ahmad was clever. He recognized that the best place to hide something was in plain sight."

❧

A week later Kevin met Mary for lunch. She was at her usual table. As he walked up, he saw she was wearing a dark red dress and ruby red lipstick. He was laughing as he sat down next to her.

"Very becoming. The color works for you. Are you going to dump those gray business suits now, go with the Mata Hari look?"

She laughed. "No, this dress will go back in the closet to hide for a few more years. But I couldn't resist. How clever to have the flash drive put in a lipstick tube. Whatever made you think of that?"

"Do you really want to know?"

"I'm dying to know."

"Once I was in a very formal business meeting. It was all men, except for our project manager who happened to be a woman. She was nervous, waving her hands a lot as she gave the presentation. Out of nervousness she reached into her purse and pulled out what she thought was a lipstick tube. She was waving it around, using it to point at some charts she was explaining, when suddenly, to her embarrassment, she realized it wasn't her lipstick at all, it was a tampon holder."

"Oh dear," Mary said. "Now that would be discomfiting." Mary called the waiter and they ordered. "I'm having a gimlet in celebration. What about you?"

"I'll have a scotch rocks, in honor of our good friend Charlie Kidd. Now tell me, what are we celebrating?"

"The lipstick—I mean the flash drive. It was a treasure trove of information on the latest Iranian UAV guidance systems. Frequencies, countermeasures, specifications, all really good stuff. It will take months to analyze it and to develop countermeasures. But it can be done."

"That's great. I'm glad we could help."

"And your young Iranian woman. Did she have any problems; did she feel compromised in any way?"

"No. She had no problems. She's worried about her mother, but feels good that she was able to see her and arrange medical help for her."

"She's a hero, you know, but we can never tell her."

"I realize that."

The food arrived and the conversation turned to Kidd. They both had stories about Kidd, how he took shortcuts and hated bureaucracy.

"He was a good man," Kevin said. "I liked him." He paused. "Of course, he found one of the best as a replacement. You know the saying, sometimes the best man for the job is a woman."

Mary laughed. "You're too kind, Kevin." They chatted for a few minutes.

Kevin stood to leave. "Thanks for lunch. I've got a busy day and have to get back to the office. Sorry to dash off."

Mary looked at Kevin as he stood there by the table. She was feeling the effects of the gimlet. There were things she wanted to say. Lately, she'd imagined herself in bed with him. It could never be; she knew about his wife, his happy marriage. She let the thought slip away.

"There are many heroes," she said, "not just Dori. Unfortunately, we can't talk about any of them." She paused. "We can't say how we really feel."

Kevin looked at her, understanding.

"Goodbye Mary," he said.

OUT OF AFGHANISTAN

Maiwand came home from Afghanistan after spending three years in-country. During that time, he compiled an exemplary work record, was promoted three times, and received a Department of the Army decoration for *Distinguished Civilian Service.* This was an award, established by the Secretary of the Army, for civilian contractor personnel who rendered distinguished service to the Army. Normally, the citation was granted for superior work performance. In his case, it was slightly different. The citation read, in part, "…for dedication to your assigned work above and beyond the call of duty, placing yourself at risk and rendering important services to local military commands." He was the only Consolidated employee to ever receive such an award.

With the winding down of some of the large overseas projects, Kevin managed to shift his emphasis to more domestic work. The United States was finally emerging from the 2007-2010 recession. Although the recession was declared over several years earlier, it took time for Federal and State budgets to recover and for consumer confidence to grow to the point that new investments in infrastructure projects started to occur. As confidence grew, more money started to flow to long-delayed projects. "Deferred maintenance" was the term used to justify not spending money on needed highway and bridge repairs, new water treatment facilities, and mass transit projects. Consolidated began to re-shape itself to respond to new opportunities.

❧

Over dinner one night, Kevin told Juliana he had an "announcement."

"My, aren't we being formal," she said. "And what might your announcement be?"

"We might have to move. Or, more correctly, we might *want* to move."

"Oh, and why is that? What's happening?"

"The company has offered me a promotion to senior vice president. Not a really big deal, but more money. There is a catch. They want me in the office in Orange County. The plan is to form a special government projects office. They haven't said I have to move, but I don't want to do that commute every day."

"So, what are you thinking?

"I'm thinking Newport Beach. We can find a place with a nearby slip. Keep the boat there, have an easy commute to work."

"Can we afford it?"

"I think so, we'll need to look around, see what's available."

❧

Two months later they were in their new home on the Balboa Peninsula in Newport Beach. It was a two-story house with three bedrooms and a roof deck with a view of the ocean and bay. They kept the master bedroom, while one of the others became Juliana's studio and the other bedroom became Kevin's office. *Seascape* was in a nearby marina.

Juliana loved her new home at the beach. The bay was a half a block away in one direction, the ocean a block and a half in the opposite direction. She reduced her work commitment to half-time, mostly on projects she could do at home. Meanwhile, Kevin was busier than ever with his new responsibilities. They had drinks with one of their new neighbors, Dortha and Clay Welsh, who lived nearby, but to the other neighbors on the street, Kevin was largely unknown.

In November of their first year in Newport, a huge Pacific storm rolled in from the Northeast, coincidentally with the high-high tide of the year. With the low-pressure area hanging over the bay, the storm surge raising one to two foot-high waves in the bay, on top of the high tide, seawater surged over the sea walls in a number of areas and flooded portions of the Peninsula. Water flowed down their street, overflowed the curb, and flooded into the small patio in front of their house. Fortunately, the water level stayed two inches below the door threshold so there was no damage to their house. Other older homes on the street, however, suffered water damage. This incident caused Kevin to think more seriously about global warming. The melting of the polar ice caps, increased greenhouse gas emissions, and rising sea levels had all seemed worries for the future. This storm changed all that. He began to wonder what could be done to protect their new home.

While he was discussing the storm with Juliana, she mentioned a new project she'd started working on at R&D.

"Oh, what might that be?"

"We're compiling a source book on global warming. For example, there are more than a dozen islands in the South Pacific and Indian Ocean that are in imminent danger of being flooded by rising seas. At some of these islands entire villages have been relocated and their former sites are now underwater."

"What's the evidence?" he asked.

"Scientific measurements indicate that the sea level remained constant for most of the last century but now, in the final decades, it has risen an average of seven inches. That correlates with the melting of polar ice and glaciers. By 2100, the rise is projected to be ten to twenty-three inches more. Many of these islands are only three feet above mean sea level, and when they flood, crops are wiped out and they become unlivable.

How do you know it's due to human activity?

"For one thing, since the industrial revolution the earth has been getting warmer and the change correlates with the increase in atmospheric carbon dioxide due to burning fossil fuels," Juliana said. "It's not just the rising sea level. Oceans are becoming warmer, so there's more energy to drive hurricanes and typhoons. As the earth becomes warmer, the temperature change is affecting entire ecosystems. Plants and animals accustomed to certain temperature ranges have to move to higher elevations. Surveys of Yellowstone National Park show that in a warmer climate fire and insects will destroy species of spruce and fir, allowing sagebrush to expand. Can you imagine Yellowstone with most of the forests gone?"

"I agree there's lots of scientific evidence, but so far the U.S. has not shown the political willpower to address the issue. You know what happened at Kyoto Conference on Climate Change in 1997—the U.S didn't sign the agreement. What can you do about that?"

"I don't know," Juliana said. "But we have to find a way to bring about change. I'm now thinking this is one of the most important challenges facing the human race."

❧

A few months after the storm, Kevin went to Washington D.C. to work on a proposal for a new Navy project. He was impressed to learn that the Navy was concerned about its coastal ports and facilities. While scientists and politicians argued about the validity of climate change, the Navy quietly set about preparing for the worst. The meeting in Washington was to prepare a proposal to survey Navy facilities along the Atlantic coast, to establish their vulnerability to sea level change, and to prepare preliminary cost estimates for raising docks and breakwaters, and for relocating shore facilities to higher ground.

One afternoon a secretary came into the room where he worked and slipped him a note. It said, "Call your office—urgent."

He read the note. "Hey guys," he said, standing. "Excuse me for a minute. Something's come up. I'll be right back as soon as I find out what this is about."

Kevin went into the hallway and used his cell phone to call his office in Los Angeles. Holly answered the phone. "I got your message—what's up?"

"It's that Mary woman," Holly said. Early on, Holly had been put off by Mary's military brusqueness. Though Mary had mellowed in her contacts with the civilian world, Holly still referred to her as 'That Mary woman.' "She was very insistent and has to talk to you. I told her you were traveling, but she said that I should get ahold of you immediately and have you call her, any time day or night. She gave me a special number to use. The nerve! What's with her, Kevin; does she have the hots for you?"

Kevin laughed. "No chance, Holly. She's actually a nice person. It's just that she forgets that she's no longer in the Air Force where she was used to ordering people around. I'll see what she wants."

He went into an empty office for privacy and called the number Holly had given him. It rang twice and then was automatically forwarded to another number with a different ring.

"Minnick."

"Mary, this is Kevin. My secretary said something has come up."

"Kevin, thanks for getting back to me. I hate to disturb you while you are away on business, but we need your help."

"What's the problem?"

"Could you put your business on hold for twenty-four hours if we needed you to attend a meeting?"

"I suppose I can arrange that, where is the meeting?"

"You would need to make a quick trip, but I promise you we'll have you back in less than thirty hours."

"When would I need to leave?"

"Tonight."

"Tonight? And where is the meeting?"

"It's in Luxor."

"Luxor, as in Egypt?"

"Yes."

"You want me to go to Egypt tonight? For thirty hours?"

"Yes."

"Mary, I promised my wife no more trips to the Middle East. She'll divorce me. No, she'll kill me if I run off to Egypt."

"She'll never know."

"How is that?"

"Because you won't officially enter Egypt. This trip will never have happened."

"But Mary, hells bells—what about me? I can't lie."

"You won't have to lie, since the trip never occurred—officially."

"Are you going to tell me what this is about?"

"We have a lead on your Egyptian friend. We think she's working on a Nile tourist boat that will dock in Luxor tomorrow afternoon. The Egyptian authorities are willing to pick her up if we can positively identify her. They'll turn her over to us if they get her. They're taking a lot of heat about the Arab Spring jailbreak and the new government wants to get some brownie points with us."

"But why me?"

"You're the only person that can do a positive ID on her."

"Shit, Mary, I have a really bad feeling about this."

"I know it's a hell of a thing to ask, but we'll cover you. You'll go on the boat as an Egyptian doctor. We're saying there is an outbreak of something on the boat and crew needs to be checked. She will never see you. If you recognize her, you'll nod your head and leave while the Egyptian cops make the grab. Thirty minutes at most, and you'll be on your way back home."

"I don't know, Mary...."

"You know, she is the last link to Beske's murder...."

"Oh Christ, I can't believe I'm going to do this. What happens next?"

"Get over to Andrews Air Force Base by 7 p.m. Give your name to the guard at the gate. There will be a vehicle waiting there to take you to a C-32 aircraft. You'll be a passenger on an 89th Airlift Wing flight. You'll fly to Cairo, transfer to a private jet, land at Luxor, and wait in a hotel until the *Nile Princess* docks. We have people in Cairo who will meet you, be on the flight, and get you in and out. As soon as the crew has been inspected, you're on your way back."

"What if she doesn't show?"

"You come home. But we think we have solid information. Unless she jumps in the Nile up-river she should be on that boat when it docks."

"Welcome aboard, Mr. Hunter," the uniformed crewman said to Kevin. Take any seat you want. Once we're airborne you can find some coffee up forward in the galley. Right now, just buckle up. We're cleared for takeoff."

As he was speaking, Kevin could feel the big jet start taxiing. It climbed rapidly into the night sky over Washington. He settled back in the seat, alone in the passenger area. Forward, he had a glimpse of the cockpit and several crew members moving about. About an hour later, the crewman who first welcomed him on board came back to check on him.

"Did you find the coffee?"

"No, I decided to pass. I think I'll try to sleep for a while."

"Good idea. I checked the flight plan and it's eleven hours. We have a tail wind."

"You guys make this trip regularly?"

"No. We just go where we're sent, anytime, day or night, when we get the call. Every now and then Command springs one of these training flights on us. The point is to make sure the aircraft and crew are always in a state of readiness."

"This is a training flight?"

"Yes. I guess the timing worked out good for you, huh?"

"Yes. A lucky coincidence."

Eleven hours later in bright sunlight, the plane began its descent. On the approach, Kevin could see the three pyramids of Giza in the distance.

The crewman walked back to check on him.

"You sleep okay? We're on final approach. I

understand that your people will have a car for you. We're going to be here for six hours. A different crew will be flying us back. Enjoy your stay in Egypt. By the way, have you been here before?"

"Yes, a few times."

"Lucky, huh? We can't leave the airport, so we don't get to do any sightseeing. Maybe someday."

"I hope you get an opportunity in the future. There is a lot of history here."

As the C-32 taxied to a stop in a remote corner of the airport, a black SUV pulled up. The driver stepped out and watched Kevin descend from the plane.

"Mr. Hunter?"

"That's me."

"If you come with me, sir, I'll take you to your aircraft."

He drove to another part of the airport where a twin engine Gulfstream jet stood with its boarding steps opened.

"Here you are, sir. Have a nice flight."

Kevin got out of the car and boarded the Gulfstream. The door closed and the plane began to taxi. With a quick glance, Kevin saw there were five other people on the plane. Three were Egyptians and two were Americans.

One of the Americans stood and motioned Kevin to take the empty seat next to him.

"Welcome, Mr. Hunter. My name's Parker. You're right on time, so I assume you had smooth weather. Were you able to sleep?"

"Yes. I guess I was tired, because I slept about eight hours. I could use a shower and a change of shirts, but other than that I'm fine."

As they were talking, the Gulfstream accelerated and made a steep climb, then turned south.

"Luxor is about three hundred miles from Cairo. We'll be there in an hour. We have a room for you in the Luxor Winter Palace hotel. There you can clean up. I've got a doctor's smock for you to wear for this operation."

Parker did not smile, so Kevin assumed the pun was unintentional.

"We don't anticipate any difficulties, but my instructions are to take care of you. The Egyptians on board will make the arrest and escort the prisoner from the boat, if you are able to identify her. They have their own transportation back to Cairo. As soon as the operation is over, I'm to get you back to the Gulfstream and you will return to Cairo to catch the flight back to Andrews."

"How many crew members are there on the boat?"

"Counting the waiters, stewards, cooks, and so on, about one hundred. Our target is one of the entertainers on board. The crew will be brought into a room where an Egyptian 'doctor' will ask them a couple of questions. The boat has security video cameras in various locations. We're going to be watching one as the crew members pass by. If you spot our target, I'll advise the Egyptians and they will detain her. We will depart immediately after that. They will be able to verify her identity. We want this to have the appearance of an Egyptian operation."

In the room, Kevin took a shower but did not shave. Parker had provided a *galebeya,* a doctor's smock, a surgeon's cap, a name tag that said "Dr. Sadat" in English and Arabic, and a stethoscope to hang around his neck. As he was dressing, there was a knock at the door. Parker entered, looked at him, and smiled.

"Very good, Dr. Sadat. You should pass muster in that outfit. If you're ready, let's go down and get on board before they start summoning the crew. Put your belongings in this bag. Leave it in the car. We won't be returning to the hotel. The crew inspections will take place before any passengers are allowed to disembark. If any of the crew members don't show up, we'll check the passengers as they disembark."

The Egyptian doctor and his assistant sat at a table with the crew manifests. The Captain, first officer, purser, and other operating crew members were first in line. The doctor asked them one or two questions, crossed their name off the list and then passed them out of the room. Meanwhile, Kevin and Parker stood apart in the security office, watching a camera that focused on the corridor leading to the interview room. After the uniformed crew members passed through, there were Egyptian waiters, cooks and stewards. They conversed and joked and look bored by the proceedings. An occasional black Nubian kitchen worker passed down the line. So far only men had appeared. The female crew and workers seemed to hang together, and appeared all at once. Kevin focused on an attractive, dark-haired Middle Eastern woman wearing jewelry, but it was not Leila. A few more women filed past the camera, and then he saw her. She had cut her hair and dyed it blond, but there was no mistaking. She glanced briefly at the camera and moved on out of view. Unlike the others, she was not chatting with anyone. She seemed nervous as she approached and passed the camera.

"That's her," Kevin said to Parker. "No doubt; it's definitely her."

Parker spoke a few words softly in a small microphone clipped to his collar.

"Okay, Kevin, we're out of here. You've got a plane to catch."

On the Gulfstream he changed out of his doctor's clothes and into his own. He and Parker were the only passengers returning to Cairo.

"So what happens next?"

"The Egyptians will take her back to Cairo and put her in prison. They will first confirm her identity and then they will interrogate her about the prison break. They'll pump her for any information she might have about the Sinai terrorists and her brother's involvement. When they've gotten all they can from her, she'll be extradited to the U.S."

"Do you think they'll get anything out of her?"

"If she knows anything, she'll probably tell them. Their methods are not gentle."

လာ

As he boarded the Air Force C-32 a few hours later, Kevin was greeted by the same crewman, now off-duty for the return flight.

"Wow. You back already? Fast trip, huh? Not much time for sightseeing for you either."

"You're right. That's how it is with these training missions."

Leaving the crewman to ponder that remark, Kevin took a seat. Suddenly, he felt very tired. When the plane began to taxi, he fell asleep.

Kevin slept for several hours. When he awoke the plane was over the Atlantic Ocean. He went forward and got a cup of coffee. As before, he was the only person on the plane, other than the crew. He returned to his seat and buckled up, thinking over what had transpired.

When Kevin walked back into his hotel room, it was near midnight. He'd been gone twenty-nine hours. The message light on his phone was blinking. He picked it up to listen to the messages. The first message was from Mary. She must've called just before he returned.

"Hi Kevin. I heard you had a successful 'meeting.' Congratulations. You've done a great service for the Agency."

The second message was from Juliana.

"Hi, love," she said "I was missing you so I thought I'd call and say hello. You're probably out with the boys having dinner at some fancy restaurant, while I'm here eating leftovers. It's 8 o'clock and I'm going to get in bed and read myself to sleep. Don't bother to call if it would wake me. I wish you were here in bed with me. Give me a call tomorrow. Love you."

❧

Four days later Kevin flew home from Washington. Juliana picked him up at the airport.

"How'd all your meetings go?"

"Fine. We're working on a Navy proposal and the next phase of the PENREN project. The client is very demanding, but seems happy with the progress being made. That's what counts."

"Did you do anything fun, go to the Smithsonian or to the theater?"

"No—I didn't have any free time."

"Well, you were out late that one night when I called."

"Yes—sorry about that. I was working, lost track of time, had a late dinner, you know how it goes."

"No, I don't know how it goes. I'd like to join you at one of your late-night dinners and learn 'how it goes,' as you say."

"Well, it's pretty boring, if you really want to know. To be truthful, it was one meeting I really would have preferred to miss."

❧

Four months later Mary called Kevin.

"You have any free time this week for lunch?"

"How about Friday?"

"That would be good. The usual place?"

"Fine."

"See you at noon." She hung up before Kevin could ask any questions.

When he walked into the restaurant she was already

there. The waiter came to take their orders. She ordered a glass of Chardonnay and a seafood salad. Kevin glanced at the menu and set it aside.

"I'll have the same thing," he said. To Mary he said, "You're not having your usual iced tea. This must be an important meeting."

"We've made some progress," she said.

The waiter returned with their wine. Kevin raised his glass to her. "Here's to progress."

"Kevin, what you did for us was truly admirable. I know it went against your better judgment and you broke your promise to your wife. But in doing so, you kept a promise to us, a promise you made to help us if you could. I got a full report from Parker. I wish I could have seen you in your Egyptian doctor's outfit. He said you looked very authentic."

Kevin laughed. "Now that you mention it, I brought you a souvenir from the trip I didn't take." He reached in his pocket and pulled out a name tag and handed it to her. She looked at it and laughed.

"Dr. Sadat—that's priceless. I suppose it's a common enough name in Egypt that no one would give it a second glance."

The waiter arrived with their food and Mary quickly put the name tag in her purse.

"Besides thanking you, I want to give you a report. Leila is here, back in federal prison. She was given a choice of telling us what she knew about Saleh or being extradited back to prison in Egypt. She confessed that Saleh had told her that they had to kill an American agent when a kidnapping went awry. It was his way of warning her to keep her mouth shut or the same thing could happen to her. Apparently, Beske tried to stop them when he realized what was happening. They killed him in the car. They dumped you and his body in the cabin. They overdosed you. You were so out of it they tied you up and left to get something to eat. When they came back and found you gone, they buried Beske and figured they'd get to you by grabbing your wife. As you know, that backfired. "It's a sad story, but at least now there's closure for all of us and for Beske's family, thanks to you."

"You know, Mary, when I sat in that huge airplane, the only passenger on the trip that never occurred, traveling six thousand miles there and back, I thought to myself, this is what the U.S. does to bring evildoers to justice. If the world knew the lengths we are prepared to go, there would be fewer attacks on Americans."

"Yes Kevin, that is probably true. But you can never talk about something that never happened."

In fact, the trip that never happened was the last time that Kevin flew to the Middle East. There was every sign that the American presence there would no longer involve "Boots on the Ground." During his campaign for a second term as president, in 2012, Obama promised to end the war in Afghanistan and bring home the combat troops by December 2014. He hedged this commitment slightly by stating that a few thousand personnel would be required beyond that date for training and advisory purposes to help the Afghanistan National Security Forces (ANSF) be prepared to maintain internal security, but that all U.S. troops would be home by 2016.

In fact, the first part of this promise was kept. NATO ended its combat mission on December 28, 2014, bringing to a close the twelve-year-long Afghanistan war. NATO joined the campaign in 2003, two years after the initial U.S. attacks.

The NATO forces, in addition to combating insurgents in Afghanistan, had been working to train and equip an ANSF force of three hundred and fifty thousand men to provide peace and security within the country. How well the ANSF could succeed in this mission was known by all to be critical. Once the NATO and U.S. forces were gone, could ANSF withstand renewed Taliban and al Qaeda attacks and bring stability to a country that had seen nothing but war for more than thirty years? This was the big question. It was not certain that ANSF could do this, and it was absolutely certain that they could not do it without ongoing U.S. financial support. Given that Afghanistan has one of the most corrupt governmental systems in the world, success became even more problematic.

Kevin knew that if ANSF failed and the country slid once again into chaos and became a haven for terrorists, the sacrifice of the more than two thousand military personnel who gave their lives—not to mention the $1 trillion cost of the war—would have been in vain.

One warm night in June 2014, Kevin was listening to CNN News. Juliana walked into the room.

"Why so moody?" she asked. "It's not like you. You've been this way for a while—a few weeks at least, maybe a month."

"Before 9/11 there were terrorist attacks by al Qaeda. You remember the U.S. Embassies in Tanzania and Kenya in 1998 and the *USS Cole* bombing in 2000, I'm sure. But 9/11 made Osama bin Laden a hero to Muslim fanatics, who became inspired to follow his example. In 2001, there were attacks in thirteen countries, mostly in the Middle East."

"We know about that. That's why Homeland Security was formed. Bin Laden is dead now, so what is bothering you?"

"On the news I heard that twelve years later, in 2013, there were over twenty-eight hundred attacks in *fifty* countries, with nearly seventeen thousand killed—and the number is expected to increase every year. They say it's inevitable that there will be major attacks in Europe and the U.S. in the future. There's no end in sight, no country can escape this terror."

"I've never heard you be so negative before," Juliana said. "What's changed?"

"Every day the world news gets worse. It seems that new threats emerge from around the globe. Iran has its nascent nuclear energy program. China is building a modern navy and becoming more aggressive in the Pacific, staking out claims to remote island specks of land claimed by the Philippines, Vietnam, and Japan. Most ominous and immediate is the threat posed by ISIS. You know they just captured Mosul, defeating a much larger Iraqi Army force that appears to have run rather than fight. Mosul is the fifth largest city in Iraq."

Juliana sat next to Kevin and put her arm around his shoulders. "Honey, we can't be the world's police force. Iraq will have to take care of its own problems."

"Julie, the problem is much bigger than Iraq. Now ISIS has announced the formation of a worldwide Muslim caliphate headed by Abu Bakr al-Baghdadi, who declared himself 'Caliph.' ISIS further announced that the known Muslim world would be divided into 'provinces' of the new Islamic State and subjected to Sharia law. ISIS has no regard for human lives—their victims or their own. Because of a schism in the Muslim world that occurred fourteen centuries ago, the Sunnis still consider themselves the true believers and Shias the heretics. The stories coming out of Syria and northern Iraq are heart wrenching. Entire families have been executed, men, women, and children, simply because they're not Sunnis. Young girls have been captured and held as sex slaves for ISIS fighters. Iraqi POWs were beheaded in public or shot in the head and buried in pits. Thousands of civilians have been forced to flee as refugees, their possessions stolen and their homes burned. It goes on and on. There seems to be no limit to ISIS's criminal and outrageous behavior."

Juliana took Kevin's hand "I know it's terrible. Atrocities happen. Think of what the Japanese did in Nanking. The human race seems unable to settle disagreements except by fighting. I know it's absolutely scary and could lead to the end of world peace as we know it, but what more can you do or we do? It's time to put aside these depressing thoughts and think about us."

Juliana was right. Thinking about the world situation was depressing. Kevin told himself that he had played his small part. Now it was up to others. It was time to shift focus, spend more time together. He owed it to Juliana.

A FAREWELL

After reaching sixty-five, Kevin began thinking about retiring.

It was time. There were many changes in the company. He was sick of traveling. More and more, he just wanted to spend time with Juliana. The U.S. was pulling out of Afghanistan. Iraq was in turmoil. The U.S. invasion had not brought peace to the Middle East. Instead, it created a vacuum and destabilized the area more than ever before.

The bright hopes of individual freedoms and liberty that had accompanied the "Arab Spring" had faded as country after country descended into the chaos of sectarian violence. Instead, a grave new terrorist threat emerged—radical Muslims that not only attacked Westerners, but killed their own women and children. No country seemed immune to violence—cowardly attacks by terrorists who were willing to sacrifice their own lives to kill defenseless civilians.

The spy ring that sought to bring drone technology to Iran had been finally exposed and defeated, in no small part due to Kevin's persistence. But in the larger scheme of things, what had it mattered? It all seemed futile in hindsight, after the Iranians captured a downed U.S. drone and claimed to have reverse engineered it.

So many trips, so many unpleasant places, not just the Middle East, but North Korea and others. So many flights, remembering the Korean Air flight shot down by the Russians, the Malaysian airplane that disappeared, another shot down by the Russians over the Ukraine. Flights with bad weather, the plane bouncing, lightning strikes, passengers throwing up, the discomfort. Getting sick in strange countries, hoping the local doctors knew what they were doing, and then hurrying home. It was enough.

He and Juliana enjoyed their new home in Newport Beach. Although they had lived there for five years already, Kevin hardly knew the neighbors or the area. Juliana would entertain him with stories of her walks on the beach and the sights she saw. One day it would be a grey whale rolling in the surf, scraping barnacles from its back. Another day, hundreds of dolphins jumping and diving a few hundred yards offshore. The shoreline was constantly changing under the influence of wind and wave. In the winter months the beach would become steep, eroded by wave action. In the summer the sand would be returned and the beach would resume its gradual slope.

On those nights when he was home, sleeping in their bed, he could lie there and listen to the distant surf, the waves crashing on the beach. During the winter months, huge South Pacific storms would send swells six thousand miles northeast across the Pacific. Eight days later, large surf would impact California's south-facing beaches. On nights when there was a low tide, the waves would break with a thunderous crash on the shore, causing a sound that could be heard for several city blocks on a still evening.

A light sleeper, Kevin would lie in bed, the sound of the surf reminding him of coves and harbors where he'd been in his boat, until he eventually drifted back to sleep.

Holly had retired and many of Kevin's former colleagues had moved on to new jobs or, in some cases, to new companies. Consolidated had been swept up in a series of mergers and acquisitions that had quadrupled its size and brought in many new faces. The top management of the firm as Kevin knew it had completely changed. There was nothing wrong with that in his mind; in fact, it was inevitable, given the success of the company. He knew this about organizations: either they grew or they died. There was no such thing as standing still. Once you stopped growing, stopped innovating, you were sure to be overtaken and swallowed by the competition.

He was offered other assignments. Once he went to Washington D.C. for six months to help resolve some complex legal claims. While there, Juliana toured the Smithsonian Museum complex, the Capitol, and its art museums, and he was able to secure a private tour of the renovated Pentagon for her.

One Saturday they visited Charles Kidd on his "farm" in a remote part of the Shenandoah Valley. Juliana and Kidd's wife Charlotte sat in the shade discussing art.

Kevin stood by drinking a beer while Kidd barbecued ribs on his backyard grill. "Do you have any contact with your old gang?" he asked. "Do you miss working?"

"No contacts whatsoever, and I don't miss working," Kidd replied. "When I left, I think they were glad to see me go. It was a time when the Agency was under a lot of scrutiny. We had missed things. Then we tried to repair our image by swinging too far the other way, if you know what I mean. Guantánamo, all that surveillance, rumors of torture, it put the Agency in a bad light."

"I don't think we can put all the blame on our national security agencies," Kevin said. "What about Congress and the president? When you stop and consider that we've been at war, more or less continuously for twenty-five years, it boggles the mind. And what have we gained? Nothing. Are we more secure? No. Have we created an entire generation of new enemies sworn to our destruction, willing to commit suicide just to kill a few of us? Yes. Sadly, that even includes women and children brainwashed to the point they are willing to blow themselves up for the cause. It's a horrible state of affairs, one that we have made worse by our mistaken policies."

"We've left a mess for the next generation, haven't we," Kidd said

"One night, about thirty years ago, Juliana and I decided not to have children," Kevin replied. "We kept putting it off, due to her job and my career and traveling. That night we just decided we didn't want to bring someone into our messed up world. We thought we'd adopt an orphan; but even that plan went away. Maybe it was selfish, but we enjoyed each other and the freedom we had. We didn't want to give it up."

It was a rainy, windswept night when Kevin and Juliana returned from Washington after being away for many months. Juliana clung to Kevin's arm as the plane was tossed by rough weather. Flashes of lightning illuminated the dark sky. Somewhere a passenger screamed when the aircraft suddenly plunged and children started crying. Upon landing, the plane skidded and braked hard before coming to a stop on the wet Santa Ana Airport runway. They took a cab. By the time they reached home it was dark but the rain had stopped. They unlocked the house and threw their luggage in the living room. They looked at each other, knowing the other's unspoken thoughts. They locked the house again and made the short walk to the beach. The air was fresh and moist from the rain. A slight breeze blew in from the ocean. A quarter moon shone through the broken cloud cover, which was gradually clearing to the northeast. The wave tops glistened in the moonlight. Out in the San Pedro Channel, they could see the lights of the three oil platforms that lay off of Long Beach. The beach where they stood was deserted.

Kevin hugged Juliana. "Funny how we both had the idea to come here, first thing," he said. "I guess we weren't aware of how much we were missing home. As interesting as it was in Washington, this is the place we belong."

Juliana kissed him. "If you spent a little more time here, took walks on the beach with me, you'd never want to leave. You might be inclined to travel less, send other people in your place when those trips come up."

"I know. Lately I've been thinking more and more about retiring. There's just a couple of other things I'd like to see finished."

Juliana poked him gently in the ribs. "You'll never retire. There will always be just 'a couple of more things' that you'll think you have to do."

"No. I'm serious. It's a different world. The challenges are still there, maybe more difficult than before. Somehow they've lost their appeal. I can't explain it—not even to myself. I feel like I just want to get in my boat and sail away, no itinerary, no fixed destination, anchored at night in some quiet cove, the boat rocking gently, or sailing downwind on a night like this, the boat's wake reflected in the moonlight."

"So do it," Juliana said. "You know I would go."

"I know you would. It's a nice thought, but it's impractical. But we'll definitely make some trips when I retire. The first one would be to circumnavigate Catalina Island. We'll spend a night in every cove and harbor on the island as we work around it. Another one I'd like to make would be to visit all the Channel Islands, a leisurely trip, stopping at Marina del Rey, Ventura Harbor, Santa Barbara, and then stay a few days at each of the Channel Islands.... "

Kevin broke off, looking out to sea, recalling other trips they'd taken when they were first married including the fateful trip to Santa Barbara Island. The sea was calm now. Moonlit waves rolled smoothly up the beach, hardly breaking. How deceptive, he thought, knowing the vast power those waves could unleash. The sea level is rising everywhere, he thought. One day it will happen here, and then what?

Juliana hugged him close. "I'm getting cold," she

said. "Let's go back to the house. It will be sheer joy to sleep in our own bed for a change." Juliana took his arm as they walked back to the house. "I like your idea of circumnavigating Catalina," she said. "Promise me that we'll do that one of these days."

§

It took another month after returning from Washington for Kevin to feel he'd caught up with all of his responsibilities and deadlines. With all the urgent matters taken care of or delegated to someone else, he told his boss he wanted to take a week off, something he promised Juliana. They provisioned the boat in preparation for an early Monday morning departure in August, planning to circumnavigate Catalina Island in a clockwise direction.

It was still dark that Monday morning when Kevin slid the hatch cover back and went down the companionway into the galley. He turned on a light. Being in *Seascape* always had a special significance for him. It was his special place, his retreat from the world that pressed in on him. Here were familiar odors, candle wax, engine smells, a faint scent of sea water in the bilge. The interior was a mixture of polished brass and varnished teak. At the navigation station he checked the battery voltage and switched on the electronics. He started the engine as Juliana came aboard. Ready to go. The ocean his open road. No limits, no constraints, the freedom of the sea.

Once underway, Juliana made coffee in the galley. She came on deck in about ten minutes, bringing a cup to Kevin. He sat in the cockpit, looking more relaxed than he had for months. There was a light swell running, calm with no wind, early morning cloud cover with the marine layer hanging near the coast. The boat was on autopilot, the engine pushing it smoothly at five knots.

"Thanks for the coffee, love. Isn't this great? Hopefully we'll pick up some wind in a few hours. I'm bypassing Avalon, going direct to the backside of the island. I figure we can hit Avalon as a last stop on our way home."

"Thanks for doing this. I felt we needed this trip." Juliana sat down beside him, put her hand on his thigh. "You were under a lot of stress in Washington. You needed to get away."

"You're right about that. You know, I've pretty much decided I'm going to retire. My first concern was finances, but the house is paid for. I'll get some retirement pay. Soon I'll start collecting Social Security. With my IRA and options on Consolidated's stock, we should be okay. We're not rich, but we should be comfortable. The next issue is, if I retire, how will you take it? Ever since you retired, you've had the house to yourself. You haven't had me in the way, tripping over my stuff, having me around for lunch, and not having your complete freedom when I'm gone for days at a time on business trips. Do you think you could stand it?"

"In a heartbeat. You can quit the day we return. You can't retire soon enough as far as I'm concerned." Juliana stood up, squeezed in between the wheel and Kevin and straddled his legs. She sat on his lap, her arms around his shoulders. "Just think of the fun we can have when you're home all day," she said, kissing him.

"Hey, be careful, I'm driving this boat and I can't see."

She kissed him again, deeply and long. "You don't need to see. I looked, and there is nothing out there, and the autopilot is driving the boat."

"In that case," Kevin said, as he started to unbuttoned her blouse, "let's go for it."

"Don't get too carried away," Juliana said, pushing his hands away from her breasts. "Wait until tonight."

"Spoilsport. You got me all excited and now you walk away."

"Time for breakfast," she said, standing up and

pulling away from him. "I've got some muffins, cantaloupe, and juice. Will that hold you until lunch?"

❧

By noon they had reached the east end of the island. On the approach, they were greeted by a large school of dolphins that followed the boat for a couple of miles, diving and surfing the bow wave. The wind had come up briefly, but was finicky, and now was on the bow, so they were back to motoring.

Juliana went below to the galley and made turkey sandwiches, put out chips and fruit, and brought them each a beer.

The sky had cleared and the sea sparkled green and blue as they sailed west along Catalina's shoreline, passing Ben Weston Point as they headed to Little Harbor.

"I want to go in there and see if there's room," Kevin said. "The anchorage is small and only has room for about three sailboats, but on Monday, hopefully, everyone's cleared out. I've always wanted to spend the night there."

It was early afternoon when Kevin turned into Little Harbor. He passed behind the reef and into the anchorage area, which was empty. He pulled forward, dropped the bow anchor, set it, and then backed up to place the stern anchor in the shallow water near the beach. Once it was set, he pulled forward on the bow anchor line until his depth sounder indicated 1.6 fathoms, or about ten feet beneath the hull. He took up the slack in the stern anchor.

"Cocktail time," he said as he shut down the engine. Juliana, who had been supervising the anchoring operation, nodded her agreement.

"What would you like? I'll fix you something while you do your log and square away the boat."

"I'd like a Margarita and some chips. I'll cook tonight if fish tacos are okay with you."

"Sounds great."

~

Dinner over, dishes washed, they sat in the cockpit under the stars, with just the faint light from the trawler lamp that hung over the salon table shining up from below through the companionway. It was a warm night and Kevin stretched out on one of the bench seats with his back against the bulkhead, a flotation cushion as a back rest. Juliana sat on the bench between his extended legs, her back against his chest. She was pointing out the various constellations they could see overhead.

"You can spot the Big and Little Dippers, right?" Pointing overhead, she said, "There are Cassiopeia and the Pleiades."

"You're good at that. I learned a few stars to use for navigation, but I can never remember all the constellations."

"Are you warm enough?"

"Yes, what about you?"

"My hands are cold," he said, as he slipped them under her sweatshirt. He pushed up her bra and freed her breasts. He cupped her breasts in his hands, feeling her erect nipples.

"Oh, honey, your hands are cold. That's not nice."

"But you're warm—and very nice." He moved one hand down over her stomach into the top of her jeans.

"Wait. Let's go to bed. I want to get out of these clothes and be comfortable."

After they made love, Kevin slept soundly. The long trip, standing at the helm, running up to the mast to raise or lower the sails, and especially the evening's passion, were all it took.

About five in the morning he heard a faint sound that didn't belong in a boat at anchor in a calm harbor. The first time he heard it, he ignored it, not wanting to stir from the warm bed. The second time, he came wide-awake. It sounded like a giant hand gently shaking the mast. He could hear the rigging vibrate. It did it for a moment, then stopped, and then repeated.

Kevin was puzzled for a minute before he suddenly realized what was happening. The boat was bottoming. He quickly turned on the depth sounder and read zero feet. How could this be? Of course, it was low tide. He ran out on deck and slacked the stern anchor line, then pulled the boat forward on the bow anchor until he had two feet of clearance under the hull. About this time Juliana woke up.

"What are you doing, running around the boat naked?"

"I had to move the boat. We were hitting bottom. When we anchored yesterday, I forgot to check the tide. We anchored at high tide. I thought we had lots of depth—wrong! It turns out there was a minus low tide."

"Any damage?"

No, I don't think so. We barely touched and I think the bottom is soft. I'll dive and take a look after breakfast."

"Great," she said, throwing off the covers. "Right now get back in bed and let me warm you up."

After breakfast Kevin put on a mask and dove under the boat. The bottom was sandy and there was no damage to the keel. They put the dinghy in the water and rowed ashore to the beach and took a short hike up to the hills overlooking the cove. It was a spectacular view of the rugged north coast of the island. A hiking trail led off towards the interior of the island. At one prominent bluff overlooking the ocean, Kevin found a handful of wooden golf tees. Somebody had been up on the bluff, practicing his drives, firing golf balls off into the Pacific Ocean.

They returned to the boat and prepared for the short run up the coast to Catalina Harbor, arriving at lunchtime. They picked up a mooring and had lunch on the boat. Kevin launched the dinghy and motored out to the point, where they snorkeled amongst the rocks and kelp.

Afterwards, they returned to the boat for a nap and then went into the little town of Twin Harbors and had dinner. Back on the boat they sat again in the cockpit, under a starlit sky. "So tell me, do you think you'll really retire? What are you going to do? I can't picture you sitting around the house twiddling your thumbs. What about your involvement in national security, your concerns about terrorists, drones, spies and bad guys? Are you going to be content to live a quiet life at the beach, no intrigue, no excitement of international travel, no responsibilities for big projects, all that stuff?"

"Yes, believe it or not. My mind is made up. I've been working long enough. As for other things to do, I might take on some consulting assignments for Consolidated. We have some government clients that would like me to consult on some special projects for them as well. I'm not sure I want to do that. Right now, the quiet life sounds very appealing. And you're sure you're okay with me retiring?" he asked.

"Yes, definitely."

Kevin leaned over and kissed her. "I appreciate your support," he said. "Think about anything that you might be concerned about; there may be things that you'll think of that I haven't considered."

"There's one thing I'd like to do," Juliana said. "We have such nice neighbors, some of whom you barely know, I'd like to arrange a dinner to announce your retirement and invite your boss and a few friends to join us."

"Good idea. I'd enjoy that."

"I'll also think about other things we might need to do. At the moment, I think I'm ready to go to bed."

Juliana came on deck in the morning, knowing Kevin was there with his coffee. "Good morning love," she said, "what are you thinking about?"

"You know, out here, we're not that far from the mainland, yet it seems so far away. I can sit here and watch seagulls diving, pelicans flying low in formation, and an occasional bald eagle perched up there on the cliffs."

"Yes, and what does that mean?"

"It means I'm able to forget for a few hours or days the depressing state of the world."

From Catalina Harbor they sailed west along Catalina's rugged shore, passing a pinnacle called Eagle Rock. Off in the distance to the north there was a low-lying island shrouded in a dark cloud. Kevin pointed it out to Juliana.

"There's Santa Barbara Island. I wonder if it has any more surprises for us?"

"I hope not," Juliana said.

From the west end of the island, they sailed east along the north side, spending nights in Emerald Bay, Moonstone Cove, and finally Avalon. They went ashore so Juliana could do some shopping, followed by dinner in a restaurant overlooking the harbor. Walking back to the boat landing, a Middle Eastern man and a woman wearing a *burqa* passed them on the street. When Kevin turned to look, they had entered a store and he dismissed them from is mind. Kevin and Juliana left Avalon at 8 a.m. and had breakfast underway. It was a clear beautiful day, but unfortunately no wind, so they had to motor most of the way until a breeze came up during the last hour. They crossed the shipping lanes just before noon, shortly after a large container ship had passed heading south for Asia. At 2 p.m. they were in Newport Harbor.

Back to civilization, Kevin thought, as he put canvas covers over the boat equipment and hatches. Back to reality—how fast time had passed, and how wonderful it had been with no schedule and no fixed destination, and the wide open ocean at their call.

Driving home, Kevin could not get the image of Santa Barbara Island out of his mind. Something about it seemed to forebode evil.

THE BOARDWALK

Back home, Juliana was energized by the thought of planning a dinner party to celebrate Kevin's retirement. True to his word, on his first day back at work, Kevin notified his boss that he planned to retire at the end of the month. He submitted the paperwork necessary to exercise his remaining stock options and to transfer funds from his 401k account to a new self-directed IRA he had established.

Near the end of August, a few days before he officially retired, Kevin had a call from Mary.

"I hear that you may be retiring. Good for you. Some people have all the luck, although I would say you're too young to retire."

"Mary, how are you? I keep watching the news, expecting to see an announcement that you've been appointed Director of the Agency."

"Not much chance of that happening. Don't forget that I'm a woman."

Without hesitation, Kevin said, "About that, there was never any doubt."

"That could be taken several ways."

"Take it the good way."

"I will. But I have a question. Now that you'll have some free time, is there any chance that you'll get bored and might want to take some short trips at government expense?"

Kevin laughed. "Remember, I took one of your 'short trips' once. It was only thirty hours as I recall—to go half way around the world. No, I really am done traveling—unless by boat, my boat, with me driving."

"Okay, I understand. I just thought I'd ask. But there is one other reason for my call. Our job gets more complicated every week. Our surveillance methods get better, then the terrorists find new ways to hide. Now we see growing evidence that ISIS is reaching out to marginalized U.S. citizens, trying to recruit domestic terrorists. I wouldn't bother you with this, but one of the intercepts had code words for Egypt and MFO and also mentioned 'New Port.' I know that's not necessarily Newport Beach. It could be nothing, or it could be something. Under the new protocol of sharing info, we pass such domestic intercepts to the Feds and they presumably inform your local PD. Please don't quote me on this or I'll get in big trouble, but watch your backside. Maybe it's a good idea to get away on your boat for a couple of months."

"Thanks for the warning, Mary. Things are normally pretty quiet here, but I'll be careful. You also—be careful."

While Kevin was completing paperwork and cleaning out his office, Juliana was on the phone contacting dinner guests and making arrangements for a small, intimate dinner party to be held in September, after Kevin retired. It was a good time of the year. The weather would still be nice, and with kids back in school, the beaches less crowded. She booked a private room at Twenty-Two Ocean View, an elegant waterfront restaurant in Newport Beach. The guest list included good friends Clay and Dortha Welsh; Kevin's former secretary, Holly, and her husband; Kevin's boss, Ray, and his wife; and Kevin's longtime friend and sailing partner, Russ Spencer, and his wife. The party was scheduled for Saturday night.

On Friday night before the party, Kevin and Juliana were in bed reading. He put his book aside and turned to hug her. "I feel so fortunate. We are together and free to do whatever we want. We can walk to the beach any time with a picnic and just stare at the water. Or, if the mood takes us, get in the boat and go to the Channel Islands or anywhere we feel like going."

"I like the fact that you're not depressed anymore," she said. "It's wonderful to see you relaxed, more like your old self."

On the evening of the September retirement dinner, Kevin and Juliana and the Welshes were the first to arrive at the restaurant. The front wall was finished in black marble. Next to the front door there was an elaborate menu in a brass case mounted onto the wall. When they entered, the hostess greeted them, recognizing Juliana.

"Good evening, Mrs. Hunter. The room isn't quite ready for you. Would you mind giving us another five minutes or so?"

"That's fine, Juliana said, "Our other guests aren't here yet. Kevin, you and Clay take a seat at the bar while Dortha and I check the room."

The bar was finished in rich, dark wood panels. There was a series of shelves behind the bar in front of a window that looked out over the ocean and the pier in the distance. There were hundreds of bottles of different types of liquor on the shelves, with the front row being made entirely of different brands and vintages of Scotch whiskey. The setting sun, shining through the window behind the liquor display, created a mosaic of different colored lights. In a separate room, the restaurant had a large cellar with thousands of bottles of wine.

The bartender stood with his back to them as Kevin and Clay took a seat. When the bartender came for their orders, Kevin noticed that the barman was not the usual one he remembered. His features were Middle Eastern.

"What will you have, Clay? This is Juliana's party and I think she's got it all covered."

"Vodka rocks for me."

"I'll have a martini," Kevin told the bartender. "Gin and two olives."

The drinks came and they clinked glasses.

"What are you going to do, now that you've retired?"

"As little as possible," Kevin said with a laugh. "Juliana has a list of things for me to do around the house. That will take at least a year. After that, we'll see. The company wants me to remain as a consultant for a while, so that will also keep me busy. The one thing I don't want to do is travel. I did enough of that for two lifetimes."

A few minutes later Juliana came to the bar and called them. "Bring your drinks and come upstairs. The room is ready."

After they left the bar, the bartender returned to the corner of the bar, picked up a cell phone, and made a short call.

When Kevin and Clay entered the room they saw the table was set with place cards for each guest. The settings were very elegant, with two crystal wine goblets, a separate water glass, black napkins, and white china. There was also a small booklet by each setting. Curious, Kevin picked one up and looked at it. His picture was on the cover. The title read "Kevin Hunter, a Builder's Life." He opened the first page and saw a short paragraph describing his early life and education, plus the date he joined Consolidated. He thumbed quickly through the other pages and saw brief summaries of many of the major projects he'd worked on.

He hugged Juliana. "This is a surprise. When did you find time to do this? And how did you manage to get all this information and keep it secret?"

"I had some help. In fact, here are two of my helpers," she said, as Holly and Ray entered the room with their spouses, followed by Spencer and his wife. More about that later. Here's the waiter who will take your drink orders, or, if you prefer, there is wine here and you can help yourself."

After introductions were made and everyone had a cocktail, there was animated conversation as the guests read through Juliana's book, joking with Kevin about some of the projects he'd worked on. He was plainly embarrassed at the attention, and was relieved when two waiters appeared to begin serving salads.

After everyone was seated, Juliana stood.

"Thank you for coming and joining us for this evening. You have all had a special part in our lives. Enjoy dinner. We'll have a short break before dessert is served. At that time, I'd like to invite each of you to share a favorite story about Kevin."

Ray stood. "I think we should drink a toast to Kevin. Here's hoping he spends more time on his boat, sailing to the islands...."

The restaurant lights flickered and went out.

No one said anything for a moment. "It must be the Edison Company," Juliana said. "They're putting the power lines underground in this neighborhood."

Kevin tensed, instinctively looking toward the door, the sudden darkness triggering old fears.

A moment later the lights came back on.

"Oh well," Juliana said, "my first thought was that we might get to have a candlelight dinner."

"That would be romantic, as long as the kitchen still functioned," Dortha said.

At this point the waiters entered the room and began serving dinner.

The food was delicious: a tropical salad with mango and hearts of palm; steak and lobster, served with potatoes *au gratin* and artichoke hearts, accompanied by a fine Cabernet and a French white Burgundy.

As the table was being cleared, Ray started off with the stories, describing how he, Kevin, and others had been stranded in Chicago after 9/11.

"When we finally got out of there," he said, "Kevin was driving about eighty miles an hour in the middle of Nebraska when we're pulled over by a highway patrolman. Here we were, three men in a rented car, driving like a bat out of hell in the middle of the night, three days after 9/11. I thought for sure we'd all be arrested, but amazingly we got off with a warning."

Holly told how on one of his many trips, Kevin lost his plane ticket. He got to the airport and found it was missing, and then faced being stranded in Honolulu. He thought he'd lost it in the cab to the airport, and he had her calling all the cab companies in Honolulu, trying to find the driver that had taken him to the airport. While she was making calls he realized it had probably fallen out of his pocket in a movie theater, where he'd gone to watch a film while waiting for his next flight. He had to scramble to get a replacement ticket in time so he didn't miss a critical flight to Japan.

After several more humorous stories, dessert was served, a slice of chocolate cake with fresh raspberries and a chocolate cookie decorated with white chocolate that read: "Happy Retirement."

"I want to thank you all for coming tonight," Kevin said. "All of you have been an important part of my life. Together we've done some interesting projects, weathered some bad times, and rejoiced in some very good times. Hopefully, we've left the world a better place with some of the infrastructure projects we've done…."

He paused. "…despite what has been accomplished, there are still many unsolved problems. The world is not at peace and we face some serious environmental issues." He raised his glass. "Here's a toast to the future generations. May they succeed where we've done a lousy job."

Outside the restaurant, Kevin and Juliana said goodbye to their friends. Dortha and Clay were the last to leave, after the others were on the way to the parking lot to collect their cars.

"Thanks," Kevin said to them. "It was a wonderful

evening, very special. You two have been great friends and neighbors. I really appreciate the fact that you joined us. Of course, don't believe most of those stories you heard—they were wild exaggerations."

"Do you want to ride back with us?" Clay asked.

"If you don't mind, I think we'll walk back. It's such a beautiful night—no wind, full moon, very romantic. Nice time to walk along the beach."

When Clay and Dortha left to get their car, Kevin and Juliana started back along the boardwalk, passing the Newport pier. There were people coming and going on the pier. Hand-in-hand, Kevin and Juliana walked slowly along the boardwalk. Behind them, a man stood holding a bicycle and talking on his phone. There was a package in the bicycle basket that hung from the handlebars. As they walked east along the oceanfront, there were a few other pedestrians, but nothing like the afternoons, when the boardwalk would be crowded with people on bikes, skateboards, and roller blades.

It was high tide and the waves were breaking far up on the shore. Near the water's edge they could see a few couples and small groups of people—lovers or partygoers enjoying a night cap on the beach, dashing back when the sea cascaded over the sand towards them. A solitary bicyclist rode by them, going in the opposite direction.

It was a short walk, seventeen blocks from 22nd street back to Island Avenue. At 13th street, Kevin stopped for a minute and hugged Juliana. "You look great tonight," he said. "You know how much I love you."

She kissed him and held him close. "I love you too." Juliana broke away from his embrace. "I don't want to seem unromantic, but let's keep walking. I've got to pee. I should've gone in the restaurant, but I didn't want to hold everyone up."

In the distance, there was the low murmur of voices, the faint sound of the receding bicycle.

A cloud moved in front of the moon.

As he started walking, Kevin heard the sounds of a bicycle approaching from behind them. It sounded like it was moving fast, and as Kevin turned back to look, he stumbled off the edge of the boardwalk, tripped and fell face first into the sand. At that moment there was a blinding flash and a loud noise.

When Kevin regained consciousness, he saw flashing lights. He looked up into the faces of several firemen who were kneeling above him, administering oxygen. He passed out again.

He awoke, groggy. It took a moment to realize that he was in a hospital room. He tried to focus to clear his vision. A nurse stood nearby, adjusting some device with tubes.

Someone sat next to the bed.

"Juliana, is that you," he said, trying to turn to see who was there. "What happened?"

"Kevin, it's me, Dortha Welsh. You're at Hoag Hospital; you've been injured."

"Where is Juliana? I want to see her."

"She's not here Kevin," Dortha said, as she started crying.

"What happened?" Kevin said. "What happened to us?"

Juliana died when a ball bearing penetrated her heart, killing her instantly. Kevin's injuries were not life-threatening and he was released from the hospital two days later. His hearing was affected and he suffered a mild concussion when a piece of the bicycle frame hit his head in a glancing blow. The police told Kevin that the assailant had packed an explosive charge with several dozen ball bearings. Some hit nearby houses; others flew out onto the beach. Fortunately, Kevin was down on the sand so they missed him. The assassin died in the attack. No one else was injured, although there were other people on the boardwalk who witnessed the entire incident.

The Newport Beach police spoke briefly with Kevin at the hospital, and interviewed him again at his home several days later. The attacker had been identified. He was a twenty-one year old naturalized U.S. citizen and undergraduate at the University of Southern California. His parents were Egyptians and lived locally. They told the police that recently they had become worried about their son because he was on the verge of flunking out of college. He'd become very religious and spent hours on the Internet. Also, he met another Egyptian who seemed to have influenced his thinking in some profound way. This man, whom the parents described as a cleric or religious teacher of some sort, was actually working as a bartender at the Twenty-Two Ocean View restaurant. He disappeared the night of the attack—just walked out of the bar in the middle of the shift and had not been seen since.

The attacker's damaged cell phone had been found on the boardwalk. The police hoped to use it to get additional information about persons behind the attack. Egyptian officials had been contacted and were cooperating with the U.S. authorities. So far, nothing had been learned about an Egyptian involvement. At this point, the U.S. authorities were considering that Kevin and Juliana were victims of a random attack by a depressed student who decided to blow himself up.

Kevin never accepted the idea that the attack was random. He thought that he was the target, and the attack had gone awry with devastating consequences.

IN MEMORIAM

In the weeks following the attack, Kevin was numb with grief. Days slipped by. He scarcely knew what he did. Juliana's ashes were in a closet in the house. He couldn't bear to look at the container. The sight of it plunged him into a dark melancholy. He felt a terrible sadness and remorse, and wondered again what he could or should have done differently. Yet, having the ashes nearby gave him some comfort; it was as if she hadn't completely left him. Eventually he would scatter the ashes at sea.

But not yet.

At night, before sleeping, Kevin took solitary walks on the beachfront. One evening he went into one of the small beachfront bars and sat down and ordered a drink. It was a Tuesday night and not much was happening. The few tourists who ventured into Newport came mostly on the weekends. There weren't many reasons for visitors to come during the winter months.

There were two other people at the bar, a young couple. Kevin noticed them when he walked in. The woman had long blond hair and colorful flowers tattooed on her upper arms. The man had dark hair, pulled back into a short pony tail. He had his arm around the woman, his face close to hers, speaking in low tones. Kevin took a seat at the other end of the bar and called the bartender over. He ordered a Manhattan straight up. As he sat there, sipping the drink, his thoughts slipped back to that night in the cabin, when he'd rolled over and found poor Beske's body. Much later, he'd finally summoned the courage to go meet Beske's wife, to tell her how sorry he was about her loss, to face the inevitable question, for which he knew he would have no answer—why?

"I really didn't know him," he'd told her. "And he didn't know me, but even so he tried to keep me from harm, and lost his life doing so. To me, he will always be a hero. I'm so sorry for your loss."

Shallow words. He knew his visit left most questions unanswered, maybe rekindled pain over her loss, but it was something he felt he had to do. When Kidd told him about Saleh, he tried to call Beske's wife to tell her that her husband's murderer was dead. The number was disconnected. Kidd told him she'd remarried and moved away.

Thinking about Beske brought to mind others: McKinsey, bright, enthusiastic, personable, hit on the head and tossed in a river; poor Frank, who loved Saudi Arabia, shot in the head as he sat at the desk in his office; the warm and gregarious soldiers of FIJIBAT, dead in a hostile desert far from their beloved island home; and then Juliana, love of his life, dead because some idiot listened to the crazed arguments of an Islamic radical on social media.

More frequently now, it happened. He would awake in the middle of the night, damp with perspiration, dreaming of the attack. In his dream, he would push Juliana out of the way, and she survived. If only there was a way to stop those dreams he thought, as he downed the drink.

The bartender saw his empty glass and came over.

"How are you doing, sir? Another Manhattan?"

Kevin thought for a moment. "Two, one for me and one here," he said, pointing to the empty seat next to him.

Then, pointing down the bar to the couple, he said, "And give them whatever they want and bring the bill to me. I've told myself that one night I'd come back here and buy everyone a drink, just like it's done in the movies."

The bartender shrugged and looked around the nearly empty room. "Looks like you picked the right night," he said, as he went off to make the drinks. He returned with Kevin's order first.

"Here's yours, and this is for your friend," he said.

After the bartender served the couple at the end of the bar, the man looked at him, waved, and said thanks. The woman looked at him, a long appraisal, then raised her glass to him. Kevin raised his glass to her. She gave him a warm smile.

Seeing the couple in the bar filled Kevin with longing. How he missed Juliana—it was an empty feeling that never went away.

Kevin sipped the drink slowly. He was beginning to feel the effect of the alcohol. He thought about going to the Mexican place down the street. Maybe get a couple of tacos, if it hadn't closed for the night. He glanced down the bar, caught the woman staring at him. She quickly looked away, staring down at the bar, but smiling again.

He finished his drink. The untouched drink next to him was symbolic, a reminder of someone who would not be joining him. He left it on the bar, untouched. He left a ten dollar tip and got up to leave. As he walked out, the woman with the tattoos turned on the bar stool and smiled at him again. The man she was with ignored Kevin, starring moodily into his drink.

"Thanks again," she said. "Have a good one."

After two drinks, Kevin decided that he didn't feel like eating. He walked over to the beachfront for the walk home. There were a few young people walking there, but it was mostly deserted. In the distance he could hear the rumble and crash of the surf as waves broke on the beach. Overhead was a clear sky, a few stars showing, quarter moon and nearby a planet—he guessed it was Mars.

As he walked, the ocean was calm, benign. Yet he knew the mysteries of the sea—all the things he'd seen. He knew how storms in the South Pacific could send swell that would build into huge seas when they reached shallow coastal areas, or how hurricanes would build off of Baja California and send mountainous waves to the offshore islands. The sea was so beautiful on a calm night like this one. It was hard to imagine the ferocity, the brutal strength of those waves, when something stirred them up.

He paused for a moment to look at the sea, the waves coming in. He knew that in all that tranquility and peacefulness, demons lived. They waited for the moment when you let down your guard momentarily. On the jetty, turn your back to the sea for a moment and a huge wave would come out of nowhere and drown you—it happened a few years ago to a Japanese couple who had been peacefully fishing. His body was found the next day, but hers—lodged in a crevice in the stones—was not found until weeks later when anything that marked it as a human had been erased by the sea. There were other things to fear besides the sea. A walk on the oceanfront could turn deadly.

Kevin was remembering other walks he and Juliana took on the beach. She was passionate in her concern that the sea level had risen ominously in the last few years, faster than predicted. "Many of the small islands in the Pacific had been inundated and rendered uninhabitable," she said. "Tuvalu, Kiribati, Vanuatu, and the Marshall Islands have seen low-lying atolls disappear. When winter storms cause huge swells to travel across the Pacific, the higher lands were flooded, as happened at Wake Island, parts of Fiji, and the Cook and Solomon Islands."

Now, no one debated whether global warming was

real or not, Kevin knew. Nations everywhere scrambled to enact the legislation and policies to cut greenhouse gas emissions. In Newport, there was a crash program underway to replace or raise some of the one-hundred-year old seawalls by twenty inches. At night, lights lit up barges in the harbor where cranes were working day and night to repair and raise the seawalls. Experts questioned whether this would be enough for more than the next three to five years.

Watching moonlight glimmer on the waves, he recalled the pleasant times he and Juliana had experienced on his boat. How those happy moments had been shattered forever by a terrorist bomb.

The world is in a perilous condition, Kevin thought. There were threats everywhere. Innocent people, like poor Juliana, killed for no reason, regardless of religion. There was no end to the killing. One killing led to another and then another and another. The cycle went on and on, sweeping women, children, and innocent bystanders into its deadly net. He had to acknowledge that he'd been a part of it. It was depressing but true.

He continued walking towards the empty house that awaited. Another glance at the ocean and his thoughts shifted again to global warming and all of its dire consequences. Dealing with the threat of climate change had become Juliana's obsession. "If we don't become better stewards of the earth and its resources, our planet will become uninhabitable," she'd told him "Religious differences won't matter, because we'll all be dead. Only life forms that can survive in a hot, dry, desolate desert will be left. When all traces of human civilization have disappeared, the planet will recover and new life forms will emerge. Maybe they'll evolve into life more intelligent than what we've been up to now."

With this thought, Kevin unlocked the front door and entered his darkened house, recalling what had been important to her. He knew now what to do. He would create a foundation to support climate change research. That, better than anything else, would honor Juliana's memory.

ACKNOWLEDGEMENTS

I owe a special thanks to Nancy Smith for the cover design and other art work and to Mark Neal for doing his usual fine job of mapmaking. I'm grateful to my "troop" of committed readers who generously took time to review early drafts of this book and to send me their blunt criticisms and many helpful suggestions:

Julie Bird
Neal Brockmeyer
Elizabeth Brooks
Dan Eberly
Florence (Johnny) Frisbie
Joe Genshlea
Jan and Gary Giovino
Raymond Holdsworth
Linda Kahn
Marie Kontos
Lou Leo
Judge Philip Mark
Cambria McLeod
Lt. Col. Grant Mizell
Bob Mosier
Tom Nielsen
Jon Nord
Lane Obert

Carol Pangburn
Kelly Parmenter
Verne Parmenter
John and Judy Remington
Donna Roff
Tessa Roper
Vicki Sabella
Susan Salot
Dan and Linda Schmenk
Lynn Smith
Nancy Smith
Robert and Carmen Smith
Russ Spencer
Howard and Mitzi Wells
Todd White
Joan Wren
Sandra Wright
Behjat Zanjani

54061910R00261

Made in the USA
San Bernardino, CA
06 October 2017